REBELS OF MINDANAO

A NOVEL

TOM ANTHONY

BEAUFORT BOOKS
NEW YORK

DISCLAIMER
This is a work of fiction. Any resemblance to actual events, locales, or persons, living
or dead, is entirely coincidental.

Library of Congress Cataloging-in-Publication Data
Anthony, Tom.
Rebels of Mindanao : a novel / Tom Anthony.
p. cm.
ISBN 978-0-8253-0514-6 (alk. paper)
1. Intelligence officers–United States–Fiction. 2. Undercover operations–Fiction.
3. Terrorists–Fiction. 4. Insurgency–Philippines–Mindanao Island–Fiction.
5. Muslims–Philippines–Mindanao Island–Fiction. 6. Manobos (Philippine
|people)–Fiction. 7. Mindanao Island (Philippines)–Fiction. I. Title.
PS3601.N568R43 2008
813'.6–dc22
2007052193

Published in the United States by Beaufort Books, New York
www.beaufortbooks.com

Distributed by Midpoint Trade Books, New York
www.midpointtrade.com

www.rebelsofmindanao.com

Acknowledgments

I want to thank my sons, Michael Anthony for his persistence over several years of pushing me to write this story and for his detailed comments and constructive criticism throughout the process; and Christopher Anthony for his inspiration to record images I observed in Mindanao.

Eric Kampmann, Beaufort Books, New York, saw something worthy of being published; Arnold Dolan, editor, Trish Hoard, copy editor and Margot Atwell, Associate Publisher, for pulling it all together.

My special thanks to:

Brigadier General Ramon Ong, Philippine Armed Forces, Retired, for vetting my work and for making corrections in four languages.

The Otaza, Payen, and Otakan families, whose names I borrowed to create fictional characters, and for telling stories around our cooking fires and on the beach in Mindanao, which expanded in creating *Rebels of Mindanao*.

General Fidel V. Ramos, for teaching me to "Care, Share and Dare," in writing and in life.

Freddie Aguilar and Sean Hayes, whose lyrics I quote with their permissions, adding song to the story.

An article published in the New York Times Magazine, July 21, 2002, "It Only Looks Like Vietnam," by Donovan Webster, quoted in my book, gave me a new perspective.

Thank you Emalyn, my source for inspiration in all things, and our daughters Emily and Elaiza.

Contents

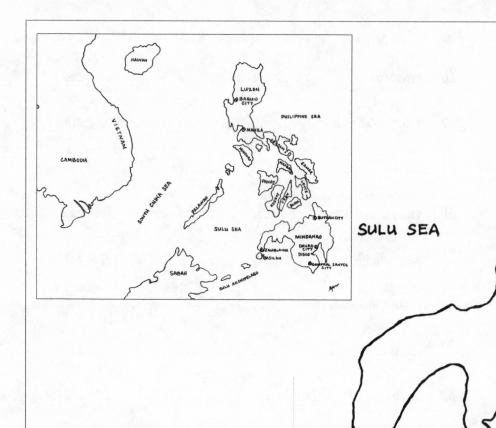

SULU SEA

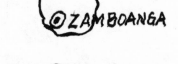

BASILAN

CELEBES SE

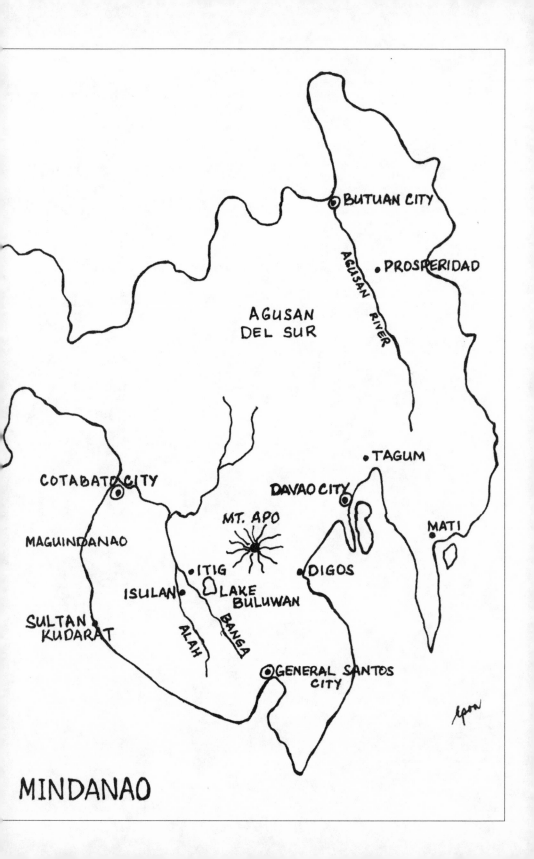

MINDANAO

REBELS OF
MINDANAO

Prologue

Today, the Philippine Archipelago consists of 7,121 islands at low tide, with seventy-five million inhabitants growing at a five per cent rate each year, speaking some seventy-five different languages or distinct dialects, less a few each generation as indigenous tribes are absorbed or become extinct. Five hundred years after being consolidated into a country forced upon them by the conquering Spanish, the separations of waters and religions still keep the peoples from melding into a single nation.

Ocean barriers isolate the islands from potential invaders but also hinder the adaptation of new technologies. Despite its vast expanse and diversity, the Philippine Islands was defined as a single nation for the convenience of the colonialists. After the Spanish, foreign domination continued under the Americans, who brought in a form of democracy. Filipinos attempted to make their culture fit their masters' with varying degrees of success and often accepted religious sects of splinter churches as alternatives to the Catholic dogma of the Spaniards. After independence from the U.S., in 1946, the central government in Manila inherited a cumbersome structure.

Of the three large island groups—Luzon, Visayas and Mindanao—Mindanao, in the south, is the most tormented. Mindanao could stand alone as a nation and has the resources to do so, with no contiguous nations to dispute the natural boundaries of the oceans. As England sent its outcasts to Australia, so Spain sent its troublemakers to Mindanao,

La Tierra del Destirro, the land of the exiles. Outlaws and undesirables from the north were deposited onto this island of Moro pirates—the Muslim terrorists of three centuries past. Over the intervening centuries, some things have changed, others not at all.

A war of insurrection has raged in Mindanao for much of the last forty years without much outside attention. Muslim rebels, who fought against the Americans when they replaced the Spanish, then *with* them to throw out the Japanese, continue their insurgency against foreigners who send in only missionaries and token soldiers. Brother against brother, Christian against Muslim, poor against rich, on it goes . . .

1

Istanbul

The blast killed a dozen worshipers at the Beth Israel synagogue in downtown Istanbul, attracting international news coverage. It was a significant event for Mahir Hakki. Now, for the first time in centuries, he thought, *we are taking the fight to them.*

The rusty old car that Mahir and his friend Jamal had loaded with explosives had rolled slowly down the hill, crashing through the door below a Star of David. Mahir was careful to push the button on the remote control a microsecond after, when only the foreign Zionists were near the car. He wanted to make sure that no innocent countrymen of his would be hurt. Mahir told his friend, "We want our patriots to understand the struggle. Then all of them will join in jihad."

Back in the spring of 2004 when Mahir was working in the only tire store the Turkish European Trading Company had been able to hold on to, Gregory P. Mount, the vice president for marketing at Goodyear Tire and Rubber Company, came to Istanbul with his wife and son, taking a sentimental journey back to where he had started out so many years before. He could not resist walking by the old store and talking to the guy there about tires.

"I remember when this was just a used tire shop," he told the worker.

Mahir replied to the stranger, "Then you would know my father, Hassan."

"Yes. An old and very good friend of mine. How is he?"

"My father passed away fifteen years ago."

The time had slipped away for Mount. He was surprised, "Mahir. Is it you? I knew you when you were a small child."

"And you sir . . . are?"

"Greg Mount, Goodyear International, retired."

"Ah, yes, you helped my father, and started the good and the bad."

Mahir explained the history of the rise and fall of the House of Hakki when Mount took him to lunch at the Sheraton Hotel, while Mount's wife and son shopped in the bazaar for hand-made rugs and hammered brass tables. Mahir let out his venom, but in a courteous way. He held no personal grudge against his father's old friend, and his mother would surely like to see the Englishman again. So Mahir invited Mount to come out to their house by the sea some day, some indefinite day in the future that would never come; their lives were not on parallel paths.

Mahir told Mount, "I don't hold you personally responsible. But your company is a part of it, the informal global conspiracy of Jews and Christians. No American can be elected president of your country nor an Englishman prime minister unless he first swears allegiance to the State of Israel, a government and a people who are the eternal enemy of Islam."

"Mahir, that is just not so." Mount was not offended, rather flattered in a backhanded way that this young man would be so forthcoming with him. "I don't think the Israelis are your enemies: they just want to have their homeland."

But Mahir was not convinced and told Mount, "The Jews had their own place, carved out of the land of the true believers, but that was not enough. Now they extend their settlements into other Arab lands, and when they have enough squatters in them, they will call a vote."

Mount saw no future in the argument, so he let it rest and asked, "Mahir, can I help you in some way now?"

"No, you can't, now. I have no hate for you. You must live your life with your philosophy, as I must mine. I must be responsible to Allah for what I do and for the consequences."

"Enshallah." Mount thought that he understood and had said the one right word.

Mahir thought to himself, all this he does not understand. "And early this very morning the country of my birth, once the heart of a great Turkish empire, signed a military cooperation agreement with Israel, the enemy of Islam. I've got to help shape the future that my son, the last of the House of Hakki, will live in."

The young rebel and the old world traveler parted forever after lunch, friendly across the generations, but the conversation confirmed for Mahir what he had already believed: there was no hope for his personal future. He made a decision. He would dedicate one year to Allah alone and the rest of his life to his family, especially to his new son. He will have done his part.

He sought out and agreed to work with Jamal, an acquaintance from school days in Istanbul. Jamal had told him about the Syrian with Al Qaeda, who would support them with money and technology. Their first assignment from Al Qaeda was easy for them. Jamal had been trained in Yemen and taught Mahir how to make the bombs. The two terrorists-in-training placed homemade explosives inside one of the old GM wrecks that Mahir fixed just enough to get to the synagogue. His homeland was becoming too intimate with their Zionist neighbors in the eastern Mediterranean, and it was time to send a clear message that Israel was not wanted as a partner of modern Turkey in anything. The Yankees thought the struggle of the Muslims would be only against Israel; it was time to introduce them to the global dimension of the war, of jihad in many countries at the same time.

By the time he personally met the Syrian, Abdul Sali, Mahir was already a committed revolutionary and an experienced bomber. He would have done his duty for nothing, but when Sali offered to pay him 500,000 U.S. dollars to undertake one new mission, he calculated he could thereafter spend all his time on the Marmora Sea, his son could someday establish a new technology business, and he would make the hajj. He accepted the assignment.

The next week Mahir Hakki was on board a freighter out of Istanbul as an ordinary seaman. They stopped in Izmir for two days to take on freight, and Mahir took the opportunity to stroll along the quay, wondering what his father had seen fifty years before when he walked on the same smooth stones. After loading, the freighter sailed on to its destination, and the smoky old ship docked on the northern coast of the island of Cyprus at the port village of Kyrenia, the Turkish enclave on the mostly Greek island. While the sailors were enjoying a few hours' leave and the chance to drink small cups of very black, bitter coffee and to dally over sweet honey cakes in the open-air cafes downtown as they watched the local girls, Mahir disappeared. Dressed in old jeans and a white tee shirt like the ordinary sailors who would be returning to the ship sometime in the early morning hours, he left with only a canvas sports bag containing his gear for the coming journey. Between a branch of the Bank of Turkey and the post office, he saw a blue Ford, as promised, driven by a man in traditional Arabian dress. Mahir immediately entered the car. The driver drove away without saying a word and traveled to the green line that separated the Cypriot capital of Nicosia into a Greek zone and a Turkish quarter known as Lefkosia. Mahir left the car at that point and continued on foot to his next rendezvous, his meeting with Sheik Kemal.

2

Duty and Honor

General Luke Hargens, in his two-star general dress blue uniform with a rainbow of medals over its breast pocket, stood next to Charlie Downs, a civilian wearing a dark blue suit. Cadets in full dress uniform marched in precise formation to military music onto the Plain at West Point. Hargens and Downs had joined up with the long gray line, the other graduates of the U.S. Military Academy back for their reunion parade. Downs teased Hargens.

"Luke, stand at attention, they're playing the Official West Point March!"

"Stand at ease, Charlie, and suck up your gut. The only reason I flew in for this is because you persuaded me."

"It's been a long time since I last met you here. You were the Commandant then; only a one-star."

Hargens doesn't remember exactly, and wrings his bony hands. "A lot has happened since then, Charlie."

"Yeah, you went on to get another star before you got that soft job in Manila. What a deal."

"You can talk. We all know what you really do."

"Too bad Thornton isn't at this parade, hearing this music—he'd call it 'The Humper.' Remember our plebe year at the academy when we all snuck off base?"

"I remember that. He talked some girl into smuggling us back long after taps. It must have been two in the morning. We were in the back seat of her car under a blanket."

"I was in the trunk."

"A ballsy thing for plebes to do."

"If we had gotten caught, no careers for any of us."

"If we had gotten caught."

"He was always the maverick. That's what I wanted to talk to you about, personally. What we couldn't do by e-mail. Our old roommate Thornton lives in Mindanao, Luke, over there where you are."

"Yeah, I know. He's gone local."

Downs had to smile, but it was fleeting. "He took on a job for me in Eastern Europe toward the end of the Cold War. He thinks he screwed up."

"He told me part of it. He gets up to see me from time to time and we'll have a beer at the Manila Yacht Club. He's ashamed he let you down."

"He didn't. But he still thinks I don't trust him. The contact he recruited was killed. He thinks it was his fault."

"The Polish woman? What was her name? He thinks he caused her death. That's why he moved to Mindanao, as far from Eastern Europe as he could get."

"He wanted to call his own shots. Couldn't do that in the Army."

"I know. When we were teaching here, he already had his honorable discharge in his rear pocket, ready to get out and be on his own."

As the color guard passed, they came to attention and saluted the flag. Then Downs nodded toward MacArthur's statue behind them, "You know there's been trouble in the Philippines ever since *he* returned, sixty years ago." Downs paused a moment, then continued. "I have some serious info for you. The Philippines may lose Mindanao."

"We paid a big price for those islands in World War II. What do you know that I don't?"

It had been forty-four years since Luke Hargens and Charlie Downs had first marched onto the Plain at West Point with their classmates, and forty years since the last time they had marched together with those same guys, their number since reduced by war, disease, and accident. When they were cadets, they would take the bus from the West Side Terminal in Manhattan north along the Hudson, cross the George Washington Bridge and then follow the Hudson River north, the river clogged just beyond the bridge with row after rusting row of Merchant Marine vessels left over from World War II, a reminder of how many soldiers and sailors had shipped out of New York on one-way tickets to win that particular war.

This trip Hargens had made in a chauffeured Lincoln Town Car, sitting in the back seat with Downs. The two had been in intermittent contact by e-mail for the last several years and knew fairly well what the other was up to personally, although they worked in different departments. Downs was a man who really knew what was going on in the world in his position as Director, Force Deployment and Strategy, a think tank within the State Department. He had worked in that capacity in Washington for the last two administrations, and although he did not usually get into the oval office, he advised those who did.

Downs had wanted to savor the trip with Hargens back up the Hudson for their reunion weekend and was glad they had hooked up to share the eighty-five miles it took to ride from Newark Airport to West Point. Hargens respected Downs by not getting too political with him, although Downs was very ready to talk about the world situation in general and Hargens had his concerns about how the U.S. Army was being overstretched. They agreed about many things, but not everything.

Downs had e-mailed Hargens in Manila, where he now served as the Commander of JUSMAG (Joint United States Military Assistance Group), the combined force of Americans who provided the muscle for U.S. diplomacy in the Philippines. He could hardly order Hargens back to the U.S., but told him they needed to have an important talk, something not suitable for official correspondence across department lines. When they arrived at the South Gate of the academy, the guard saluted the placard on the front windshield and waved them through.

At West Point that weekend, during the official reception for the class of 1964 at the Hotel Thayer, Hargens made the time to talk to as many of his classmates one-on-one as he could—a fascinating collection of individuals, all from the same mold but each one unique after having followed different paths. He walked around the Point four or five miles each of those three days, covering the grounds alone in civilian clothes, reminiscing. One walkabout he made in the early pre-dawn hours when the academy grounds were quiet and dark, lit only softly by the area lights. He thought he would be stopped by military police security, but instead they just saluted him; it must have been something about the way he walked at that unusual hour, and how he held his bearing; they knew he had to be an old grad. He walked by monuments to Patton and Eisenhower, Lee and Grant, and shortly before dawn he looked up to see MacArthur, perpetually carved in stone, cold hard stone, looking toward his landing in the Philippines, keeping his promise to return. And next week Hargens would be returning to the Philippines.

Hargens got back to the Hotel Thayer just as early breakfast was being served. He was not tired, his body still on Western Pacific time, twelve time zones out of phase. He would get tired later, but now he was too excited. He went through the buffet line and sat down alone at a table for two by the window, the Hudson far below seeming not to move. Downs walked over and they exchanged firm handshakes and a kind of masculine half-hug.

"Thanks for being here," Downs said.

"Thanks for pulling me back." Hargens was quiet and sincere. "You really harassed me into making the trip, or I wouldn't be here." The weekend was turning out to be more meaningful for him than he had anticipated. "But I have to admit, a football weekend here is really some-thing to see."

"Luke, do you remember where you were on the day the last heli-copter left Saigon?" Downs was ready to talk.

"I was already a lifer and back in the States, in the Career Course at Benning. Where were you?"

"I was teaching here at West Point before I got out of the army and started at DOS. Thornton was here teaching then too, German language."

"So tell me, Charlie, what is it that's eating you up?"

"OK, here it is. Some Turk, a smart, determined guy named Mahir

Hakki, is carrying five million in cash from Syria into Mindanao. Al Qaeda intends to finance an Islamic revolution."

"Oh boy—they could do a lot with that. Like win the war. So why don't you just have your CIA boys take him out?"

"Can't. The President doesn't want to hear about it. He's in too much trouble overseas already. Too much going on. And President Cayton of the Philippines can't tell his guys the whole story. They'd just keep the money and finance themselves or, worse, the insurrection. We need a consultant we can trust."

Hargens brought Downs up to date. "OK. I get you. I had dinner with Thornton last week in Manila. He lives in Mindanao, owns a small construction company there."

"I had our guys check him out, Luke. He still looks like a Ranger."

"He always kept in shape; not that big but he wrestled, played football. The girls always liked him."

"Yeah, he liked them too; part of his problem. Do you think we could get him one more time?"

"I don't know. He's living well now, never did get married again. The last time I saw him he was wearing a safari suit with some kind of bead necklace and looking ten years younger than you Washington types, still has blond hair. It would take some convincing. He thinks you don't trust him after what happened in Eastern Europe."

The two old roommates grew quiet for a moment, gazing down at the Hudson, silent and gray, remembering. Then Downs continued, cautious because he was speaking out of school, crossing department boundaries with an unauthorized plan. "Luke," he started slowly, but then decided just to lay it all out. "We need Thornton. The CIA informed the State Department that Al Qaeda intends to instigate revolts and stage terrorist attacks simultaneously in several countries within the next month or two, and to set off dirty nuclear weapons within the U.S. at the same time. Their theory is that if we're kept busy at home, we won't have the will or the means to handle other conflicts in the world at the same time."

"They may be right. Glad you D.C. guys are wising up."

Downs continued, ignoring Hargens' sarcasm, "We know that Al Qaeda is sending the cash from a source in Syria into Mindanao very soon. They want to create chaos, but we don't know exactly how they intend to do it, or how they plan to get the money to Kumander Ali, the leader of the rebels. It's enough to be the catalyst for a revolution in a poor country if they use it effectively, or should I say if they corrupt enough people."

Hargens took the opportunity to needle Downs. "Why Thornton? Why don't your DOS buddies negotiate with the rebels, give them the opportunity to screw up in yet another country they know nothing about?" He hit a sore point.

"I'm not fooling around." Downs said testily. "But you hit the nail on the head. State and Defense agree this is not an assignment for the CIA. There is already a huge stink about those few dozen Special Forces troops from your JUSMAG tromping around in the jungle over there. If it got out that we'd involved the CIA in Muslim Mindanao, it would cause so much trouble it could easily escalate the civil war—or at least cause enough controversy to get the wrong guy elected president there. Can you imagine 'Yankee go home' demonstrations in Manila?"

Hargens got serious too, "Yes, I can. We've had riots already, right under my window at the embassy. The new generation always forgets the sacrifices of the old. So what do you want me to do?"

"Using your JUSMAG Command in Manila, persuade Thornton to create a small team, recruit a few locals if he has to—you can help him—and take out the Turk. Just do that, quietly. Then the Philippine Army can win the civil war on the ground."

Downs continued. "Luke, my contacts tell me that local papers have reported U.S. troops are moving into Davao City proper; that's not a very good idea, you know. They have no real mission. They'll just be targets hanging around the bars when off duty, and probably screw up the peace that exists there now. You have a problem."

Hargens followed Downs' downward gaze toward the distant river, then faced his friend and said quietly, "We all have a problem."

"Yeah, I know, but you're assigned there, and it's happening on your watch. Don't lose the Philippines. MacArthur would get down off his statue and come after both of us." Downs paused a moment, and his tone changed. "Come on, let's walk up the hill."

"It might be a long time until we meet again. What else can I do for you before one of us gets buried here?"

"Luke, we need to have Thornton take out the Turk. He's the right guy in the right place. He's done it before for me. You, JUSMAG, give him the support he needs on the ground. Let him keep the cash. Nobody here, or in the Philippine government, would need to know about it."

"I get it. All this is just between you and me, right?"

"Right. Thornton can make it happen. Wonder what he's doing right now."

3

The Lady Love

The Lady Love, a videoke beer bar, was set between the Christ Our Savior pawnshop and the Jesus Is God ink cartridge refill station in downtown Davao City, Mindanao. During the day, the Lady Love could hardly be noticed. Its unpainted door had unpainted cardboard windows. A banded stack of partially rusted corrugated steel roofing sheets leaned against the wall beside the doorway. Candy peddlers moved in front of the place among the parked vehicles and along the sidewalk offering their sweet wares with smiling, toothless grins. Street hawkers offered to sell places to park. For a few pesos they would not scratch patrons' cars with a key or a knife while they were away. But at night, the pink neon sign was turned on and its pale glow made the place look cozy and inviting in contrast to the darker surroundings. Inside, a long wooden bar ran down the entire left side, tended by Morris O'Neil, a moderately grouchy Irishman who owned the place and promoted it especially to foreigners, using a video karaoke theme. The high bar stools were comfortable, and a quorum of regular expats, the single guys at least, would show up and complain, network their business deals, or promote their latest scams.

Morris poured the beer. His waitresses could serve drinks, but he controlled the cash. Morris was now in his twelfth year of paradise and along the way, as a matter of course, had married a Filipina. But now divorced for some years, he made do for feminine company with his pick of the young dance girls and waitresses he hired. At the bar he put in his time listening to the guys across the flat wooden confessional; it seemed they all had basically the same story, and he could recite his stock answers back to them while doing the business of delivering booze and burgers.

Thomas Thornton, a bit tipsy, sat at the round corner table reserved for regulars with Hank Starke, his foreman in the construction company Thornton had started when he arrived in Mindanao some years back. Thornton and Starke went back a long way together, back to the job they had done for Charlie Downs that had gone so sour. Since then they had met others of similar disposition from sundry national origins who eventually found their way to the Lady Love on Claveria Street.

Wolfgang Moser, a German national from the former German Democratic Republic who had washed up on the beaches of Mindanao after the end of the Cold War, occupied a bar stool near the table. Moser was now a D.J. with his own radio program on a local station. He completed the trio who met nearly every afternoon at the Lady Love.

Thornton kept up with the local news by reading the free copy of the *Mindanao Times* tucked into a rack on the wall. Today's front page reported that the popular mayor of Davao City, Eduardo Fuentes, interested in improving the city's cash flow from tourism, had recently approved through a city council he greatly influenced, if not controlled, a new ordinance permitting nude dancing, as long as the girls were not minors. Thornton raised his voice so O'Neil could hear him behind the bar. "See this? You should do your part to spruce up things around here."

"I'm making my best efforts to improve the scenery," Morris answered, then told him about the great-looking twins who had shown up recently, shortly before business hours. He had hired the two girls on the spot to work at the bar as entertainers. Only one of them had a birth certificate verifying that she had attained her eighteenth year, and hers was dated the month before. The other had no documents, and since one would not stay without the other, he turned them both away, with regrets. The next day they came back, with good photocopies of two documents, proving that Jade and Jasmine were born on the same day. Forged? Morris did not care. He filed the copies, and if there were ever any police questions, the documents, and a few free beers, would probably resolve the issue.

Thornton was curious to see if Morris would adopt the *hubo hubo* (completely nude) trend or stay more sedate for a conservative clientele. "So, what do you have them doing?"

"The twins put on a good show, Southeastern Asia style, you know."

"You mean, a short step from prostitute?" Starke wanted to know the score.

"Not at all. It's a line they never cross." Morris had set the ground rules. "I think they're sisters, and they're definitely more than just good entertainment; they're tastefully erotic and provocative, yet *almost* untouchable, if you know what I mean."

"You have to keep it conservative, you know." Moser was fishing. He put down the newspaper to get into the conversation.

Morris' heavy black eyebrows rose at that. "Conservative? Any 'conservatives' walking along this street at night are not going to come in here in the first place. We'll have a good show, but not get too naughty. Wait and see." O'Neil slapped the ceiling fan mounted above the bar to get it to work and returned to washing beer mugs, checking for lipstick smears.

"We have time. We'll see." Thornton decided to stay for a while and ordered another pitcher of beer, sharing it with Starke and Moser.

To make a stage, Morris had raised a curved platform a foot off the floor in the far rear corner opposite the bar. The warm-up act started, as a plump girl with hairy ankles bounced to a Beyoncé number. "Some of the guys like her, what do I care?" Morris told the bar in general and slapped the fan again.

The big girl left the stage, and softer music started. A statuesque young woman appeared, languidly rotating in front of a full-length mirror as "Greensleeves" played through two speakers bolted to the ceiling at opposite corners of the dance area. She danced to a slow instrumental version of the old classic, leisurely removing her clothing while twirling slowly in front of a mirror until she was wearing nothing but bright green sleeves that ran from her fingertips not quite up to her shoulder. The rest of her bare body shimmered from a light coat of extra virgin olive oil thinly spread on her slim torso. Then, miraculously, she stepped through the mirror and continued her dance back and forth through her own reflection until she split into two identical and discrete images of herself. Long legs entwined and two arms with green sleeves caressed two naked, mocha tan arms as she seemed to stroke her own image. Jade wore one of the green sleeves on her left arm; Jasmine wore the other on her right. When the soft, green filtered light reflected off their shimmering bodies, the image of one young woman became two as they rotated skillfully, dancing in small circles, intertwined with each other, sometimes one and sometimes two distinct forms, using the green sleeves to conceal, then to emphasize their small breasts and hard nipples. While they danced, each let her nearly waist-length, pure black hair swing tantalizingly across the other's naked body until the music ended and a brief silence filled the room.

Backstage, after they had showered and toweled off the olive oil and perspiration, replacing the moisture with fragrant Oriental perfumes, the two dressed in bright red mini skirts, black shoes with six-inch-high spike heels and sheer, black silk shirts with long sleeves fashionably rolled up a few folds and the top two buttons unbuttoned. The twins helped out at the bar between dances, serving beers and brandy. With the purchase of a full bottle of Emperador for twenty bucks or the peso equivalent, one or both of the twins might join customers in the separate videoke rooms in the back to sing together, if they were in the mood. Maybe some touching went on sometimes, almost accidental, if they met a nice guy. They were tall for Mindanao girls—taller than the short, squat Morris, for example—but thin and narrow across the shoulders, which accentuated the firm points under their blouses. They never wore bras. The twins seemed to dance mostly for fun, but they got better tips whenever they served drinks or danced with the guys and got a little bit too close to them. The Lady Love, after all, was not famous as a strip club; it was more of a meeting place for a clique of foreigners.

This night, Starke, using his best manners, stood when the twins returned, clapped, and with a sweeping gesture invited them to sit. As it was still early and not busy, they accepted. Jade pushed in between Thornton and Starke to sit, her mini skirt climbing her thigh. There was little room for Jasmine to sit, but, obliging, Thornton loaned her his knee as Morris delivered four shots of Jack Daniels, one of which Jade accidentally spilled almost immediately on Thornton's lap, making them all laugh.

The door to the outside opened, causing Thornton to shade his eyes as two men walked toward him. He looked up sleepily, straightened himself a bit but continued to sit.

Hargens squinted for a moment, his vision adjusting as he and another man, also in civilian clothes, approached Thornton's corner table.

Thornton recognized his old West Point roommate and shouted, "Luke! How the hell did you find me?"

"Hey. You told me, Davao City."

"You know where I live, but here? Let me guess, from our spook ex-roommate, Charlie Downs."

"Partly. It was easy, you cut a broad swath and you leave a bloody trail."

"It was Downs."

"Well, of course he has his own sources. Last week at our reunion, which you missed by the way, I retold a few of the stories you told me in Manila and nothing surprised him. He must have had his guys check on you down here. Sorry to interrupt your 'duties.' But, let me introduce Major Hayes, our military attaché temporarily assigned to the consulate here in town. Hayes, my oldest friend, Thomas Thornton."

"How do you do, Mister Thornton." Hayes thought for a moment. "Funny, I haven't seen you around town."

"I thought the same thing, maybe we run in different circles."

Thornton introduced the others. "Gentlemen and soldiers, meet Hank Starke, retired army sergeant. Luke, you remember Downs talking about him. He worked in Eastern Europe with me. Runs my construction projects here."

Starke, nuzzling with the dancers and drinking beer, gave a casual salute and popped off with a loud, "Hooah, General!"

"And my other friends, leaning against the bar over there are Wolfgang

Moser, our local German D.J., and Morris O'Neil, this is his place." Moser tipped an imaginary hat toward the men, and O'Neil nodded and went back to drying glasses.

"So what brought you to Mindanao, Luke? Your first time in Davao, and no advance notice?"

"You. We have some catching up to do, but it doesn't look like you have much room for us." Hargens checked out the dancers, who Thornton had not bothered to introduce.

"Anyway, it was time for me to make a trip to Mindanao. Can we have a talk?" The girl sitting on Thornton's lap was too interested in their conversation for Hargens.

Thornton disengaged himself and stood up. "Sure. You buy the beer," and moved with Hargens to the far end of the bar. Major Hayes pulled up a stool beside them, briefly exposing a holstered pistol as he sat, which explained the reason he was wearing a sport coat in the tropics.

"When Downs and I met last week at the Point, we talked about you. Downs had an idea. Now that I see you on your turf, I have the gut feeling he was right. So please listen to me. We have a deal for you, working for us. Major Hayes would be your point of contact. Interested?"

"Maybe. What's the deal?"

Hargens took command and started in his official briefing voice. "Al Qaeda has infiltrated Mindanao, supporting the insurgents. We need someone who travels in different circles, as you say, someone we can trust, someone who can do what you did in Eastern Europe, before you dropped out of sight."

"I'm out'a here." Thornton set down his glass with a thump, spilling a few drops of beer, and started to leave. "Downs doesn't trust me after that."

Hargens grabbed Thornton by his safari jacket. "Wait. We trust you. You don't trust yourself. We need your help. It's time to do your duty, again."

Hargens was convinced Thornton was the guy they wanted for the mission, and time was getting short. "I have a job that needs to be done, directly for me, without CIA involvement or knowledge. The State Department is OK with this, thanks to Charlie Downs being involved. Major Hayes here will provide some limited support in the field.

"Between you and me, the CIA screws everything up. They don't know the territory and could embarrass the U.S. more than help."

"You don't surprise me by saying that." Thornton was getting interested. "What do you need? Want me to operate a safe house for you in Mindanao?"

"More than that, your place could become an *unsafe* house. I want you to go after a target, a Turk, named Mahir Hakki. Al Qaeda recruited him to bring in enough money to seed a revolution. Just take him out, quietly, and then the rest of the job can be left to the Philippine Army."

Hargens continued. "Thornton, there could be some good incentive in all this for you, like that retirement fund you never earned anyplace."

That seemed to pique Thornton's interest. "Luke, you've attracted my attention."

"We can help you locate the target," Hargens continued. "Hakki has exactly five million U.S. dollars with him, mostly in hundred dollar bills. Make him disappear." Hargens zeroed in for the kill. "And Tom, maybe you did not do all you could have for Charlie on that Eastern European assignment, maybe you should have continued to serve. And maybe you can help him and me now. Maybe you can solve our problem—and your own." Hargens was sincere and convincing. "Charlie still trusts you, you know."

"And what do I do with the cash after I get this Hakki guy?"

"We don't care if the cash disappears. That would be the best solution for all of us, the U.S., and the Philippines."

Thornton considered the general's offer. "And you would give me some support in the field?"

"Not much. That's the deal. But Major Hayes can show you some new toys we have, and he can get you some local assets."

4

Elaiza

Philippine Airlines flight 193 angled upward, arching out of Changi Airport and over Sentosa Island, leaving Singapore receding into the mist as Elaiza heard the captain announce, "Mabuhay, and good morning ladies and gentlemen, our flight is expected to arrive in Manila on time at 1:47 PM, Western Pacific time." She looked out her window, saw Sentosa Island as that small strip of beach, the southeasternmost chip of Asia, where she had had lunch only yesterday, sparkled green and grew smaller.

Flashes reflected off flat surfaces in an area of buildings that is now a war memorial but once was Changi Prison, one of the many Japanese POW camps where thousands of captives were tortured to death or expired alone: British and Australian citizens-citizens of the lost empire on which the sun never set, until it set in 1945, Americans, and her own countrymen.

As the pilot continued with the usual boilerplate notices that she ignored, Elaiza Otakan plugged in the earpiece of her iPod to block out the cabin clatter. The slow beat and haunting melody of the song she listened to captivated her, and the lyrics made her think it was written just for her:

> dreams, rushing in, knowing what the end is, did you get everything you asked for, dreams, rushing in, dance floor, dance floor. Dreams, rushing in, tick tock, tick tock.

She took off her Nikes and pulled her white-cotton-stockinged feet up onto the seat, sitting on them like the college girl she could almost pass for, flipping through the airline's monthly magazine. The tune suffused her brain, mixing with her recent memories and future plans. She thought about what her American boss, Major Hayes, had told her on the phone when he called from Manila the day before, and wondered what he wanted her to do that was so important to have her fly back to the Philippines before her job in Singapore was done. He wanted her to meet him in Davao City, where all the trouble was brewing. What possible urgency could there be to derail her important assignment to track the state visit to Singapore by the Philippine President? It was her first overseas assignment out of Manila for the Americans, and she had wanted to do it right. Something important must have happened. Her boss organized his time well, writing details down in that leather-covered diary he always carried with him. The major was not inflexible, but rather hesitant to make sudden changes in plans without a very good reason. Or, maybe it was because she was the lowest-ranking Philippine citizen working in her department, and the youngest. Maybe they just wanted to check her out, to see how she performed.

Major Hayes had given her the iPod for her twenty-ninth birthday present last month, and Mrs. Hayes let her download some of her CD's. They told her she could make good use of it on her Singapore trip. She could listen to the latest hip-hop tunes while she lounged around the hotel pool, they said, as if she would have any time for that.

The flight reached cruising altitude and she rearranged the small foam rubber airline pillow under her head and sat back up straight in her economy seat, trying to get comfortable for the long flight.

As her mind drifted, she remembered when she was just eighteen and traveled overseas for the first time, coming to the city she was flying away from today. It was good that she knew Singapore; the Americans needed someone who spoke the languages and knew her way around. It was a big opportunity for her to show her worth.

She had left her village in Agusan del Sur in central Mindanao for Singapore to escape that Japanese madman. Mr. Ono was actually a great benefactor and probably thought of himself as a humanitarian, but he had been mad enough to cultivate a young Filipina girl, starting when she was barely twelve, thinking he could eventually take this young virgin with him to live in Japan. That was the madness part; everything else about him was gentleman. After she graduated she had sent him a letter, thanked him for having paid the church school's tuition for her high school education, returned the support money he had sent to her, and left for Singapore to fulfill an *au pair* contract with a rich Chinese family whom she grew to know and love.

The Japanese owed the Philippines billions in reparations for the rape and pillage of the islands during World War II. Now, almost sixty years later, who had won that war? Elaiza considered her educational advancement as part of the spoils of that lost war. Japanese businesses were sitting on the land, owned factories, controlled major sources of food and raw materials, and set low salaries for the men and women they employed. Not just the Japanese, of course, but also the Germans, the Dutch and even the World War II victorious Americans participated in the downward bidding.

She dozed. Her neighbor, a bit too loudly waking her, asked, "Are you going home?"

Reluctant to start a conversation, Elaiza simply answered, "Yes."

"Me too! I've been working for Toshiba for two years. I'm an electronics engineer. Going back home." Her fellow traveler was a proud guy.

"That's great. Welcome back." She thought that would end it.

But the engineer continued, "What did you do in Singapore? Were you a maid?"

The assumption took her back. "No, I was on a business trip for my employer."

He was a religious person, and talked to her about God's blessings, which gave them the opportunity to work overseas and to send money back to their families and churches.

Elaiza and her engineer neighbor debated their country's future while they ate the cold-plate lunch served to them some hours into the flight. She asked how he thought their country could break out of the vicious economic cycle. She thought but did not say that the church kept the people quiet, the "opium of the proletariat," and it also kept them over-populating the islands, putting millions into the work force in the last decade, with little useful work available. Proving once again the validity of the law of supply and demand, wages were low and the majority of families had trouble affording food every day. The irony: Christian values that encouraged large families bred unemployed workers, and the hopeless and landless ones in the provinces tended to become Commu-nists, joining district leaders who promised a shared title to the fertile fields of rice and fruit. She hardly listened to the engineer's explanation of religion as a business philosophy; she had heard so many versions of hopeful stories in a land where there was mostly bad news.

When she finally told him, "Excuse me, please, I'm very tired," and plugged her earpiece back in, he got the message and returned to reading his book.

Elaiza had found the way to make her own future. Thanks to her good education and excellent language skills, she was fluent not only in English and Tagalog, and had good enough Chinese that she had learned from the kids she cared for, but also knew several local dialects from her home island of Mindanao. Before the embassy job, she had always planned for any eventuality, starting with her first Singapore adventure, which she saw as a step to personal freedom. She would never let herself have to depend on anyone.

She saw the Philippines not as a developing country, but rather as a disintegrating economy, a banana republic in the purest sense, ham-strung by a primitive infrastructure and arcane attitudes. How could her country make it into the world-class society the forward thinkers visual-ized? How does one implement structural changes that conflict with the old cultural values? That's what she had wanted to hear from her Pres-ident in his speech tomorrow. Professional, living wages would have to be paid to government bureaucrats and officials to encourage them to be honest, which meant taxes would have to be increased to cover the costs. But higher costs of doing business meant that businesses would relocate elsewhere—Vietnam, China, Bangladesh, anywhere else—putting still more desperate workers into the streets, adding to the growing constituency for the Communists, or worse yet, Muslim Communists.

In fact, it was being reported that revolution in the Philippines was imminent and that conflict with the Communists and their New Peoples Army, NPA, was near, at the same time that the underpaid and prone-to-insubordination Philippine army was in rebellion against the current president and his regime. She realized that the salaries of even the well-educated were oriented toward bottom feeding; educated professionals could not afford to send their kids to college unless one of the spouses went overseas to earn a few dollars or euros as cleaning women or nurses. So the entire system in the Philippines was ripe for corruption. A small, or larger, cash "facilitation" presented with a wink would ease documents through the system, secure a position for a professional, find a parking place, or clear legal or illegal goods through customs. It was pervasive. No wonder that a junta of old army generals was threatening yet another coup, adding to the less than world-class image of her homeland as seen by the rest of the world. Well, maybe she could help do something about it some day, another reason for her to have taken that electronics course the Americans sent her to. It felt good to do such things, and even better to get paid for it.

The pilot came back with welcome news: "Good afternoon, we are 114 nautical miles from Manila's Ninoy Aquino International Airport. The weather is good; the temperature is 88° F. We will be landing at 1:51 PM local time." The aircraft was going into its final approach pattern. Before landing, she selected the same tune as before on her iPod, the words so appropriate:

> *When approaching an airport a pilot must call at least ten miles before approaching, tick tock, what you do and what you think you can do, what you are and what you do, looking out at pebbles on the dance floor, what you need is what you get, tick tock, dreams rushing, knowing what the end is, dreams rushing in, dance floor.*

Would her dreams come true in the end, she wondered, as they flew in low over the Great Smokey Mountain Range, the deprecating name Filipinos gave to a high stack of trash coincidentally located along the flight path. The dump, home to hundreds of destitute, was a colorful pile steaming with last week's rotting garbage and smoldering from the combustion of whatever the bright red and blue plastic bags contained. Green scum floated on stagnant pools between shanties with rusty corrugated steel roofs pushed together to form a village. She had flown into the dirtiest city in Southeast Asia, the contrast more vivid with the image of Singapore, the cleanest city in Asia, still fresh in her mind.

She had a too-long layover, waiting for Philippine Airlines to announce the inevitable delays for her connecting flight to Davao City, sitting on uncomfortable benches in the holding pen in front of gate nine, she had time to continue to think and remember.

The afternoon thunderheads were beginning to form when they called her flight to Davao City, and in an hour and a half she would be back in Mindanao.

5

The Turk

Sheik Kemal looked up and nodded at his visitor, motioning him to sit down. Mahir, not easy to impress, was impressed. Sheik Kemal was the epitome of a sheik in Mahir's imagination, wearing a long white robe and a red and white headscarf with a black braid (possibly an important member of a Saudi tribe), plain black socks, simple black shoes, and a solid gold Rolex President weighting down his left wrist. The sheik tore a leg off the grilled chicken that had been served on newspaper lying in the middle of the low table before him and sucked on it. He looked up at Mahir and made a sweeping gesture of welcome. "Our friends in Istanbul have told me about you. Join me in this meal and we will talk."

Mahir sat down opposite Kemal and pulled off the other chicken leg. They exchanged pleasant conversation for a while until the sheik eventually described the undertaking proposed for his guest. Mahir's eyes gazed around the room while he listened, and Kemal took it to be indecisiveness, rather than the contemplation it was. Mahir's mind worked best while he focused off into the distance.

Sheik Kemal, concerned about Mahir's commitment and motivation, asked, "Do you want the job?" He needed a decision, or he would have to move on to the next candidate.

But Mahir had his own question first: "Why did you choose me?"

"You are devout. You have met Abdul Sali and he approves. You can't be traced, and you have proven yourself," was the honest answer.

"There must be many like me."

"There are. But you speak English. That will be important where you will be going."

"Where will I be going, if I agree to go?"

"To Mindanao."

"Oh, yes, part of Indonesia."

"No. Just north of there, a short boat ride after Borneo. The southern Philippines."

"For how long? What would be my mission?"

"You will be on jihad for Allah for as long as it takes you to make a delivery."

"And then? What about my family?" Mahir was still asking the right questions, and the sheik respected him for it. He had taken some time to think while they ate.

Sheik Kemal visited Cyprus often, but he was born near and lived in Al Khobar, Saudi Arabia. Not related directly to the royal family by birth, he was a heroic leader and a charismatic figure. On occasion he still would ride among his tribe on the horse he transported into the desert in a custom-made trailer from his mansion in the city. The King of Saudi Arabia had confirmed local authority to a rival sheik for a big chunk of Eastern Saudi, rather than to Sheik Kemal. But Kemal had the real power. His clan accepted him as their leader in the ancient sense, with power derived directly from the land and the tribesmen who herded their goats and sheep on it.

Sheik Kemal also had money, indirect oil money. There were lots of ways to make money from the oil fields, and a percentage of most transactions in his informal fiefdom came to him in U.S. dollars in cash. He did not even have to ask for it. But he made sure that things ran smoothly for the ARAMCO operations in their oil fields. He also got a share of the profits from the importers of goods from other countries, what he called a "purchase commission." Sheik Kemal explained to foreign corporations that if they paid him a percentage of their sales he could facilitate business transactions—he could make them happen. The police had little to worry about in his villages, and the infrastructure functioned well. Because he and his tribesmen controlled the land, even if the administration in Al Khobar had the legal power and official sanction of the king, he, Sheik Kemal, was respected and not bothered by the concerns of the governors. He was a priest in the sense that all Muslim men are priests, men of God, and he was also an ulama, a scholar learned in the laws, because he had studied the Koran and applied its teachings in all that he did.

Kemal now asked Mahir. "Are you willing to leave your family for a month, for a year, forever?"

"I am willing to take on this mission so I will not have to leave my family again, and so we can live in quiet honor in our home." Mahir summed up his feelings.

"But would you die for your beliefs? You know we would take care of your family." Kemal's direct question and inherent promise surprised Mahir, but he answered spontaneously, "In the name of God the Merciful, the Compassionate, I am ready to sacrifice my life for Him."

Kemal was impressed with the devotion and passion of the young man, and thought about how men like the two of them could change the world. Precisely because he had the power of money and of the people, he believed it was time to make that power felt and to alter the way things would be in the future in Saudi Arabia, indeed in the world. The Saudi government was already fearful of being overthrown. Their ambassador to Jordan had stated recently as an official position that rule by the royal family of Saudi Arabia had been an institution for the last 250 years and that tradition would not change for the next 250, even as the kingdom accepted new technologies from the industrialized world. When Kemal heard the report on satellite television, he was angered that the government of his country was so far out of touch. A cartoon character popped into his mind from the TV programs his children watched, and he visualized the pressure building in Aladdin's lamp. He believed that once the genie of people's power popped out, it could never be put back. It would be the end of the monarchy, the end of the king and his family, and the beginning of popular rule under the laws of the Koran.

Of course, the new democracy would not have a European or American model. Sheik Kemal wanted to be certain that the new Saudi Arabia would take a shape similar to those limited, benevolent democracies in the neighboring emirate states, or perhaps Turkey, the homeland of the young man seated in front of him. Change was inevitable; the king would eventually die and there would be a new ruler. Sheik Kemal's purpose in life was to make certain there would not be another king, but a great emir, perhaps himself or another of his kind, a follower of the true prophet, not an admirer of the decadent West of Jews and Christians. The new emir would not be like the present officials, who drank alcohol and went with prostitutes as soon as they left the kingdom on a business or government trip.

He turned again to the young man from Turkey. "I know of your work in your homeland. It will be more difficult in foreign lands."

"Yes, I accept that fact. I understand that the cell chief wherever I am sent will be my leader. I willingly accept my role." Mahir admired Kemal's goals and vision and was comfortable in making this war his war; he would be on jihad. But also, he wanted the personal reward he would receive, or that his wife and son would receive if he were killed while engaged in the holy war. He accepted by telling the great leader sitting in front of him, "I have seen what you have achieved in your country, huge laser-guided machines grading the desert and constructing irrigation systems to leach the salt of centuries from the land, making it arable again, and systems to take salt out of seawater. I see what a strong leader can do. I see your vision, and I want to go on this mission for Allah."

"Hakki, for a thousand years people like you have gone on their missions to protect Muslim lands. Now we are in danger of losing the war won by Saladin on the plains of Syria in 1187. Those who refused to listen to the prophets, the Jews who sit on Arab land, Americans who have invaded our heartland, and the monarchs who rule the countries where the holiest places are located, must be thrown out. Your mission is very important in the new war." The sheik was effective in motivating Mahir by mixing personal stories with political facts as he saw them. "We need men like you."

Mahir was ready. He looked Kemal directly in the eyes and said, "I will go. When do I get the details?"

Sheik Kemal's contacts in Istanbul had cleared Mahir; and he had a good feeling about the young man sitting in front of him. He told Mahir, "Your mission is to deliver the resources to wage war in one of the places where the Jews and their American lackeys are most vulnerable now. Other teams like the one you will join in Mindanao will also be striking on the same day in other lands. We will make the world a field of blazing grass with too many hot spots for the enemies to put out. And for once and for all, Enshallah, we will also rid my nation of kings and return to the law of the Koran."

Mahir continued to look for clarification of exactly what he would have to do. What were the "resources"? Would he need to smuggle a nuclear device, or carry biological weapons on his body? "What is my part?" he asked.

"You are not a Saudi national, but you are a Muslim." Kemal was still not being specific as he tested the Turk. "You are about to commit to a great cause, and you will obtain riches for your family. Your part is to carry the fuel to those who will light the fuse." Sheik Kemal and his cohorts knew what they wanted to achieve, and Mahir seemed to be the perfect instrument for them. They did not want to use a Saudi national or to be personally connected. The sheik continued, "The time is right to make the island of Mindanao, in the Republic of the Philippine Islands, a separate and independent Islamic state, separate from their oppressors, the government in Manila and their American allies. With that success achieved, Indonesia and Thailand will follow quickly. The fires burning there will be our signal to rise next against the royal family here in Saudi Arabia. Americans will lose their will; they will be overextended and demoralized. Even the overseas Jews will not want to spend their hoarded money and will go back to praying and counting their shekels."

"I know what you say is true. I have seen the effects of imperialism and capitalism in my own land." Mahir continued to say the things

Kemal wanted to hear. "The Americans have become weary of sacrificing their futures, their precious retirement funds, to gain only what they call the 'hearts and minds' of foreigners in countries that have no relevance to them. I have studied about this during my training."

"Yes. They pretend to build roads and bridges to help the native peoples, but it is just so they can move their Hummers around. Al Qaeda and our strike force in Mindanao, the Abu Sayaf, stay one step ahead of them. The infidels build it; we blow it up. But now they have killed a loyal leader in that place, a true martyr whom we have been supporting, the great Abu Sabaya, shot with four of his warriors. We will avenge their deaths and call the people to fight with us against global Zionism." He continued to sketch out his vision for Mahir, without exaggeration. "The Americans will relive their lost war in Vietnam, an experience they so fear that it divides them even now. They could not hold their will together sufficiently to defeat a few rice farmers in one little country, they have lost their war in Iraq, they are confused now in Persia, and they will have no stomach and no capability to make a difference in the Philippines, in Indonesia, in Thailand, in the world. Our time is now."

Sheik Kemal was emphatic with Mahir. "Our mission for you, our mission together, is to establish an Islamic government in Mindanao, independent of Manila. We will create a global caliphate as Mohammad envisioned; we will establish the *Islamic Republic of Mindanao*. With our victory, we will embarrass the Philippine government and the president personally. Politically, they will have to withdraw from the Philippine Security Initiative or lose Mindanao, or if they do not negotiate, we will simply take over Mindanao by force. Either way, same outcome, we win, they lose."

Mahir confirmed that he knew what was going on in Southeast Asia. He said, "I comprehend; I read the newspapers and watch the television news."

Sheik Kemal nodded. "Good. We will spread discontent; then we will win revolutions everywhere. You will carry five million American dollars in cash to our attack team."

It was obvious to Mahir that there would be great risk attached to this assignment. His basic motivation was his duty; he could someday make the hajj knowing that he had performed a great deed for Allah. But the immediate job was just to haul money, and he did not understand why the sheik, with all his contacts and operational capabilities in other countries, needed him for what seemed to be such an easy task.

"Why not just transfer it electronically to someone you trust?" he asked.

Sheik Kemal was becoming more open with Mahir. "First, it is too much money to transfer at once; it could be traced by American electronic surveillance measures, and stopped. Yes, over time we could transfer it gradually in small amounts, but we do not have time, our operatives in the field need it all now. Also, I do not trust some of the people along the electronic path the funds would follow. Our armed men in the field must have it in cash; they need cash to put into hands, not electronic credits in a bank."

"If you do not trust others, why do you trust me?" Mahir asked.

"I do not especially trust you without reservation, but I have checked on you; I know your friends and what you have already done. When a man kills once, it is easier the second time." The sheik demonstrated that his intelligence was accurate.

"And we know your family." Sheik Kemal said it gently, but the message was clear.

Mahir had another question. "If you do not trust all our brothers in that country, I also cannot trust them completely. What happens if I am the one who winds up the hostage? What is *my* fall-back position?"

The sheik hesitated a bit; of course he had to track Mahir separately from whatever the simple field soldiers would report about him, as they might form their own conspiracy. Yet, if he had to get an independent message to Mahir directly, how would the Turk know it was genuine?

Sheik Kemal pointed to a large rock in the corner. "That stone is from the battlefield of the great victory of Saladin. I take it with me to remind me of my quest. Remember that stone. And yes," he told Mahir, "yes, I have a fall-back position for our interests. If I choose to use it to help you, you will know whatever you are told is from me if you are presented with a green stone and a white flower."

Mahir did not like obfuscation, "Just tell me what it is in simple terms." He was persistent with the sheik.

"I did tell you in very simple terms. What could be more fundamental?

With the complexities that may evolve, my simple answer will cover any instance. It is elemental—green stone and white flower. That is my signal, and you will know the message is from me. Leave it at that. It is easy to remember." Sheik Kemal obviously did not want to elaborate, and it was time to stop talking. Mahir would have to accept and work with what he had. Kemal told him, "Probably you will die, but we'll take care of your family. When you pick up two bags in Syria, I will transfer 250,000 dollars to your account that day."

"At the end of my mission? What if I live?"

"Live or die, when Kumander Ali informs me that he has received the bags in Mindanao, I'll wire another 250,000."

Mahir considered, looked the sheik in the eyes and said, "I will do it."

The next day, Mahir left Lefkosia and crossed the green line into the Greek part of the Nicosia. As he used his Turkish passport, he was not looked upon suspiciously; many transient workers made this crossing daily. Later the same day he was on a Middle East Airlines flight to Damascus. The Syrian contact who met him at the airport gave him a new passport, identifying him as an Indonesian citizen. Mahir appeared passably like the Indonesian shown in his passport identity. From here on he would travel on a round-trip ticket out of Damascus; one-way tickets always looked suspicious to airport officials. The next two days he spent at the Sheraton Hotel in downtown Damascus, paid for in advance by someone he never met, where two duffel bags were delivered to his room. The second day he received confirmation that 250,000 American dollars, half of his earthly reward for the mission, had been paid in advance and received in London into the old account set up by his father many years ago at Barclay's Bank, Ealing Branch. When he left Syria he had a new name on a new passport and five million U.S. dollars in hundred dollar bills packed neatly inside the two bags that he checked to be transported in the baggage compartment of the aircraft as ordinary luggage. Several porters and customs inspectors in airports along his travel route would receive good tips to let the bags pass through untouched. After connections through Bangkok and Jakarta, where he was met by a nameless person who passed him on to the next nameless person, his final contact put him on a fishing boat that was headed out to the Celebes Sea for a week. He was lodged in the crew's quarters, where he always had a bed to sleep in because one or another of the crew would be on duty. He had no work to do on board, and after three days of playing solitaire he became bored. The fourth day out they were met at sea by a smaller diesel-powered boat that looked as though it could move fast. He went the rest of the way in this *banka,* another twenty-four hours, with fewer comforts than before.

The last day passed slowly. After midnight, when the sea was calm and the moon was still buried below the horizon, the crew assisted him out of the *banka* and into a one-man rubber raft. He took with him only the waterproof duffle bags with the money and the small bag that he had hand-carried on his flights, and paddled the last hundred yards to shore. Feeling calm and committed to his mission, Mahir walked awkwardly over sharp irregular coral formations the last few feet to the beach, pulling his floating kit behind him in the first low light of the rising moon.

Zamboanga, in southwest Mindanao, is one of those South Pacific visions of a volcanic island, where mangrove roots protect the white sand beaches from a possible tourist onslaught. After the coral and the mangrove, thick undergrowth, chest high, impedes progress. Then the rain forest begins.

If all these obstacles did not keep the tourist industry from setting up sex clubs and four-star restaurants on the pristine sands, the threat of kidnapping for profit by the Abu Sayaf does, and precludes property investment in any business undertaking. The shore was empty.

Mahir pulled his gear behind him and quickly waded up a waist-deep stream, whose bed allowed him to avoid the mangrove spikes at the shoreline and to escape the possibility of being seen on the open beach. Silence prevailed at first while he waded forward, but when he stopped to adjust his equipment, the sounds came, birds of many voices, the rustling sound of something heavy moving unseen from lower to higher ground in the underbrush, high breezes stirring leaves above, and breaths of air moving strands of barbed vines to grab at his clothing. Hungry insects similar to mosquitoes and creatures like mantises he had seen before, only healthier and better fed, permeated the brush around him. Smaller species of flies and mosquitoes that seemed to have evolved precisely to enter through the tiniest cracks in his insect nettings buzzed continuously around him. They seemed to savor the insect repellent they sucked off his skin whenever exposed, drawn to the poison like an illegal recreational drug.

Who was watching him? The intelligence from Al Qaeda cells in Indonesia, passed halfway around the world to Damascus and back to him by radio while he was on the boat, would soon be outdated. Perhaps he would get new information from the mysterious contact Sheik Kemal had hinted about. Mahir had been told that small tactical units of U.S. Green Berets were located with Rangers of the Philippine Army somewhere inland from his present position, and would be delighted to catch him with cash in his possession. Mahir ducked under the canvas tarp he carried with him and turned on his mini-flashlight to check his map against his GPS readout. He determined his position and identified the particular river, nameless on the map, which moved past him as the tide began to move out and its drop to the sea became more pronounced.

He walked up the stream, his feet sucked down on each step forward by the decomposing vegetable mush on the bottom. He felt leeches sniffing for his blood. A short distance from the shore, where the coastal road crossed the river, he reached a concrete bridge and passed under an overhanging branch. He punctured the rubber raft, weighted it down with stones and pushed it under a waterlogged block of wood. Then he stashed the two big bags under the bridge and waited to meet up with his next contact.

There was little traffic crossing the bridge over his head, and no pedestrians were likely to enter the water here, certainly not at this hour. Just before daylight, he heard brush moving and a human presence descending the bank at the northwest corner of the bridge, part of the agreed-upon recognition signal. He observed from his hidden position, and then approached the stout soldier who would be his guide. Mahir Hakki was about to join the Abu Sayaf in their revolution.

6

The Embassy

Fort Bonifacio is the final resting place for 17,206 American soldiers, with neat rows of crosses and Stars of David extending in sweeping, circular rows around the central monument. Thornton did not want the number of dead buried in the American cemetery to increase, not even by one. And Philippine Army Colonel Reginald O. Liu did not want to add any names, especially his own, onto the crosses reserved for Filipino soldiers resting forever in the adjacent cemetery. But there was a good chance that because of what they were about to do their names could be engraved on stone here sooner than either preferred.

Liu and his driver, Staff Sergeant Willie Rivera, met Thornton's flight from Davao City, and the Filipino officer and the American civilian saluted each other with big smiles. Since he had arrived in the Philippines, Thornton had been in regular touch with Liu, mostly by e-mail. He regarded Liu as a near genius, whose wit and humor inspired all who knew him, his friends, superiors in rank, and especially the men he commanded. On the few occasions over the years when Thornton had flown in to Manila to visit, he usually stayed with Liu, at least when he was traveling alone.

From his teaching days at West Point, Thornton remembered Liu as the sharp, young foreign cadet who had an intense desire to learn and excelled in the study of what for him was his third language, German. That was a long time ago. In recent years, they had become comrades. When Liu presented Thornton to one of his cliques of military buddies or political alliances, he introduced him as "My professor, he taught me everything he knew." And Thornton would respond, "Yes, see how far it got him." It was a trite, self-deprecating act, but it drew smiles and opened avenues for more serious conversations among the close-knit hierarchy of Filipino military officers and businessmen.

"*Willkommen in Manila,*" Liu greeted his former teacher.

"Hey, Reggie, thanks for being here. What's up?" Thornton was not sure if he would be met by anyone at the airport, let alone the colonel.

"What's up is dinner and the game on a big screen TV at your embassy. Hargens clued me in on your plans."

Thornton threw his overnight bag into the back seat of Liu's government black SUV and himself with it. Thornton was staying at the old Paco Park Hotel downtown and Rivera drove him there after dropping Liu off at Philippine Army headquarters on the way. The insurrection in Mindanao was heating up, and Liu was heavily involved in contingency planning for possible military operations.

Later in the afternoon Rivera returned to the hotel, with Colonel Liu riding in the front seat and obviously on a mission. Liu was in action mode, wearing combat fatigues and a web belt with a .44 Magnum holstered and obvious, not his usual uniform for riding around town. Thornton jumped into the back seat and asked Liu, "Off to war, are we?"

Liu relaxed noticeably once they were underway and took off his weapon, handing it to Rivera to hold for him while he and Thornton were having dinner at the Manila Yacht Club. It was coincidentally the weekend of the annual Army-Navy football game, which provided a convenient explanation for an unusual assortment of Americans and Filipinos to meet without drawing much attention from the press or the curious. This year's celebration started at the fancy club with the old grads of the U.S. Naval Academy who lived in the Philippines hosting the West Point graduates. The Army and Navy alumni, divided today not by country but by school affiliation, included American Embassy staff, active-duty U.S. and Filipino officers, as well as several members of the Philippine Congress and prominent businessmen who had followed civilian paths after their military service ended. Several other officers also were wearing their fatigues rather than dress uniforms, indicating that something definitely was up.

After dinner, Liu and Thornton hung around drinking coffee until it got to be 3:30 AM Manila time, or 3:30 PM on the U.S. East Coast, where the game would be played. From the club they drove to the nearby U.S. Embassy to watch the contest live on an Armed Forces Network satellite hook-up. They found seats in the rear of the room around a big conference table; a bunch of Navy guys were at the other end. A few younger men and women from the Philippine armed forces and the U.S. Embassy staff joined the revelry after 4:00 AM, when the embassy started office hours in order to overlap with Washington before the end of the workday in the U.S. Even Ambassador Richardson himself came in to watch the game and to have his early morning coffee before the office workday began.

General Hargens entered from the hallway leading back to the political section of the embassy and plopped down beside Thornton, asking him, "How do our chances look against Navy?"

"Not good this year, Luke. Our athletes can't weigh more than 250 pounds, you know; they couldn't survive in combat charging up a hill with rifle, steel helmet, flak jacket and forty-five pounds of gear in 100 plus degree heat—something the Navy guys don't have to do—so our football team can't compete against class A schools." Thornton lamented the state of football at Army, a situation they both understood. "What's new with our little project? Should we firm up plans?"

"Some new info from the CIA."

"And?" Thornton was curious.

"The Turk carrying the cash left the Middle East and has already landed in Mindanao. Neither the CIA nor Philippine Intelligence was able to track him after that. Charlie wanted me to let you know."

Liu, sitting beside Thornton, was watching the game but listening to the Americans. They were all on the same page regarding the Mindanao insurrection. "As usual, your CIA is great with theory but useless on the ground, especially here, in my country. Did you study my report?" he asked Hargens.

"Yeah. Your boys aren't any better. And if they were, they'd just keep the cash."

Army scored a touchdown, and there was excitement around the room as the Navy grads hooted and the Army grads cheered, with good-natured heckling from both sides.

"In my years at West Point, we never lost this game," Liu commented.

"During my years we never won. Staubach was their quarterback and Bellino carried the ball," Thornton said.

Hargens got serious with Liu. "Reggie, I have to tell you, I would not like it if your political buddies got hold of the five million the Turk has."

Colonel Liu stood up, offended and getting red in the face, "But your guys can't get it either. You're not even supposed to be in Mindanao," and left the Americans to join the Filipino officers at the other end of the table.

Hargens took the opportunity to update Thornton. "Liu's an honorable guy, the best of the bunch. Let's help him stay that way. OK, here it is. You know Al Qaeda is waging worldwide war against us. In the Philippines, they're using this Turk to get money to the Abu Sayaf, their local cell in Mindanao, who will use the cash to control the New Peoples Army, the Moro Islamic Liberation Front, the Moros, and to mount a revolution. If they win the war, they'll install a radical Islamic government. The Abu Sayaf is on the State Department list of foreign terrorist organizations. You can be sure if they see the U.S. government putting our noses in here, they'll just toughen their position and move quickly to make something big happen."

Thornton wanted some clarification for himself. "If only the Filipinos would do it themselves."

"They've been trying for forty years to control the Moros. Never will happen; too many different interests, with corruption all along the way. Money makes it worse."

"What exactly do you want me to do, if the U.S. can't be involved?"

"That is exactly why I need *you*. I said we could get you close to the

Turk, but then it'd be up to you. This is the best I can do and still let
you keep whatever you can confiscate. Can't let too many politicians,
theirs or ours, know about our deal. I have to trust Liu and even his
boss, Congressman Galan: at least we know them, they're sitting here
cheering on our team with us right now. Keeping your mission outside
the CIA umbrella gives you an opportunity; but *you* have to make it
happen. You'll have help from our technicians as STAGCOM. I've
approved that as the operational name and concept for you as a consultant, but after tonight you're not going to see me for a while. So, good
luck. Stop Hakki before he delivers the money to the rebel leaders. And
whatever you do, don't let the Philippine Army get that money. They'd
use it to throw out President Cayton just as he's coming around to supporting our foreign policy. That's part of your mission. Otherwise we
wouldn't need you: we'd just let those guys at the other end of this table
get it. Keep it away from them too; keep it away from everybody."

Thornton was silent and stared at Hargens while the wheels turned,
then said, "OK. I got it. Until we meet again." Thornton broke off his
quiet discussion with Hargens before the others could realize they were
talking about more than football. Then he noticed another civilian at the
conference table.

A State Department employee far down the chain of command, John
Robert Mundy had been assigned to the local embassy staff a month
earlier, sent to Manila after working the Philippines desk at State as an
area specialist for the last five years. Mundy moved into a chair around
the curve of the table to sit beside Liu and watched the game for a full
quarter and a few Navy touchdowns before he thought it would be a
good time to get involved with the men seated near him. He had overheard their political discussions, and politics was his profession. During
a time-out on the field and after some social chatter, Mundy made his
move and asked Liu, "Colonel, how is our war against the Muslims
going on down there in Mindanao?"

Colonel Liu did not answer, but asked, "Is that an official question,
Mr. Mundy?"

"No, not yet, but I'm interested in any news from down there, where
the action is, and you may call me John Robert, Mundy answered.

Thornton left Hargens to listen to the new guy who liked to be called by

two first names and kept saying "Down there in Mindanao," unintentionally supporting the impression of the Mindanao separatists that Americans
saw Mindanao as just another piece of geography, "Down there, somewhere," not really an important part of the Republic of the Philippines.

Thornton could not keep quiet, and in a low and controlled voice told
Mundy, "Mindanao is big enough to stand alone as a nation. And many
down there want it that way. Mindanao could become another
Afghanistan or Iraq. Instead of making the hajj to Mecca, Muslim warriors will go on jihad 'down there' in Mindanao. Let me tell you,
Mundy, the rebels will get the same credit from Allah for dying 'down
there' as dying anywhere else in the world, fighting Americans here in
the Philippines, or wherever they find us.

"If you would please, either John Robert or Mr. Mundy if you want
to be formal. My experience and information assures me that we will,
with the cooperation of the Philippine people, win this war against terrorism. We have a political environment here within which we can help
create real peace in the Philippines." It sounded like stale rhetoric to all
the veterans around him.

"Mundy," Thornton answered—and John Robert Mundy took
Thornton's intentional affront to his name preference in silence—"when
our government sends a novice like you here, and you make statements
like that, it just forces the Moros to choose up sides, with the other side,
with the Communists."

Thornton thought this Mundy guy was a jackass, not because of
what he had just said, which revealed his ignorance, but because he had
said much the same thing in a widely quoted TV interview. His public
statements about Mindanao on behalf of the ambassador sounded
simple-minded. It seemed to Thornton that the most creative the State
Department could be was to send out representatives to shake hands
with children and pass out Bibles. All they got were photographs of poor
tribesmen smiling into the cameras for press releases about cooperation.

Liu entered the discussion in a more tactful way. "I saw this article in
the *New York Times*. It shows you in words from one of your own newspapers what you are getting into," Liu passed the *Times* article around the
table. When it reached Thornton, Hargens moved in from his left side
and read over his shoulder:

Yet as these images vividly show, a specter beyond terrorism seems to hover over Basilan. This ghost is the American military experience in South Vietnam, where, beginning in 1961, U.S. advisors arrived for an open-ended stay in Southeast Asia. Fourteen years and 58,000 casualties later, American forces finally left South Vietnam, abandoning a mission that most Americans had concluded was misguided and not winnable.

Hargens passed it on to Ambassador Richardson sitting next to him to read.

"Are you sure you can stay the course with us for as long as it takes?" Liu, for personal as well as professional reasons, wanted to know the answer to his question.

Martin Galan, not just a congressman, but also the National Security Advisor to the President of the Philippines, felt it was time to get a little bit serious. "The Philippine Army has some problems, Ambassador, General. We could use some help."

Thornton responded, "Congressman, your country is secure from foreign intervention up here in Manila, if it does not implode from internal corruption, but you would lose the southern third of your country, a major source of your food and foreign exchange, if you lost Mindanao."

The Ambassador thought it was time to cool things down. "Mr. Mundy, here, was assigned to the Philippines by State as an observer, so let's get him out into the field to observe. I need to know what is really going on in Mindanao."

"It may be a paradox." Liu was now baiting all three of the Americans. "If you Yankees were not fighting your personal global war, the insurgents here would have no one to fight against; but if we Filipinos don't have your help, we can't defeat them."

"A lot of people agree with you, Reggie." Thornton had thought a lot about the problem, and it bothered him. He lived in Mindanao. "Luke, why doesn't Defense get tough? The Abu Sayaf admits officially that it is involved with the Moro National Liberation Front, and both are definitely linked with Al Qaeda."

"Do we Americans have to sort it all out for our allies?" Hargens stirred the pot.

Ambassador Richardson could not restrain himself any longer and gave the State Department position. "We're *not* involved in politics in the Philippines, not in protocol or in substance; we have left all the negotiations between the Philippine government and the Moros to be mediated by Malaysia. We stay out of local politics."

Liu was not convinced, "You *are* involved if the Moros *think* you are involved. You guys keep talking way too loud about the Moros hooking up with international terrorist groups. Best to leave them alone and to talk in a civilized way, with some cultural sensitivity."

The *Times* article had made Thornton think, and he gazed for several slow minutes into the near distance at a dark wood-paneled wall holding framed photographs of MacArthur returning, of a former president of the Philippines, of a Filipina female spy executed by the Japanese, her name forgotten to the world but remaining a legend to those in the business, and of other forgotten famous people coming gradually into focus while his memory connected disjointed events. He did not talk for a while as he quietly watched the Navy team pile up touchdowns against his alma mater.

Ambassador Richardson leaned into a new discussion with Hargens, somewhat uncomfortably, knowing that he would have to walk a tight diplomatic line within his portfolio for their ultimate boss, the President. The ambassador had been briefed only about STAGCOM's official role in Mindanao and Thornton's deal with Hargens to locate the Turk, and was curious about the consultant who seemed to know everyone around the table. "I'm very interested in your opinion, your personal view of the present situation in Mindanao, Thomas." The ambassador was aware that on this specific mission actions would be taken without the involvement of the CIA.

Thornton, surprised to have been called by his first name, waited to consider what to tell the ambassador, then gave a short report. "The word is out that U.S. Special Forces are moving into the Davao City metro area proper. Olive drab trucks are obvious driving around town. This will send a bad message."

"That's not true! Our troops are assigned to Zamboanga only. The trucks you see were gifts from us to the Philippine Army. We know better than to upset the most stabilizing influence in Mindanao, Mayor Fuentes."

The ambassador asked to change places with Hargens and spoke directly into Thornton's ear, visibly upset. "If Mayor Fuentes is embarrassed and can't keep that city quiet, all of Mindanao could erupt. We'll have a chain of dominos fall if Davao City heats up and the NPA moves in. It would be real civil war—an excuse for the Muslims in the western part of the island to band together, and it could upset the entire strategic direction of our foreign policy."

"Mayor Fuentes will have more than just a lot of headaches trying to hold down Muslim discontent." Thornton could tell the ambassador the truth; he had no agenda to hide. "He might not survive himself."

Ambassador Richardson was plainly concerned about how the American involvement had been reported in the Mindanao press and wanted to change the message. "I will make a forceful statement to the press." He was getting testy, but his irritation wasn't directed solely at Thornton, who just happened to be handy.

"Big deal, Mr. Ambassador," Thornton answered him anyway. "Maybe you could get the Manila papers, the *Star,* the *Inquirer,* and others to print your press releases, but so what? Few people in Mindanao read those papers, except me and a maybe a few other expats. Mindanao cares little about news from Manila."

"Your suggestion, Mr. Thornton?" Richardson asked, calming down.

"Use Wolfgang Moser, a guy I know in Davao City, as your vehicle. He writes a daily local news column for the *Mindanao Times,* the same local paper that printed the reports you are aware of. He also has his own radio program. He's lived fourteen years in Davao City and can get the word out to those who're not convinced; he has real credibility partly because he's not an American. He's an Austrian citizen now, and a foreign correspondent for the *Kurier* out of Vienna, to boot."

The Ambassador called in his Public Information Officer, introduced Thornton to her, and told her to direct specific news releases to Moser. By the next week Moser would be reporting a whole new version of the news, starting his news segments with "In a statement issued today by the U.S. Embassy . . ." This would be the first time *The Mindanao Times* or its sister radio station had had direct news from the U.S. perspective to report.

The ambassador's action relaxed the tension around the room, and by 6:00 AM only Liu and Thornton on the Army side and Philippine congressmen Galan, Zobrado and Dureza from the Navy were still present, their coffees now cold and the game over.

It was Galan's turn to issue an invitation. "Will you grunts be joining us for breakfast? General? Thornton? Colonel Liu?"

"Sure, Navy won, they buy, right?" Hargens saw an opportunity to talk privately to the ranking civilian in the Philippine defense hierarchy. "Martin, this might be a great time to talk."

The Navy guys' choice for breakfast was the Bayview Hotel, near the embassy. It was only about 300 meters across the street, but everyone rode there in their chauffeured cars with bodyguards. Manila by night or near dawn is an even dirtier city than usual. The early morning beggars were just waking up, and the semi-pro prostitutes were almost ready to give up for the night.

The breakfast buffet was opening, and Hargens walked through it with Galan, telling him, "Your government has asked JUSMAG to help you defeat the revolution, but you won't let us use our troops. What the hell is your logic?"

Galan was evasive. "It's political, Luke, not tactical. I just do what our President tells me to do."

"Me too. Our president's objective is to keep the Philippines in our camp."

"We are in your camp, Luke, but if you butt into our business, the next generation might vote us out. Too many GIs hanging around bars. Good luck to all of us when they elect the next semi-pro karaoke singer. You guys may no longer be welcome here." Their plates filled at the buffet table, they sat down and joined the others.

Galan had run for president in the last election but withdrew when the current president's position looked solid. He was a sharp guy and a good man, and always ready to talk politics. Over breakfast he gave his opinion: "The Abu Sayaf are not a political or religious movement, they're just a bunch of hooligans with a constituency."

But Hargens saw a military reality. "Gentlemen, we share the same problem. If the Abu Sayaf get that five million, it could swing the balance. We don't want to lose a third of the Philippines. By the way, we can take out any target you give me. If your President can convince ours and I get an OK, just give me the coordinates."

Galan could not let such a statement pass, "But none of your combat troops on the ground! There must be a better way."

Thornton and Liu looked at each other while their bosses argued and shared the same thoughts: political factions were so out of touch and far apart that it was impossible to resolve their differences. And now the country had a civil war to fight, and the two of them were in the middle of it.

After breakfast, as the group broke up and began to go their separate ways, Hargens pulled Liu back for a moment and gave the colonel something to think about, "How does this sound to you, Reggie? Who would you rather get the cash, them, us, you, or your old German language teacher?"

7

Ugly Maria

Ugly Maria came by her name honestly. The Tagalog culture incorporated the name Mariafe into its language as a pleasant and fancy-sounding word, a melodious and Spanish-rooted name for ladies. Mariafe was meant to imply the Virgin Mary and faith, the precise Spanish translation. But when she told her name to the infiltrator under the bridge, Mahir slightly misunderstood the meaning. He spoke some Spanish at a conversational level and misinterpreted her name as Maria fea, Spanish for ugly, a name much more suited to her attributes, and once he repeated it in camp, it stuck and the others picked it up permanently. She never noticed the continuing but unintended insult, nor would she have cared anyway.

There seemed to be two distinct body types among the women of Mindanao—either the slim and graceful brown girls with perky breasts, tight butted and boasting world-class ratios, or those with belly girth broader than the bust, due to heredity and a diet of pork fat, rice and indifference. Mariafe Van Wert was an example of the latter and emphasized her androgynous ugliness by cutting her hair short, which made her virtually indistinguishable from the bulky males, especially because she habitually wore unisex shirts and trousers.

Mariafe had difficulty engaging in extended conversations, but was street savvy and had found a way to get a foreigner to marry her, sight unseen, through an Internet service. An aging Dutch fruit importer from Rotterdam, Hans Van Wert, intrigued with seeing the land where his produce originated and in need of a caretaker before he died, flew to General Santos City for the ceremony, after which they moved into a three-room house in Mariafe's village. He did not last long. A few months after his untimely death, Ugly Maria used all the money she had squeezed out of him, investing it with her mother in a *sari-sari* store with a single bedroom above the retail shop. Her new general store was strategically located along the road through her village in the province of South Cotobato and advertised "Foreign Goods" on its hand-painted sign. Mariafe lived there with her even less fortunate mother, and they worked together selling canned food and dried fish. Her jealousy soon turned into a hatred for all Europeans. When the owner of the hardware store next to her offered her a hundred U.S. dollars for a month's work driving jeepney loads of cargo into and out of Davao City, she took the opportunity, which also gave her the chance to do some wholesale buying for her own store in the metropolitan capital of the neighboring province.

She had heard about the Spanish who occupied the Philippines for half a millennium before the American colonialists took control of the country after a lucky war won mostly back in the Caribbean Sea, and thought both must be to blame for her plight. When she first heard about the Abu Sayaf from her cousin, it sounded like a good gang to join and, in her mind, a chance to hurt the imperialists and the Christian zealots who she was sure were the cause of her woe. Of course, as a woman in a Muslim war camp she would be treated neither well nor as an equal, but she did not notice or care, and the men gradually began to think of her as one of their own.

After she was recruited by Lateef, the squad leader of more than two dozen Abu Sayaf warriors, she began to spend weekends hanging around his camp whenever she was not working in her store or hauling cargo. Sometimes she would travel with the squad when they went on combat missions or to Abu Sayaf headquarters for training. It was she alone who met Mahir under the bridge and led him inland.

The two of them, an incongruous pair, remained together throughout the hot day in a lean-to shelter they made near the bridge to protect them from the sun. Shortly after dark, a four-man patrol led by the apparently underfed Abu Sayaf soldier with only one name, Lateef, picked them up. Thin, with skinny muscles rippling under his brown skin, he wore military trousers and shirt, sleeves rolled up. To signify his mujahadeen status, he had tied around his head a white headband with a red spot in the middle, which made him look like a kamikaze pilot before his last flight. Lateef led the returning patrol into the rain forest and ordered Ugly Maria to take the point, the first to push through the underbrush. From behind, Ugly Maria appeared powerful, squat and bow legged, and her muscled legs pumped her up the hills. The patrol easily followed her, focused on the faint reflection of the moon off the round, balding spot on the back of her head.

On Mahir's second night in Mindanao, the Abu Sayaf patrol traveled only five miles from their rendezvous to an established campsite. The place looked as though it might have been set up as a primitive camp challenge on some reality TV show, but it was the only home to more than thirty Abu Sayaf warriors, plus their women and assorted kids. Now that Mahir had joined him, Lateef's next goal would be to steal enough dynamite for the bombing that would show everyone that the Abu Sayaf were a power to be reckoned with.

Mahir watched two of the Abu Sayaf soldiers work on a laptop computer. He asked Lateef, who spoke English, if they were able to pick up a satellite signal and connect to the Internet directly.

Lateef explained the level of his soldiers' ability. "No, they're just trying to learn how to play games. We have to go to the mall in General Santos to connect to the Internet." Mahir felt lucky that he had a GPS device that worked.

The camp headquarters was a native hut, a wooden platform raised on stilts the height of a man to make it easier to see snakes attempting entry. The single room was square, long enough for two men to stretch out along a line on each side. Pigs, chickens and possibly usable trash were kept below the living area. The second floor had no walls, rather only a waist-high barricade to keep people from falling out while they slept, and a roof of woven grass. This is where Lateef and Mahir came to discuss their objectives and to make plans.

Lateef asked, "What are your instructions about giving me the money?"

"I must deliver it to Kumander Ali."

"We need some cash now," Lateef told Mahir, and went to open a bag.

"Wait. Sheik Kemal instructed me that Kumander Ali was to decide how and when to use this. He can't make another shipment before the target date," Mahir said.

"Ali sent me as his agent to get you. You must help our cause now. Then we will deliver these bags to Ali together," Lateef told him.

Mahir was not certain what to do. He realized Lateef could take the bags anyway if he chose to, so he replied, "You can have it, but I will need Ali's confirmation to the sheik, then my job is done."

"You are on jihad! Your job is not done until we have defeated the enemy."

"My job was to deliver these bags to Ali. I am not involved in other matters."

"You must be involved. We will need to pay for supplies to accomplish our first mission. Then we can move on to meet Kumander Ali. It is the only way you can get to him."

Mahir saw he had no real option, since he was alone in Lateef's armed camp. "Take what cash you need. You will have to answer to Ali yourself," Mahir told Lateef. "But I want a signal from Sheik Kemal."

"Very well. I will handle those matters. We should also spend some of this money to keep our pursuers busy here while we move to attack Davao City."

It was common practice for the Abu Sayaf to pay their pursuers, the poorly paid and loosely organized Philippine Army soldiers, to stage an attack with an arranged outcome and a fake objective. They would attack, pretend defeat, and leave behind guns, ammo and supplies, picking up a cash bundle left for them in the combat area. The next day the two enemy forces would again assume their antagonistic roles, both sides better off for the exchange, both paid by foreigners, with everyone making it through another day alive and fed. Thus the communist rebellion had reached its thirty-sixth year and would so continue if not for sudden global interests demanding a religious and political resolution, a visible victory rather than the informal live-and-let-live stalemate.

Lateef opened the bag. He was surprised at the sheer volume of the bills and took out one banded stack. Speaking English, their common language, gave Lateef an idea. Here was a man he could trust, who was beginning to trust him. He was a man who did not care about the money itself, but rather his duty.

"We will need you to be our communicator," Lateef told him. "Some of our people speak a few of the dialects, and some only speak their own tribal dialect. English is the common tie among our leaders and of course for negotiating with Manila. You will be a big help to Kumander Ali after we link up. After our victories you can lead the negotiations with them."

Mahir accepted his new role, and it put him in a position from which to keep watch on the money until his final reward was in his bank account. "I'll stay with you at least until you have joined with Ali and the tribes in the north." That was the most he wanted to commit.

"Then, at that time," Lateef told Mahir in accepting his offer, "Ali will signal Damascus to release the second half of your payment."

Lateef called in Ugly Maria, and she squatted down with them and the other mujahadeen. Lateef explained, "Ugly Maria will go with us on patrol. She does things others do not like to do." Maria was flattered. Mahir thought of her as Lateef's right-hand man.

8

STAGCOM

In her hotel room in downtown Davao City, Elaiza awoke after a good night's sleep. She had been put up at U.S. government expense, and had enjoyed the evening before, dining alone in the hotel restaurant. Now she was having coffee and croissants by her open window overlooking the park. She enjoyed living upscale in the city where she had once studied, living not so well then.

Major Hayes, her boss, had called just before nine AM and instructed her, "Meet me at the consulate at 1100 hours. General Hargens is back from his U.S. trip and has assigned me to be the handler for a guy he hired to help us here; I hear he's done something like this before. He's an older guy, knows Hargens from way back. I don't know yet what all Hargens will lay on us." He explained that the JUSMAG (another one of the government's endless proliferating acronyms) would be debating in Manila at that very moment how to implement whatever Hargens had ordered and then signed off, "I'm on my way to pick the guy up at the airport."

"Meet you at the consulate," she answered, and then had time to finish her breakfast in leisure. She was already in her new tight miniskirt and a pink-collared black top with a small design on the breast that looked like a paperclip. The Penshoppe logo meant something around this town. She knew she looked good.

Thornton's plane was late arriving in Davao City, as usual for the domestic airline. When he strode into the luggage area, he saw Major Hayes standing tall in uniform with hair cut short enough for white scalp to shine through. "Thanks for being here to pick me up. That wasn't necessary."

"No problem, we know you must be tired after your all-nighter in the embassy."

"I slept on the plane."

"OK. I need to get you to the consulate ASAP, but thought we could make good use of our time and talk along the way."

In the crowded airport terminal, Hayes' cleated dress shoes clicked along the airport corridor. Thornton asked, "So, what's new since yesterday?"

"General Hargens has a surprise for you. Did he tell you about our new technology?"

"Yes, he mentioned it, no details. Said I should get with you."

"OK. Good." They left the terminal and got into his official, but unmarked, car and left the airport.

Thornton turned to Hayes. "How long have you been in country?"

"Three-year tour, half up. You? You retired army?" Hayes was not all that curious, but wanted to be polite.

This officer had a plush assignment, and even got full overseas pay for it, Thornton thought. If he could have gotten this kind of cushy job, he might have stayed in the army for a career. "Yes, and no, did my time in the army, but only nine years, resigned, no retirement package," Thornton said, "still doing my time in business."

"You know about politics here. There's a whole chain of officials between the national congress, which approves the money, and the guys on the ground who do the work." Hayes continued his briefing as they rode. "Each level needs their participation percentage."

"Participation percentage?" Thornton had heard the expression, but wanted to get Hayes's version.

"Yes, say there's a government project that gets funded. This is a cash economy, so a lot of cash is moved around physically. As it moves from Manila out to the country, some gets retained at each level, a percentage kept for personal use."

"Makes life here interesting." Thornton encouraged Hayes to continue.

"I wish we could just go in there and do the job," Hayes said.

"Using our own assets would make it a whole lot easier for all of us, and them too, I know, but it's not allowed. The Philippine government has to get the credit. And that's OK with me."

"Me too. Let them do it." Thornton had his deal and was not interested in getting his name in the *Philippine Star,* or on some stone at Fort Bonifacio.

Hayes took Thornton to the Davao City Consulate, an old, drab building, not like the embassy in Manila—this place was for work, not for show—and to a downstairs workshop; a basement with no windows and poor lighting, "Need breakfast?"

"I've had breakfast, twice, but could go for another cup of coffee." Thornton appreciated the offer.

As Hayes poured a coffee for Thornton, Elaiza walked down the steps in front of them. The two men looked up to see first high-heeled shoes, then lean, brown legs, and a red miniskirt, as she descended into view.

Hayes made the introductions. "Mr. Thornton, Elaiza Otakan. She can explain the TIAM technology better than I can. Hargens has assigned her to work with you in the field. Elaiza is a JUSMAG civilian; security clearance OK for what we're doing here. Elaiza, Thomas Thornton."

Thornton said quietly to Hayes, "I see what you mean by local assets."

Elaiza ignored Thornton's comment and nodded in his direction; her intonation of his name had a slight accent. "Your first name is Tomas?"

"Yes, Thomas, or Tom. And your name, is it Muslim?"

"Cultures get mixed up in Mindanao. I have some Spanish and Japanese blood in me, but I'm mostly Manobo." She answered factually, pulled her iPod out of a pocket sewn into her leather belt, placed it on the table and began to lecture in a professional tone.

"Well, Tomas, we've added GPS capability onto the circuit board of my iPod, concealed it inside."

Elaiza sat down and handed the device to Thornton, who examined it, unimpressed. "Interesting toy. Just give me a cell phone with GPS. I'll call Hargens and tell him where I am. What do I need you for to take out one guy? I don't need a handler in Mindanao; I need some muscle."

"Easy guys, you just met." Hayes smiled but wanted to make the two learn some respect for each other. "We just had Elaiza wear this device on a trip to Singapore and back." Hayes paused, a bit reluctant to tell Elaiza. "Before your Singapore trip, we modified your iPod again. We upgraded its GPS capability before we sent you to Singapore. We needed time, data, and distance to calibrate it for your characteristic movements, your height, weight, average footstep, and simply the way you move."

Elaiza fidgeted in her chair, obviously troubled by the news, but stayed professional. "You mean you tracked me in Singapore?"

"The first prototype already installed before your trip to Singapore was a normal, military GPS. Then we installed a new device onto the iPod's circuit board, a newer TIAM (Tracking Integrating Accelerometer Module) microchip. It tells us much more accurately where you are. And where you've been. Footstep by footstep."

Elaiza was obviously hurt. "Don't you trust me?"

"We trust you, we just didn't trust the software and wanted to check it out. Somebody from our staff needed to make the Singapore trip anyway. So we killed two birds with one stone."

"I'm not anybody's bird. You could have told me."

"That might have made you act unnatural and ruined our test results. We'll download the data and see how it worked."

She had little to say to either of the condescending bastards at the moment. She had been so proud to be trusted to make the trip to Singapore. "I can read a map; with the GPS I could give you coordinates pretty quickly," Elaiza told Hayes.

"Good idea, Elaiza." Thornton asked Hayes, "Major, why not integrate voice technology on the same circuit board?" Thornton was also puzzled. Once the government gets involved, simple things get complicated. "Why do they make the equipment unnecessarily sophisticated?"

"To be accurate." Hayes laid it out. "The TIAM is different from old technologies and reduces human error. This device can track your every

footstep, even between GPS signals, and store it until we have a signal."
Hayes wanted to get Elaiza back on board with him; she was the best he
had in his department. "You ready for a coffee, Elaiza?"

"Latte," was the short answer from Elaiza. She did not like what had
happened without her knowledge.

Hayes continued. "We could have added voice capability, but Elaiza
would still not know her exact position, to the accuracy we need. And
with the old GPS you'd use up the batteries too quickly. We would
rather conserve power to transmit signals to the satellite. After a few
hours of use, there would not be enough power left to receive and to
send voice, but with TIAM and saving battery power, we will always
know where the carrier is. All Elaiza has to do is carry the device
strapped on her hip, and we will know the precise path she has followed;
we will see every footstep taken. Her Singapore trip data helped us calibrate the device."

Thornton was interested now and asked Hayes, "How do you
achieve that kind of accuracy? If you call in artillery, we want you to be
right on target." Thornton knew artillery and what even one volley of
105mm rounds could do to a hillside or a town. Air Force munitions
were even more powerful.

"While in operation, the device continuously sends a signal that our
satellites covering the South Pacific will pick up. Of course you will
know *approximately* where you are on the ground from your map reconnaissance, but we will see every step you have made on our computer
maps in the embassy."

"But how would we communicate a target's location? You only know
my position." Elaiza wanted to be sure she was not considered expend-
able cannon fodder.

"You will draw a line on the ground with your footsteps. You would
only need to walk back and forth on a straight line pointing toward the
target. If you call for a fire mission, first walk a small, two-meter circle
on the end of an imaginary arrow where the feather would be. Along
the arrow, take one step to the right to make a notch on the line for each
fifty meters in front of the arrow head to pinpoint the target." Hayes
explained in simple terms how to use the TIAM. "We will take out any
target you point out to us this way. Drawing the circle will call for a fire

mission. After you have identified it, we will take it out within three minutes, if we have the right aircraft in position and target approval. No need to communicate further; just get down and cover your head. Better, get out of the way as far as you can by moving perpendicular to the line of the arrow. The TIAM will track your movement."

"Knowing what will be coming down, you can expect to see some rapid movement along the perpendicular." Thornton would heed the major's warning if the time came.

"And it still looks like an iPod." Hayes, the technician, was proud of his work.

"*My* iPod," Elaiza continued to jab at Hayes for not telling her what she was carrying to Singapore. "And what is this target you're talking about?

Thornton liked that they were becoming a team, knew they could be starting down a dangerous path. She needed to know. "I've signed on with General Hargens to take out one Turk who is carrying some cash to Kumander Ali. I'll take care of him when the time is right. You track him with that thing in case we need help."

"Well, I guess that's it then." Hayes escorted the two STAGCOM operatives upstairs to the glass door and shook hands with Elaiza, slapped Thornton on the back and said as a farewell, "See you in the field."

"Not today." Thornton held the door open for Elaiza. "We first have to locate the Turk before we can get the cash. Try to get us some useable intelligence."

"I'm working on it. I'll get back to you when I have something. You two get busy. You need to find some muscle for your operation, some muscle the others at the embassy don't need to hear about." Hayes waved a goodbye to them both.

Elaiza picked up her reconfigured iPod and buckled it back on her hip.

Standing in the street, Thornton and Elaiza had to wait a few minutes until his driver showed up with Thornton's well-worn Pajero. They now saw each other in a new light. They had to work together on this unusual assignment, and they didn't know each other. Thornton broke the ice. "Let's check you out of your hotel. You can stay at my place in Toril while you're in Mindanao, lots of rooms there, and my staff takes care of everything. It will save you bouncing back and forth into the city in a jeepney every day while we get set up, and it will make our work a lot easier. Tomorrow we can find the muscle Hargens says you control."

"OK with me, Kapitan Tomas." Elaiza parodied his name, a gentle poke at his ego, and got into the air-conditioned vehicle, content to get out of the humid early evening heat.

9

A Message for Mahir

Mahir had time to think as they moved. He was not seen as a leader in his community back in Turkey, but rather as a mechanic. His role in this country with the Abu Sayaf would continue to evolve after they had attracted some attention, especially if their first mission proved successful. Then friends and enemies alike would take him very seriously. He was honored to have been asked by Lateef to go with him and Ugly Maria on a special assignment.

In the early evening twilight, the raiding party reached the cement factory where there was a large stock of dynamite that the company used to blast for raw materials and also sold to some of their customers in the construction business. The attackers set themselves up inconspicuously around the entrance to the factory and waited for the night; they would not need guns for this job, only knives and hand tools.

At the front gate of the factory, unlucky Carlito "Lito" Perias was the security guard on duty. While two part-timers worked in the back after normal hours to load a truck, he sat propped up on a plastic chair at the gate, quite a handsome figure in his neatly pressed navy blue pants and starched white uniform shirt with a badge created by the security agency to make him look official. A girl from the village sat beside him until it got late, fanning him with a hand-made reed fan. She was beautiful, almost seventeen, one of the village girls with dreams, her wildest one to marry a uniformed security guard, a professional of substance who earned the equivalent of six dollars a day, a good potential provider. After evening turned to night, her mother walked by and picked her up, both of them dreaming of how good life could be if the girl would someday marry Carlito. He was their hero.

From their position, the Abu Sayaf attack squad watched Lito for a while. Behind him in the yard, a scrawny worker loaded a flatbed truck. His co-worker inside the warehouse would stack an eighty-pound sack of cement onto his head, and he would balance it and carry it, hands free, out of the warehouse and drop it onto the bed of the truck. They loaded the whole vehicle this way. The workers did not notice the two men and a squat third person crawling up to the gate.

Maria wanted to kill Lito. But Lateef thought it would be more useful to keep him with the patrol, alive, as he could serve as a useful ruse. As the factory's security guard, he might be suspected of being the perpe-trator of the theft of the dynamite and the truck it was being loaded into.

Lateef and Mahir advanced into the yard and killed the two laborers just as they finished loading the truck. It was easy. Each took one of the tired workers from behind and used his knife to finish off his target quickly.

Lito became Ugly Maria's special guest. As soon as he came around, he began muttering never-ending prayers to Jesus, which did not endear him to his Muslim captors and simply bored Ugly Maria. Lateef made him drive the empty flatbed truck stolen from the yard. They put a gag over Lito's mouth, to get some relief from his babbling, and while he drove, Lito looked at Ugly Maria with fear, though she thought he was admiring her. The patrol moved into hiding before dawn.

The third night after Mahir's arrival in Mindanao, Lateef reposi-tioned his command outside General Santos City, near Digos, preparing to make the next move to an attack position nearer Davao City, 125 kilometers farther north. They stopped for food and San Miguel beer at an open *ihaw ihaw* that provided television for entertainment, the volume turned loud to show the quality of the sound system. They ordered rice with *viand,* the *viand* being whatever fish or meat, or possibly only a vegetable, was available in the kitchen. Some of the men watched a soap opera on TV and the exaggerated and romantic stories made them giggle. Mahir could not follow the dialog, so he studied the surroundings in silence. Two young girls were quietly working in the kitchen, preparing the food. They were solicitous toward Lateef, who obviously had been here many times and knew everyone in the restaurant. Mahir watched the girls move and felt pleasurable awakenings within himself as they circled about the kitchen in tight, ankle-length skirts and sleeveless blouses, their faces covered for religious reasons.

Lateef announced that they would spend the night here, and after evening prayers, ordered more rounds of beer and a bottle of brandy. Two of the younger Abu Sayaf warriors, pleasantly drunk, put a video CD in the machine and started singing along with old Beatles songs.

Mahir sat quietly in the dark and as the night wore on, the restaurant work stopped and the staff joined the videoke party. The two girls grew quiet, and as the others grew louder they moved closer to where Mahir was sitting in silence. They conversed easily with Mahir in English, and after they become comfortable, one asked, "How do you like working for Lateef?" Obviously, they were a part of his support structure.

Mahir was cautious in his reply. "I haven't been with him long. I don't know him well."

"We have known him since we were children," one of the girls said.

Mahir had difficulty telling them apart in the dark, and asked, "Are you sisters? Do you work here?"

"Yes, to both of your questions," the other girl replied from the nearer darkness beside him. It was warm and humid. They dropped their veils to talk to the new warrior. "I am the older, but only by ten minutes. This place was our father's until a soldier from the Manila army killed him. Our mother runs it now—this is all we have, except for what Lateef gives us."

"We're happy that you will help us with our war," the younger sister said to Mahir from the other side of the table they were now sharing. Mahir was surprised that they were aware of Lateef's mission, and he must have evidenced suspicion in his silence.

"We know who you are. We were told to say our names to you and that you would understand."

Mahir was shocked. Could others spot him as easily and ruin his mission? Why did Lateef not have this under control? While he was thinking, he looked at them again. The twins suddenly seemed to be more grown up.

"Don't worry," the one beside him said, "we were told to tell you that if anything goes wrong, this is the place you should find your way back to. We are the answer to your question to him."

Mahir thought back to his request of Sheik Kemal and the cryptic response he received, something about a green stone and a white flower. "Then what is the answer to my question?"

The answer from across the table was Jade and the nearer one told him Jasmine, and Mahir realized he had received the message from Sheik Kemal that he had been waiting for. His family was safe and the first installment had been received by them.

Lost in thought, Mahir looked around him. The younger warriors had returned to the stolen truck, and Ugly Maria was asleep on the floor, snoring and slobbering over the two duffel bags. Lito, still bound, had fallen asleep on a bench. The small TV was tuned to a game show that Mahir could not understand. When Lateef started to nod off, he found a corner to sleep in, leaving Mahir alone at the table with the two girls.

"We were born here. That's our mother working in the kitchen. This is her place, now, because of Lateef." Jasmine explained.

"But since we're eighteen now, we have new work, in the city." Jade seemed excited to have someone to speak to about her experience.

Jasmine confirmed, "We dance. It's fun. The money helps our mother."

"Especially when the great festival, Kadayawan, starts next Thursday, then we'll be back in the city. It's not far by bus."

"But now's a slow time, and we came back here to help."

It was obvious to Mahir that the twins knew everything, and he relaxed. "I heard about Kadayawan. Lateef told me. That's the time we will attack."

Jasmine made it clear she knew what was going on. "We know. You may need to return here, if there is a problem."

"Or maybe if there is no problem." Jade moved closer to Mahir, touching his thigh with hers as they sat. "Do you have a wife?" she asked.

"Yes." Mahir answered, becoming confused.

"Is she as pretty as we are?" Jasmine touched Mahir's hand. "Many men say the girls of Mindanao are very special."

Jasmine closed her hand around Mahir's and felt no resistance as she gently coaxed him to stand.

Jade wanted to be included and began to tow him gently toward the steps to their room. "Maybe we can explain better upstairs."

On the second floor, Jade and Jasmine slowly undressed each other while Mahir watched, then they undressed him and demonstrated why Muslim men are permitted more than one wife. Mahir was at first reluctant, thinking about his loyal wife and his infant son. But the physical reality was near and his family far. His desire became irresistible when they let their long, soft hair fall down and around him. He stopped thinking. He could not stop himself as the three became creative on the floor, their only bed being a thin pad covered with a single bed sheet.

Early the next morning the sisters were gone. But now he knew where to retreat if he had no other option. It all made sense now. The answer to his question was apparent, and it put his mind at ease that he had given Lateef access to some of the money. Sheik Kemal had kept his promise.

Lateef pulled his team together and this time drove himself, with Lito sitting bound-up between him and Mahir. Ugly Maria and the other men rode in the back, perched on the load of dynamite, now covered with a tarp.

The rest of the week they stayed in a new camp at a resort between the lake and the ocean, a few kilometers south of Davao City. The Abu Sayaf soldiers brought to camp the usual supplies of mangos and durian and other tree crops from the forests around them, which the farmers donated to the cause, willingly or unwillingly. The stolen truck was made into a handsome parade float covered with fruit and flowers shaped into a towering, purple peacock, innocent and lovely, but blocks of dynamite were tightly packed into its bowels. That would make a nice present for the mayor of Davao City at the Kadayawan festival. Neither the Philippine National Police (the PNP) nor the Task Force Davao—the local army contingent—would challenge such a thing of beauty slowly moving into the assembly area for the extravaganza called Kadayawan.

10

The Mango Tree

After she showered, Elaiza pulled a long red tee shirt over her head as a full-length dress and went outside to sit on the patio off her first floor room. Thornton's place in Toril, a village west of Davao City, was nice enough, small but with four bedrooms, she guessed. He apparently had a master suite on the second floor. Her small room must have been for one of the servants. She thought he must have two or three, probably an entire family working for him; in the Philippines, that would not cost much. She looked around her room. The few personal things lying about showed that others lived there. They must have pushed together into the other rooms to make a place for her.

The aroma of sizzling pork fat and onions meant someone was cooking a hearty breakfast in the "dirty kitchen," the outdoor cooking area in the back. She walked around the side of the house from the patio to the source of the cooking aromas.

Thornton was making fried eggs and ham. He looked interesting but out of place, wearing old jeans, well-scuffed Tony Lama boots and a safari shirt.

"Good morning, ready to go to war?' she asked.

"Magandang umaga," he answered, smiling, "not if I can help it. Let's try to do this job as quick and easy as we can."

"Do you mean the STAGCOM mission, or breakfast?" Elaiza teased Thornton, who gave her a warm smile.

"First one, than the other," he responded. "Breakfast sounds better than STAGCOM, but we're stuck with the acronym, not as bad as Strategic Support Command, the name Hargens *wanted* to give us."

"It sounds silly." Thornton thought she looked like a schoolgirl when she talked that way.

"Well, General Hargens created the name for us while I was with him in Manila. It sounds official and gives our team status with the paper shufflers at the embassy. They had to name the operation something to get the project funded."

"And you're the boss, right, Kapitan Tomas?"

"Yep. It's my command. First one since Vietnam. Just you and me—a young woman and an old guy—taking on an entire insurrection." Thornton winked at her. She turned her back and made it clear she didn't like to be winked at.

"You know there will have to be more than just me." Elaiza wanted to be professional. "My boss told me you needed some men with guns, a few really good warriors who know their way around. Maybe I can hook you up with the Otazas, Manobo natives from Agusan who can shoot and fight."

"If you say so, I'll check them out. I have another guy joining us, if I can convince him. He's younger than me and older than you, a retired U.S. Army combat veteran. We worked together before on a project like this, and we work together now in my construction company. We should be able to train the guys you get."

"I know you have to count on me to provide your 'local assets,' as you Americans refer to the people who work for you here. I want only to recruit from my region, from my tribe, that's where I have contacts I can trust."

"Right. Thanks. The man I want is Starke, Hank Starke, he would be my tactical leader, our First Sergeant.

"We'll see how he works with my guys. Nice place you have here."

Thornton and his company had built the house as a model home. First it served as his showroom and office, but as the business grew he took it for his own. Now, in the early morning and over breakfast, still tired after having spent most of the previous day traveling and then getting briefed at the consulate, Thornton talked with Elaiza about the mission from General Hargens.

Thornton had already accepted the deal, and Elaiza had been assigned to him as part of her job, but he wanted to sense her active involvement and personal commitment. While it was still cool, with an early breeze coming in off the Celebes Sea, Thornton quietly talked about his meeting in Manila with Hargens. He told her about the Turkish terrorist who was bringing in money from Syria to finance revolution in Mindanao, and that someone highly placed in the American government wanted his help to take the guy out.

Damn him, just enough info to get me involved and not enough to answer my questions, she thought, and broached the subject by asking, "Kapitan Tomas, it sounds to me like you have already decided on something, I see from how you squint and focus your eyes when you talk. What would you do if I didn't come along?"

Thornton told her the simple truth. "I would still do it, you know. But you're a volunteer, you could go back to Manila, or simply quit. I wouldn't want you on this mission unless we're in it together, as partners. I need you."

Elaiza wasn't satisfied with his sketchy answer and asked him, her voice the slightest bit skeptical, "Why such a change in attitude toward me? I thought you wanted some muscle. You've been out of the army a long time. Why not let your old army buddies and younger volunteers fight this war." She looked up at him with her brow wrinkled.

"It's not an army thing. Downs's position in our government now is much higher than an army job. He gets some of his information from the CIA, but doesn't believe all of it. He doesn't trust their competence on the ground, certainly not in Mindanao. Here, they're clueless, but they don't know they're clueless, a fatal combination.

"And as far as my Army buddies are concerned, my old roommates know me. I did a job for a guy named Charlie Downs in Eastern Europe one time, as the Cold War ended. There were some problems.

"But you're a combat veteran, right?"

"Yes, even wounded in the Tet offensive when the First Air Cav Headquarters in An Khe was mortared, but I didn't want to go to Viet Nam and if I could have gotten out of it, honorably, I would have. It was a waste of time."

Elaiza saw that he wanted to talk, and was quiet as he continued. "I reported to the office of the Vice Chief of Staff of the U.S. Army in 1967 and told him I thought we were fighting the wrong war in the wrong place at the wrong time. I actually used those words, long before they became trite. The old general listened and was quiet, then called me to attention and said, 'Captain Thornton, you are going to Viet Nam!' Somehow, having told the Vice Chief of Staff what I thought, I felt OK with going. I had made my statement. I served my year there and got out after a tour back at the Point teaching German. I enjoyed being an instructor and teaching a foreign language, but that was not a career path for me. Got out as fast as I could for a career in international business. I still got to travel, but that led to complications. I left a wife and child behind to take that assignment in Eastern Europe for Charlie Downs, who was in the CIA then."

"I thought you were a businessman. I didn't know you were an agent."

"I'm not, never was, not a professional. I was a businessman, but they needed a businessman. Their guys on the ground were too conspicuous."

"Just like here, it's easy for us to tell who they are." Elaiza had to agree with him. "Missionaries, someone as obvious as Santa Claus in the jungle, or big white guys in blue jeans bumbling around the hotels and bars."

"I'm a big white guy in jeans."

"Yes, but you don't pretend to be anything else."

"That's why Hargens and Downs came after me, again. Elaiza, this shouldn't be a difficult thing for us to do. It could earn me enough dollars to really disappear, or reappear wherever I want, anywhere."

"Well, I like it here; and I can't take any money. I'm a government employee."

"You won't like it here if Mindanao becomes a war zone. But if we take this guy out, I can keep the cash, and you will surely be promoted."

"But how will you do it? You're just another Yankee who doesn't speak our language too well, you can't hide, and if the CIA is lost in the woods, you will be too."

"No. I won't be. I know my way around in the *bundok* a lot better than you think I do. And Hargens and Downs know it. They know that when the time comes I'll make the decisions they would like to make, but can't in their positions. I'll make the right things happen this time, for sure. I think that with a team of men from your tribe, if we organize them and give them the right tools, we can keep the Turk from delivering the money to Kumander Ali. That way we all win, big."

"We'll see. I hope to be able to convince Uncle Pedro. Maybe he could get his brothers, the Otaza brothers. But I want to hear more about the deal you made."

"It's straightforward. The U.S. Embassy in Manila has tracked the infiltrator as far as his landing in Mindanao. He's a Turk, Mahir Hakki, and he has hooked up with the local Al Qaeda cell, the Abu Sayaf, headed up by some joker called Lateef, and they're moving around and already active in Maguindanao and Sultan Kudarat provinces."

"They've been doing things like that for years. So what?"

"This time it's different. The Turk has five million U.S. in cash. If he can get it to Kumander Ali, they can use it right now to start a revolution your Filipino brothers might not win." Now she had the essential background and information.

"How would you end the fighting, forever? What would you do?" she asked.

Thornton pretended to be serious, but had a slight grin. "*Mais il faut cultiver notre jardin.*"

"That doesn't sound like German." Elaiza's brow wrinkled again.

"No, French. Voltaire. The last line in *Candide*. 'Let us go work together in the garden.'"

"More riddles."

"Maybe. Here's another. Life in Mindanao is like that mango tree." Thornton pointed to a huge tree growing across the street from them and told her the story.

Evenings when the moon rose early it would outline the ancient mango tree on the opposite side of the road, its branches reaching upwards at sharp and variant angles to form ominous shapes. The tree must have been only a seedling when the Japanese invaded Mindanao, perhaps one of hundreds in a commercial plantation. Now it stood alone. Some said the tree was split when it was a seedling, as a marker by the withdrawing and defeated Japanese soldiers who had hidden gold under it, so they could find the tree when they returned. There were many legends of gold stolen by the Japanese and hidden in Mindanao. But the Japanese never returned, and over the generations the split tree grew, the forks divided just above the ground, growing into two huge trunks of equal size a yard thick and standing sixty feet into the sky.

After the yearly monsoon season, the mango tree burst forth with thousands of small, sweet mangos that struggled to ripen in the sun, but few managed to hang connected to their mother tree long enough to turn golden. Every day the tree was attacked by its only natural enemy, the young men who lived on the other side of the wall. Early in the morning on their way to work, at noon when they sneaked some *shabu*, illegal crystal meth, or when they returned in the evening and gathered to smoke, they would assemble behind the wall. When the farmer who owned the land was not there, the hoodlums would charge across the cornfield planted around the tree to throw anything heavy they could find at its fruit-laden branches. With stones that returned to earth to be used again, heavy wooden clubs, and rusty tools they attacked the old tree, violated its branches and brought down the unripe, green fruit still attached to the young outer branches of the cruelly assaulted tree, mangos that had to be eaten immediately or would soon rot in the heat after they split their skins when they hit the ground. Some of the more enterprising boys climbed the tree to its higher branches where from their perches they shook the outer limbs and dozens of green mangos would fall, delivering them to the giggles of the men below. At least once a year, one of the hooligans would accidentally fall along with his harvest, breaking a bone falling from such a height, and there was rumor of a death some years past. The young men ate the unripe harvest on the spot, before the farmer could chase them away. The boys thought it was great sport to get free fruit and to outwit the old farmer.

The farmer and his lame wife lived directly across the street from Thornton's house, at the end of a two-acre cornfield, in a shack against the hollow block wall the farmer was gradually constructing around his cornfield and his mango tree to keep the young men out. His wife sold their crop of sweet corn, roasted one ear at a time to passersby from the window of their shack. The farmer rotated crops, one year corn and the next year peanuts, which his wife would fry slowly with garlic in a pan, add some salt, and sell, one small paper bag half full for five pesos. They would have sold mangos from their tree also, if they had any. At one time they had considered the old tree to be their retirement fund, since the harvests of the golden crops would be greatest when the aging farmer would no longer be able to work the cornfield. But the gangs of shabu-addicted thieves always beat them to the crop. To secure his future and his mango tree, the farmer would invest any pesos left in his wife's cash box after they purchased necessities to buy a few more hollow concrete blocks, which he cemented into the extending wall. For the last ten years the war was waged between the farmer and the marauding bands of mango thieves. With the farmer now nearing retirement and looking forward to securing his pension, the wall was nearing completion, but rather than stopping the marauders, it just made them more inventive. They hid behind the wall, and when the farmer was in one corner of the field hoeing corn, they struck at the tree from the opposite corner, trampling the corn seedlings from every direction until the farmer's basic existence was threatened. He gave up the idea of ever having a retirement funded by the mango tree.

With that Thornton paused. After sitting in silence, Elaiza said, "Maybe we can do something to help change that." The story made Elaiza think. "Let's get moving, Kapitan Tomas."

Thornton liked the way Elaiza said his name, not Thornton or Thomas like everyone else, but a name she conjured, with a flourish of old Spanish music. "So be it. We're on our way to Agusan."

11

The Dam on the Agusan

The group of Elaiza's young cousins from Davao City made their trip look harmless, but Thornton worried about them being in the line of fire should the group be attacked or stopped and examined for ransom potential. Occupying the low-horsepower, brashly painted jeepney—an open-air public transport adapted from old American jeeps that legally carries twelve or illegally as many as can fit in it—they slowly rode up the long, winding incline out of the Compostela Valley and into the province of Agusan del Sur. Travel became hazardous as the oncoming traffic careening in downhill spirals toward them had trouble maintaining control of their vehicles. The saddle they eventually crossed over was the watershed where streams first flow north into the valley of the Agusan instead of south to the Gulf of Davao.

Thornton wondered if unseen adversaries knew where he was, whether a rebel noticed him among the colorful band of natives and whether they believed this apparently tranquil domestic scene was posed, if they were watching. Today's trip may have been a dumb idea, Thornton thought, but since he had encouraged Elaiza to recruit men from her extended family to join STAGCOM, he had to make the trip so they could get a look at each other. Of course the Otaza clan, the Manobo family on her mother's side, had heard about Elaiza's prestigious position with the American Embassy and knew she was involved in some things she could not talk about. Exactly what she was doing they were not sure, but she traveled to other countries, and anything "overseas" was a goal they all dreamed about. Anything was better than working in the rice fields or banana plantations in the steamy heat along the banks of the Agusan River.

A young boy, skin burnt almost black by the tropical sun, hurried along the side of the road, happy with the flapping stack of dry coconut fronds balanced on his head, and proudly taking them home for the family cooking fire. Thornton watched other images roll by. A thin, evenly brown young girl trotted behind her mother, followed by a single member of an indigenous armed force mounted on a horse of acceptable character and carrying a newer looking M-16 rifle. The single component of military dress signifying his membership in any kind of organized unit was his floppy camouflage hat. But everyone in the jeepney knew that the rebels, in this area the NPA, the communist New Peoples Army, controlled this province in central Mindanao. The NPA owned this land.

The jeepney continued north, more slowly now as an eight-wheeled trencher leased by the Japanese multinational Marubeni was laying fiber optic cable alongside the main highway and obstructing progress. Eventually that cable would bring Internet access to the inhabitants of the tree houses along that road. The hope was that the next generation of children would become just as literate and able to compete for overseas jobs as their brethren in the big cities. If they had been hooked up to the Internet today, they might already have the news that Thornton did not, and the villagers might not be quite as happy as they seemed to be, waving at the stranger as he passed by in the jeepney.

Bringing the kids from Davao along on a holiday junket was meant to serve as a cover for Thornton. But some eager NPA patrol might take an opportunity to make a name for its leader if they had any idea that an American was in their domain.

There was no obvious place to stop and eat, until they found an unnamed roadside stand with only a dirty, hand-painted sign advertising "Grilled Chickens" in Visayan and English. Fresh lemon grass gave a sweet aroma to a rich fish soup with rice. A few extra kilos of steamed white rice were served cold with smoky-tasting taro root. Three street chickens, somewhat burned, were torn apart by greasy fingers and eaten by hand. Lunch for about a dozen Otakans, Otazas and Thornton added up to a total cost of $19.37.

Thornton shaded his eyes to watch a large bird soaring high above rice fields bounded by banana trees in the near distance and a mountain range on the horizon.

"That's Kabayan, the only Philippine eagle living in the wild." Elaiza followed his gaze. "A few more are in captivity, near here in Malagos. Eggs are being incubated there. Maybe someday they can release more. When I was in school, we had projects to save the eagles. Even the President came down to see."

"It's so quiet and peaceful."

"It won't be if you guys mess it up."

"Maybe we can keep it this way."

"What do you really think will happen, Kapitan Tomas?"

"We'll win another war. I'll get the money. What do you think will happen, Elaiza?"

"It will be like it has always been. Foreigners come and go, and we are left to fight each other over and over again, brother against brother."

As they drove on she grew melancholy, and Elaiza told Thornton her story. The flood of '89 took all their crops with it, and forced the family for the first time to work for others, in this case the Sime Darby group and their Chinese partners who planted coconut and rubber trees on what was left when the water went down. The Otakan family started over. While her father worked on the new dam, Elaiza's mother sold dried fish and sundry items in her *sari-sari* store by the road, in exchange for gold flakes found by her customers in the clearer streams rippling into the Agusan. Elaiza was the youngest child, and slept with her hand on her mother's breast, seeking security stolen by the flood. Sometimes she pinched her mother's breast when the bad dreams came.

The next year, just as normalcy was returning, things got worse. The Otakans were playing a May Day softball game against the Otaza family, a happy rivalry and a great excuse to roast a pig. Elaiza's mother hit a long ball, and struck her head on the plate sliding safely home. As she lapsed into and out of consciousness, Elaiza sat fearfully beside her, touching her still beating breast. It took almost two months for the brain to swell until, without the relief of an unaffordable operation, the unavoidable end came. Elaiza's father continued to work on the dam, and the eight children had to be portioned out among older uncles in nearby villages. It would be a long time before Elaiza felt secure enough to slip her small brown hand under anyone's shirt again.

Elaiza continued to reminisce. Eventually, their troupe reached the dam on the Agusan River, the dam that Elaiza's father had helped to build with pride as the foreman of a carpentry crew using bamboo moulds to shape the concrete now holding back some of the river's force. Their northward journey ended, and the cousins spent the remaining morning in the village, Elaiza reminiscing about her youth, Thornton absorbing a new life, so foreign to his past and so full of uncertainties. Backed up against the dam where the road abruptly ended, Thornton thought maybe he had traveled as far in life as he could without turning around, in more ways than one.

Elaiza's extended family in Agusan were curious about the big white guy and why Elaiza had brought him there. Thornton, Elaiza, and the noisy children who were along only for the ride clambered up the steel grill steps on the side of the dam as though it was a tourist attraction. As a matter of concern, Thornton tried to observe the opposite shore, obscured where the brown water disappeared beneath overhanging palms. It was quiet except for bird noises and the gurgle of the water floating illegally-cut logs downstream to some secret saw mill.

Walking near the dam on a sticky mud path, Elaiza showed Thornton the coconut wood house built on stilts where she had once lived with her family. They climbed the ladder to the single room, where the bare hardwood floor of native yakal had been polished smooth by genera-tions of bare feet. An open window framed palms standing quietly in regular patterns. Dark brown smiling children climbed up the closer trees, holding on to the trunks with their hands and grasping branches with their toes, smiling back, wanting to be a part of the extraordinary event of a blond stranger in their domain. On the hard-packed dirt floor below the raised hut, women in knee-length sarongs, hand-woven in twists of black and red with bright white strands, and younger girls comfortably topless until they went into the village, were chopping the tops off coconuts to collect a refreshing drink of coconut water to offer their guests. Outside the house, eggplant, okra and a few stalks of corn grew in an area fenced off with flat bamboo sticks wired together. Half a dozen skinny goats with fat udders stretched full of milk nibbled at underbrush outside the fence. In some villages, the goat owners made a kind of cheese from the rich milk, but here it was reserved for the young goats, to get them to an age where they could be roasted over an open fire for birthday parties.

Although Thornton found the day interesting, he was worried about time, about when the Abu Sayaf would make their next move, and asked Elaiza, "Why did you bring me here? Couldn't we recruit these guys in a civilized place?"

"No. Being here is important. If you want the Otazas to work for us, you had to come to them first."

Pedro Otaza, wearing floppy sandals, blue shorts and an almost white tee shirt, sat with his four brothers on logs or stools eating rice from a common bowl and scooping up pieces of fried pork with their fingers, laughing and smiling about whatever one of the others said, and drinking beer from cans while passing around a bottle of cheap brandy. The younger Otazas trusted Pedro to handle the planning. Elaiza introduced Thornton who shook hands with each of the Otazas in return and took a long swig of the brandy they offered.

"I hear that you and your brothers know how to shoot?" Thornton said to Pedro.

Pedro stood up with his .22 rifle and moved to the outer edge of the circle of people, took aim and a small bird fell from a nearby tree.

"We shoot birds with our .22s to feed the dogs. It's not difficult. We're good shots. We also have experience with knives, with our bolos."

Thornton asked, "How do you defend against an upward thrust?"

Pedro stood up and drew his bolo while Thornton tested him. "This is thrust, parry, slash." Pedro adequately countered the standard moves in their mock combat, a stab from above defended by a raised forearm, a forward thrust parried and deflected.

"But have you actually fought other men?" Thornton asked.

Pedro showed Thornton his left hand. It had a fresh cut deep into the meat between his left thumb and index finger and had been sewn back together with a piece of cotton cord of the same texture and tensile that Americans would use to sew up stuffed turkeys at Thanksgiving.

"Sometimes you have to defend with your bare hands. It's better than being stabbed."

Thornton looked at Pedro's wound. "Who fixed that for you?"

"I sewed it together myself. Luckily, I'm right-handed and could use my fishing net needle." Pedro tightened the cord, poured brandy over the wound, and caught the run-off excess in a cup. He looked for a moment at the few drops of blood in the brandy, and drank it. "No reason to waste good Tanduay."

"If his brothers are like him, I think we have our team," Thornton later told Elaiza.

"He'll drive the jeepney back to Toril. It will give you a chance to get to know each other. His brothers will do whatever he says." Elaiza had already talked with Pedro.

When it was time to start back, family members respectfully pushed into the jeepney. One of Elaiza's young cousins, the pubescent Jenyvie, crowded into the front seat and sat on Thornton's lap. She was fascinated with the strange guy she saw as a great albino *carabao* in dark sunglasses, but also wanted to escape the squeeze of the other dozen or so cousins pried into the back rows of seats with their parents. Elaiza debated with the curious child in Visayan and after a few minutes the girl squeezed over the seat and joined her cousins.

As they drove on, the tinny sound from the jeepney's radio entertained the travelers with Karaoke-suitable Rod Stewart sound-alikes, interspersed with news from the province capital. Things were heating up again in Zamboanga since the well-publicized arrival of the U.S. advisors now engaged in a joint military exercise—named Talon Vision—with the Philippine Army. The happily singing load of kids and cousins were oblivious to the news, which Thornton listened to closely. All the radio stations in Davao City were reporting the elevated threat of terrorist activity and Mayor Fuentes had announced a red alert for the upcoming holiday parades. Task Force Davao and the local police would be putting up roadblocks and opening the trunks of every passing car to check for explosive devices.

The road they traveled was a rehabilitation project under the administration of the previous president, but it was still a two-lane muddy path. During the past few years over five million U.S. dollars had been spent on construction but almost no work had been done. The money sent down from the capital dissipated somehow along the way, as it filtered through the various layers of government on its path from Manila to Mindanao. The intended economic impact of immediate construction, jobs and the pathway for produce to move to the seaport of Butuan, the gateway to the impoverished province, devolved into just another slush fund program of graft and bickering. Maybe the vision of the NPA, the communist idealists, had some merit for this large island, divided by religious and commercial differences and unable to compromise with a central government so far removed from them in distance and in philosophy.

The stops along the way back to Davao City from the dam made Thornton nervous. Each stop ate up too much time and exposed them to close inspection whenever they were outside the jeepney.

North of Tagum the jeepney stopped along the road and the passengers moved respectfully into a small cemetery. "Please come with me." Elaiza invited Thornton to join her family and he followed her down a narrow forest path, scratching his head slightly on a low-hanging limb. Elaiza checked out the scratch, taking his arm for a moment to show him the way.

"This is my mother's grave. We all stop here whenever we return to Agusan."

Thornton looked for birth and death dates on a tombstone, but the grave was covered only by a primitive, uneven concrete slab, with no dates or names.

Elaiza brushed shoulders with Thornton as they stood there, silent, thinking that someday she'd lie here beside her mother. It seemed to Thornton that she leaned ever so slightly against him for a moment of support and comfort.

As the group left the cemetery, Thornton took Elaiza's elbow and escorted her back to the jeepney. While she was fussing with the young girls to get back into the vehicle, without being seen by Elaiza, Thornton talked aside to the caretaker standing by the gate, an older man who seemed to be permanently camped by the entrance and nearly ready for a place there himself. The caretaker asked Thornton for a few pesos tip, which he received, along with an unexpected offer.

"Can you contract to fix up the Otakan grave?" and offered the man five hundred dollars in cash.

The caretaker beamed, "For that, I can do anything you want."

Thornton made a sketch in his notebook and tore out a page, which he gave to the caretaker with a combination lock he kept in his canvas backpack. "When the project is finished, put this lock on the compartment in back of the tombstone," and gave him the open lock.

Thornton jumped back into the jeepney as Elaiza made a place for him beside her.

South of Tagum, Thornton received a text message on his cell phone: "U.S. Consulate, Davao City, reports explosion, a taxi rammed through the gate, exploded, area sprayed with blood, crater blown into pavement, several known dead, the Homeland Security Officer on site. Confirm." He punched in "Roger, Out" to acknowledge receipt.

"Kapitan Tomas," Elaiza's intonation showed her concern, "I know that frown means something not too good."

"I'll explain when we have some time alone. The Abu Sayaf hit our consulate, but no need to disturb everyone else. Let it rest. Hayes is OK." From now until they arrived back in the isolation and relative safety of Toril, Thornton felt that the Muslim insurgents could sense them, small ants crawling along on the sticky, muddy road.

Pedro continued to drive the jeepney, and when they stopped Thornton gave him the additional duty to stay close and to watch—not near, but close—with his bolo sharp but hidden. Thornton hoped that in the coming days Pedro would recruit his Manobo brothers to work with him on the mission he was about to commence, now made urgent by the news he had just received.

Thornton decided it was too soon to brief Pedro, but Elaiza needed to know now. Following the bombing, there could be insurgent activity on their return route, which meant she would have to re-direct their return to Toril and back to what he hoped was his safe house. Even though he was wearing a bush hat and unnecessarily long sleeves, anyone could see from a distance that Thornton was a white guy. But Elaiza blended in, or would if she didn't dress quite so uptown. Even under the most flowing native skirt, it would be hard not to notice her form when she moved, lean muscle tightened by hand-to-hand combat training and laps around the gym back in Singapore or Manila. They both would need to think more about their dress habits.

As the afternoon wore on, the Otakans and Otazas began to depart and return to their homes in nearby villages, except Pedro, who would stay near Toril, and some of the cousins from the city. While Pedro dozed on a bench in front of the restaurant, Thornton showed Elaiza the saved message from Major Hayes: "Abu Sayaf blew up consulate; dozen killed. Get back ASAP. Carefully."

She put her head down, straight black hair swinging forward, hiding her concern. He could almost feel the GPS signal searing into her brain. This territory was her home, and she knew where the paths and roads were and were not.

Elaiza woke Pedro and spoke intensely to him in Visayan, giving him all the information he needed to know at that moment. Thornton's cell phone vibrated again. He said nothing but showed Elaiza the new text message: "US Attaché and 20 civilians dead, suicide bomber with them, blast at Davao Airport, return. STAGCOM."

In Manila, the U.S. Embassy issued a warning to U.S. citizens not to travel in the Philippines.

Elaiza looked at Thornton seriously. "It's started."

12

Sergeant Starke

From the small balcony of his apartment overlooking the Davao River, Hank Starke watched a river ferry, a larger *banka,* picking up passengers at the Bankerohan wharf. Men and women alike wearing blue jeans and tee shirts, the contemporary unisex dress code in Davao City, crossed above the brown water on a narrow wooden plank to board a boat that would take them on their commute upstream to an inland village or to the provinces across the river and away from the city proper. Directly below the balcony in the alley, two squatting women wearing conical, hand-woven grass hats were grilling chicken parts on a hand-made grill set up in the street and conversing. A short-legged, obese, brown and white dog wearing a leather harness settled in beside them, arched his back and strained, placing a smooth, nicely tapered shape next to the women. It did not disturb the preparation of their food.

Before the relative cool of the morning turned into the predictably sultry day, Starke pushed through the curtain of hanging plastic beads that separated the open balcony from the living area. The beads produced a soothing, clinking jingle. He boiled a pot of water and made three cups of weak black tea with double sugars. As the twins began to twitch and stretch out in their drowsiness, he placed two of the cups onto the small rattan table beside their shared bed. Starke liked their unique relationship and would regret the day it would end, as all things must, but for now, why should he give it all up? The twins had been living with him, on and off, since that first night. He had come to suspect they might not be actual twins, maybe sisters, or maybe just friends. He didn't care.

While he watched them, he contemplated the deal Thornton was suggesting. Should he get involved in a lot of potential trouble with his business partner? Should he try to talk him out of a mercenary deal? They had a good enough business, and neither wanted another tragedy like the one Thornton had lived through in Eastern Europe. He didn't talk about it much. Starke thought, "This is not my country. My country doesn't care about either me or this far-away place. All my friends back in Ohio are totally ignorant of this place, this culture, even that these people exist. My best bet is just to continue like I am."

Starke had been a wrestler in high school before he joined the army, and was still remembered as a sparkplug in the beer joints around North Canton, Ohio. His center of gravity was so low that it seemed theoretically impossible according to the laws of physics for him to be upset, let alone pinned. Not fat, but stable and broad based, with Popeye's arms and a wrestler's wrists, when he went on the attack, narrowing his eyes, adversaries felt the challenge, and most eventually succumbed.

As he aged, Starke began to look like Larry Csonka, the Hall of Fame fullback of the Miami Dolphins, with a rounded face and what would be called a pug nose if it were at all cute and not just pushed up. He was somewhere in his forties, and it was evident that his black hair had once been thick, but it was now thinning in front with an ample supply clinging in back, left uncut to grow long where it existed and then pulled forward over the barren space. When he emerged from a pool or the sea, the longer hair formed pointed peaks falling outward to give him the appearance of having used a crosscut saw to trim the outline. His deep-set eyes did not twinkle when his brows furrowed, but when he threw back his heavy head in laughter, you saw a man you would like to know better. His unusual features were not unattractive to the local ladies, his pensive stare being interpreted as sincerity, which it was, although perhaps not always sincere in the innocent way the ladies supposed.

The twins tolerated him, and he took care of them. The week before, Jade had developed a lingering cough at night. The next day all three had the flu and fevers. Starke decided to take himself and the twins to a doctor to get an antibiotic prescribed. He had never really been sick since arriving in Mindanao, and had had his annual physical at the Long Beach Veterans Hospital during his last trip stateside, so he had no personal doctor in Davao City. Jasmine located a public clinic and gave five pesos to a boy to run ahead and hold a place in line for them. Dozens of small shops in what was supposed to have been a parking lot constituted en masse the neighborhood marketplace for the barrio. The door to the doctor's office was located between an open-air tobacco stand and a vendor selling dried fish. Jade held her nose. Cigarette smoke drifted into the clinic. A young man was waiting in line, holding his right hand, which had almost been cut off, wrapped in a bloody towel. A pretty young woman with her left foot growing where her knee should be was breast-feeding her baby while she balanced herself on a short crutch. The place was dusty, and brown dirt collected on the ridges of the reception desk. A fat, sweating woman wearing a tight pink tee shirt and jeans, made up a medical history for Starke and the twins, writing the information onto a lined tablet in pencil.

Eventually, they got to see a woman doctor who seemed professional and competent. She prescribed vitamin pills and some herbal medicines, which the fat woman dispensed as they left. The total cost for the doctor and medicines for the three of them was less than thirteen U.S. dollars. Within a week, all three were cured.

When she saw that Starke had entered the living room, Jade got up and gently pushed him into the big easy chair and sat on his lap holding her cup of tea on a saucer. "Thanks for being so thoughtful. It's not just the tea; I like that you take care of me. Of us."

"You're no trouble." Starke rocked back and balanced her strategically. "I like you two, too."

"Do you like us more than your wife?" Jade purred like a cat.

"You know I have no wife." Starke knew he was being gently harassed.

"I want to know why you left her. Her skin was whiter than ours. I've seen her picture." Jasmine liked to tease him, too.

"In America, guys like girls that are tan. You look tan to me. I like you the way you are."

"But your ex-wife looks pretty. Do you still love her? You still send money to her." Jade joined the hazing session.

"It's the law. I made a divorce settlement." Starke wanted to change the subject. "I have to support my ex-wife and her husband."

The twins looked at each other for a second, then at Starke, covered their mouths with their hands and giggled.

Starke was having fun, and rocked back in his chair. "You two girls going to work early today, is that what you told me?"

"Yes, Morris has us working early today, starting at noon. His regular waitresses are taking a day off because once Kadayawan starts we'll all work fourteen-hour shifts. But they work harder than we do, we have breaks when we're dancing. They have to carry food and pour drinks non-stop." Jade set her tea back down and massaged Starke's head.

"I'll see you then. I may be meeting Thornton there later."

"Oh him. I don't like him." Jade surprised Starke.

"Why is that? You hardly know him."

"Because he wants you to do things for him, things he doesn't want to do himself. That means he's taking advantage of you."

Jasmine had joined them and was sitting at Starke's feet, checking out the pedicure she had given him and touching it up, "I think so too. He'll get you in trouble. It's better that you just stay here and enjoy life."

Starke closed his eyes and breathed it all in, not caring what they said about Thomas Thornton. He began to doze, and the girls steered him back to the bed where they continued their massage until he snored.

Starke's cell phone blinked and vibrated on the cardboard desk he had rigged up beside his chair on the balcony. He left his nest with the twins and picked it up. "Hank, you awake?" It was Thornton. "Can you meet with Moser and me?"

"Sure Bro,' my calendar is all blank." Starke sounded wide-awake.

"I'll be at the usual place. Maybe I'll even buy you a beer."

Starke knew the usual place and answered, "I'll get myself all shined up. My girls in the next room have to work there today anyway." He hung up and continued to enjoy the fresh air, reading yesterday's newspaper.

He thought again about the job Thornton was offering him, an interesting undertaking that appealed to his adventurous side, with potential for real wealth for himself, but with the inevitable risk of paying too big a price if he lost the game—not only a chance of being killed, but, if not that, the distinct possibility of a serious wound far from medical facilities, or being captured by the Abu Sayaf and held captive for a long time, if they would ever release him. It had happened to others before. Any time lost could never be regained. But he could win big; one last consulting assignment, and he could upgrade his digs here in the city, put his share into a conservative bond fund, and maybe even set up a bar over in Mati. Considering his life at the moment, taking a chance with STAGCOM seemed a reasonable gamble.

It was late afternoon when he walked the short distance up Claveria Street to the Lady Love. He stood in the doorway for a moment with the setting sun behind him, waiting for his eyes to adjust, then walked carefully toward the source of the 80s soft rock music. Halfway across the floor, his vision was restored and he waved to Jade and Jasmine who were dancing together to a quiet number, as he steered toward the trio lounging around the far end of the bar.

"How is it out there? Rain start yet?" O'Neil greeted his customer.

"Yeah. Cow pissin' on a flat rock. Just another day in paradise. Hi guys."

Thornton had been speaking with Moser in German, but when Starke came up to them, he nodded toward two men sitting at the other end of the bar. "Something's going on with those two Australians, Hank, they're drunk, and they've been eyeing your girls."

As the twins ended their dance number, one of the sailors waved a bank note in the air and said in the general direction of the stage, "Here pretty pussy, here pretty pussy."

Starke was standing only a few feet from them and heard clearly. But he thought it best to keep things quiet and calmly told the sailor, "Take it easy, Davao City is a quiet place. What are you here for anyway?"

"We're here for good cheap pussy and bad cheap booze, just like you. We like those two gettin' off the stage," the man waving the money mumbled back.

"That's not for you tonight. Let 'em alone, they're just trying to make a few pesos." Starke defended his protégées.

"Get lost, they look good to me," was the response.

"I'm not getting lost, you guys are the new ones here." Starke was still calm.

Without warning, the first sailor threw a punch that was automatically deflected by Starke's karate chop, and his counter punch caught the sailor along the side of his head, stunning him.

The other sailor stood up to help his buddy, but Thornton had had enough of the nonsense and blocked him with a hard flat hand into the chest that momentarily stopped his breathing. Starke ended the day for the man facing him with a short, powerful jab to the face.

Trying to regain his breath, the sailor who could still speak gave up and helped his buddy stand, saying as they decided it was best to leave, not to the men but to the twins, "We'll see you later, both of you and both of us." But the sailors had had enough of Davao City.

13

The Schloss Code

Elaiza entered the Lady Love as the two drunken sailors staggered out. When she pushed one of them out of her way, he stumbled and bounced off the door casing. In the bright light of the late afternoon, the two sailors squinted and tried to decide which way to go on Claveria Street.

Morris O'Neil put a pitcher of beer on the bar. "It's on the house, gentlemen. Thanks for keeping it quiet in here."

Starke clapped Moser on the back and asked O'Neil, "My pleasure. How about putting some of that into one of your cleaner mugs?"

Wolfgang Moser was not the kind of guy to get into a fistfight, and was happy to go back to his conversation with Thornton, chatting with him while exchanging a "prosit!" with the free black beer, an improbable scene anyplace else around town.

Elaiza joined them at the bar. "Reporting as ordered, Kapitan Tomas. This must be STAGCOM headquarters, huh?"

"Hi Elaiza. You could say so. Hank Starke here has signed on, I think, and this beer-drinking German will help us, I hope."

Elaiza nodded around Thornton toward them. "How do you do? You guys are an interesting crew. Kapitan Tomas, why did you invite me here? I don't drink."

"I know. Wanted you to get to know these guys."

Elaiza accepted a mango juice and took a sip.

"By the way, I like my new nickname. How'd you come up with that?"

"History. Five hundred years ago Kapitan Tomas Monteverde, from Spain, brought desperados here, like you."

"Well, I've been called a lot worse." Thornton had to smile. He really liked this girl. Then back to business.

"Wolfgang, lay it out for her, please. Tell her about the Schloss Code."

Moser appeared reluctant. "Well, young lady, against my better judgment, maybe I could put things into my radio show. Thornton here wants me to teach you some German."

"Let me guess, the best way to do that is while drinking?" she asked.

Thornton wanted to explain. "It was my idea. Tell her about it, Wolf."

Moser still sounded unsure, "Thornton thinks I can mumble into the mike in some German dialect and give directions."

"But I certainly wouldn't understand."

"No one else would either," Thornton explained. "That's why you're here. Take out your pencil and learn some Deutsch. I'll drink the beer."

Thornton left Elaiza with Moser and joined Starke, who was not in a hurry to hear what Thornton wanted to discuss, but Thornton got to the point and asked him, "What would it take for me to get you comfortable taking chances with my new team? You might have to lead them in combat."

Thornton knew he had more work to do to get Starke motivated and on board with STAGCOM without any reservations.

"Did I hear you say a cool one million U.S. dollars? That share of confiscated booty would make life here a lot more fun." Thornton had mentioned the possible share that was on the table for Starke. Starke shifted his weight around and took another sip of beer. He visualized taking the twins to Hong Kong for a week, maybe with a side trip to gamble in Macau. It more than passed through his mind; it stuck there.

Starke ordered a shot of warm Johnnie Walker Red Label to sit beside his cold beer as Thornton began to persuade, looking for signs of emotion.

"Hank," Thornton began, "Elaiza thinks she can recruit a Manobo crew. What do you think?"

"Manobos are tough; I'd take a squad of them into combat. They'll need some training to develop discipline so they don't all run around in circles in a combat situation like young boys at play, but I can teach men to follow orders. I like the girl too, she has spunk." Starke pounded ketchup over the cheeseburger that Jade (or maybe it was Jasmine?) slid to him across the bar while he thought about the operation.

"So, are you in?" Thornton wanted Starke to make a commitment, internally and personally, to the mission itself.

Starke asked, "How long do you think it will take to get that Arab guy and, my idle curiosity, what will you do with it all?"

"If it takes much more than two weeks, I'll be very surprised. The Abu Sayaf must do something soon, or their support will be whittled away," Thornton told Starke, who was now paying close attention. "Or their leaders in the field will use up the money to live on and after that not have enough left to fight a war."

"OK, so much for the Abu Sayaf, how do you see the New People's Army fitting in?" Starke wanted to understand the relationship between the two groups.

"The NPA have the troops, thousands of men with guns; the Abu Sayaf has money and leadership, but only a few hundred men. If the two get together," Thornton explained, "they can control this island."

"How could they get together? The NPA are communists, the Abu Sayaf are Muslim. They have opposing theologies. Just like the communists and the Catholics in the old days behind the Iron Curtain. Remember?" Starke was suddenly a philosopher and theologian, and had been listening.

Thornton had his theories, and had shared them before with Colonel Liu to test them. "They'll forget those differences when the issue is their perceived freedom, and once they find a charismatic leader who promises them *Liberdad*, add a few U.S. dollars, they'll do whatever he asks.

Just like in the old days, buddy. Yes, I do remember. They would be told their local chieftain would represent them in a new federal congress of some sort. Think about it." Thornton had thought about it, and the picture was not pretty.

"OK, I'm thinking." Starke got back to the immediate issue, "So what do we do when we find them?"

"First we track them, have to stay close on their heels. Elaiza will stay in communication with the embassy. When we have the opportunity, we take out the rebels, keep the money. After we've removed the cash and hence the temptation for certain corruptible officials, we tell the Philippine Army where they are, and Colonel Liu can have his way with them."

Thornton left Starke to his ruminations and went to where Elaiza was scratching something on a piece of paper with Moser.

Wolfgang Moser, an unlikely transplant to Mindanao from East Germany, was a disc jockey for 90.3 FM Radio Mindanao. His show, "European Classics," introduced Beethoven, Puccini and especially Strauss to a growing audience that extended to all of the island as his listeners erected makeshift FM antennas, frames shaped like Catholic crosses that implied a larger than expected Christian population within the predominantly Muslim communities in far western Mindanao. Moser's five minutes of news on the half hour reported events, but he was determined not to get deeply involved in politics. Five journalists had been assassinated in Mindanao in the last three years, nineteen throughout all of the Philippines.

Moser had lived seven years in Davao City, since meeting and marrying a Filipina when they were both studying at the University of Vienna. After earning her degree, she brought her new husband to live in Davao City and, after the fall of the wall, got his aging father out of East Germany to join them in the tropical sun. Thornton enjoyed his conversations in German with Moser and his family. They were unlikely to be comprehended by eavesdroppers, and Moser knew it was a hobby for Thornton to keep up his language skills.

When Thornton first heard Moser's radio show, he took the initiative to meet him, and they quickly found areas of common interest, thereafter meeting weekly downtown for lunch and philosophy. After he got to know Wolfgang's father, Thornton was allowed to call him Vati, and he enjoyed drinking a beer and singing songs Vati himself had forgotten, but remembered again with the first few notes, no matter how off-key Thornton was. No one else enjoyed their music, and it offended some, but when he heard the words, Vati would remember lost loves, hardship in the snow, and that Russian prisoner of war camp where he was lucky to be fed pea soup twice a day for a year, and his old red eyes would swell up.

Thornton had introduced Moser to the Lady Love, and sometimes they stopped by with the early crowd for a few bottles of beer, or a bottle of bad and overpriced Spanish red wine served too cold, and a hamburger. They sang German marching songs, and played with Austrian and Bavarian dialects. They listened to the Schlommel music, reminiscing about the hills around Grinzing from their days there and the more famous music of Strauss, the latter the only music that was likely to be played on the air by Moser.

When Thornton had unveiled his idea to create a code in German, Moser told him he could not put his radio station into some sort of espionage game. This was not communist Germany, and the Cold War was over.

Now, talking to him with Elaiza listening, Thornton explained to them both, "Wolfgang, what if, for example I, or Elaiza here, or your own wife, got lost in the boonies. Wouldn't you help them find their way home?"

"Of course, but you're talking here about undertaking a for-profit venture with political ramifications."

"Well, I'll make it easy for you." Thornton tried to put his friend at ease, and in the process to educate Elaiza as well. "Just imagine, imagine you could tell them over the radio, during your program, what direction to take, and you could do it secretly."

"Why a secret? If they're lost, they could call me on my cell phone. What's the problem?" Moser was puzzled, and Thornton thought for a while about how to explain it to him.

A large man, English maybe—Thornton could hear the language but not the accent—entered and sat at the other end of the bar from them and ordered a Jack Daniels with a San Miguel Pils. Thornton spoke more quietly, revealing the details of his idea. "Just imagine that our

STAGCOM patrol was lost, I mean 'misoriented.' It would be *unhealthy* for me if the terrorists out there knew we were communicating."

"Yeah, another terror alert was announced today, a Yellow Alert for Davao, with Kadayawan coming up this weekend." Starke showed he was still following the discussion. "Terrorism is an unhealthy event around here."

"Well, Abu Bakar has been convicted, and this Himbali has been taken out, just last week. That hits the Abu Sayaf hard." Morris was also getting interested.

"The loss of their leaders will inspire the Abu Sayaf to retaliate," was Elaiza's opinion as she listened to the men while she sipped her mango juice.

"The Abu Sayaf are buying new hired hands, as we're sitting here," Moser said, "and all of us are already targets. Thornton, back to your theoretical question. Of course, I would have to help." The D.J. was obviously intrigued. "But what would stop an assassin from walking right into my studio and popping me?"

"They wouldn't know what you were saying," Thornton told him. And he went on to explain, "German is very different from the dialects in Mindanao; Wolf, you could literally cough into the mike and communicate a message."

Starke digressed, reading the newspaper: "Have you heard of the Magdalo? The coup plotters?"

"It doesn't matter to people here who runs Manila," said Elaiza. "If some cadets recently graduated from the Philippine Military Academy want to throw out the old order, who cares?"

Starke risked sounding negative, but shared his opinion. "The plotters only hurt themselves, those Tagalogs. But the Philippine Army will retaliate here, in Mindanao, the two-faced bastards. Look in today's paper: 'A battalion of Philippine Marines boards a transport ship at navy headquarters in Manila to fight the Abu Sayaf in Mindanao."

At this point the big guy at the other end of the bar seemed to come alive as Jade and Jasmine began to dance again. He tipped them to do a number for him on the raised platform. The music got louder, and the group of expats and Elaiza at the bar were forced to speak in less hushed voices when they resumed their conversation.

From his perch on the end stool, Starke watched his twins, whom he took more than a paternal interest in protecting and preserving.

Elaiza watched them too, with mild curiosity. She asked Thornton, "What does all this have to do with me and my iPod, even 'upgraded' as it is?"

"Listen to this for a while, see what you think." Thornton was still intrigued with his idea of a code. He might actually need it sometime, it was more than just an exercise in semantics. "When I was in the army in Germany, I lived near the small town of Kitzingen near the smaller town of Iphofen, famous for its dry Franken wine—you know, it comes in a *Bocksbeutel*, those bottles famous for being shaped like goat's gonads? Well, I won lots of bets, with Americans and Germans both, that I could tell from one taste which side of the mountain behind Iphofen the wine came from, north, south, east, or west. They took my bets, because all the wine looked exactly the same, in the same little green bottles, just with different vintner labels, and they all came from about a five-mile radius. I almost always, I would say always, won."

"How did you do that, a foreigner, an American?" Moser had not heard this tale before from Thornton.

The twins had come over and loitered around Starke after their dance, oozing their natural sexuality, warm skin just a little bit moist and evaporating hints of perfume. But Elaiza's cold stare discouraged them from any snuggling, so they retreated to a front table to sit and flirt with the guy who had tipped them.

Thornton went on. "It was easy. There were four wines from very different grapes, the *Mueller-Thurgau, Riesling, Kalb* and *Sylvaner*. They grew on different sides of the mountain. The east and south got lots of sun; the north not so much, and it got cold much earlier in the autumn on the northern slope. On opposite sides on the mountain the soils were very different, loam, clay, sand, and limestone. The wines were as different as a red from France and a white from Italy. I won the bets."

"The point is?" Starke asked.

"We create a simple code using strange German words. Elaiza, you'll need to make notes of key words, *Thurgau* will mean north, *Sylvaner*, south; *Kalb*, east; and *Riesling*, west." Thornton was thinking as he spoke. "Use difficult and long words like *Neuschwanstein*, crazy Prince Ludwig's castle near Fuessen."

"OK, but what good is a code?" Elaiza was getting curious.

"Moser could easily, and in secret, give us directions on the air; since no one would be specifically looking for secret communications, it would be simple." Thornton turned to Moser. "Wolf, you could announce something like, 'Three callers tonight have requested Mozart's '*Eine Kleine Kalb Sylvaner Kalb*,' slurring the words a bit into your mike. I would interpret that as, 'Move three kilometers east southeast.' Nothing to it."

"But anyone who knows music or German, would figure out something was strange." Moser was understandably skeptical.

"Yes, eventually, but it would work for a week, and that would be long enough. You know all the people in Mindanao who both understand German and know something about music, and they are not the ones we care about deciphering a code. Worst case scenario with those who could be suspicious, laugh it off as a contest you were running to see if anyone noticed. Or put them all to sleep with some Mahler."

"OK, but where would I get the information to help you?"

"From Major Hayes; he's assigned here in Mindanao during our mission and is hooked up with the U.S. Embassy tech guys in their lab by cell phone, or even land line. He could be in the station with you, giving you the messages we need." Thornton pulled it all together in a way that made Moser comfortable.

They then devised a code with these key elements: *neunzig grad*—ninety degrees; "I have had three requests for"–three kilometers; *Bach rechts*–the stream to the right; *Fluechtling, Gefaehr hinter Dir*"–fugitive, danger, rear, and so on. The cardinal directions would come from the Iphofen wines. Wolf could announce a musical piece as old Austrian Schlommel music, and "cough" a few words in Viennese dialect that would hardly be noticed even by someone fluent in German, let alone Visayan.

"OK, so we have a code, and Moser can give you, or whoever has the iPod, messages. What good is it?" Starke asked.

"The embassy, and therefore our armed forces, will know Elaiza's exact location. And I mean exactly. If and when she moves in a specific way, she signals back to the embassy by the steps she has taken. Each step will be recorded digitally on a map overlay. The iPod is a radio and a GPS device rolled into one. I'd like to leave it at that."

"Pretty slick." Moser was impressed. "I always thought you were a CIA professional, or something like that."

"Moser, I'm just a businessman, but working with Elaiza, and also with Starke here, I hope I can pay back some people I owe for when I was, shall we say, more involved. I still have some personal confidences to keep. And it's just better that that's all you know. Don't get more involved. I'll tell you the whole story some day."

"OK, I wasn't that curious anyway. But I would like to know what you think you three can do by yourselves that the entire Philippine Army can't?" Moser thought he had hit the nail on the head.

"That's one of the things I'll tell you some other time. Let's let it rest there for today." Thornton raised his glass in another toast, signaling that he did not want to talk any more about that subject.

Starke was feeling the alcohol only slightly, but the twins' near presence, his buddies around him, and the interesting conversation put him more at ease and fascinated at the same time. Without asking any more questions, he went into one of the videoke rooms with the twins and a bottle of brandy.

When Starke was gone, Elaiza declined a beer from Thornton, and ordered a sparkling grape juice, then said, "I got it. We can use the code to direct our team around, but no one will know what we're doing."

Thornton confirmed her conclusion, "Yes. We get close to Mahir Hakki, you turn your uncles loose, and we make him and the cash disappear. It should be easy."

14

The Mission

Sergeant Henry Starke arrived in Toril in time for breakfast leftovers with Thornton and Elaiza, plopped himself down and completely filled one end of the table, all decked out in tactical black, except for the design on his tee shirt featuring an off-white bald eagle, wings stretched by his girth. He belched in satisfaction, as was the local custom he had adopted as his demonstration of being simpatico with the natives, then tapped his fingers showing his eagerness to get on with the business at hand.

It was still cool, the morning salt breeze mixing the essence of yesterday's jasmine with the faintest hint of today's durian crop on its way to a nearby open market. Starke passed around a newspaper he had bought on his way there, with the report of the bombings at the airport and Sasa wharf, showing photos of shattered windows and a searing picture of a dead girl in a pure white dress splattered with blood, still clutching her small doll. It put steel into Elaiza's heart.

"If they can kill that child, they could kill my child someday," was her low growl.

The woman who worked for Thornton came and cleared the dirty dishes away. Thornton took out a map and spread it on the table. He explained, "OK, here's the situation. Some idiots in the Defense Department wanted to send U.S. troops into Davao City proper, 'for training' of course, but General Hargens was able to get that mission cancelled. Hargens asked me to help him, just for a short time on a very focused assignment. And I am to keep it all quiet. Only a few will know about our mission and the details."

"How we gonna do it, Thornton?" Starke asked; the experienced trooper got right to the point.

Thornton told him, "We need to find the Turk with the money and finish him, without letting the world know the U.S. is involved in internal affairs in the Philippines. The Filipinos have to get the credit for winning their own war. Elaiza here works for our embassy and will keep in direct touch with a U.S. Army officer who is our only official contact, her boss at the embassy, Major Hayes. He works for Hargens. Our job is to get that Al Qaeda cash before the Philippine Army does."

"What's our security, Kapitan Tomas," asked Elaiza, "how do we keep our plans secret and cover ourselves? I don't want to see any more photos of dead little girls or boys."

"Me either. Our primary means of contact, of course, is by cell phone in areas where there is reception. It's low tech, but relatively secure. I doubt the Abu Sayaf has the technology here in the field to intercept any communications, and if they did, and understood our English, they would not be able to react fast enough to have it matter. So Major Hayes and I talk directly on my cell phone."

"But we also will have a back-up," Thornton continued. "Elaiza is not only our liaison with the native troopers, but also our communications expert. The geeks in the embassy will know where this device is, when Elaiza is wearing it, down to an accuracy of a few feet, much better than any normal GPS and so accurate we can use it to call in an artillery or air strike."

Starke was atypically quiet and a bit confused. He asked Thornton, "What do you know about the whereabouts of that money carrier?"

Thornton let him in on the latest he had from Hayes. "We assume the Turk is with the Abu Sayaf in the southwestern, mostly Muslim half of Mindanao, the ARMM, the Autonomous Region of Muslim Mindanao. They will want to hook up with the NPA in northeastern Mindanao, the Moros in the West, and the Moro Islamic Liberation Front with their breakaway renegades, the Moro National Front as well, here in the south. The NPA has armed troops on the ground in the north and east. If they all get together, they will start to think they can achieve their objective, an independent Islamic state of Mindanao. A civil war could not only break up the Philippines, but also move the world in the opposite direction from what the U.S. President and the President and Congress of the Philippines want."

"But the Abu Sayaf say they are not responsible for the blowing up of that little girl, I heard that announcement came from Eid Kabalu himself. If the Abu Sayaf was making trouble, he would want you to know it was him doing it." Starke was up to date from reading newspapers in the Lady Love.

"I believe him, but I doubt that my own countrymen will *want* to believe him." Elaiza got into it. "I think your CIA wants to connect terrorist acts here to the Bali bombings by the Al Qaeda, whether it's true or not. The CIA likes to take out the easy targets even more than they like to get the *correct* target. They want to connect the Al Qaeda terrorists to the deaths of those Australians in Bali, keeping the Aussies on your side. Nobody really cares about my people."

"Neither the U.S. nor the Filipinos want to commit significant combat troops in Mindanao, I agree with that much," Thornton told them all, "but we may have to. The U.S. already has 500 Special Forces rangers on the island helping your countrymen. The Philippine Army is not well trained, has poorly functioning equipment, and their rifles are so old that the rifling is worn out and they don't shoot straight. A percentage of the soldiers are paid to do nothing, or have sympathies and families with the other side. It's discouraging. Filipino soldiers can't find their way back to their own camps or just don't want to and wind up wandering around in the jungle. It's more profitable for them to work with their enemy. Consider if they had to find, fix, and destroy the Abu Sayaf elements now in South Cotobato along with the irregulars out there in the boonies. How good would they be? We don't know which ones are with us and which ones are against us. Or they work their 'pay to raid' programs."

Starke got into it. "With all due respect, if the U.S. Special Forces troops running around on the island can do nothing, what makes anyone think just two unusual guys and one girl can?"

"Want to try me sometime in hand-to-hand, *boy?*" Elaiza bristled at the "girl" comment.

Starke groused, "Sure, meet me at the gym sometime."

Thornton had to chuckle at his friends' teasing, but moved the discussion along. "A large combat force would be easily noticed and would not work. The Abu Sayaf will just hide; they want to keep their guns, their power. But a paramilitary unit like STAGCOM has a better chance of success because they won't know we're following them."

"Why do you think so?" Starke was not convinced.

"Consider how the rebels view their political situation. Consider the difference between to disarm and to be disarmed," Thornton told the sergeant. "If the Philippine Army, or worse yet, American troops assisting the Philippine Army, move into the provinces in force and physically take their guns away, the MNLF fighters and the others will resist. The Muslims in Mindanao will join the communists, put on their Che Guevara tee shirts, and say they are the Army of Liberation, or some new acronym for the same old theme, of simple desperation and the desire to be free of Manila, whatever that means to them."

Elaiza didn't like Thornton's apparently condescending attitude, but realized he overemphasized to make his point, "But if they disarm *themselves?*" she asked.

"Yes, that's the big difference." Thornton looked at her while she spoke, then turned to Starke. "That's exactly my point."

Starke had been in counterinsurgency operations in his past career and picked up the thread. "If they're not paid for fighting and if they're not forced to give up their guns by some outside government foreign to them, they'll melt back into the jungle because they simply have to find food to live. We can just ignore them and the revolution will dry up through lack of interest."

"But we can't create a Christian crusade against their Islamic jihad. That would mean civil war in Mindanao." Elaiza wrapped it up.

"You got it." Thornton took the lead again, "Now we know who the enemy is and what his mission is. He doesn't know about STAGCOM. There is just one key guy for us to take out as far as we care, so with stealth and secrecy, our small team is more likely to get him than a bunch of uniforms bumbling around in the brush." Thornton laid it all out for them.

Starke answered, "If he knows nothing about us, we have the tactical advantage."

Elaiza furrowed her eyebrows. "How do *we* know *where* he is?"

Starke followed along in the conversation, "And if we find him, we just bump him off as soon as we get him, right?"

Thornton turned and looked directly at Starke. "Wrong, we'll have to find him, and follow him, and keep the money from reaching the NPA leaders."

"And then defeat them so they'll not be able to bring the tribes along with them into the revolution," Elaiza concluded.

Thornton agreed, "Yes, if we can accomplish that mission Hargens—and especially someone back in D.C. I owe a lot to—will be satisfied. Then the official powers that be can get involved and defeat any larger insurrection, and without international embarrassment."

"If he really has five million U.S. dollars, he can create a lot of attention here." Starke could see the money being spread around. "So why not just eliminate him and forget about it?"

"Because," Thornton explained what Hargens had told him, "The Al Qaeda in Syria would simply send someone else with more money. But if we track him and wait until he gets to Kumander Ali, the NPA leader, and take Ali out too, then the Abu Sayaf get embarrassed and lose their support base, after all the promises they will have made. That leaves the Philippine Army a short time frame to come in and mop up the hangers-on."

"Again, what do we do with the money, can we keep it?" Starke intended to be sarcastic, but Thornton took his question seriously.

"Yes. That's the deal. No one back in Manila or in Washington needs to decide what to do with the captured money. Some unit of the Philippine Army can declare victory in a field campaign, the NPA resources dry up, and the Abu Sayaf is bankrupt. Then the squabbling rebel groups won't be able to unite, lacking the capability to support a force in the field."

"What's the downside?" Starke asked.

"We die, for example. Nobody will come after us if we're captured. Or we just wind up wasting time."

"Who knows about all this?" Elaiza had been paying attention. "In our government in the Philippines, I mean?"

Thornton thought it was a fair question with no risk for his team to be informed; they had the right to know most of the details.

"Very few people, the National Security Advisor to the President of the Philippines will have to know. Liu, of course. The President himself will say he was not aware. Cabals like this go on all the time, as you know. And one senior officer, whose name is best kept secret, will know. That's all."

"How do we find this Al Qaeda agent?" Elaiza asked.

"As you know, he's already here," Thornton reiterated. "But intelligence sources could not track him after he landed and, we suppose, joined the Abu Sayaf. But they will show up and do something obvious. They will want to make a lot more noise than the three bombings this week. When we hear it, that's where we'll go. It will happen soon."

Starke looked at Elaiza then at Thornton, "I have only one more question. How do we split the money?"

15

The Otaza Brothers

"Ok. Let's start now. We have a lot to do, right, Kapitan Tomas?" Elaiza liked to play name games; she never lost at Scrabble played in English, which was not even her mother tongue. She knew by now that Thornton was a U.S. Military Academy graduate and had been an army captain. In her school she had learned about a certain Kapitan Tomas de Monteverde, Philippine Maritine Academy, an officer in the Philippine Navy centuries before, who married the daughter of Don Damaso Suazo of Davao City nobility. Monteverde was an early settler in Mindanao, and brought the concept of the fresh water fish farm to Davao. Now a main street and a residential area of Davao City were named after him. So it seemed appropriate for her to call Thornton Kapitan Tomas as he had brought Elaiza back to Davao, and their assignment had taken her in a new direction in her life.

"Yes, we do. It will be an important day. I want to get Pedro and the other Otazas on board with us and together with Starke."

"Your Sergeant Starke looks eager now, working out and jogging. By the way, Pedro has a large family back in Agusan, if you need more troops for our venture," Elaiza reminded Thornton. "And being family who live in the same village they know each other better than most brothers."

"Thanks, we'll see. We have to keep STAGCOM as small as possible, just enough men to do the job, no more." Thornton was pleased with the prospect of having a potential team of irregulars who knew and trusted each other. "Ask Pedro to get his four brothers here now; see if they'll join up with us."

"Pedro's nearby. I'll get him moving." Elaiza was picking up the ball quickly; Thornton liked that.

Elaiza made a call to a *sari-sari* store, a temporary stall built next to the gutter on the main street where a woman sold general merchandise and foodstuffs in small quantities, asking her to locate Pedro and to have him call her back. He would be near the store, waiting for Elaiza's call. Pedro was living in a lean-to he had erected against the concrete wall surrounding Our Lady of Prague monastery, overlooking Davao City. He preferred staying on his own in the improvised shelter since he had ridden in from Agusan with Elaiza and Thornton, waiting to see what Elaiza would want him to do after the terrorist bombs had gone off.

Waiting for Pedro to call back, Thornton suggested, "Let's have a pig roast on the beach; a big party with music should be a good incentive for them all to get here quickly."

"OK. Great idea. I'll set it up." Elaiza was starting to identify with her job, in spite of her earlier reservations. "They can meet Sergeant Starke and get to know him." A few minutes later she received the return call from Pedro and explained the situation to him.

"I can have my brothers get into Davao, but it interrupts Robelyn's marriage plans," he told her. He sounded uncertain.

Elaiza had an inspiration. "How about, bring them all, with their families, and we'll have the wedding on the beach, Manobo style?"

"Deal." Pedro answered quickly, and he started to talk faster and louder as he discussed arrangements with Elaiza. "Tomorrow soon enough?"

As soon as he hung up, he left the *sari-sari* store with a proud strut that made his old sandals flop audibly as he prepared to make a quick trip to

Agusan to round up his brothers. He would be remembered as the one to invite the whole family to a special occasion.

The rest of the day Thornton and Elaiza continued to plan, with books and maps spread out on the long table set up outside on the second floor balcony of Thornton's house in Toril. It seemed each learned from the other as they practiced translating the Schloss Code and studied the capabilities of the TIAM.

The next afternoon Pedro showed up in Toril with his four brothers from Agusan del Sur. They came with their families, seventeen people arriving twisted and cramped into a twelve-seat jeepney. The extended Otaza family brought with them, tied with ropes on the roof of the jeepney, a fat sow past her litter-bearing years, who would show up later on the beach for dinner, cardboard boxes full of fruit, and a few skinny gift chickens to be kept alive in a crate until the next day. The new arrivals had not eaten during the five-hour trip so they all got together for a lunch of rice first. While the children and their mothers finished the rice, Juanito, the youngest Otaza brother, slaughtered the sow, catching its blood to make *dinuguan* by frying the intestines in it. Later the assemblage took the pig carcass to the beach at a place that Elaiza had arranged. The men chopped the pig into one-inch cubes with a sharp bolo while the women started three charcoal fires smoking under a palm tree near the black sand beach. The cooks flopped pieces of fatty pig meat onto makeshift grills formed from rusty construction re-bar found at nearby construction sites and overcooked the meat, eating the blackened, greasy chunks by hand, with great satisfaction. The crew was lucky to have several pans of burned meat left over for the next day, as well as the *dinuguan,* which apparently was better after it aged for a day or so. The band of Manobos, including all five of the Otaza brothers now, could live comfortably as squatters where branches of short trees hung over the beach.

Starke enjoyed watching the preparations, somewhat amazed by the native customs. "Pedro and his brothers seem to be having a good time," he said to Elaiza.

"Wait 'til they start to sing!" Elaiza knew what was coming.

"Excuse me. I think I'll try some burned meat, with rice . . . and maybe a long swig of brandy."

Thornton opened a few bottles of cheap Fundador brandy, and soon the cooked meat started to smell not so bad, even to Starke. The five Otaza brothers started to sing. Vicente played an old guitar mean, by ear, reviving American pop music of the 1950s, even though he himself was only in his early thirties. Reymundo looked exactly like Chuck Berry in 1959 with his sweptback pompadour, and he sang old time rock and roll at the semi-pro level. Of course, Thornton remembered when, and sang along with the remix of Platters hits. Pedro sang tenor and played percussion on anything. Tonight he chose the rice pot upside down and two spoons. He sang loudly, and in tune. Two of the young Agusan girls had beautiful soprano voices and pressed in to sing beside the men. The musicians and the audience sang louder, and Pedro had to make a list in writing on a note pad of their torrent of requests to get them all in. It was a unique opportunity to bond, and Robelyn's wedding was the perfect occasion for all their purposes. The dinner preparations and songfest signaled the start of the ceremony, the highlight of the evening.

In the old days, it was assumed among some of the tribes that the man is too timid to propose marriage to a woman, so marriages were arranged after a suitable dowry was agreed, as much as a horse and a few carabaos, perhaps with a hand-carved betel nut container added to the pot to seal the deal. Virginity was important, without which the dowry was greatly reduced.

Pedro himself beat on the ceremonial brass *agong* as the groom danced and gradually settled in beside his bride to join her in eating a large bowl of rice with boiled birds' eggs. A priestess chanted in the Manobo dialect to Timanum, the Supreme Being, who some thought lived in the ocean and some thought lived on the mountain; they were not certain where he lived, but the frequent earthquakes seemed to prove he lived in the earth. The priestess prayed to a *manong,* an exquisitely carved wooden idol representing the Supreme Being, and the marriage was sealed. The bride and groom danced together around the fire while the *agong* accompanied modern instruments; variations of Chuck Berry styles seemed to creep into the musical legends of the tribe.

When the mood cooled with the night, the participants in the ceremonies gathered to give thanks also to the Christian God. Pedro asked Luz, one of the older of the young girls, to sing something religious, and she gave full force to *Oh Holy Night,* backed up by Vicente and a chorus of almost two-dozen voices. Singing seems to be a Filipino birthright, and the impromptu open-air choir sang with talent and force. When a quieter time came, Thornton got the Otaza brothers together and sat with them by the fire under the leafy banyan tree that protected them from the light drizzle that was starting. Elaiza translated while he laid out his plan and his offer to Pedro and the four other Otaza brothers who were not yet committed.

"Gentlemen, I have a dangerous job to do. I need some help, and would like you to work with me. You do not have to trust me, just trust your niece; Elaiza will be with us all the way. And your brother, Pedro, has already agreed to work for me."

"We are here already." Reymundo was ready to get involved. "It's easy for us to stay. The women will go back to Agusan and take care of the land and animals."

"Good." Thornton wanted to put them at ease. "Master Sergeant Starke will help me train you for this specific mission, although I know you already know your way around. He has combat experience and can help you. Think of him as your point man on patrol. I will lead the overall operation with Elaiza handling communications between us in the field and the people I work for." Thornton did not tell the Otazas the details about his deal with Hargens; if he got the money, he'd take care of them in a fair way.

"I've seen your ability with firearms, and I'm comfortable with how you handle yourselves and your bolos, knowing what your brother can do. STAGCOM will provide new rifles, good rifles that shoot straight. Do any of you have licenses to carry?"

There was some grinning and chuckling.

"Mr. Thornton, we're not even able to get government identity cards." Vicente got involved in the fun. "When we were born, no one wrote anything down. We don't have birth certificates. We are born, we live, we die, we disappear, and we don't have documents for any of these events."

"You won't need documents as far as I'm concerned. I just want to know if I can count you in with STAGCOM. "STAGCOM" sounded official and was short, easy to say, and seemed to reflect the masculinity of the Otazas.

"Mr. Thornton, we have already told you we're here, and so are our families. You are with our family. What more do you want?" Vicente's acquiescence seemed to seal the deal as no objections were heard from the other brothers.

"Your word is enough for me." Thornton realized that he should not talk more about the mission during the wedding celebration, now winding down. Who better and what greater commitment could he find? He turned the meeting over to Elaiza and Pedro, who laid out the assignments and explained that each team member could come away from the mission with some American cash. More than the money, and more than any projected new wealth, their blood relationship cemented loyalty, for the duration of the mission at least. Thornton considered his STAGCOM team now complete.

Pedro continued to talk with his brothers after Thornton finished. Pedro always talked, whether he had something to say or not. Elaiza translated for Thornton. A lot of what Pedro told his brothers was not logical to Thornton's way of thinking, or even correct, but he kept talking, and his musical chatter made his brothers and the entourage of family comfortable. They would have to relate the import of the meeting to make everyone back home comfortable with the pending absence of their men. Thornton was glad Pedro had brought his brothers in from Agusan. He instinctively liked and respected them, and all together the five Otaza brothers appeared to be a gang of potentially mean guys. Judging by the lengths and widths of scars here and there, the four younger brothers had as much experience with the knife as Pedro, and Thornton wanted them on his side.

Silence settled in for a few minutes as the fire turned to bright orange coals. Pedro suddenly asked, "Just who are we looking for, and why?"

Thornton gave some of the background and related it to their Augusan homeland, "You know about the Al Qaeda and their faction that oppresses you in Agusan, the New Peoples Army."

"Yes, of course, the bastards tax anything that moves on the road, and our government looks away." Reymundo had some personal experience with the NPA when he took rice to the markets in town to sell. Illegal checkpoints stopped him to collect taxes for the support of NPA combat troops in the field.

Sitting cross-legged and barefoot, more a rice farmer than a mercenary, Eduardo had a similar view. "Yes, of course, we know about them, but we also know not to talk about them in our village. The NPA in town share information with our neighbors and some of the impatient soldiers are always looking for a rich Chinese merchant to kidnap for ransom. We don't like them, but they also keep foreigners out. That is good."

Thornton finally told them what the brothers needed to know: "We have only one man we must eliminate to get our rewards. The government forces can do their own work without us. Can you kill just one man, a foreigner wandering around in Mindanao with two big sacks of money?"

The Otazas' smirks and silence were their obvious answers.

Starke took another slug of brandy from the bottle and gave it to Pedro to pass around, saying sleepily, "I think I'll just stay here," and curled up on the beach to go to sleep by the dying fire.

Thornton and Elaiza had their team.

That night, Elaiza went up to Thornton's second floor suite with him. They talked quietly for a while about the day's events, and she watched him sip a glass of Australian red wine, listening to classical music and Moser's late night program on the radio. She was tired and fell asleep in her chair on the balcony. Thornton lifted her, and a lingering aroma of her perfume, *Innocent Angel,* and natural perspiration surrounded her; he weighed her firmness as she stirred slightly in his arms, placed her in his bed, and covered her with a thin sheet. He returned to the balcony and spent the night sleeping uncomfortably in the chair.

Thornton awoke early. A horizontal strip of early morning purple separated the new day from the smooth, black water of the Gulf of Davao and outlined the mango tree, hinting of its history of torment. Preoccupied with thoughts about doing his job for Hargens, he sat alone on the balcony until Elaiza woke and joined him, only a little bit embarrassed that she had spent the night in his bed.

From the balcony on that pleasant morning, as the sun rose, Thornton and Elaiza watched the somber old farmer, head bent over, walk across the field with his axe and cut down his mango tree. He had finally given up.

Elaiza said quietly, "The story of my island."

16

Kadayawan

The third Thursday of August is the first day of Kadayawan, the festival giving thanks to all the Gods for the crops of flowers and fruits. The harvest is always good in Mindanao, a patchwork of mango and banana plantations crowned with pink and white waling-waling orchids. The word *Kadayawan* was created for the annual occasion, a composite of the Visayan words *dayaw* and *madayaw,* implying excellent harvest and good fortune, and the festival showcases its essence in sound and color.

Long before the formal start of the Kadayawan ceremonies, young boys carrying torches pranced among the camps and the cooking fires of the participants. They were up before dawn, unable to sleep any longer with all the noise and excitement of the final preparations. The boys were already in parade dress, blue and red pants resembling pajama bottoms, loosely fit at the waist and tight from thigh to ankle, embroidered with intricate designs, and short-sleeved shirts in contrasting colors open in the front exposing bead and shell necklaces jangling on their youthful, hairless chests. Just after dawn, dancers and marchers from neighboring towns and villages came out of their lean-tos erected in bare spots against the hollow block wall on the football field where the parade would assemble.

As the early rays of the sun broke through the thin, low-lying layers of charcoal smoke, the female dancers began to put on their costumes. Some of the women wore painted masks incorporating long black and white feathers extending upward in spirals, meant to resemble the famous Philippine Eagle, Kabayan, possibly the last of an almost extinct species and a vivid symbol of the free spirit of Mindanao. Young girls in long, bright red and black skirts with interwoven golden yellow strands and slit up both sides showed long trim legs as they moved forward. In a loose order of procession, they joined the short, skinny negritos, the aborigines with black skin and reddish, kinky hair who inhabited the southwestern part of the island. The younger children carried woven grass baskets filled with dwarf vegetables and unfurled bright paper strip banners, tugged along by a humid breeze.

The vivid colors and happy sounds of the assemblage contrasted with drab garbage stacked opposite the wire mesh fence, blocking the football field from the road where street children begged for a few pesos from the early onlookers. A pile of plastic and moist cardboard burned in smoking, flameless combustion, drifting toxic hydrocarbon fumes into the assembly area. While the dancers were doing their pre-dawn primping, the Abu Sayaf advance team arrived in downtown Davao City, inconspicuously traveling by intercity bus. For his role, Mahir was the best dressed among them, wearing conservative but expensive street clothing. He had shaved his full beard, keeping only a trim moustache. He walked around the plaza and began chatting with the city employees on site. For a thousand-peso tip, the parade official at the gate let him register a float as the official entry of the European Importers Union—a phony organization, but the application form looked genuine enough to the guard, and he could use the money. Mahir spoke English rather than the local language and looked like a distinguished gentleman to the official.

Opposite the shoeshine stand on the wide boulevard, two early birds, Thornton and Elaiza, ordered cappuccinos and casaba cake at the *Blu Gre* coffee shop. Elaiza read from the paper, "Mayor Fuentes is concerned about security for the parade; he's issued another alert and cancelled weekend leave for the police."

"Good. And they're patrolling already, look." Thornton pointed to a tough-looking senior policeman, who gently scooped up in one arm a young boy running into the street where he was not permitted and then set him gently back down on the sidewalk. The lad continued his happy tour of the parade route and the officer returned to issuing gruff instructions to his subordinates.

"And this is new." Elaiza continued to read, "The Office of the President is convinced that the 'Oakwood Incident,' that attempted coup by disgruntled army officers, was not terrorist sponsored, unlike the threatened bombing attacks in the southern islands which the Abu Sayaf are instigating."

Thornton agreed. "It's not likely that those whining young lieutenants from Manila are behind the attacks here," he said. "They have no support base in Mindanao."

"You sound so superior."

"Would you rather have me be inferior? I don't think I'm so superior, but if someone tells me that two plus two equals five, I'm not simply going to smile sweetly and say, 'Oh, that's nice.'" Thornton couldn't be quiet when Elaiza played the culture card, even when he knew it would start an argument.

He continued: "Those junior officers don't realize the harm they're causing to their own country, especially to the workers and professionals who pay for their educations at military academies and their government salaries and pensions until they die. What juveniles. And what was the best they could do in their uprising? They took over a hotel inside a shopping mall. They can't think any bigger: incompetence even in protest."

"Yes, that was the Oakwood Hotel, or what some call the Magdalo Incident." Elaiza still wore a frown.

"I guess they were protesting the corruption of their generals. Maybe they would rather report to some Muslim mullah." To Elaiza, Thornton still sounded as though he was preaching to a lower caste. She radiated silence.

"There are so many wandering zealots in the country, with different group names. And each local tribe also has its own charismatic mini chief who wants more. That's about as far as they have thought this through." Thornton was rambling mostly to himself.

Elaiza didn't disagree, but didn't like his attitude. She wanted to make him think. "But what if they ever unite? All those tribes and factions?"

"Add in the mix of religious cults, and you have a civil war in the Philippines that Manila can't win," Thornton concluded.

"But the trouble now is from outsiders."

"Yes, Elaiza, but only until they become insiders, and get some fire-power. What is an outsider, anyway, someone from another country? Another village? A different church?"

"If they get the firepower, you can expect a war. Look at this article, it's official, the president's team negotiating with the communists admits that peace talks have broken down." Elaiza read as they finished their coffees and the street in front of them began to fill with people waiting for the parade to start. Gradually her frown relaxed into a mere dimple on her forehead.

Kadayawan was the optimum opportunity for Lateef and Mahir to get into Davao undiscovered and to blow up a big part of it—or at least to hit some very significant targets. The Abu Sayaf could make a real statement. It wouldn't be just blowing up some poor people's bus stop this time or bombing an almost empty fishing wharf and killing a few innocent young girls. All Mindanao would hear about it. By the time Lateef had arrived with the explosive-laden truck, Mahir had baskets of flowers and a dozen boys recruited to insert and arrange the fresh orchids. The awkward vehicle could not have been moved the long distance from the resort into town for the parade in its final form, and its sponsors were not trying to win any award, but the float needed to appear genuine for the parade. The crew got busy, and their activity blended into the chaos around them.

Now Lateef slipped the rusty vehicle, reconfigured into a flower-covered float, into the metro area, unchallenged by the armed men at the Task Force Davao check points who waved them through with holiday smiles, even despite Mayor Fuentes' alert of the continuing terrorist threat. It had been easy to conceal the three tons of dynamite in the stolen flatbed truck, now containing an underpinning of internal supports of wood 2" by 4"s. Over the framework, orchids and fresh fruit were tied into a curved surface of chicken wire mesh, shaped into a towering purple peacock and crowned with thousands of *waling-waling,* the most beautiful and famous of the Mindanao orchids. The float slipped onto the football field and into the place Mahir had staked out earlier.

When they had a chance to talk alone, Mahir asked Lateef, "Any problems moving in?"

"No. Little curiosity was shown. Everyone is involved in their own work, and they'll stay that way, Enshallah."

"This day will start the revolution."

"You cannot have a revolution without the people. Why do you think all these people will join up with us?"

"Look how many men in the street you see wearing Che Guevara tee shirts. They will join."

"These poor people have nothing to lose. They will all join us when they know they're fighting Zionism and Yankeeism." Lateef did not seem concerned that he was soon to kill many of his countrymen indiscriminately.

Mahir answered, "You make good sense to me. The struggle is not just about autonomy here. We must have true Islamic republics everywhere, under the laws of the Koran."

"Yes," Lateef agreed. "We must do what we will do today not only as the Abu Sayaf of Mindanao, although we will profit greatly ourselves, but also for the children of the hopeless. We will decide what they need, and we will provide for them."

Mahir and Lateef were ready.

Thomas Thornton and Elaiza Otakan had moved to stand in front of the Gingerbread baked goods store next to Banco de Davao on Monteverde Street, where early parade observers were eating sugary bread and drinking Nescafé. The customers threw paper wrappers and napkins into the street as soon as they consumed their snacks. The hot breeze dried out the debris and blew it around their feet. The two were not concealed, but they were not too obvious leaning against a post where some shade was offered from the cover of a narrow balcony above. Thornton always stood out in Davao City because of his white skin and light hair, gray now mixed with blond. He contrasted with any surroundings—crowds of dark *Dabawenyos* or dusty architecture. The first marching band passed them playing "As the Caissons Go Rolling Along," probably not knowing it as the official song of the U.S. Army Artillery; it was an easy tune to march to. Teen-aged majorettes, not yet grown into their long legs, gamboled in flossy short purple and white skirts, the colors of their school, the College of the Immaculate Conception, coincidentally also the colors of the *waling-waling* orchid.

During the parade and before the horse fights in the afternoon, street hawkers did brisk business selling fresh durian, the fruit unique to Mindanao that smells like rotten grapefruit mixed with rancid cheese, and has a unique, almost sweet, indefinable taste. When the spiny husk is cracked, men, women and children run toward the scent. Some foreigners like it OK; some can't stand it; but it is an authentic essence of Mindanao, and its aroma now mingled with wood smoke and flower fragrances along the route.

Morris O'Neil would not open the Lady Love until noon, and the real business would not start until after dark. He was surprised to see Hank Starke out and about, and especially surprised that the twins were with him at such an early hour, but he assumed they would have time for a nap after the parade, and Kadayawan was too spectacular to be missed if you were in town. He had to admit the twins looked radiant today; perhaps he could generate a little promo for his place with them. He bought two small masks, just large enough to cover their eyes, and bright green to resonate with the green sleeves image they projected at the club. He gave the masks to them saying, "Here girls, get into the mood and add to the atmosphere."

"Thanks, I'll wear it." Jade was openly pleased. "I can accessorize." The deep green reflected off her jade necklace.

Morris had not seen the string of jade gems before. "Good idea not to wear something so obviously expensive in the club: the clientele would expect you to give *them* tips," he teased.

Jasmine wore no jewelry at all but, like her twin, looked delicious in the early morning sun in a bright red, tight-fitting dress and high heels accented with a necklace of fragrant, pure white jasmine, so appropriate for this day.

Morris could hardly resist a mock lecherous and conspiratorial stage whisper to Starke: "I can only imagine those two wearing nothing but green stones and white flowers."

Starke got him back. "Sometimes I don't have to imagine." He invited the three to join him at a table outside Beau's Café for a cappuccino. Some of the other customers, especially the males, nodded signs of recognition, or perhaps mere approval, as the girls more sashayed than walked to their seats.

Morris saw Thornton and Elaiza standing on the opposite side of the street and gave them a thumbs-up sign. The street between them was filling up.

Elaiza always looked different from the other women, Thornton thought, comparing her to the girls with Morris. She could wear a miniskirt or hot pants and still not be mistaken for a japayuki—the girls kept by some old Japanese executives for their lengthy "business trips" in Mindanao. Japanese were hardly noticed, unless they had such a female with them. Everyone noticed japayukis on the street, partly because of the way they overdressed. The bricklayers and carpenters all noticed Elaiza when she walked by too, but in a different way. She was dressed hot, but greeted them in a way that was not provocative. They liked her when she jogged by their construction sites in the morning and recognized her later when she went out to dinner with Thornton.

"If they put an explosive device in this crowd, they'll kill hundreds," Thornton thought out loud.

"At least." Elaiza furrowed her brow. "We would have to check out every object in the parade concealing a volume of more than a cubic meter, I suppose."

"Yeah, plus anything along the route or in the assembly areas large enough to conceal explosives. The local police will be swaggering around in full uniform, but I think they're too polite to ask questions." Thornton was not impressed with the security precautions.

Elaiza was more hopeful. "One good thing," she said, "is that Task Force Davao has kept an eye on everything coming into town from the indigenous regions as they cross the checkpoints entering the town proper."

"Big deal. They have a few guys with guns watching a dozen big trucks a minute drive by their outposts," Thornton said. "Those checkpoints only function with a military attitude *after* an incident, then they shut down all traffic and search every vehicle, when it's too late and after the insurgents are long gone and back in the boonies."

"We can't do much about it, so stay suspicious," Elaiza warned him unnecessarily, and checked her butt pack where she kept the TIAM with her fatigue uniform and field gear, just in case.

"Who are those hefty ladies in street clothes on the reviewing stand? Why aren't any of them in costume?" Thornton asked Elaiza.

"It's beneath them to wear costumes; they're the sponsors of the main event. The one with her hair tied back is the chairperson of the cut flower export group, and the one beside her is the head of the dried fish export commission. They put this all together to promote the export of cut flowers, mostly orchids and roses, and products from the agriculture and fishing industries. They don't want to be thought of as natives and so have adopted leftover Spanish names and customs." Elaiza was not impressed with the dignitaries. "They put lotion on their faces to make them white. Do you think the Turk is here?"

"Yes. Somewhere. If he blows something up in Davao City, it will be the biggest statement the Abu Sayaf will be able to make for months; the next best choice would be around Christmas. He doesn't want to wait that long. Look, the parade is starting to move again."

"Oh, you should like this, I hear the *agong*." Elaiza rose up to stand on her toes, stretching her lean calf muscles taut; Thornton noticed.

Dak a dak dak boom boom, dak a dak dak boom boom. The musicians struck their sets of nine cast bronze *agongs*, time set by the largest *agong*, the bandir, as big as a cooking pot, the lesser *agongs* as small as teapots. Brass cymbals and hollow wood drums covered with carabao hide generated a combination of crashing and thumping sounds and the enthusiastic but unrehearsed musicians intertwined the emotions of sex, anger, hate, and jealousy. Women danced as they moved forward, followed by the musicians. The men joined them and emotions intensified. Every step had a meaning and importance: life, love, planting, and harvest. The beauty of the women was striking: mestizas, mixes of Spanish and tribal bloods making the next generations of mocha beauties taller, but inheriting the bright white teeth of their native ancestors. The shiny golden brown figures with long black hair made the parade sparkle. Some waved to the spectators from their perches on the floats; others danced in the street with the musicians and marchers.

"Oh, oh, I see a problem," Elaiza said suddenly. "There are only a few floats moving forward now as I watch. More will be coming, but there are also lots of big parchment figures being carried along by the marchers. There must be sufficient volume, more than a cubic meter, of empty space available inside them."

"Let's be more careful of the really big ones, supported by some undercarriage or on a vehicle: disregard those being carried by one or two people. Explosives would be too heavy to carry the entire route. If our suspects are here, they'll be after more than taking out a few people in a suicide mission."

From the Maragusan Valley, the source of the Agusan in the north, came the Mansakas. The Tagabaawa were in from Mount Apo, just outside of Davao City to the west, and Manobos from the Compostela Valley, including Pedro Otaza and his brothers in the city with their families for these few days, all happy to have the chance to be involved, and especially the Mandayas, the most numerous of the local tribes from the areas immediately east of Davao City and extending down the far peninsula to Mati and hence Samal Island. Atas and Obos were lining up. B'laans and the Muslim and almost-Muslim tribes like the Kalagans, whose religion is a mix of the Islamic teachings of the Koran and primitive tribal customs, added their distinctive rhythms. Other tribes having varying mixes of Christian and Muslim beliefs and legends formed into their parade positions. All together, the street dancers constituted a primordial mixture of color and sound, fueled by tribal superstitions.

Elaiza saw Pedro and his four Manobo brothers carrying painted and feathered bamboo sticks used in their dancing. She knew that sharp bolo knives were concealed inside the hollow poles and that the native wooden carvings strapped to their backs for decoration were in reality heavy arrows that could be thrown as spears for short distances. But today they would not have a chance to use either; the threat was of a different nature.

Thornton and Elaiza both saw it simultaneously and didn't need to say anything to each other. One large float moved forward on wheels, a towering *waling-waling* purple goddess of the harvest, offering a symbolic durian a meter in diameter; a sphere of golden flowers was stuck into chicken wire that, despite its apparent lightness, bounced and jumped, stretching taut the steel cable holding it. Suddenly the float stopped in front of the reviewing stand and the driver dismounted to look under the vehicle as if he was attempting to fix a problem, but he rose from the undercarriage, turned, and walked away from the route of the parade at a brisk pace. The sphere of flowers swung back and forth on its wire and then, just in front of the plump ladies sitting with the mayor, the flower goddess and her durian globe both instantaneously disintegrated with steel shards and orchid blossoms alike propelled from the center of the sphere and then from the entire vehicle, moving outward at great speed and with the silent beauty of an exploding star at the edge of the universe. The sound and the shock wave hit, and shrapnel shredded dancers, the elegant ladies on the stand and Mayor Fuentes.

Pedro's team was not touched, and their first reaction was to turn immediately to help the injured. Thornton's first reaction was to tend to Elaiza, slumped behind the concrete post where they had been standing, stunned, some spots of blood on her arm.

"I'm fine, I'll assemble our team behind the bank. Where's Pedro?" She spoke urgently to Thornton.

"He's on his way here, I see him." Thornton held her, but looked around, alert to whatever would come next. What he had seen shocked him; the attackers had exploded the dynamite device directly in front of the mayor's reviewing stand, the ball exploding as it swung through his line of sight. Mayor Fuentes was more than just the mayor of a city, he was the mayor of the largest city in Asia, by surface area if not by population, and he was an important and powerful national leader. Through his five terms as mayor, Christians, Muslims and others regarded him as a man of the people. He had earned great respect for his policies, his implementation of modern methods and for himself as a humanitarian. Manila had looked upon Fuentes as the Governor of Mindanao.

Thornton and Elaiza saw body parts scattered like so much hamburger in streaks radiating out from the explosion's center. The aftermath of this catastrophic event was chaos. He squeezed Elaiza's hand and said, "See that taller man throwing down his mask? Why is he so calm? It has to be the Turk. Get to Sergeant Starke. I'm following that guy." Thornton was already moving.

"No. If you're going after him, I'm coming with you." Elaiza stood up, running with him.

"You'll be better with your uncle than with a white guy in this situation. Give me your iPod!"

"No! I'm keeping it from now on; it's my job. And I'm going with you. It's only calibrated for me. I can use it to signal our position." Elaiza was not going to be dissuaded, and there was no time to debate.

"Then hurry! Let's see where he goes." Thornton grabbed her arm and they ran together from the site of the explosion through puddles of blood, amid pain and confusion.

17

Pursuit

Even before the debris from the explosion settled, Mahir considered his immediate assignment with the Abu Sayaf hit team successful, and not just for the message it sent. The unusually high death toll for a single terrorist bomb attack would be a plus, but he also considered the event to be the start of the larger mission, the beginning of a new and historic jihad to turn the island of Mindanao into an independent and fundamentalist Islamic nation. Kumander Ali, the leader of the Abu Sayaf for all of Mindanao, would be pleased and perhaps would honor him when they met.

Moving away from the blast, Mahir and the rest of the hit team walked slowly but deliberately, looking straight ahead without curiosity. The horrified spectators and participants ran either toward the sound of the explosion, or directly away from it, depending on their individual dispositions; none of the innocent bystanders were just walking. Mahir discarded the mask he had been wearing and instantly became just another pedestrian, not much different looking than the others, except a bit taller, as he reached the stolen jeepney.

But Thornton had seen him. Some members of the terrorist strike force following along the parade route as back-ups had walked at the same pace as the parade until the malevolent float reached the reviewing stand and exploded. But when, immediately after the explosion, five people suddenly dropped the parade masks they were wearing and began moving at a purposeful pace converging toward a single point, it made them stand out, obvious within the crowd to Thornton. Although they tried to take on the visages of casual observers or participants of the parade, to look like five innocent people all wearing black jeans and shirts with various logos, their movement toward a common destination directly outward from the destroyed float gave them away. Thornton saw them as a cohesive group and deduced from their purposeful actions that they were the perpetrators. The taller one had to be Mahir Hakki.

He pulled Elaiza along and followed the Abu Sayaf at a distance, trying not to be noticed and staying in the early afternoon shadows as the enemy attack team withdrew.

Thornton saw Ugly Maria calmly approach a parked vehicle across the street and swing her heft onto the back of the jeepney, its rusted license plate numbers further obscured by strategically placed lumps of mud. She was the last to return before the Abu Sayaf squad departed the city, heading south back to the staging area. Harold, one of Lateef's men, drove. He smoked a cigarette, blew the horn from time to time for no reason, and together they looked about the same as the other loads of people trying to get out of the general area as expeditiously as possible. They needed the jeepney for transportation into and out of Davao City, but the false image of normality could last only a short distance. Such smaller jeepneys would not normally commute a long way; it was too far for such a smoke-pumping, inefficient vehicle in normal commercial operation. Just after Toril, they pulled into the Lake Forest Resort, where they were still registered and where they held Lito, their hostage from the cement factory, who had been uncomfortably sitting on a sack of cash while the hit squad carried out the attack. Lateef had decided to keep Lito with them, at least during the time they would be active near

his village. Lito was terrified, but cooperated. Most of the time Abu
Sayaf hostages were eventually released, he thought, and he had many
Muslim friends in his village, including one of them who was now
holding him by force. Surely this could not be a kidnapping for ransom
plot, as he obviously had no money. So he couldn't understand what
was going on. Abu Sayaf irregulars Jun and Bong had guarded him at
the resort while the hit squad had done their business in Davao City,
and the two warriors were now well-rested and ready to assume their
key roles in the move on toward Digos later that night. For now, they
would take the early evening guard while the returning attack team
rested following their bumpy withdrawal from the attack.

Thornton had seen the loaded jeepney depart as sirens began to
sound behind him. It was good that Elaiza was with him, if she could
keep up. She had the iPod and could connect with the embassy to report
positions and get information. He asked, "How badly are you hurt?"

"Really, not at all. Just some cuts from glass or metal that was thrown
around. Not serious." She was easily staying with him as they walked
briskly.

Because he was a white guy and an obvious foreigner, Thornton was
able to stop a taxi on the outskirts of the city. The driver would expect
a big tip from a foreigner during a moment of such urgency; news about
the blast was already on the radio. Thornton told him, "Just drive, I'll
point."

This seemed to make perfect sense to the cab driver, assuming that
his passenger could more easily direct than explain where to go and to
get out of the area.

When they saw the rusty vehicle of the Abu Sayaf, Elaiza took over
and ordered the driver in his own dialect, "Follow the old jeepney!" The
jeepney puffed its way south, with the taxi following at a distance.

When Mahir, Lateef and their squad pulled into the resort area, it
seemed to be their immediate destination. Thornton and Elaiza had the
taxi drop them and they left the roadside to enter the brushy foliage.
They climbed the wire fence around the resort just in time to see the last
two of Mahir's men disembark from the jeepney and enter a reed-
thatched cottage on an empty beach on the Gulf of Davao, near the
center of the Lake Forest Resort.

The jeepney had entered the tourist facility unchallenged through a sentry-guarded gate, the private security for the resort. The Abu Sayaf had no need to have their own man on alert, as the resort management did not suspect them of being the terrorists the radio was reporting on. The rental cottages for tourists were directly on the black sand beach; the lagoon behind them was an artificial lake created by diverting the flow of a small stream. The lagoon blocked off the approach of any police or army unit that would come after them, but it also blocked the men's own escape. They would have to choose a more difficult route around the lake when they resumed their move back toward Digos.

Although Task Force Davao acted quickly to seal off Davao City proper, Mahir and the Abu Sayaf squad had already arrived back at the seaside resort by the time the order was implemented. Because they had checked in as tourists some days before and had gone out and later returned in the same jeepney, there was no suspicion about their movements. There had never been a question about the truck, as it was apparently part of Kadayawan. Now they would abandon the jeepney, leaving it parked in front of the two cottages they had taken for their accommodations, the bill having been paid a week in advance. The entire team would disappear when the night was darkest, after 2:00 AM, when Lateef knew there would be no moon. The squad spent the early evening trying to rest. Events of the frantic day had strained their physical and emotional limits and had drained their energies, but none were able to sleep immediately after they returned, although resting was exactly what they needed to do. Only Ugly Maria slept, making guttural noises and slobbering saliva onto the floor mat. The others gradually nodded into slumber.

Thornton had found a patch of garden crops surrounded by vines growing on a wire fence and stomped out a clearing where he and Elaiza could observe the cottages. "You rest for a while, later it will be your turn," he told her.

"Right, like I can just go to sleep after all this," she answered, but curled up with her back pushed against his and closed her eyes.

Thornton planned to stay hidden there in the fast approaching night, the sun setting quickly this close to the equator. He wanted to take out that tall dark Arab, leave him dead, but mostly he wanted the money without having to get into hand-to-hand combat with several rag-tag Muslims. He knew the U.S. had the capability to do the job with one high explosive bomb and pinpoint accuracy based on Elaiza's tracking with the TIAM. Then they could walk in and claim the bags of cash. But, after all, it was not just about the money; Thornton knew he had to get Kumander Ali too if he was going to make Charlie Downs happy.

Shortly after midnight when the world had turned charcoal black, Elaiza took her turn on guard; Thornton could doze off for a while. When she initially heard more than saw the squad of Abu Sayaf leave their beach cottages, she quickly awakened Thornton. "I believe I see the silhouette against the sea of a taller man who could be the Turk."

Thornton squinted, "I think you're right. Let's go."

The Abu Sayaf squad pulled out slowly, not leaving the resort through the gate, but around the lake and parallel to the Davao-Digos highway, then stealthily overland through the brush, where they did not expect to be seen after they entered the thicker growth.

Six hundred meters down the road and south of the resort, the hit squad paused. When it was quiet on the road with no traffic or pedestrians moving in either direction, they crossed all at once in a line parallel to the road, pulling along the stumbling Lito tied by a leash around his neck, with Ugly Maria tugging at the other end of the short rope.

Thornton and Elaiza waited as long as they could before crossing the road without losing direction or being seen. They paused almost too long, but the night was dark and their target moved slowly. It was easy to follow them now. The Abu Sayaf moved cautiously, but made some sounds while tramping down brush. Thornton went first, and Elaiza followed him along the new path bent through the high grass, and later through thicker underbrush and then the jungle itself. The torment of the mosquitoes and the flesh-cutting grass blades gave way to volcanic black mud swamps. When the footing turned solid again, it was a short-lived blessing, as the trek up steeper terrain drained valuable moisture from their bodies and they had no drinking water to replace lost fluids. Thornton could continue to follow the group, he supposed, but he would have to keep them in sight in the minimal ambient light.

On the outskirts of Digos in the province of Davao del Sur, about

seven miles from the resort where they had started their trek, Lateef
stopped and checked his map. Thornton saw them all kneel or lie down
and take up defensive positions, indicating that these soldiers were well
trained and disciplined when on patrol. Elaiza took advantage of their
halt to turn on her iPod again, with one earplug speaker in use. She
tuned in to Moser's program as the D.J. was nearing the end of his show
for the night. She waited for Schloss Code messages, prefaced by something like "For my loyal listener Luv-Luv . . ." It didn't matter what
name he gave; the key words "My loyal listener" would indicate to
Elaiza that the message was for them. The Chopin First Piano Concerto
was playing. Then, after the predictable requests for Strauss's "Blue
Danube," Moser announced, "And for my loyal listener, Magda, in
Bislig," and some mumbled words in German: "Zwoa Kalb Thurgau
Kalb." It was the Schloss Code.

And later after another similar dedication, "Silvaner Fluss."

The two messages literally were the code words for cardinal directions and the words Zwoa for Zwei, meaning "two" and Fluss for "river."

Elaiza and Thornton listened, and figured out that Starke and the
Otazas were located two miles east northeast on the south side of a river
from their present location, which had been tracked and reported to
Major Hayes by a text message from the embassy; Hayes had then
passed it on to Moser for encoding and transmission.

"Elaiza, it's working! The Schloss Code works. Starke and your uncles
also took the road south after getting our position. When we need them,
they'll be near." Thornton was relieved to know that Starke and the five
well-armed, definitely motivated, and well-rested Otaza brothers would
be ready to move out within minutes after he gave the order.

Looking at his map, Thornton drew a semi-circle on it with a two-
mile radius from the point where the code told him STAGCOM was
positioned. He was situated on that curved line, two miles on a back
azimuth west-southwest from where it intersected with the point where
the river crossed the highway. Thornton now knew that with Elaiza's
help in communication he could direct STAGCOM. He felt reassured.
The insurgents had no idea that they were being followed, so Thornton
held the strategic advantage. After the message was received, Elaiza
moved four paces backward on the line of approach and then forward

again, with two side paces notching the line. She was right back where she had started, but her movement was detected by the TIAM, mounted along with the GPS device on the iPod circuit board. By prior agreement with the embassy, her movement signaled, "Your message received and understood," and "those I am following are dead ahead along this line one hundred meters." She did not draw a circle to signify a fire mission; Thornton wanted to take out Mahir himself, with STAGCOM. No international mess, no questions.

Thornton had covered himself with a small canvas tarp he had folded into his back pocket, to keep the light of his small flashlight contained while he did map reconnaissance, and it had made him sweat even more than when he had been moving through the stagnant night air. He now folded it back up. Mosquitoes smelled his warm blood and took out their frustration on the netting hanging loosely from his safari hat.

Beside him, Elaiza was sweating. The scent of *Innocent Angel* was gone, and she had changed into the fatigue outfit she kept in her butt pack. She had covered her face with a scarf to protect herself from the thirsty insects. There was some movement of the air, but it was not a cooling breeze; it was hot, wet wind. They were thankful when Mahir began to move again, continuing south, and they followed.

When the last star began to fade, the Abu Sayaf halted. They would need to find a place to spend the day, to "lie dog," the tactic of waiting quietly and in concealment until after dark, before continuing. The general area had been reconnoitered on their way north through it a few days before, the local inhabitants were few, and even fewer lived inland away from the road.

"Our patrol needs to find a place to survive the heat; the day that is coming soon will be hot," Mahir told Lateef, wanting to know his tactical plan. "Maybe this high grass is not enough shelter."

"And we will need fresh water if we are to continue, fresh, running water which should be easy to find in this region; water runs away in all directions from the summit of the big mountain. But we do not want to be walking back and forth in the open carrying water." Lateef understood their situation and led them to the luxury of a grassy mound under a broad-leafed tree floating like an island on a sea of savanna grass with a small stream running through. It would do, and it was just in time as they could discern recognizable forms beginning to take shape in the blackness of the dying night.

Thornton saw the spot they chose, and made a similar plan for the coming day, opting to stay near the tree line from where he could observe them, a scant distance of less than a hundred yards separating them, elevated in a copse of broad-leafed scrub brush raised a few feet above the grassy plain.

Elaiza, breathing hard, had some good news. "Look what's here. These are "paco"—salad ferns. We can strip fronds off the young and tender plants and eat them for the moisture they contain, as well as for nourishment."

As soon as they settled in and felt concealed, they collected what they could and stuffed more ferns into a plastic bag for later, if they had to move out suddenly. "Wherever we find more growing along our way, we should eat as much as we can on the spot and collect what we can carry with us." Elaiza set herself to the task.

During the night's trek, they had not been able to see well, and there was no opportunity to pause. Now the paco ferns would be all they would have to eat or drink for at least the next twenty-four hours, and they were thankful. Their position was tactically good. Thornton and Elaiza were located where they could observe the resting Abu Sayaf, but could not be seen themselves. However, the great disadvantage was that they were not near even a small rivulet of fresh water.

Thornton tried some of the bland-tasting ferns Elaiza handed him, "I'd call this good luck. Dinner and drinks in a comfortable place, and where we're concealed from the enemy. And this is the second night we've slept together."

Elaiza couldn't help smiling at Thornton's humor, "*Unintentionally* slept together! The first night was *more* uncomfortable for me." But she lay down near him as they settled in to get some rest before the next grueling trek. Still, she found it difficult to fall asleep, uncertain about whether the apprehension came from the danger of their situation or because of the physical presence of the guy she felt next to her.

18

Delusion

Mahir did not like Lito, but respected him for the way he reacted to his captivity and was at least curious about him, a kind of academic interest. So he tested Lito, who was tied up and kneeling beneath him in the camp, "Stupid Christian, why does your kind of people come to impoverished lands like this and start new churches? Why give new names to old ideas? Do you think you can invent your own church?"

"I did not invent any church. I am just a security guard." Lito knew he was being taunted, and he chose his words carefully. "Outsiders come to new lands for business and to spread their religions. In Mindanao, this was done by both the Muslims and the Catholics, except the Muslim traders arrived here first."

"Prisoner, Jesus Christ may be your God but he is not mine. The God of Abraham is Allah."

"People call their God many names in many languages, but I think they all mean the same God." Lito needed a tactful answer, so he answered slowly and deliberately.

"How can you be so arrogant as to think so? That is your personal arrogance, nothing more. Abraham was the trusted friend of God, and he deduced there must be a God, thus did God reveal himself to Abraham. And Abraham was not a Jew or a Christian; he was a man of God, a Muslim. What rules you Jews and Catholics make do not apply. Our destiny is the will of Allah." Mahir did not like the attitude of his prisoner and was determined to set him straight.

"I do not know the rules of the Jews because I have never met a Jew in my entire life. And I am not familiar with the rules of the Catholics. I only repeat what the missionary told me." Lito was getting worried by his captor's rising anger.

"Catholic or not, you are all unbelievers. Who is this guy John? What salvation, doesn't salvation just mean washing with water?"

"We baptize into the faith with water as a symbol, but it was the blood sacrifice . . ."

Mahir lost patience with what he saw as blatant stupidity and almost shouted, "Blood sacrifice!" interrupting Lito. "You mean like slitting the throat of a goat, or even young children bought from their parents for the purpose of pouring their blood over a new stone bridge to make it last longer? Yours is a religion for the insane. You preach peace, but you attack Muslims who are already living in peace."

"God is angry because his law was violated in the Garden of Eden. Only Christ could atone for our sins by dying on the cross. Jesus is God and came here to die for us."

"How can he be God if he is the Son of God? It does not make any sense. We know Jesus was a great prophet, but we also know the final prophet of God is Mohammad. Enough of this. Why do you Christians continue to sin against God by killing Muslims? Do you not get it? Your way will never work. The same message has been sent over the genera-tions; happiness comes from worshiping Him only." Mahir continued, getting more disturbed with the direction of the discussion. "You Chris-tians are still fighting the Crusades, coming into peaceful lands and killing us so you can go to heaven. It is time for your missionaries to go back to Kansas and Mississippi and convert the inhabitants of their own poverty-stricken cities. Start there! Why do they come to Mindanao, or Afghanistan, or Turkey? Because they think we are more stupid, easier to convert than the lost souls in their own country? Will they get a higher rate of conversion here? Your missionaries should stay in your homelands and leave other people to their personal superstitions, if that is what you think their beliefs are."

"But I did not come from another land." Lito stated the obvious. "I come from the north of here, where I was born, and only came to the city to find work."

"Even sadder for you, you do the work of the Yankees and the Zionists, against your own people." Mahir spoke while quietly counting through his string of a hundred beads that he always carried, especially useful in situations where there was nothing else to do.

"But I am just a poor security guard."

Mahir was not being kind to the hobbled prisoner. "Look at these men with me. To have a home with a metal roof and a daily income, or to own a jeepney, would make them rich men. They have nothing and would not eat tomorrow if they were not members of this squad and humbly received the gifts of those we protect as we move through the land." The captor was losing his desire to continue the discussion, but did not replace the gag in Lito's mouth, which obviously caused discomfort. Mahir was bored, realized he was tired, and shortly fell asleep. It was not so easy for Lito to rest, but he began to doze after the sun passed its highest point of the day and began to decline.

When Lateef observed that the light was fading, he ordered the team to prepare to move out for the second night's march. He called Ugly Maria before the others awoke from their afternoon sleep and instructed her, "The Christian is no longer of use to us as a hostage and tonight will be a difficult hike for us. Get rid of him and I will pay for you to have another of your tribal tattoos put on your forehead when we reach our destination."

Ugly Maria understood the message and, before the rest of the party began to assemble their equipment, proceeded with her assignment. Lito was dozing, not quite awake. She replaced the gag and pulled him into the grass by his hair. She applied her usual technique; she flipped Lito around and from behind sliced his jugular vein open with her short, sharp utility knife and completed the incision from ear to ear. It was quick. Lito looked surprised as he felt the life pumping out of his body with red, bubbling liquid spurting down his arms and torso and he knew he was dying quickly. Ugly Maria pushed the living carcass into the brush so its kicking would not disturb the men's meal of dry fish, warmed in the sun on the grass near where Lito had been sitting. The unfortunate security guard, just so much heavy baggage, would not be continuing with them.

The patrol moved out of camp shortly after nightfall.

19

The Chinoy

Colonel Reginald "Reggie" Liu had built a new, modern home in Manila with his wife, Trisha, on grounds next to Fort Bonifacio, near the headquarters of the Philippine Army. They were planning ahead for his retirement, which was scheduled in two years unless he succeeded in being promoted to general officer rank before then, giving him the chance to continue his career. They also had a home in Albuquerque, New Mexico, partly as an investment and partly as a future second home so that whenever Liu finally did retire they could be near their son and his wife. Many Filipinos, even family members of senior professionals and politicians, sought work overseas to supplement the relatively low salaries at home, including senior army officers, especially the ethical ones. In fact, during Liu's overseas assignments, Trisha had spent years working as a pharmacist in Santa Fe while Reggie fought the battles, overseas and alone. Liu was a gentleman, well respected by his contemporaries, his seniors in the army, and the men he led.

He was one of a select few officers from the Philippines who graduated from West Point, returning to his native country to fulfill his army obligations. His government sent him overseas again to attend the German General Staff College in Hamburg for a year. Liu spoke fluent German already, having studied it at West Point. Of course he spoke excellent English and several Filipino dialects: thus after a tour as the Defense Attaché to Korea, he had become something of a linguist. He even spoke passable French. But language was only one of his areas of intellectual interest and ability. He had graduated from Case-Western Reserve in Cleveland, Ohio, with a master's degree in mechanical engineering, and he later taught engineering courses and thermodynamics at the Philippine Military Academy in Baguio. This was in addition to duty assignments as a professional officer, among them commanding an infantry company and later a battalion in the field.

Liu was now nearing the end of an assignment as military advisor to the Philippine congress, reporting to Martin Galan, Chairman of the Committee on National Defense, with whom the President consulted closely on military matters. Galan held the highest congressional office with direct access to the military, and, according to the laws of the Republic of the Philippines, civilians were supposed to control the military.

Newspapers were already reporting that Galan would be selected to become the next Secretary of Defense, but he had received no official word yet. The stories in the *Philippine Star* were a positive omen for him; it seemed that if the papers floated a theory that sounded good, the regime would go with the flow and make the rumor a reality. Galan had a real chance for the promotion, and great implied power already. The military would simply do what he said; they read the papers.

Liu had his personal opinions and issues with Galan, who was more than his boss; he was the man with whom he most often spoke his heart. In his official government position, Congressman Galan was far senior to Liu, but they had known each other since childhood, and then reconnected in the army, when both were stationed in central Luzon. Galan went back to Manila after his three years of military service and created for himself a successful civilian career in business, opening a private bank with a network of branches throughout the country. Satisfied in many ways with his business success, he chose to serve his country in another role and made a courageous—because in the Philippines politics is a dangerous business—move into politics, and in his fourth term, took on his new role as a senior trusted advisor when his political mentor was elected President. Liu thought Galan was incorruptible, not subject to the crazy schemes that abound in the Philippines. He could not imagine him being involved in a junta, coup d'état or revolution.

Liu and Galan met at least once a month at the Aristocrat, a downtown Manila restaurant that dated back to the time when Spanish culture was omnipresent in the Philippines. This time Liu arrived first, in uniform, and was immediately shown to the best table. Galan arrived a few minutes later in smart civilian dress, a light blue barong tagalog over black trousers, a style favored for formal occasions and that, when worn during the day, was an indication of higher class. They sat opposite each other after shaking hands and exchanging smiles.

Looking out over Manila Bay across Rojas Boulevard, Liu mused, "What happened to the Spanish language? It is so beautiful and essential. All you Pinoys have Spanish names but you can't speak a word of it."

"No, but at least they gave our forefathers Spanish names or we would still be just Bong, Dong and Jun." Martin Galan knew about Liu's interest in languages and jested with his friend.

"Even my Chinese ancestors seem to have run out of names, so my parents called me Reginald. It sounded like an English gentleman to them, I guess," Liu responded.

"And here we sit, speaking English in a Spanish restaurant next to the American Embassy while our national language is Tagalog." Galan pondered one of the dichotomies of the Philippine nation, the diverse culture, or rather the collection of different cultures that make up the nation and simultaneously keep it apart.

"Or is it? I thought our national language was English."

"Maybe it should be, and at least it's an official language, but can you get a Cebuano sergeant to shout commands in English to a Tagalog in the heat of an attack when they are pinned down by heavy automatic weapons fire, or when they're supposed to attack? He'll revert to the language he knows they will understand," Galan said. "We have to teach them better."

"You need to appropriate more money." Liu, thinking like the professor he once was, gave it right back to Galan.

"I know English must be taught in schools, but patriotism and nationalism are not tied to any one language. We both know that English is not essential for daily living here, perhaps, but it is indispensable for global involvement and awareness, not just for our officials but for those who elect them." Galan was turning serious and philosophical. "And for the workers who go overseas. They need to learn it also."

Galan was touching on one of Liu's lingering doubts about the future of democracy in his country. He put a possibility to Galan. "Think about the kind of government our voters will choose next. They might elect the best neighborhood karaoke singer rather than a statesman."

"They better elect a statesman soon, or there will be no state. Even now, groups in Mindanao blame the Kadayawan bombing on disgruntled military officers who want to overthrow the government because of corruption," Galan responded. Now they were getting to the real issues. Galan manifested his discontent when he did not answer Liu, but twisted the fancy restaurant's red cloth napkin into a knot.

Encouraged by the direction their discussion was taking, Liu vented what was on his mind to Galan. "To get to the root of the problem, we must admit the truth. Some younger officers think all of us are corrupt, skimming off government cash and property for ourselves." Liu believed in the constitution. It was a trade-off he made willingly; between greed and duty, he had chosen duty.

"They have a point, or did at one time in recent history," Galan admitted, "but those young officers who raised their own flag over a fancy hotel and thought they were protesting for a new morality in government were not thinking about Mindanao. It never entered their minds. They were only thinking about the northern half of this country."

Liu supported Galan's opinion. "They were not thinking at all, and their silly antics just encourage the insurrectionists to push our nation into a civil war."

"Reggie, I expect soon you will be a general officer." Galan surprised Liu. If Galan wanted him to be promoted, he could make it happen.

"And I suppose some day you will be President," Liu said, returning the compliment.

Galan fidgeted, but only slightly, and changed the subject. "We have to change the way we appoint our top generals."

Liu was glad to have his own personal opinion reinforced by a man he respected. Galan continued, "Now, the Chief of Staff is appointed only for a year or less, more as a reward for loyal service than a recognition of competence. Once appointed, he brings along his cronies and promotes them to general officer rank, then soon after that a whole new flock of fledgling one-stars all retire and get their pensions and staff for life, a huge cost for a poor country. Better we appoint a younger man to be the chief and let him serve long enough to implement an agenda. Someday you could be that man, postpone your retirement for more stars; mentor your successor. In the meantime, you could help elect the next president."

Liu liked what he heard. And so would many of the younger officers, the ones who served loyally and with little recognition. "You're right, Martin, a lot of the officer corps right now are simply pissed off. Better we act sooner than have to react later to another internal revolt." Liu wanted to show Galan his support.

Galan paused, refolded his napkin and replaced it neatly on the table. "There's something I want to talk with you about, Reggie, in that regard. I need the right man to command an expanded force in Mindanao and the Visayas to prevent the MNLF from taking over the southern Philippines. The peace talks are stalled, and the Moros have lost their patience. They are not accepting the obvious presence of American troops in the indigenous lands. Do you remember our conversation after the Army-Navy game at the U.S. Embassy, with that Thomas Thornton and the U.S. Embassy staff, especially the reps from their State and Defense Departments?"

"Yes, Thornton is an old acquaintance. We both graduated from West Point, different years, of course." Liu wanted Galan to get to the issue. The waiters were standing ready to serve dessert.

"Apparently some things have started to roll between Washington and Manila. Both governments believe it is in their long-term best interest to thwart the global presence of Al Qaeda, and we have definite proof of a major initiative underway at this moment in Mindanao. I want you to lead our forces there on the ground. You will report, in

theory, to Lieutenant General Roland Villarreal who heads Southern
Command, but you will actually get your orders directly from me.
Check in with Roland when you get to Davao City: he'll work with you.
I will be, unofficially, working with the U.S. Embassy: they have the
intelligence-gathering mechanisms, satellites and tech systems, and some
special forces on the ground now, "training" our rangers."

Galan paused to let this sink in and to wait for questions. There were
none, so he continued, "We will need to act *immediately* on the intelligence we get from them, I mean within *minutes* of receipt, so I will either
be in the operations room of the JUSMAG personally or in direct contact with the Americans by telephone all the time. Our president has
secretly approved all this, but we have to keep it quiet. Go by Army HQ
and coordinate all this with the Chief of Staff, then get to Davao City.
Roland is instructed to give you troops and logistical support, but will
let you command—for better or for worse, you'll be on your own."
Galan laid out the problematical assignment for Liu, by its nature full of
the possibility for disgrace and embarrassment if it got fouled up and
little reward if it went perfectly.

"What's new about the threat in Mindanao? Why me? Why now?"
Liu wanted to confirm Galan's commitment to him, and test the depth
of the congressman's authority. He saw his first star either within his
grasp or slipping away—he was not sure which.

"The Abu Sayaf has some new money. Hot money; no way to trace it."

"I am aware of that, and understand the U.S. interest in having
Thornton make it disappear before they can use it."

"Since the execution of that Muslim terrorist in Indonesia, Al Qaeda
is now targeting bars and night clubs, churches, any place the cowards
might be able to kill either a lot of people or, even better, a lot of tourists.
The Kadayawan bombing in Davao City is just the start of their plan;
there will be more incidents. They're after softer targets to make a
louder statement. It's not just about going after our military, which
might be too difficult for them," Galan continued. "Their cells are functioning independently world-wide. No central control from Al Qaeda in
Iran or Afghanistan is necessary. We need to pursue a second front
against their clandestine cells. In Mindanao, for example, that Octagon
gang, one of the cells, goes after rich Chinese, kidnapping unsuspecting

wealthy citizens for ransom. Can you imagine, according to our intelligence, the MNLF has 12,000 men under arms in the North, the NPA has terrorist influence in the East, and the Abu Sayaf has training camps in the West? Only Davao City proper had been quiet, until the bombs and then the major catastrophe at Kadayawan last week. We lost the only powerful and charismatic leader we had in Mindanao when they killed Mayor Fuentes. I will give you the power and the authority, exclusively; you report directly only to me. So try to avoid snoopy seniors. You know the routine."

Now Liu had the entire concept of the operation laid out clearly for him. It was a request, but it was also an order, given to him in friendly language and demeanor by Galan. Liu probed. "I suppose if anything goes wrong you blame me; if it goes right, you get the credit?"

"Reggie, you're beginning to understand politics." Galan smiled in a mock conspiratorial tone. Then he shocked the straitlaced Colonel.

"The Americans just want to make the money go away so the Abu Sayaf is not funded. They don't care where it goes. Instead of this Thornton guy winding up with it, think about how much good we could do for our country if it wound up in some small bank in the middle of Mindanao, say, in somebody's name, not yours or mine of course, but in someone's name who would support the right choice for the next president. Wouldn't that make a lot of sense? Think how much good we could do for our country. We could resolve all the problems we've just talked about." Galan had his arm around Liu's shoulder as they stood up and walked out of the Aristocrat, the last luncheon guests to return to the heat of an early afternoon in Manila.

What Galan told him sounded wrong to Liu, yet Galan's hopes for their country were the same as his. Wasn't this why he had sacrificed his best years?

As a last stop before he left Manila, after he had gone home and picked up his already packed combat kit and said goodbye yet again to Trisha, Liu went as ordered to Malacanang, the seat of the Philippine government, to meet personally with the Chief of Staff of the Army, General Ramil Ortiz. Although only a Colonel in rank, Liu was well known and respected throughout the army, partly because he had taught "thermo" to many of the younger army officers in their academy days in Baguio. General Ortiz was aware of the official mission assigned to Liu by Galan, and now he confirmed its importance. Reiterating the need to act discreetly during any military operation, Ortiz told Liu that he would get the necessary support on the ground from General Villarreal in Davao City, but he also wanted to brief Liu personally before he departed on his assignment.

Ortiz came right to the point. "We have got to sort out the Davao blast, find out who did it and eliminate them. Some of the overseas press, and even some regional rags published out there in the provinces, are conjecturing that the Kadayawan disaster was carried out not only by our own citizens, but also by members of our armed forces. Some suspect a coup is coming. We have empowered a Truth Commission to buy some time while they investigate the root reasons for the Davao City bombings. We don't have much time. Meanwhile, the world views us as a banana republic. We must change this image, and we must change the facts, very soon."

"All this I know, sir. And I will do my job." Liu was honored, but needed to be tactful with Ortiz. What he was doing was not exactly according to protocol. "What reliable intelligence do we have? Exactly who do we think were the prime movers in the Davao incidents?" he asked.

"Not good intelligence, locally. Maybe Abu Sayaf, maybe NPA, but we have information from the U.S. that Al Qaeda is funding the local terrorists. But we can't publish our version of the story without some hard proof, preferably some dead bodies, with documents. It must be made clear that no one in our government is sponsoring revolution in Mindanao. If that were the case, civil war throughout the Philippines could happen, even here in the north, at great cost in lives and to our progress as a nation."

Liu took their discussion in another direction, "I understand the church is also raising questions. The Christians do not want to become Muslims."

"And vice–versa, I am sure. We can't comment about such matters even in jest. But we certainly need to take into account commercial business interests also," Ortiz continued. "Merely the threat of civil war shuts off foreign investment, and then the peso crashes, our country can't afford to pay the interest on our foreign debt and the whole house of cards collapses."

Liu was sitting in the old, burnished rattan chair opposite the general's desk, a chair he had occupied several times before when the situation was happier. He waited for the Chief of Staff to continue.

"Colonel Liu, Reggie, there will be some American involvement, I have been informed, but we must keep it low-key. Whatever you do must look like a Philippine Army operation, undertaken by our loyal citizen soldiers against a foreign threat to our country. You know there are American troops in the area now. The Americans are in the field—but in Zamboanga, not in Davao."

"The Vice Mayor, replacing Mayor Fuentes, is waiting for you with General Villarreal in Davao City. We know from the Americans where the Abu Sayaf patrol is stopped at the moment, so try to get there immediately, take charge of the field operation, and eliminate that renegade outfit before all Mindanao blows up!"

Colonel Liu left for Davao City in a C130 with a small cadre of rangers and support teams, and extra equipment to help out the existing Task Force Davao. He was intensely aware of the immensity of his assignment all the way south.

Davao City had been a small, dirty town lying on the two banks of the Davao River for the centuries of occupation, first by the Spanish and then the Americans. But during the last twenty years it had experienced rapid growth as territory was annexed and population multiplied. Tribespeople moved in from the jungles to taste city comforts and foreigners came from everywhere to seek their fortunes. Now it was a big dirty city lying on the two banks of the Davao River. There was not as much trash lining the streets or as many open sewers running into gutters on every block as before. Progress. Hovels built long ago on stilts above garbage dumps, where the freshly arrived natives from the country could literally live on the garbage, had been bulldozed and concrete shops with apartments above them put in their place. More progress.

Liu landed at the new and modern Davao City airport and was met by Vice Mayor Miguel Mandosong, accompanied by the bodyguards of the recently assassinated Mayor Fuentes. The arrival protocol was under the nervous control of Mandosong, who was actually now the mayor in fact, if not yet accepted by the people or even by his own subconscious.

"Colonel Liu, I am at your service, and hope to bring you quickly to the headquarters of Task Force Davao. They are ready to move against the enemy."

Liu nodded to Mandosong politely.

They drove with sirens and blinking lights through the choke points where police officers controlled the traffic entering the city along any of the corridors of approach, closely inspecting vehicles with tinted windows or questionable license plates. A heavy-duty 2 1/2 ton dump truck loaded above its wooden stakes with hard, green, fat bananas being moved into Davao City for export to world markets, was forced to move off the road so the official vehicles could whiz by. The rushing convoy scared and scattered the weavers seated at the edge of the highway who were piecing together rugs of romblon, the fibers of a plant that grew profusely along the Davao seacoast. Tricycles hauling pedestrians bumped up onto the curb.

The officials arrived at the headquarters of Task Force Davao less than half an hour after Liu had touched down. Three-star General Villarreal, commanding all army forces in the south, was a man who had been contending with the insurgents in Mindanao, especially the inland areas of the west and north, for the last three years. The Task Force reported to him, and he used it as his personal tool for special actions.

"Colonel Liu," he welcomed a man he had known for years although they had not often met, while he hardly looked at the nervous Vice Mayor, "Task Force Davao has two full infantry companies already mustered and sitting in trucks with their engines running. You don't need any written orders."

"I understand, sir." Liu knew when to say as little as possible.

Villarreal took Liu by the arm and led him over to the window, while Vice Mayor Mandosong sat and drank a Nescafé, thankful that the officers were taking charge of the insurgent question. He would have his hands full in handling the city administration itself.

"The Chief of Staff called and briefed me," said the general. "You will have all I can get for you, but I still have to defend Davao City from

God knows what will happen next. This small force of two companies is all I can let you have now. But they are both commanded by capable officers and are well equipped. Good luck. Don't waste time. Don't delay anything by contacting me to approve your plans, just stay within your operational area; Galan will tell me whatever I need to know."

Liu gritted his teeth almost hard enough to be heard, said nothing, gave a casual but respectful salute and left Lieutenant General Villarreal to drink coffee with the nervous man who would soon be appointed mayor of the third largest city in the Philippines. Liu commandeered the car of the mayor-to-be and left to take over his new command, the Task Force Davao.

20

Jihad

The Abu Sayaf had lightened their load. There was no more stupid Christian to haul along with them, and they also dumped tools and equipment they had needed only for the Kadayawan bomb, which, praise Allah, had been a great success. Still, forward movement by the patrol through the undergrowth was slow. The experienced tribal warriors under Lateef's leadership, who was alternating with Ugly Maria as the point man, knew how to move through the thick brush, looking overhead from time to time to see where the higher, broad-leafed trees did not cover over to intermesh and obscure the sky from view under the canopy. Seeing the sky above, the warriors could move directly ahead without bumping into tree stumps. Using the techniques of the practiced land navigator, they followed a straight-line azimuth, taking a jag a bit to the right, then moving parallel along the line of their intended course, than a jag to the left, checking the azimuth on their compass and moving forward once again parallel to the path laid out on their map.

The warriors wore tight-knit, smooth-textured and lightweight black denim trousers, made by Levi's in China, and long-sleeved shirts of various colors. One of the troopers had a light blue shirt imprinted "Lee USA" in large black letters, not the best or the most correct uniform, but complete body coverage was more important for protection from mosquitoes and other hazards. Long vines with wait-a-minute hooks grabbed any fabric or flesh they caught. Plants that seemed to have nerves reacted by closing around feet like an octopus on land. Lateef had assigned an M-79 grenade launcher to one of the men, who wore a skullcap with a lazy "W" stitched on it in yellow; he looked tough enough to use the weapon. To give them all some kind of military identity, Lateef ordered them to wear yellow armbands. They were an army in uniform and on the move.

After they emerged higher up out of the grassland, Mahir made his way nearer to Lateef. They had moved a long distance, making much better time after they reached firmer and higher ground, and he wanted to know their position. Mahir asked him, "Have we reached Isulan yet?"

"No. We have a long way to travel, another night's march," answered the patrol leader. "We are still in the highlands and need to cross the Banga, then we will turn north and continue to the other side of Koronadal City to the point where the Banga and Alah rivers meet. There will be our rendezvous with Kumander Ali."

As they moved on, giant bats flew over them making eerie, flapping sounds in the absolute black of night. They heard OV10 ground attack planes and MG520 helicopters of the Philippine Air Force flying unlit in the night sky, searching for them, but Lateef knew they could not be seen under the tree canopy. The next day the newspapers would report around-the-clock searches for the insurgent paramilitary forces that perpetrated the Kadayawan massacre and would discredit persistent reports that the Philippine Army was in revolt. Armored personnel carriers continued to drive back and forth on the highways as a show of force, burning precious diesel fuel, tying up traffic and accomplishing nothing more. The insurgents were not on the highways. The central government of the Philippines would continue to demonstrate its confusion, a confusion that might permit the rebels to take over all of Mindanao.

"You hear the aircraft. Are you worried about them? They must be

Americans," Mahir asked Lateef as they made progress and it was easier to converse.

"I'm not worried. Not unless they pinpoint our location. They fly all night. It's just a demonstration," Lateef told him. "We take them out sometimes."

Mahir was surprised. "How can you shoot one of them down with just your rifles?"

"It's not easy, and we often miss; but they only have a few aircraft, so the loss of one is a major event. We can't fire where they can see the rifle blast, especially at night. But when helicopters fly over us, they are looking ahead. We position ourselves high on a hill or mountain but below the tree line, and immediately after they fly past us, the entire squad will run back up the hill and fire directly at the rear of the departing aircraft, aiming two meters above it to allow for the bullets' fall along their trajectories. We fire all we can and then run quickly back below the tree line. It only takes one bullet in the right place to cause a helicopter to go down. We have three kills." Lafeef was proud to explain their tactics.

"How did you figure this out?"

"We saw it in the field manuals we have. We can't read the Russian words, but we understand the pictures. I train our teams myself," Lateef explained to Mahir.

"But on the ground it's important that we evade them; we can't make deals with the Americans. Their soldiers are here for short tours they call training exercises. While they're here they make a lot of noise, attend the tuna festival in the city, and run off with bargirls at night when they're off duty. Soon they'll be gone, and we'll go back to business as usual with the local police and army leaders who live near our villages. They will not wake up until the war is over and it's too late." Lateef had worked informally with the enemy a long time and did not think their cozy relationships would change. "They're not the real enemy. America's our real enemy."

Mahir considered Lateef's statement for several dozen footsteps, then asked, "Who do you see as your real enemy?"

Lateef continued to advance a few minutes before he answered, "Weak leaders." He paused, and then continued. "In the past I pinned my hopes on the Moro National Liberation Front. But the Manila government sent weak people to negotiate with us, and we also appointed weak leaders to make *our* case for autonomy. There was no progress, and when war came it divided the Muslims in Mindanao; it did not unite us. The MNLF didn't know what it was fighting for."

"What are you fighting for now?" Mahir asked.

"For self-determination, for our own identity and for our own country. When you meet Kumander Ali, he can explain better than I can. He is a strong leader. He split from the MNLF to create a true Islamic movement."

Exiting the rainforest but still without the benefit of moonlight, Lateef's patrol paused. The cargo carriers pulled up into the middle of the force and set down a sack of rice and a smaller one of sugar, a small power-generating set, a plastic bag of documents and training manuals in Russian, radio equipment, medical supplies, and boxes of various kinds of ammunition. They considered themselves well equipped for guerrilla actions or a lengthy bivouac.

It was late night now, and Lateef collected his Abu Sayaf team under an island of several coconut palm trees within the greater expanse of the rainforest itself, where they would wait for a messenger from the MNLF. The messenger would take them to Kumander Ali's headquarters at the secret location in the triangle where the rivers met. Joining them at the juncture would be other tentative allies like the NPA, the long-fighting communists, and other Abu Sayaf units. The Moro fronts needed the money Mahir carried; they already had the muscle.

One of Lateef's men climbed a palm tree in the dark and cut bunches of coconuts out of the cluster near its top. After the men chopped them open with their bolos, they drank the coconut water from the husks; the nourishing nectar seemed to flow directly into their blood streams and quenched their thirsts. Next they scooped out the rich coconut meat for a meal. When finished, they politely placed the coconut husks neatly upside down by the trees, to show the farmer who owned them that they had not stolen the coconuts, only taken what they did because of necessity, as was permitted.

Settling into position in his camp, Lateef was unaware of Thornton's presence a scant hundred meters behind him. He took the time to indoctrinate Mahir on the goals of the Abu Sayaf for the Philippines. "Brother Mahir, we will declare war on the United States and their Zionist masters, and you will be with the first to fire a shot in the new war of freedom for Mindanao!"

Mahir knew that Lateef had learned to play combat games on the Internet and that he had fired an M-16 while he was in an Al Qaeda training camp in Afghanistan. Because of his training, Lateef considered himself a pedigreed techno-warrior. He had proudly signed up for the great cause, the jihad, knowing "We will win the global war," as he often stated in orations to his men.

Mahir had traveled in Western countries and knew something of world geography. He wondered where Lateef thought the troops would come from to invade and occupy the expansive lands to the east like California, Alaska, Mexico and other territories of the unbelievers. He thought Lateef's goals might be overly optimistic, but said nothing to discourage him.

Lateef lectured, "God speaks directly to men. I hear his powerful words and rich language." Mahir felt Lateef was speaking his mind, not just what he had learned from study. Lateef continued, "To my way of thinking, we and our Muslim brothers will win the great war by starting new cells in many countries simultaneously. There is no need for us to communicate with the others, no need to send troops to sit on their lands. The example here in western Mindanao will be the spark to start fires in the countries of the enemy."

Lateef had seen personal deeds of the unbelievers that affronted his sensibilities, and he told about his experiences. "I saw in the resorts of Palawan white people drinking alcohol and their prostitute women walking in the street, exposing their naked, shaven legs and arms. The decadence must end." He carried with him a copy of the Koran in Arabic, the only true language of the Koran. Even though he could not speak or read Arabic, except the words he memorized for prayers, Lateef knew what the Koran said about women walking around uncovered. When he came in from patrols and returned to his village, all the women were covered from head to toe whenever they left the house, even if they were going to work all day in the sun on a banana plantation.

Shortly before sunrise, Lateef and Mahir faced Mecca together and prepared to make the first of their five prayers of the new day. While on jihad, they were required to pray only three times each day, but they tried to keep the strict law of five times unless they were actually in combat. They had safely reached their objective for the day, the Liguasan Marsh, a delta of small streams and low land, looking on the map like the veins of a stripped tree leaf, an inhospitable swamp overlapping the uncertain borders of Maguindanao and Sultan Kudarat. They were thankful for the blessings of Allah.

21

Serendipity

The STAGCOM team, minus Thornton and Elaiza—who were on an arduous trek pushing inland through the bush on foot in pursuit of the Muslim revolutionaries—were waiting. Pedro had driven Thornton's Pajero up the main road out of Davao City and crossed over a saddle in the foothills south of Mount Apo. Preparing to stay overnight and perhaps for several days, the team took up a position along the main road, located near a unit of Task Force Davao that was sealing off egress out of Davao to the southwest. STAGCOM consisted now of Hank Starke, who had assumed tactical command in Thornton's absence, and the five Otaza brothers.

Pedro and Starke were in the front seat with their elbows propped out the open windows of the parked vehicle. "When do you think we can get into action?" Pedro asked Starke.

"Don't get nervous. I know you want to get the job done. We just have to wait in position right here for now. When the time is right, Thornton will tell us what to do," Starke told him.

Pedro looked out at his brothers asleep in hammocks strung up between trees outside the vehicle. "When will that be?" Pedro asked. "As soon as we know where they are, we'll surprise them, right?"

Starke liked Pedro's enthusiasm, but needed to channel it. "Surprise is a great advantage, I agree with you, but let's get ourselves and our equipment prepared, and be fresh to intercept those murdering bastards when the time comes." Starke wanted to keep Pedro and his brothers motivated, but also to make sure they didn't act recklessly.

"Maybe we'll hear something before morning. Major Hayes will call us when he gets an attack order for us from Thornton, then our mission is a 'go' and we move out immediately. But I have no idea when that could be. When you don't know what else to do in the field, sleep is always a good idea. You'll be rested whenever you need to hit the ground. Then you can move fast." Starke was an old soldier, and Pedro knew he was right. Dusk dissolved into a quiet night, and they dozed off.

Back in Davao City, Wolfgang Moser was on the air, hosting his regular evening program and sending out greetings and special requests to listeners throughout Mindanao. Major Hayes sat beside him, waiting to hear from the embassy operations center with something to forward to Thornton, wherever he was. A simple phrase sent over the open air waves by Moser during his show would at least let Thornton and Elaiza know that the signal from her iPod had bounced up to the satellite and been received and understood by the intelligence officers at the American Embassy in Manila. As soon as he heard from them, he would create a message for Moser to integrate into his broadcast.

Hayes and Moser talked between selections. "How do you interpret that last news report you just read, Wolfgang? Do you really think we will have civil war?" Hayes asked.

"It's not a rosy picture." Moser looked for the precise words in English. "The politicos, both in Manila and Washington, know they've got to stop the terrorists before any more tragedies like the Davao City bombings occur. And they haven't heard yet about the messy death of that hostage, the Christian security guard. You told me about it, but I can't report it, not until I receive it officially and his death is confirmed. But the story will eventually get out."

"Two or three people are killed every day around here, on the average. Why is his death so different?" Hayes had read local newspaper stories about civilians being murdered, a few Abu Sayaf killed, or AFP soldiers lost in action. "You read the news on the air."

"Well, several things are new. The Americans are involved in combat in the Philippines this time, which is against this country's constitution, and I bet is not known about by most Filipinos. It's probably also kept secret from most Americans and even the American Congress. The world is getting very strange, Hayes—hard to tell who the bad guys are." The German shared his doubts with the major. "It's time to decide what is good and right and then to act decisively."

"Take it easy, Wolfgang, all wars are not Blitzkriegs. Timing is important. We have to wait until the Turk and his Abu Sayaf buddies link up with the local insurgents, so the whole network can be exposed and exterminated, or our entire undertaking will be a waste of time. Whether STAGCOM gets the money and gets away with it is not the issue for either the U.S. government or the Philippines. We've got to help our friend. If all Thornton does is take the money, Al Qaeda will just arrange for another shipment to be carried in by some new emissary."

Moser didn't quite understand. "But if the joint task force of Philippine Army and the police forces hit exactly at the right moment, and hard, perhaps once and for all they could wipe out the separatist movement."

Hayes didn't know what to say, didn't know how much Thornton had told Moser, so he probed, "With all that power, why do you think they need STAGCOM, two foreigners who don't speak the language, and Elaiza's five uncles?"

"Hum. Well, I understand why Thornton asked you and me to work the Schloss Code with all this secretiveness."

"OK, educate me."

The German had a realistic perspective: "If any politicians got to the money, they could go to jail. Or get bumped off."

"Bureaucrats here do lots of things they could go to jail for. Why would they get politically correct and cautious all of a sudden?" Hayes knew the informal ways to get things done, involving pesos and personal connections.

"Because they want to win this war themselves; but your countrymen don't think they can. America is busy 'building democracy' in other countries. American politicians think the Philippines is in their back pocket, but they assume too much." The German continued, "Some of their military leaders, like Thornton's connection, General Hargens, know better, but nobody listens to them. So the top guys have to act, as they say, clandestinely."

The major was reassured to hear that Moser was so well informed. It put him at ease knowing that he could talk more openly. Hayes stood, propped against a high case of old VHS tapes that Moser used in his program and listened to the music.

"Want a beer?" Moser asked him. He wanted to help the lanky American relax while they waited. "Help yourself to one out of the cooler." The record he was playing was almost over, and he would soon have to cut back to live commentary.

"Sure." He got a San Miguel for himself while Moser switched to his on-air voice, using more of a foreign accent than normally, what he called his sweet voice, to introduce Vivaldi. Soon the sounds of the "Four Seasons" were on their way to all of Mindanao, where there were only two seasons, summer and monsoon, and he had time to talk with Hayes again.

"Major Hayes, OK, I understand why both the Filipinos and the Americans needed Thornton and his team, but why would *he* want to get involved?"

"There's a sizable cash reward, as you know." Hayes again tested Moser's knowledge of the operation. Thornton had revealed that Moser had his confidence, but Hayes wanted to be sure he was not telling the German something new. The look in Moser's eyes gave no indication of surprise.

"I have that impression. But I know both of you guys; I've seen you together and apart. You're not poor, but you will never be wealthy; that's not what drives you army guys. This is not a money thing for you. It's about that Eastern Europe deal, isn't it?" Moser let Hayes think while the music played, then turned to his microphone and spoke to his public, reading some text messages. When he had the chance, he continued, "It's about what happened to that woman too, isn't it?"

Hayes became more at ease; he had guessed correctly that Thornton had few secrets from Moser. When the D.J. pulled his headphones off for a few minutes, he continued. He wanted Moser to know. "Although Thornton was in Vietnam, he was not involved in close combat. But many of his West Point classmates did the real fighting, and some of them were killed.

He had some kind of staff job, and he certainly did not volunteer for combat. His Purple Heart was incidental; he just was in the wrong place at the right time."

"Well, good for him. During those years I was having a ball at the 'Uni' in Vienna. I wouldn't have liked to have been in his combat boots." That war had little relevance for Moser or for most Europeans.

"Some of his classmates went on to become generals. He became a businessman." Hayes continued.

"Everybody must follow his own path, Major Hayes. Generals fight wars so businessmen can build nations."

"Idealist. I still think it bothers him, but he keeps it to himself. Except for this Hargens guy, and Charlie Downs. He can talk to them."

"Maybe he hasn't figured it all out yet for himself. Let the clock tick a while longer. He'll get it right." Moser put his headphones back on just as the music ended and he had to ad lib for a while until he found his notes and the next record to play.

When the music started again Moser continued. "I've lived here a long time; my wife is a native. Mindanao would be a much better place to live in if *everybody* would leave it alone."

Then it came. Hayes's cell phone vibrated, and he read the text message from the embassy, a series of key phrases to be forwarded in code to Thornton. Hayes worked out a script in English for Moser to incorporate in an innocuous way into his reading of the requests and song dedications. He handed the text to Moser, who translated the key words into German. After the music now being transmitted was over, Moser would send the message over the air using the Schloss Code.

* * *

Trailing the Abu Sayaf, Thornton and Elaiza heard unusual rustlings ahead of them, but the patrol no longer seemed to be moving forward. The rebels were making an opening with their bolos chopping a semicircle of open space, a cul de sac at the end of a tube they had pushed through the jungle, where they would put up nets and string hammocks. When the noises ceased, Thornton correctly took the silence to mean that the patrol had halted, and so he did as well, a scant hundred yards to the immediate rear of the insurgents.

"Elaiza, let's sit down here, it's waiting time again. We need to rest when we can."

They settled down on the ground facing opposite directions, their backs propped against each other as before, and made themselves as comfortable as they could.

"Hook up the iPod," Thornton whispered. Elaiza plugged in the earpiece, tuning it to Moser's regular program on 90.3 FM, Radio Mindanao. They dozed, reclining close together as sleep came, intermittently. Then finally, about midnight, the coded message came, and for the second time the Schloss Code worked. The D.J.'s night program was nearing the end when the message for Thornton came through.

"And for my loyal listener Herr Handkuss in Isulan" . . . A pause . . . Thornton knew that the improbable name Handkuss, Austrian dialect for greeting a noble lady by kissing her hand, was tonight's signal. It told him the embassy knew Elaiza was with him in the jungle and confirmed with those few words that STAGCOM was ready to hit the Abu Sayaf whenever he gave the word. From his map reconnaissance and only one key word from Moser, Thornton deduced that the Abu Sayaf patrol was headed toward Isulan. Lateef was leading his team as straight as he could through the brush in that direction. The message also confirmed that the spy satellite had picked up Elaiza's slight back and forth movement and that the embassy had correctly understood her transmission.

Moser continued his program, and between the next two requests mumbled in German, "Silvaner Silvaner Riesling," the cardinal directions for south by southwest and later, after another dedication, the single word, "Hauptstrasse."

Using his flashlight under his tarp, Thornton studied the map. The coded message he had received was clear: the STAGCOM team had moved to a new location on the main highway, south by southwest of his position, and that they knew where he was. Starke had relocated

STAGCOM into an attack position near the spot where the Abu Sayaf had set down for the night. Thornton would observe the enemy patrol to be sure they stayed in place, then hike over to STAGCOM and lead them in a surprise attack just before dawn. The Abu Sayaf outnumbered STAGCOM, but they would be asleep and it would be easy to take out the Turk, and get the big bags he had with him.

Thornton dozed off, but a few hours later woke up quickly as was his old army habit, wide-awake moments after being sound asleep. It was well after midnight and above the trees floated a skinny silver sliver, the concave semicircle of a very new moon, unexplainably bright. How could it be so bright with the sun rising soon behind it? Could it be the reflection of the South Pacific upon it, or was it a phenomenon caused by the relative positions of the sun and moon? It just did not make sense, he thought, but it was unique and beautiful. Elaiza stirred beside him, pushing against him in her sleep.

Thornton awakened her. "I have an idea. This might be easier than we thought."

Elaiza was groggy only for a moment.

"Elaiza, send a signal. Confirm our receipt and understanding of Moser's previous transmission."

Elaiza twice moved back and forth five steps directly along her previous path. The tracking device was calibrated to her person, to her dimensions and footstep characteristics. The TIAM component traced her every footstep with or without a continuous GPS connection, then the module sent its stored data in batches whenever it could connect to the spy satellite. The intelligence team back in the lab at the U.S. Embassy in Manila would get the data, and know how old each bit of information was. From the raw data, the computer would show Elaiza's exact location and her precise movements as well as the time each footstep was taken, and then chart her trail on a large-scale map the techies could see on their computer screen. By her movements on the ground, Elaiza was confirming back to them that she knew the location of Starke and STAGCOM.

"Should I draw the circle?" Elaiza asked.

"No." Thornton told her, "I want to take them out with a surprise attack by STAGCOM." He did not want Elaiza to send the signal for a fire mission from the air force. "We don't need additional help; Mahir and his Abu Sayaf buddies are settled in for a while, probably planning to spend the entire day tomorrow hiding; it's almost morning already.

"We'll get to Starke and the men, and attack; we're close enough to get STAGCOM and lead them back before the Abus move out again. We can at least kill enough of them to take over the camp, get to the money, and get out of here. Leave the rest of that Muslim hit squad for Colonel Lui and the Philippine Army to mop up. The good guys would win again."

"When do we go?" Elaiza was standing up and tucking herself together.

"Wait for the beginning of early morning light so that we can find our way to Starke and your uncles on the highway."

"I can't sleep. My mind is racing, and it's uncomfortable."

"Try counting sheep."

"Is that what you did on your farm in Pennsylvania, growing up?"

"No, it's just a saying in English, something to do to make yourself get tired and help you go to sleep. We had cows. It was boring enough though, that's why I left."

"I see. Let me guess. You left home when you were a young farm boy, and over and over again you left women behind, greener fields and younger crops to mow, whether you loved them or not, even whether you had kids or not with them."

"You left your home too, for greener pastures."

"It's very different. My mother died, and my father had to work on that damn dam to support eight kids, but you, you are an orphan by choice."

"An orphan of choice? I never disavowed my parents."

"You left your own family. How can anyone trust you?"

"What was the name of that Philippine Eagle?"

"You mean Kabayan?"

"Yeah. Kabayan. They want to release young eagles to fly free. Birds fly. Try counting sheep, you need some sleep before dawn."

Elaiza relaxed. Later, comforted by his presence, she slid her hand under Thornton's shirt, resting it on his chest until first light finally came. He noticed.

After the long and uncomfortable night, they left their position and moved as quietly as they could the five hundred yards to where they expected to find Starke, Pedro, and the rest of STAGCOM on the main road.

Thornton was sure Lateef and Mahir's patrol was asleep, or too far away to detect their presence.

All were except one. He had awakened with a mild stomachache and walked away from the camp to dig a hole and deposit the results of his indigestion. As he was returning, he noticed Thornton, an obvious white guy in the dark jungle, and his smaller companion. The accidental sentry followed the suspicious characters and saw them reach the main road at a culvert bridge four kilometers south of Koronadal City.

The Muslim returned to the Abu Sayaf camp and woke Lateef to report the sighting of a white soldier just outside their camp, moving toward a group of vehicles, maybe a contingent of the Philippine Army. Lateef immediately guessed the entire situation and was sure the news was a gift from the prophet. By early morning he and Mahir had planned their ambush.

* * *

Thomas Thornton and Hank Starke shook hands silently, directly meeting the other's gaze, not exactly smiling but each relieved to find the other in good shape. Elaiza smiled at Starke and punched him in the belly; he gave her a bear hug. STAGCOM was complete again.

They were only seven men and Elaiza Otakan, but well armed and dedicated, a potentially lethal team, unquestionably highly motivated.

Thornton and Elaiza had located the Abu Sayaf patrol. Killing the Turk Hakki would derail the insurrection and earn them the money, an ideal situation for Thornton. But then what? If Thornton was ever going to regain Hargens' trust, let alone Charlie Downs,' he needed to do it right.

If STAGCOM could catch Kumander Ali with the money before he had a chance to distribute it, the Philippine government would gain a major victory against the revolution. It sounded simple, but it wasn't.

Colonel Liu had to be on the scene and in charge when it happened, but not come away with the cash either. That was what complicated Thornton's job.

Thornton asked Starke to get their men organized and ready to move out. The old top sergeant left Thornton in the command post and checked out the Otazas on the M-16s he had issued them. He had taken the five brothers into the brush just off the road to try out their new rifles by shooting birds for target practice. Pedro, and especially Reymundo, were great shots, well practiced with the .22 rifles they owned back in their villages in Agusan, and they also applied the expertise learned from their practice with hand-made slingshots, which seemed to sharpen their eyesight. The Otaza brothers quickly picked up on the M16 in single shot mode, not yet rapid fire, and the birds made a savory addition to the food for the dogs that seemed to appear out of the nearby village and preferred to hang around the command post rather than raiding the local garbage dump.

Thornton erected two hammocks within a small grove of hardwood trees for himself and Elaiza. He knew she was dead tired. In the meantime, the rest of the men studied Thornton's crumpled map and field notes and deliberated–had Mahir hooked up with Ali? Was this an ideal time to attack?

22

LZ Koronadal

Sixty miles to the north, a washed-out Vietnam-era Huey helicopter gifted to the Philippine Army by the Americans years ago and in its last years of operational capability, penetrated the air space of South Cotobato province and headed inland over the coast toward the landing zone designated LZ Koronadal. When he got a message about the approaching helicopter, Sergeant Starke and the Otaza brothers got busy clearing an open area to make a landing zone near where their Pajero was parked.

John Robert Mundy was on board the Huey and was not happy that his flight had been ordered to go by way of Davao City to pick up Major Hayes. Hayes, in turn, was not happy to have a civilian along for the ride in a possible combat situation. They engaged in unfriendly discussion on the flight.

"Mundy, I've asked the pilot to go into Koronadal from the south so the Abus won't get a shot at us, they may have a ground-to-air missile."

"Major, please refer to me as John Robert Mundy, or Mr. Mundy. That's what I'm called in the embassy," the D.C. official huffed back.

"Right, Mundy," Hayes responded, insolently ignoring the name preference, "Welcome to the field."

Mundy scowled. "Where was that trooper killed?" was all he asked, changing the subject.

"In Zambo, but we're not going there," Hayes told him, referring to the recent death of a U.S. Special Forces lieutenant farther south. "We have a handle on that situation. We can avenge his death right here."

Mundy represented the official U.S. position as the Department of State saw it. He had Charlie Downs' reluctant approval and gloated that he spoke for the Department of State in the field, obliging Hayes to hear his insider's opinion. "The Philippine government has taken the position that they won't tolerate terrorists in Mindanao, but it's just talk. The national police and the army together have no real power in the villages or in the jungles, no ability to control events on the ground. They just kind of drive around on the main roads and worry about traffic control. We have to change their attitude."

"We can't win the war for them, a few dozen of us in a nation of seventy-five million," Hayes said. "I know that."

Hayes had to tolerate Mundy. They were on the same side after all, and both knew their mentors, Hargens in Manila and Downs back in D.C., had their hands full deflecting the slap-happy military types whose only solution was "Send in the B-52s and bomb them back to the Stone Age."

"The civilian government has to formulate a winning strategy. Without a real plan, the Philippine military can never gain the approval and support of their nation," Mundy continued with his personal insights into geopolitical rationale. "Who knows what bunch of old retired soldiers will get together over a few beers in the officers' club at Fort Bonifacio, baptize themselves a junta, and form a new government." He paused. "DOS wants to know what's going on, and that's why I'm here."

"I wondered why," Hayes mumbled mostly to himself, and said, "You guys at State got the Philippines to wave their flag in Iraq some years ago, only to pull out their troop commitment of fifty-one men because one truck driver got captured. It would have been better for everyone if they had never sent any troops to that war in the first place. When the

MNLF sees how the Philippine leaders buckle, they'll use the terror tool." Hayes was not forgiving; he had lost good men in combat.

"We know about the tools of terror." John Robert Mundy was calmer now; after all, Hayes was a fellow countryman. "If Al Qaeda gets away with terrorizing Mindanao sufficiently to cause regime change with a few bombings, you can expect to see them using bio weapons and dirty bombs back home, or in Indonesia, Japan, Europe, you name the place, the next target."

"The politicians in Manila are getting desperate." Hayes had heard some loose talk around the embassy. "I hear we're ready to sign an agreement to cooperate with the Indonesian military; that would sure help us seal off access into southern Mindanao."

"Can't talk about it." Mundy was proud of what he knew that Hayes did not.

"I don't think you see the big picture about their Iraq pull-out," Mundy said. "The Philippine president was running for election at the time. If he had not given in to the demands of the Muslim kidnappers and they had beheaded that driver, he would never have been re-elected. The voters would have elected some comedian who couldn't find Iraq on a map, let alone govern the Philippines and administer a foreign policy."

Hayes was concerned about the way the war in Iraq was going and harbored an old resentment. "I still don't like that they sent a paltry few troops to 'help Iraq.' It took two of our guys to protect each one of theirs—two real soldiers we had to take out of combat. The Philippine contingent had no tactical capability. I don't think they were ever sure which way to point their rifles."

"That's simplistic, and wrong," continued Mundy. "They were truck drivers, like our own truck drivers in California, or Korea or Germany. They weren't there in a combat role. If we recognize we're in a global war, then we have to cooperate with the ASEAN pact members as allies."

Hayes radioed ahead to Colonel Liu to coordinate their rendezvous, and the Huey took up a flight path to approach the landing zone. The pilot descended on a sharp angle downward to the minimal landing area carved out by the Otaza brothers, the tops of the surrounding palm trees slapping against the helicopter's skids as it approached and set down. Mundy ducked down and trotted under the wash of the helicopter blades as he held onto his steel helmet. Hayes stepped off the aircraft and walked upright to salute Colonel Liu, who had just pulled up in his jeep.

Liu had arrived at the STAGCOM forward position only a few minutes before Hayes radioed and quickly selected the TFD command post on a low hilltop a hundred yards away. It was shortly before noon. The two infantry companies of Task Force Davao were with him and stretched out along the highway in their trucks waiting for him to issue orders.

Both Hayes and Mundy respected Liu, but for different reasons. Hayes liked that Liu was a professional soldier; Mundy liked him because he understood geopolitics and spoke in those terms. Liu needed to cope with internal politics in his own country, while taking advantage of any assistance that the U.S. could give to his cause, including this small STAGCOM irregular force. The Americans could be a useful and flexible tool in situations he wanted to keep off the record, as well as providing intelligence directly from the U.S. Embassy in Manila. STAGCOM was just what he needed when he was told by his superiors not to report details. He would tell the whole story only to National Security Advisor Galan, who did want to hear details, like what bodies were left on the field, preferably enemy bodies, and how they happened to become bodies instead of prisoners. Galan would not want to hear bad news.

Hayes briefed Colonel Liu, both of them ignoring Mundy as they walked away from the LZ and toward the STAGCOM Pajero. "Using our new technology and with Thornton following them on the ground, we have that Abu Sayaf patrol targeted, including the Turk with the money cache. They're located exactly 467 meters to the north northeast of this command post."

Thornton walked up to greet his friend. "Hello Reggie. Welcome to the *bundok*," using the Tagalog word which had evolved into 'boondocks" during the last century of Americans fighting insurgents in the Philippines, back in the period when General Douglas MacArthur's father was the U.S. commander in the islands.

Liu smiled back. "Thornton, I see you and Ms. Otakan here work well as a team. Thanks to you, your handlers in Manila have fixed the enemy for us."

Elaiza positioned herself between Liu and Hayes. "Thanks, Colonel. My upgraded iPod did the job."

Liu acknowledged the young woman in army fatigues. "I should say, thanks both to your work and the two of you being in the field and on their tail."

"Can you confirm that the Abu Sayaf haven't moved since you came in from the field?" Mundy looked at Thornton.

"Welcome to the zone of operations, Mundy. I'm sure you'll be at home here." Thornton smiled back and answered his question. "They're down for the day. Based on their habits, from my observation, they don't move during daylight hours once they've settled into a position."

"I wasn't sure you had received the last position confirmation from the embassy, Mr. Mundy." Elaiza looked short, standing next to all the tall guys, especially Mundy, who was wearing a steel helmet that added to his over six-foot height.

"I'm sorry, Ms. Otakan, I couldn't communicate with you once I was airborne, and knew I'd see you here. Thanks, your code system worked." He turned to the group. "So, if they haven't moved since Thornton arrived here, then we have them fixed."

"I expect they're where Elaiza reported using the TIAM." Thornton had been thinking about how he and STAGCOM alone could have done the job quickly. With Liu and the Task Force Davao now on the scene, he would have to work with them. "Major Hayes, your German must be getting better. I understood everything Moser said."

"Moser did the talking. I just helped him sketch out what he was going to say before he translated it." Hayes asked, "How many of them are there?"

"Good question." Liu didn't know what he was up against. "But first, Ms. Otakan, using your codes and the radio was a great idea, well-executed. Good job. But without being right on their butts during their trek here, we would have no idea whether there is a squad or a company-sized unit there. Thornton?"

"The patrol we followed had seventeen in it," he answered. "We were able to stay close enough to them to be sure. They have six Garand rifles, two M203 grenade launchers and the other nine have M-16s. No AK-47s or RPGs."

"That fits the Abu Sayaf signature, small units, moving at night," Liu responded, and with his eyebrows encouraged all present to comment.

"How does the rebel unit here fit into their overall order of battle, Colonel?" Mundy asked.

"The Abu Sayaf is a partner of the Jemaah Islamiyah, a local cell of Al Qaeda, but something new is going on. I call it the 'unseen hand' that funnels resources all the way from the Middle East into this remote province," Liu explained.

"The Abu Sayaf is a spent force; they have no national organization, no popular support," was Hayes' analysis.

"That's what we thought too, but now with this 'unseen hand,' as the Colonel says, things could change. They're gaining momentum, and the initiative," Mundy conjectured.

"Time to turn that momentum the other way." Thornton saw the thinking was getting all muddled—too many interests and opinions involved. He was ready to do the job without the TFD; in fact, he wanted STAGCOM to do the job, alone, and lobbied Colonel Liu. "Reggie, this is a small unit operation. STAGCOM can handle it. No need for you to get your hands dirty." He tried to convince the TFD Commander.

"I've thought about that. You'll notice that I have kept my men on hold, not deployed, until we agree on our approach here," Colonel Liu responded, thinking that he could save his power for a more decisive opportunity.

"Let's review," said Mundy, wanting to stay involved. "We have them pinpointed. We have options: call in an air strike with smart bombs, employ artillery, or just continue to follow and observe, and perhaps most importantly, deduce where they are headed and therefore what might be their final goal. We have the luxury of waiting until they get to wherever they're going."

"We have the drop on them, but do we have a chance to encircle them all?" Liu considered the value of a quick and easy victory, indulging himself in thinking about getting his first star after all these years.

"Not good enough for you," Thornton reminded Liu. "A quick win might be good enough for my purposes, but your job wouldn't be done. For you, Colonel, and your country, it's not just about the unseen hand carrying in the cash—although that aspect could be good for me personally. You want to eliminate all the Abu Sayaf cell leaders here. Then Al Qaeda in Syria or someplace else will not have some other terrorist cell to which it could provide more money. We cannot take out the source of the funding, but you can take out the operational leaders here. They'll be harder to replace. Let STAGCOM handle what we have here. I'll get my reward, and maybe a place to live in Mindanao that's safe. Then you'll have time to clean up."

Liu liked the idea of a win–no lose scenario. He pondered his decision a few minutes while pacing slowly in a small circle. "O.K." He wanted to be decisive. "What do we know for sure?"

"We have STAGCOM right here and ready to go." Elaiza was the first to respond. The men turned to her, a bit surprised that she had taken the initiative.

"Right." Hayes, the link to the U.S. Defense Department and hence with access to U.S. intelligence, turned to Liu, " We think they are all headed to an NPA camp someplace north of here. But we're not sure how they want to use the cash the Turk is transporting. Shouldn't we wait to find that out?"

"The NPA wants to overthrow the government of the Philippines, you know that. Not just mess around this time," Liu said, showing his concern.

"Well, if not all of the Philippines, at least they want to take over Mindanao. There is more and more talk about a Republic of Mindanao, or some kind of new federation with or without Manila and the rest of the Philippines, but we don't know the grand strategy of the insurgency at this time, if indeed they have one." Hayes was sharing the strategic analysis of the military types in the embassy and back in Washington. "They may have bigger objectives," he continued. "Your government, and your army especially, must stop treating terrorists like ordinary criminals, like wife beaters or drug peddlers. Terrorists are best disposed of as soon as they are found, right here in the field. No need to hold them for trial."

"They feel the same way about you, Major Hayes, and the rest of you Yankees," Liu retorted. "The Abu Sayaf doesn't want to have to haul captives around or feed them for very long. And I am not in a mood to take much more bullshit from them, or from you." He was in command of the joint operation. It was his country and his terrain, and he had had enough discussion. He would handle it. He made his decision. "We attack today, sooner rather than later. We'll take prisoners if we have to, but in the Philippines we know how to interrogate. We'll find out what we need to know."

"Easier to decide what to do after a victory than after a defeat, right Colonel?" Elaiza's question expressed her opinion. Liu stared at her hard.

Hayes had opinions based on his own combat experience. He proposed, "Then we should attack before dark, or they could move on. Thornton is no longer following their every step."

"Captain Agustin, join us and put up a field table." The commander of Liu's A Company had been standing at a respectful distance from his commander.

Liu and his staff took out their maps and began to make plans with the three Americans and the Filipina who worked with them looking over their shoulders. Thornton supplemented what they knew by overlaying his personal observations onto their maps. He recommended what he thought would work best for TFD as well as for himself. "Reggie, you make some noise from the highway. We, as STAGCOM, go in and mop up; make them disappear. Then we disappear; we were never here. You declare victory and go back to Manila."

"You don't need to overemphasize. I get it." Liu, processing the information, then decided and told Thornton, "No. We'll hit them at 3:00 PM. STAGCOM will *not* be involved. Gives us time to assemble an overwhelming force and time enough to execute before dark. By nightfall we will have seventeen of them either way, KIA or captives. Agustin, move out."

This was not the time for Liu to play politics; that would come after the victory. Mundy, the observer, observed, and said to no one in particular, almost as if to confirm to himself, "I want to see how the new Task Force Davao will handle this job," not aware that less than half a click away, Lateef and Mahir and their small force were already starting to move quietly into attack positions on the western side of the road touching the landing zone where the Filipino officers and the Americans were talking.

Thinking they had the advantage, Colonel Liu and the others took their time working on their maps and operational plans. Liu gave permission for the TFD troops to light up cigarettes while waiting for orders. All felt confident, and Captain Agustin started to walk purposefully back toward his men in the convoy.

"Major Hayes . . ." John Robert Mundy started to say something that Hayes probably would not have agreed with when automatic weapon fire whistled bullets through the gaggle of officers gathered around the command post. Liu instinctively spun to his right and ducked below a twisted tree trunk. Agustin pulled out his .45 pistol as he initially jumped up and then came back down behind a stack of bags filled with some kind of grain, and aimed his weapon in the general direction of the noise, but he didn't see any targets to engage, only flashes of light from within the brush.

Thornton heard the firing of the M16's and for a moment assumed it was coming from his STAGCOM guys practicing, but when he looked in their direction he saw immediately that two of them had been wounded by gunfire. Grabbing Elaiza by the arm, he ducked down and ran back with her to check on the Otazas.

They found Pedro taking cover near where their hammocks were strung up. When Thornton saw that the firing was coming at them from the tree line, he realized that the Abu Sayaf patrol they had been following had ambushed them. Pedro did not want to be pinned down, but Thornton pushed him behind a tree. "Lay down some suppressing fire toward where the flashes are coming from. Give the TFD troops a chance to get out of their trucks!"

Elaiza bolted over to her two cousins, Eduardo and Juanito, who had been injured. A hollow-tipped bullet had shattered Eduardo's shoulder. Cement fragments from a foundation wall had peppered Juanito's left arm enough to draw blood. Elaiza and Juanito dragged Eduardo out of the direct line of fire behind the wall to bind up the wound, stopping the blood flow and holding the shoulder together. Elaiza stayed with the more seriously wounded brother until a medic could come up from the main group farther down the road an hour after the action ended. The rest of the STAGCOM squad fired into the source of the bullets coming at them. Task Force Davao was caught in a crossfire, and their plan to attack had been preempted.

Captain Agustin was pinned down and did not have the opportunity to signal to his troops parked along the highway. But a sharp young sergeant rallied a few riflemen who had been smoking beside the vehicles and led them cautiously forward. The rest of the regular army soldiers were still inside the trucks and could not be effective at the moment. Agustin motioned to the sergeant to hold a position near the first vehicle and to lay down fire toward the attackers. The men who had not yet disembarked stuck to the floors of the trucks, frozen by fear and doubt. Before they could compose themselves, two M79 grenades hit the first and second trucks from close range turning them into clouds of blue-black smoke with fiery centers.

Captain Bautista, commander of the second company farther back in the column, crawled forward. He had not been a part of the briefing and was totally confused. He grabbed the men he could find who were outside their vehicles and deployed them into defensive positions on the western side of the road, while the burning first two trucks were still being peppered with automatic fire.

The Abu Sayaf patrol had continued firing for another thirty seconds after scoring the grenade hits on the truckloads of confused Task Force soldiers, but now Lateef assembled his troops and together they ran through the brush around the outside perimeter of the firefight and away from the marshland toward the west, withdrawing along the paths they had used on the approach and quickly putting some distance between themselves and their ambush victims. Suddenly Lateef looked back and saw his last man shredded by a volley of accurate fire. When he heard shots to his eastern flank as well, they seemed to be partially surrounded, at least on two sides. Lateef understood tactics as well as the AFP; he had learned from watching them for years, and considered how to press the advantage he had achieved. He signaled his patrol to turn to the right and to give two bursts of random but rapid fire south.

His tactic worked. The Task Force Davao troops who had counterattacked

ducked and stopped firing, confused. Having only recently awakened
and still dazed from the explosion, they didn't know which direction to
maneuver and established a defensive position while waiting for orders.
Captain Agustin, with a squad of men he had hastily assembled on the
road, moved forward into the brush far enough to see the backs of the
Abu Sayaf as they sped away, and fired after them.

Two more men were lost to Lateef, but he saw the location of the
squad of riflemen pursuing and wheeled into the underbrush, taking an
offensive posture after he rotated his force in a counter-clockwise quarter
circle relative to the advancing Task Force troops. He could see more
TFD troops crossing the road. Mahir caught up with Lateef and the rest,
dragging a dying or already dead comrade. From where they paused,
they fired one last volley from their M16s, causing the TFD to pause
momentarily. The Abu Sayaf, less than a platoon-sized force, slid farther
into the jungle and retraced their steps back to where they had camped,
deciding it was time to get out of the area.

Ugly Maria was the rear guard, the last one out of the area and not
in much of a hurry. She saw John Robert Mundy, in dark green jungle
fatigues, crouching behind some low foliage and quietly approached him
from his side unseen, giving him a direct blow on the temple with the
tire iron she kept with her for just such a purpose. It dazed Mundy. Ugly
Maria did not want to burden Lateef with either a hostage or a decision.
A broken and sharply pointed limb on a hardwood tree helped her
decide. Two of the Abu Sayaf turned back to help her hoist Mundy up
and impale his twitching body on the long spike of wood, the pain of the
stabbing wound causing Mundy to regain consciousness just as Ugly
Maria used her favorite knife to slice open his belly.

For the rest of the day and into the night the Abu Sayaf slowly but
steadily continued their way due north between the Banga and the Alah
Rivers, toward the prearranged meeting point with Kumander Ali. The
Alah drains Lake Sebu in South Cotobato province and flows through a
broad plain parallel with its brother river, the Banga. Parallel mountain
ranges channel the two sibling rivers north until they join to become the
Mindanao River, which continues to the seaport of Cotobato City.
When he reached the river junction near the border of the province of
Sultan Kudarat, Lateef ordered his men to take up defensive positions

within the triangle formed by the rivers, leaving only their southern flank exposed to pursuers. Mahir and one cargo boy were well guarded in the center of the new camp, holding the vital stash of U.S. dollars that would seed the revolution.

23

Task Force Davao

Colonel Reginald J. Liu had been professionally humiliated on the field at Koronadal in a sloppy battle that caught him unprepared, and he was angry. He was perspiring not only from the heat and the humidity but also from frustration, sweat trickling down his face, a face more rounded now than when he was younger, eyes peeking from behind pudgy and slanted eyelids reflecting the half of his ancestry that was Chinese and narrowed by years of squinting down a rifle sight. Liu may have put on a few pounds, but his legs were muscled and powerful from training and leading soldiers in combat. Now he was being tested again. One minor American State Department official had been killed and two of the STAGCOM irregulars wounded, one seriously. Liu had also lost five soldiers. He commanded a field force far superior to the enemy paramilitary group that had attacked him, but their smaller force had beaten him in the first encounter of what would become known as the Mindanao Civil War. Even with high-tech, secret American intelligence and electronics surveillance technologies providing exact knowledge of the enemy's position, the Abu Sayaf had gotten the jump on him. Maybe it was pure dumb luck, but it counted. And he had absolutely no excuse why his security elements had been unable to detect the Abu Sayaf.

Twenty-six dusty, recently re-painted 1982 vintage deuce-and-a-half trucks of Task Force Davao, Philippine Army, were positioned along the road behind him, containing a large infantry force that he had not been able to deploy at Koronadal. Too late to avoid the defeat today, he ordered the rest of his troops to dismount—the soldiers who had not been stuck on the floor of their trucks. Liu moved them into defensive positions on the main highway south of Koronadal and put his trucks into a motor pool, well guarded. He ordered the mess unit to set up cooking fires and the entire battalion-sized force to get settled in for the night, with a perimeter guard well motivated to stay awake after the deaths and wounding of their comrades earlier in the day. Liu had already seen to one of the most difficult responsibilities of a commander that he had to accept. He had shipped the bodies of the dead and the living wounded back to Davao City along with letters hand-written on bond paper for their families.

Hayes wrote his official report to be flown back tonight to the embassy in Manila. The hard copy documents would keep company with John Robert Mundy's cold, mutilated body in the helicopter on its return trip.

Liu established his command post by sandbagging an abandoned soft drink stand he had commandeered at the south side of Koronadal. Moments later, his two captains and the two Americans, Hayes and Thornton, joined him. The wrinkles on Liu's brow tightened, and so did his grip on his coffee cup as be began describing the situation. "This is just disastrous. Our first engagement in a real conflict since the breakdown of the P.S.I. treaty agreement, our first combat against the Abu Sayaf away from their home base of operations, and we get spanked. I am going to ask for special authority to initiate *punitive* actions against this enemy, not just defensive posturing."

"From where we see it, and the way Manila and Washington will see it," Major Hayes responded, "is that we no longer have a few foreign terrorists loose in the countryside; we now have a real threat to stability.

Hell, that's wrong, we no longer have stability. You have a civil war on your hands."

Thornton gave his perspective. "You're both overstating what we have here. We've been following one Turk and a few confused farmers who think they're revolutionary warriors on jihad. Without the money the Syrians sent here with that Turk, they couldn't find food to live on except for handouts from missionaries, unless they stopped their terrorist activities and stayed in one place for a while, planted something, and waited for it to grow. Even with the Turk and all that money, the Abu Sayaf are just a few recently barefoot tribesmen. They couldn't gather a quorum in an outhouse."

"They have shoes now, Mister Thornton," Liu responded, objecting to Thornton's condescending comments, whether he was a long-time colleague or not. "They might not wear white socks under heavy and hot combat boots, like you consultants, but they have weapons and money and they are near to achieving a kind of cooperation among themselves, the MNLF, the NPA and the others."

Captain Agustin got the attention of his commander and reported to Colonel Liu, "Sir, we have in the Southern Command alone at least 6,000 troops available in Mindanao and the Visayas. If you ask for them to be put into the field, we could be ready for serious combat within four days."

"The Abu Sayaf are in their realm now, Captain." Liu reverted to his military instruction voice, "in their milieu, they are experts of evasion. We have not had much success over the years, frankly."

"Yes sir," Agustin responded. "I see their resurgence. I don't like their renewed efforts. That's why I'm ready for action as soon as you order it."

"Well, we have the Abu Sayaf patrol located," said Major Hayes. "STAGCOM tracked them, and we know where they are. We can bring in a long-distance air strike and take them all out twenty-four hours from right now, if you get your government's permission to ask for our support."

"That is preposterous." Liu did not take a second to respond. "This is not just about that small Abu Sayaf patrol, and you know it. We have to use them to find Kumander Ali."

Lui continued, "There are many different kinds of rebels scattered over many provinces. Most of their members have not been to school, do not have documents that attest to their births or marriages, can't read or write, and wouldn't know Karl Marx from King Kong. New Peoples Army sounds cool to them and they might pick up some loose change from kidnapping for ransom under that flag, but they do not identify with the labels you invent for them. But we still can't blow up a few individuals together with a whole town. You'd create a dozen martyrs and a million enemies. This is not Vietnam, and it is not Iraq. Ali wants to band together small groups of families, the kind that would fight us at night while they harvest pineapples at the Dole plantation during the day. You can't tell who is a rebel just by looking at him. They don't have universal enemy codes implanted on microchips inside them that you can read from space."

Major Hayes offered his perspective to Liu. "The NPA rebels are *communists*, scattered over three or four provinces. If all their scattered groups combined, they still wouldn't unite with the *Muslims*. Islam and Communism don't mix."

Colonel Liu continued as though he was teaching at the Philippine Military Academy again. "The Abu Sayaf will not have any more luck organizing the communists than we've had educating them. The scattered NPA will never join together, and so we have to defeat them piecemeal in the field, one renegade band at a time," Liu concluded.

"They might not unify this month or even this year, maybe not until their kids get on the Internet, then they can all get together asynchronously," said Thornton, thinking about how the future would look. "They won't need to see each other in person or know their real names. The next generation of insurgents will use web cams and create cute nicknames for themselves. They'll find a way to connect."

Liu stared hard at Thornton a long five seconds, then responded. "By accident or by genius, the general area they have chosen for continuing this confrontation itself is a uniting factor for them. They are located at a strategic confluence of three territories, South Cotobato, Maguindinao, and Sultan Kudarat. Together that makes up most of the Autonomous Region of Muslim Mindanao, the ARMM. If you add Basilan Island and the islands that trail off toward Indonesia, islands that surely would go along with anything decided here, as Basilan is the home base of the Abu Sayaf, you have a nation. Combine all that geography with Agusan and Lanao del Sur, the rest of Mindanao, and you have a country three times as big as Kentucky in size and four times larger in population."

"That makes your next action strategic, and you will need to make it decisive." Thornton summarized what they all were thinking. "And remember that the larger war could turn on one little firefight, one small incident. Like today's."

"As much of history is decided," Hayes said.

Thornton moved on. "Colonel Liu, it's you who decides the objective for TFD. Your objective decides whether I can be involved, and how."

"I know that. Here is how I see it. To move my task force quickly long distances, I am constrained to stay on the roads until the decisive moment, but we have significant firepower and the advantage of superior forces."

"Yes, so to achieve your objective, you don't really need STAGCOM," Thornton said.

"STAGCOM is of little value to me in major combat involving massed units charging each other. There may be a time you can help me with small unit missions. But the major threat to us is not the NPA's combat power. The threat to my nation comes if they organize the people, all the people of Mindanao, to follow a rebel leader politically."

"So STAGCOM represents an opportunity for you." Thornton wanted to set the Colonel up for what might happen later. "Consider, Reggie, at the opportune time, you step aside. I am your opportunity. You win the war, STAGCOM slips in and the bounty money disappears, and you then can win the peace. The cash is a divisive element because it might permit the NPA to consolidate."

"Thornton, you have your own ideas. You want to pursue them first for your own selfish reasons." Liu was talking frankly.

"Tomas, let the professionals do their job." Elaiza just had to say something to him. "It's not worth dying for."

"I don't intend to die for it, but before Liu blows them up with his artillery and spreads the cash all over the jungle floor, I would be happy to clean up the mess for him."

Thornton turned to the colonel. "Reggie, listen to me; we can both get what we want out of this."

"No promises, Thornton, other than that I will do my duty. If there is no conflict with that, maybe we can help each other. We'll see." Liu was closing the discussion.

After his briefing, Elaiza asked Colonel Liu to help her with the seriously wounded Eduardo. He had not been evacuated with the other wounded soldiers because officially he did not belong to any of their units. The medic had looked him over, and the news was not good. His upper arm was shattered, and would have to be amputated just below the shoulder, or he would not survive. Liu called for a medivac helicopter and told Elaiza, "OK, I'll get this fellow taken care of. We'll send him to Davao Doctors Hospital, it's close by air, and he'll have his best chance there." Elaiza stayed with her heavily medicated uncle until the chopper picked him up.

At the command post the TFD leaders wrote out the details of an operations plan. They defined their mutual tactical objective: to tie down and then destroy the Abu Sayaf along with any elements that had joined the movement in Mindanao. They would track them into Sultan Kudarat, where they were now heading, trap them between the Banga and the Alah Rivers, and wipe them out.

The next morning, Task Force Davao, commanded by Colonel Liu and now reinforced, started out of Koronadal on the main road north, this time with armed riflemen, fingers on triggers and rounds chambered, on top of each vehicle. A helicopter overhead kept watch on their flanks to give warning of the possibility of an ambush. Liu rode in the front seat of his jeep, the middle vehicle in the convoy as an armored Humvee led them up out of the swamplands and into the foothills. The colonel's driver said to his leader, "With that cover above us, there's no way we could be surprised, but neither could the enemy we're following."

Liu knew his driver was right, said nothing, but thought, "One helicopter. Of the forty helicopters owned by the Philippine Air Force, only seventeen were serviceable, wrecks from the Americans' old wars." According to a recent report he had seen, the Air Force somehow needed a work force of several thousand men and women to maintain the aircraft. Typical mismanagement, he thought. If only the Philippine Air Force had the funds to buy new helicopters, the flying relics could be consigned to the scrap heap. He sighed in resignation and returned his attention to the road ahead.

Careening downhill from the opposite direction at over thirty miles per hour, a two-wheeled motorcycle with outriggers followed the hyperbolic arc of the highway's outward curve, balancing five human passengers seated on each outrigger. It narrowly missed hitting Liu's jeep. Liu began to see more of them transporting passengers between villages and intermediate destinations along the highway between Koronadal and Lake Buluwan.

"Are there no buses or jeepneys here?" asked Colonel Liu.

"Very few, sir," replied his driver. "That is the primary means of transportation around here. For a fare of four pesos, passengers are carried wherever they want to go, as long as it is along that highway—and not only passengers, but also cargo."

Following Liu, Starke drove the Pajero with Elaiza dozing in the front seat between him and Thornton, the Otazas spread out in the back two rows of seats. Looking out of his window at passing scenes, Thornton saw the sleepy eyes of a long, fat hog tied to the outrigger of a bicycle, looking back at him, questioningly. He surmised that the pig, a full-grown hog, roasted, with rice, would feed an enemy platoon for a week in combat.

Liu had decided not to close the road with checkpoints, as that would also shut down the economy of the region. That would not be good politics, so the road stayed open. Travelers could just as easily be defecting from the NPA as going to join another subversive cell, and the last thing the AFP wanted was to create more enemies and more hatred.

The advancing task force left the two-lane paved highway and took a dirt road westward toward the projected position of the Abu Sayaf. The column was now moving at a walking pace. Liu ordered most of the troops to dismount and sent out patrols on his flanks to move parallel with the main force. The road, which had started out as generally passable, became incrementally worse every mile the men moved—from hard-top to hard-top with potholes to a hard-packed, ungraded and unmaintained dirt road to a condition in which the road was barely distinguishable from the rest of the terrain.

In the Pajero, Thornton shared his growing concern with Elaiza. "I don't like traveling along this so-called road. The mountain villagers have had months to place land mines. We know they do that."

"But any mines would get Liu's vehicle first, before we roll over them," she answered, alert to the dangers.

"Not necessarily. The mines could be in the middle of the road, allowing the vehicle wheels to pass on either side, but if we just happen to slip, it's curtains." Thornton had seen it happen.

He was thinking out loud, formulating, and when Liu's men dismounted from their vehicles, so did STAGCOM, except for the slightly wounded Juanito, who was now driving the Pajero.

"Elaiza, time to turn on the TIAM," Thornton reminded her.

"It's on, you have us on your map?"

"Yeah, I got it. Liu will want to engage any rebels wherever he finds them. And he will want to win. That could be a big encounter. I want to get our target before he does."

"And he's OK with that?"

"I don't know." Thornton turned his head toward Elaiza. "I'm not sure what; but something must have happened in Manila to affect his attitude."

"Meaning something about the money?" she asked, wondering what really was puzzling him. "Is that it?"

"He wants the Turk too, but only incidentally." It sounded hollow to Thornton himself when he said it that way. He knew Liu wanted more, but was not sure what.

"We have a better chance alone to find the Turk than Liu and TFD do, what with their making all that noise and show. We know where Mahir is headed. We can make a beeline toward their destination and cross paths with them eventually." And turning to the Sergeant, he said, "Starke, you and the four Otazas who are still OK, come with me."

With that, STAGCOM became a hunter-killer patrol. "If Liu pauses or procrastinates, we attack Hakki."

"Elaiza, take the Pajero and drive to Bual with Juanito. That's close enough to rejoin quickly and far enough away to avoid action. I'll shadow Liu until he fixes the Turk in place. Pay a family there to stay with them, cover the Pajero with banana leaves or something like that and take care of Juanito and yourself." Thornton then walked away from her after issuing his orders.

It hurt her. Every time he walked away now she wondered if she would ever see him again, surprised by the depth of her feelings. It seemed to her that he always walked away from the people who cared about him. There would have to be a last time, and she wondered if this would be it. "When?" she asked.

Thornton knew he would see her again. Or would he? Uncertainty was a part of their relationship. He looked back; she was looking straight ahead over the steering wheel and did not smile. He strode off with apparent confidence but felt a knot in his belly. Then he turned around and walked back to the Pajero and held her close, pressing her face into his chest.

"You win. From now on, we'll always be together." He surprised himself by what he had said. "Come on. Juanito, you heard what I said, take the vehicle to Bual."

Elaiza was already out of the Pajero and walking briskly after Sergeant Starke, before Thornton changed his mind. Thornton was eager now to leave Liu and get on with it. He caught up with Elaiza as STAGCOM moved away from Liu's column. She chugged along beside him, and Pedro slid into file with his three healthy brothers falling in behind them. STAGCOM moved into the jungle and away from Liu and TFD.

Thornton saluted Liu as he passed him, and Liu gave Thornton a wave goodbye, and turned his attention forward. TFD eventually reached a saddle in the mountain range where the province borders met. The road became better and more traveled as they descended, first becoming two ruts that the wheels of the trucks fit exactly, then a packed dirt road. Open coconuts sliced in two were lying alongside the road to dry and become a cash crop for the local residents. As no one owned the land here, the farmers collected the coconuts from the trees that grew wild, and after drinking the coconut water or selling it along the road as fresh buko juice, they husked the nut and chopped it open. The split halves were laid by the road where the farmers could watch the crop to shield it from stray pigs. The white coconut meat would dry in the sun and become copra, one of the few steady sources of cash for the indigenous tribes living in their ancestral domains.

Task Force Davao now consisted of 376 infantry soldiers, hastily organized out of the existing force augmented by two companies from the 603rd Infantry Battalion, usually stationed just west of Davao City. Manila had also promised that more troops would be made available and were on the way by truck up the main road, arriving at least as far as Koronadal by the next afternoon. Liu ordered his troops to dismount, turned the now empty trucks around and sent them back toward Davao City to pick up the additional reinforcements and to bring them up from the rear, joining him later when his main force continued forward. As he advanced slowly in his jeep in the middle of his dismounted troops, the intelligence he had to guide him in ordering an attack was quickly becoming yesterday's news. He did not know what he was up against: just a Turk with a bag of money and a bunch of Lumads? Certainly more than that now. How many NPA had infiltrated behind him on those curious bicycles, or simply on footpaths, through passes in the high mountain ridges?

Liu and the column, spread out and centered along a dirt road through the marshlands, continued along the sometimes crowded path. The oncoming foot traffic now consisted of local farmers following their carabao and goats along the road, meeting the column of soldiers coming from the opposite direction, both herds constricted by the narrow way. The farmers, in this region a Muslim minority resentful of Christian domination, just looked at Liu in his jeep, smiled pleasantly or gave vacant stares, curious about the column of advancing soldiers and suspicious of their intentions.

Liu's slow-moving caravan eventually reached lower ground, crossed the bridge on the Banga, and entered the province of Sultan Kudarat in western Mindanao.

24

Sultan Kudarat

The mujahadeen gave Mahir and Lateef more of a welcome than the two had expected. Mahir thought he would be treated as the foreigner he was, but he felt more like family than in many places he had visited in the primitive areas of his own homeland, back in Turkey. Mahir was considered locally to be a member of Abu Sayaf, especially since he accompanied Lateef, a now-famous Abu Sayaf leader, and he enjoyed the status. The village, a cluster of a few dozen palm frond-covered farmers' huts that might possibly have a name assigned to it on some map, had one muddy road that was the town's thoroughfare. Sitting in front of the third hut on the left were two women, smiling almost toothlessly, with only a few big white ivories showing when they smiled, picking lice out of each other's hair with their fingers and a small comb. Mahir watched them as he passed by. It seemed to him that only the women picked out their lice; the men did not bother.

A smoldering, acrid smoke hung over the camp of the other rebel soldiers already there as the Abu Sayaf patrol moved in to join them. The men were burning plastic pipe scraps and old Styrofoam chunks to heat water and cook rice at scattered individual campfire sites. Burning the plastic seemed easier to some of the soldiers than using the dry wood that was lying around them. The smoke smelled distinct from an ordinary wood fire and somehow seemed modern to the new enlistees on their way in. Many of the recruits looked very young, not old enough to shave. Minors were being freely recruited now; their parents had trouble feeding them at home and felt honored when their children were selected to serve. Young women were recruited also, but if they were too young to be used in combat or were not big enough to carry weapons and ammo on long marches, they were delegated to becoming overseas workers or "entertainers," sold for sex slaves to some foreign brothel after being exported out of Mindanao through Indonesia, a short boat ride the opposite way from where Mahir had entered.

A youngish looking man wearing a red and white head band and quasi-military uniform came out of a hut farther toward the center of the village and approached Mahir, not smiling, and asked, "Have you brought me the money?" The man had recognized the Turk, whose facial features and height set him apart from the others.

"Yes, I have it, less what Lateef has used already," Mahir said. "I just need a receipt from the proper authority, then no problem."

"I am not running a government-licensed business here, we do not have accounting records." Mahir realized he had just met Kumander Ali, the leader of the breakaway Moro Islamic Liberation Front, who stated the obvious.

"A hand-written note from you will be fine, in any language. I need something, your excellency." Mahir hoped there would not be a problem now, and there was not. Kumander Ali said nothing but came back later with a few short phrases written in English and a few characters in rudimentary Arabic. It would do.

Mahir called up the men who had been carrying the two canvas bags, and passed them on to the man he had recognized from the photograph shown to him back in Damascus. Mahir was relieved that his job was done but pleased when Kumander Ali invited him into his hut with Lateef.

The three squatted on the slatted wood floor. Kumander Ali ripped open a cardboard box and offered warm cans of San Miguel Pilsen beer, recently stolen from a delivery truck.

Ali needed Lateef's confidence as much as he needed the money from Mahir. The Abu Sayaf represented by Lateef out of Jolo and Basilan were necessary allies for Ali if he wanted to reach his goals in this province, and then in all of Mindanao. He considered what to do next, and whether Mahir, the new guy, could be involved. Other rebel leaders would be joining them to determine how best to work together to leverage the new funds. Ali needed to involve the other factions, and perhaps the Turk would be a useful catalyst; foreigners aroused interest and gave authenticity. Ali wanted full control, and the Turk could help him gain it.

Anxious to return to his family in Turkey, Mahir was focused on getting out of the country as soon as possible, but as he listened to the other two men attempt to find common ground with each other, he thought about how he might be able to make the best out of the situation personally. After all, he had already invested his time in this unusual venture and had taken considerable personal risk. If the wrong Philippine National Police or Army officer got hold of him, he might easily be "shot while trying to escape." On the other hand, if this bunch of rebels ever found a way to work together, they could create a whole new country for themselves, give it a new name, design their own flag for the next edition of school textbooks to be printed around the world, and he would be one of the few foreigners who could profit under the new regime. It also occurred to him that those twin sisters back near Digos might make good wives for him in this country; he would not need to tell his Turkish wife about it. It was just a thought. He had been away from home for a long time.

Over the next few hours, Commander Aldrin Bumbog, a senior official of the NPA, and a man named Mehmet Al Zein, speaking for the Moro National Liberation Front, showed up at the shack and sat down on its porch. They had never met each other before, although they had heard each other's name. Ali and his followers had split away from the MNLF the previous year, and Ali became Kumander Ali of the Moro Islamic Liberation Front. He had broken with the MNLF because he thought Al Zein lacked the spine to fight. But now Kumander Ali was philosophically inclined to get back together with Al Zein, his old rival.

Times were different now. It was a momentous event to have the important leaders of the Mindanao insurgent forces opposing the Manila government gathered together here in this small village. Bumbog and Al Zein had heard about new money coming in and wanted their share. Ali brought one of the canvas sacks out of the hut and gave a stack of hundred dollar notes to each of the men, more money than they had ever seen. There was ten thousand U.S. dollars in each stack, a miniscule portion of what Ali had, but it made them happy. The leaders could satisfy their followers and feed them for months with this windfall. Now the leaders would decide what to do next for the benefit of all.

Kumander Ali started the meeting as the emergent and apparent leader. "We will achieve our freedom, and we can save some of these dollars for better use later. It is easier for us to pay the common soldiers two cans of sardines, or sometimes shrimp paste, every day; it's cheaper for us, more useful for them and they can sell or trade one of the cans." In other words, it was easy for them to steal the simple supplies they needed to compensate their troops; they decided to keep the money for better uses.

But Lateef, as the Abu Sayaf representative, pressed to know what the money would be used for, and especially how his band would get their share. After all, the Abu Sayaf was the conduit for the funds. He asked, "Now that we have succeeded and have a victory in sight, we should move boldly. What is your plan, Kumander Ali?"

The idea had occurred to Kumander Ali months before, but this was the first time he verbalized it to anyone. "If we rename ourselves NPA, the New Peoples Army, it would help us unify." The Moro leader explained their situation. "Despite years of working to uplift the plight of the Bangsomoro peoples, our officials have never worked together. But we have common goals. If we now show we are united, it would demonstrate to Manila that we are also powerful."

"To the rest of the world, none of you have credibility yet," Mahir informed them. "It would be useful to show solidarity."

"OK with me whatever you name this coalition," Bumbog concurred, speaking in his dialect, "I will not insist on any particular name from our point of view."

After storytelling and a few self-conscious jokes, Al Zein made the major concession. "It is acceptable to call our combined forces NPA. The MNLF agrees to accept this name. It's simple, short, and sends a good enough message."

Ali realized he was witnessing a historic breakthrough, and pressed on. "There is one imperative; we must have an election to gain legitimacy."

Bumbog joined the confederation with a simple statement. "Then simplicity is best, I too like NPA. It will be easy to remember during an election."

"Three simple letters are much easier to sell to voters, no matter what their language is," said Mahir, facilitating the consensus. The Abu Sayaf bosses in Basilan and Jolo would be pleased with his work in the field and would report his success to the Syrian, he hoped. He kept his satisfaction to himself.

Kumander Ali pushed the insurgent leaders to move forward with urgency, still not hinting how much cash he had available, "Within the next several weeks we will have our best chance to get everything we all want." He had to be careful how he phrased his words because these leaders, and surely most of their followers, were not able to verbalize complex ideas, such as war plans. But they could understand money.

"If you pay ten U.S. dollars per vote, the citizens will show up and check NPA," said Bumbog, moving the meeting forward again. The others raised their eyebrows and chins simultaneously, a kind of reverse nod indicating an affirmative answer.

"Get all your villages to vote, and we will have a new country, I promise you." Kumander Ali started to summarize, to see if there would be objections. Silence indicated that the confederacy was formed. Henceforth, they would be known collectively as the NPA, the New Peoples Army.

Mahir now felt he should be free to leave; the newly formed NPA could decide how to spend the money he had turned over to Ali. He had won his personal battle and was confident that the Syrian would transfer the rest of his earthly reward to his account; Ali had already given him the hand-written receipt that the Syrian demanded as verification. All Mahir needed to do now would be to retrace his steps; he could find his way out with no time pressure against him, thinking again that maybe he would have a chance to stop off at that resto-bar along the road where the two sisters worked. To get to the sea he would only need to follow the coast.

But Mahir realized that he was with a team now. He believed in the mission, and he wanted to see his team win. He wanted to be the victor for once in his life, against a worthy opponent, in fact a numerically more powerful one. It would taste good to be one up on his global enemies in economic and religious philosophies, to make up for what had gone on back in Turkey. Maybe he could even wind up owning a fruit plantation or an export business in Mindanao and connect that business back to Istanbul. He would have the cash to invest. His allies here would rather work with him after their victory, he supposed, and they would need some help representing their interests to the world. Wild thoughts began to race through his mind. So he decided that he should stay on for a while and continue on jihad. Victory in the war of theologies would wipe out the Christian missionaries and Jewish businesses; both would be replaced by the new Muslim order.

Kumander Ali, the leader of the reconstituted NPA, took on increased authority with an army in which he would command thousands. As a gesture of thanks, he assigned about fifty men—two truckloads of soldiers—to Mahir to command. Although he had little formal military education himself, Mahir imagined getting his men together for training. After all, he had recent, real combat experience compared to his other subordinates, whose primary activity was limited to the monthly collection of tongs, extortion from miners and loggers who worked in their valleys. The barefoot soldiers assigned to him may have been in some squabbles with the PNP and the AFP, but the most they could boast about was sniping or kidnapping. One man, the most experienced, had held up a hardware store and stolen an M-16 rifle from a PNP officer who was there buying nails for personal use.

Mahir hoped he could organize and lead the men assigned to him to one specific place and get them to shoot their rifles in the same direction: such an outcome would be achieving a high enough level of discipline. Many of them did have rifles. They also had one 60mm mortar tube, two 12-gauge shotguns and several dozen rounds of mortar ammunition. They had never fired the mortars and did not know how, but they carried them everywhere they went. Mahir thought he could figure out how to employ the mortar tube, but then he still would not know how to aim this indirect fire weapon. Maybe someone could figure out how to convert the mortar rounds into car bombs or strategically placed IEDs—individual explosive devices—or to make a dozen coordinated suicide bomb attacks. That would certainly put a big dent in the enemy's will to fight if the explosions were in the right places, like theaters or churches. He would lose twelve NPA soldiers in the deal, but they were not much good individually anyway, and the NPA could recruit more. He would ask for volunteers who did not have rifles, like the knife carriers or ammo porters. If all they had was a bolo, they were better employed to take a few of the enemy with them in suicide attacks and die while on jihad than to continue their march unarmed.

Since Bumbog and Al Zein had accepted Kumander Ali as their tactical leader in the field, Bumbog decided to test him. "Now that we're united, what do you recommend we do first?" Bumbog wore an aviator's flight jacket that he had taken from the dead co-pilot of a downed AFP aircraft and kept the collar turned up to look cool.

Ali had a surprise answer. "I have given it much thought. Suicide attacks have value, but timing is important. At this moment we have the Philippine Army confused. Now is the time for us to do what we have waited for. It is time for us to announce our war. Our next move is tonight. Near here in Itig is a radio station operated by a broadcasting company out of Manila. Tonight, we take the radio station!"

Kumander Ali had already discussed this plan with Lateef and assigned him to be the patrol leader, since he had been in a firefight recently and could do a better job with his experienced cadre than any leader of the raggle-taggle herd of new recruits wandering in who didn't know each other or even speak the same dialect. It would be difficult to ever forge the motley assemblage into a disciplined combat unit, let alone do it by nightfall. So the task fell to Lateef, who kept the same core team he had brought with him, including Mahir because they had fought together in a successful skirmish, and joined by nine of Ali's personal security guards, but not Ali himself. The mission to take the radio station was important, but it was grunt work. They made their plan as simple as possible, and it should be easy.

The patrol would also include Ugly Maria. Kumander Ali had ordered her to cover her body, especially her face, at all times whether in the village or on patrol—perhaps not only because of religious tradition—but she refused and told him to go to hell. He didn't make an issue of it, and none of the others admitted to being offended.

Lateef and the attack squad left the village shortly before 10 PM using four *habl habl,* motorized tricycles, typical inter-village transportation in the area, to approach Itig town center by road. One tricycle at a time they rolled silently past the AFP checkpoints along the road. The soldiers paid no attention to the numerous and ubiquitous tricycles and stopped only cars and larger vehicles for inspection. They parked on the dirt basketball court, the wide spot in the road in the center of all villages, where the patrol assembled for their mission.

Radio FM 99.3 broadcast until midnight every day of the week. Seven minutes before scheduled sign-off on this particular night, Mahir, Lateef and the rest of the Abu Sayaf hit squad burst through the door. Lateef pressed a short knife to the neck of the program manager, nicking it and drawing a drop of blood. He calmly told the terrified man, "Walk fast out of town, do not look back or ever return. Your announcer inside stays with us." The terrified man complied, perhaps walking a bit faster than even Lateef expected, and the NPA had its radio station.

What they had captured was a two-story wooden building, a diesel generator, a transformer and an FM transmitter of sufficient strength to reach a parabolic area of geography that covered the western coast of Mindanao 90 miles north and south of the station and extending 75 miles inland. In effect, it covered the four provinces that would constitute the core of the new country, the Islamic Republic of Mindanao. Residents who did not listen to the station personally would still get the news, delivered by word of mouth as fast as traffic or pedestrians moved; *radyo de baktas* was the "walking radio" that kept everyone informed.

The next morning when the early crew and later the office staff arrived, they were told the property was now an asset of the NPA. The temporary flag cut from a red tee shirt with a black portrait of Che Guevara flew from a bamboo pole. Two of the boys who did clean-up work and cooking asked to stay on, as did one of the D.J.'s, and they were accepted into the revolution. When the D.J. signed on the next morning, he announced for the first time, "Radio Free Mindanao is on the air," and informed the listeners that he would no longer play decadent foreign music. The first song he chose was Freddie Aguilar's vocal version of *Mindanao,* then several selections of tribal gong and drum music, followed by Imam Ali announcing prayer time, which would thereafter be done five times daily. The Koran was read by religious leaders between more old folk songs. On the noon news, Radio Free Mindanao announced the formation of the Islamic Republic of Mindanao and called for elections to be held on the 40th anniversary of the founding of the NPA, the communist New Peoples Army. Choosing this auspicious date should help get the scattered NPA elements still hiding in the provinces to join efforts with the coalition. It was just thirty-one days away, the sooner the better. They did not care about how many people actually voted, just as long as those who showed up voted the right way and a public event demonstrated to their constituents and to the world the strength of their movement.

25

Rebellion

Colonel Liu was livid. How could a bunch of farmers and a few terrorists announce *Radio Free Mindanao?* What the hell will they do next? His boss in Manila and certainly the President of the Philippines and shortly after that the Western world would be shocked to hear that a new radio station out of Sultan Kudarat, the predominantly Muslin western province of Mindanao, was playing Muslim folk music around the clock and readings from the Koran. Prominent ulamas, Muslim religious leaders of the province, were invited to preach on the air in support of kidnapping for ransom and other coercive means to collect revenue for the logistical needs of the cause. A massive exodus of the Christian population out of Mindanao could be the drastic consequence. This scenario the central government in Manila could not accept.

When he heard the first broadcast from Radio Free Mindanao, Liu was riding in his jeep on the transverse road forming the base of a triangle at the junction of the Banga and the Alah rivers, where his infantry presently contained the main NPA force. He had to get to his command post to go over the situation with the captains assigned to Task Force Davao. Together they would need to figure out what to report to Manila. Maybe the President would let the U.S. Air Force take out just that one target. The situation had escalated to such a point that President Cayton might be willing to accept the political backlash. It was better than losing Mindanao. Liu fidgeted beside his driver in the front seat of their jeep while it bounced along, continuously knocking his knee against a loaded M-16 rifle secured in a bracket between them.

Every time his nervous driver heard the metallic clank of metal against metal he instinctively beeped his horn. Frustration increased with each delay as they swerved slowly in and out of pedestrian traffic. Master Sergeant Rivera had driven his colonel everywhere in peace and in war for fifteen years, and now, down this backwater road, he was confounded that his periodic beeping had little effect on the civilians blocking passage. The jeep had to wait at the outskirts of a village while a midnight-black water buffalo dragged a sled loaded with equally black mud off the road, every wasted minute adding to the colonel's consternation and making him more restless.

The task force commander knew exactly where the Abu Sayaf was; he could hear them on that damned radio station they had captured in Itig. He had reported back to Galan in Manila that he had the main NPA force cut off in the triangle, but his credibility had been damaged by that one, small Abu Sayaf patrol that had slipped out and seemed to roam around at will, even taking over a radio station. His task force needed to put a stop to this nonsense and eliminate these damned *insurgentos,* as they had been called since the United States' first counter-insurgency war in 1902, when the American army of occupation in the Philippines became a cause for Muslim revolutionaries to band together for the first time. Now, over a hundred years later, the new and continuing insurgency was no longer limited to opposition of foreign intervention in the country. Much worse, a large part of the country had declared independence from the republic. How could those semi-illiterate bandits and extortionists simply declare themselves to be a new country!

As soon as Liu arrived back at his new field command post near Isulan, he swung out of the jeep and marched to the table under a canvas tent where his staff was drinking coffee and smoking. Liu remained standing after they came to attention and saluted, letting them also stand for an uncomfortable minute, not giving them an immediate "At ease."

"How did they take that radio station? We had them isolated in the triangle, Bautista! What the hell is going on, Captain?" Liu confronted his subordinate officer.

"It can't be the same force that attacked the radio station, sir. The main NPA contingent was confused and wandering into the triangle," the young captain reported, with no outward emotion, looking straight ahead at the large, hand-drawn map of Mindanao nailed to a board on the post holding up the tent.

"It was the same in my area, Colonel Liu," said the other young officer, supporting his comrade, "a major force was directly in front of us, and they are still in that position. They were not capable of mounting an attack as far away as Itig."

"I think that's it. You said 'major force.' Sit down." The officers sat. Liu put them at ease. "It would not take a large effort to capture a radio station, only a patrol. But I can still hear them on the radio!

"It would have been easy for a small hunter-killer guerrilla patrol to move through the jungle or at any time along the highway without our detection, especially during the night. They would have local guides with them who know the territory," Colonel Liu concluded.

"Yes, sir." Captain Bautista risked calling the Colonel's attention to his earlier command. "You ordered us not to close down the roads to civilian traffic. A small unit could drive into Itig, unnoticed."

"OK. Get me Manila on a secure connection." Liu could not wait any longer.

His call was put through to Martin Galan immediately, who told him right off, "I have this from the President, Reggie, take your task force and move now and wipe them all out. We may have political costs to pay later for going on a punitive expedition, but political memories fade quickly, and a breakaway state may stay broken away for a long time. We need to move now and be decisive. CNN is making us look like fools."

Liu answered with a "Yes, sir," and once again saw either promotion to his first star and a probable fast track to more promotions after that, or disgrace and perhaps even jail time if the Abu Sayaf were not defeated. Galan could later deny he had authorized what some might consider extralegal or even unconstitutional methods that resulted in the loss of life, whether of Philippine soldiers or innocent indigenous tribe people.

"I'm counting on you. I'm on my way to the presidential palace now, and I can keep things quiet for a while. What do you need to get the job done quickly?" Galan was now talking on his cell phone from inside his car; Liu could hear Manila traffic puffing and beeping in the background.

"I need firepower. I need boots on the ground, lots of them. And I need artillery. The quicker you can get them to me, the quicker I can execute your orders."

"OK, I'll handle it. Keep the road behind you open."

"Roger, out," Liu responded and returned to his meeting.

It fell on Colonel Liu as the Task Force commander to state realistically to his captains how he saw their current situation. He stood up and started to speak in his military academy lecture voice again, "The Abu Sayaf, the MNLF, NPA, NFD, CPP, MILF, ICI, BILF and the rest of that alphabet soup of loosely related groups of obscure and hopeless causes have achieved some degree of unity. If they can organize and coordinate, and formulate realistic political objectives, they could actually win independence. Mindanao is in rebellion!" Liu ended his lecture, sat down, and changed the tone of his voice to outline his objective for the coming battle.

"We must attack and severely degrade the ability of the insurgents to conduct war. Foreign terrorists are fighting a civil war against our law-biding citizens, tricking them into an alliance they do not understand. We must defeat their ability to control the countryside. We need to make them hurt so much that they will not try to revolt again." He could not mince words; the officers immediately subordinate to him had to understand that he did not want to take prisoners, but he could not say that directly.

Major Hayes had walked into the tent. When Liu stopped speaking, and the other officers had left, he addressed the colonel, "Well spoken, sir. If I may give my opinion, you know I am here only as an observer.

But I can encourage you. I heard our president speak to your congress last year. He told them that our two nations have made the choice together to defend ourselves and not to be intimidated by terrorists. This Abu Sayaf group pretends to act for God, but no religion tolerates murder. My country supports your effort to wipe them out. But you did not hear that from me. And you will never hear it from our ambassador."

"Thank you, Major Hayes." Liu leaned back in the folding chair that Master Sergeant Rivera had brought out for him. "My superiors in Manila have informed me of actions taken by the U.S. to cut off fund transfers to Abu Sayaf leaders and to block their bank accounts. That makes the insurgency desperate for the money shipment moving in now. They will resolutely defend it."

Hayes pulled up a chair, unhooked his armored vest and sat down. "I think you have your forces spread too thinly. Consider massing against specific targets. Make it difficult for them to survive in the jungle."

"We try to surround NPA units whenever we locate them, Major, but they disperse swiftly. They go back to their farms and villages, and hide their guns." Liu was telling the American advisor the simple facts. "They operate in small and isolated units, you know."

"Yes, I know, Colonel, but not this time. I have new intelligence for you. General Hargens asked me to pass it on. The NPA is pulling out of the triangle. STAGCOM tracked them."

"If true, that's a new tactic for them, moving together and coordinated."

"Yes, it is. You need to improve your maneuverability; don't just stay on the highways. But right now, you know where they are, so go after them before they all move out of the triangle."

Liu reminded Hayes, "The communist insurgency has been resilient. We push, they give way, then the rebels snap back when we leave an area. But I think something is changing. If an elite NPA force is massing around Itig, they're changing their focus and will engage in mass attacks."

Hayes thought about the bigger political picture. Peace negotiations between the MNLF and the Philippine government had been going on endlessly. Now generations had passed since the Philippines had actually fought together with the Americans against a common enemy, the Japanese, which united them. But after the end of World War II, the most recent of three generations of Filipino Christians and Muslims fought each other and the jostling for power did not satisfy either party. "Your rebels here are getting impatient for change. They've been fighting you for a long time, and now even talk between you has stopped. They'll try something new." Hayes thought it was a good time to lay it all on the table.

"I can't help that; the insurgents unilaterally backed out of the peace negotiations. And then they changed their mission and their methods," the colonel responded.

"OK, but the AFP has 80,000 infantry soldiers throughout the country available for combat, and supporting units such as artillery and combat engineers, against only 7,000 NPA. What does it take? What's wrong with you?" Hayes, the advisor and observer, would have liked to have had an overwhelming advantage like that when he went into combat in past conflicts in Iraq and Afghanistan.

"I hear your message, Major." The tone of his voice when he said 'Major" contained more than polite impatience. "Maybe now, for the first time, you will see what the AFP can do." For the rest of the briefing, the American major was silent while Colonel Liu made his plans.

Shortly after noon, Liu was satisfied, he wouldn't wait for reinforcements. He dismissed his men after ordering them, "Move at the times I have assigned; Bautista and your company, just after nightfall. Agustin, be ready before sun-up tomorrow. Now, go get your men ready. The time has come."

26

The Triangle

A t the Task Force Davao command post beside the road, a dog barked someplace in the dark. It would soon be dawn. Colonel Liu put on his fatigue uniform, packed up his combat gear, pushed aside the canvas flaps and left his tent. He had already been awake for two hours, knowing he should be resting but not able to sleep. During his operational briefing the day before, Liu had assigned the troops available to him into two strike forces, each led by one of his experienced infantry captains and consisting of about 150 riflemen. Now it was time for action.

Major Hayes saw Liu walking across the packed-down, moist mud between their tents and approached him. He surprised his older ally with a sincere compliment, "Colonel Liu, I want to tell you, I respect your professionalism and wish you well today."

"Thank you. I've lived through years of disillusionment—Filipinos fighting Filipinos. Perhaps that can end soon. You're welcome to follow the action, but don't get involved." The ground rules could not be repeated too often.

As task force commander, Liu did not want to mix Americans together with the Philippine troops. He didn't want CNN to report this as a joint operation; in fact, he hoped they would not report it at all. If he achieved a well-publicized victory over the Abu Sayaf, it would call attention to the fact that the struggle continued and that stability in Mindanao was a myth. And obviously a reported defeat at the hands of the insurgents would be far worse.

Liu might put up with STAGCOM. He could find a job for them; Thornton had some firepower, and STAGCOM could disappear quickly. It would cost him nothing to employ the Americans; they had their own incentives and objectives. Thank God they were in the bush and out of his way at the moment; he would not have any explaining to do no matter what happened. Major Hayes did not bother him; he could tag along and "observe."

"Right, sir," Hayes replied to Liu's request to lay low. "I understand; I won't be noticed." Hayes had worked with Filipino officers in the field before and knew well the limitations placed upon him by the Status of Forces Agreement between the U.S. and the Philippines. Leading a team of American Green Berets during training exercises the previous year, he had instructed Filipinos in small unit tactics and knew the score. From his perspective, Hayes thought his most difficult task in the past had been getting the trainees to act like alert, seasoned professional soldiers rather than the tired veterans who had been engaged in anti-insurgency operations for ten years or more, with hardly any chance to visit their families. The Filipino soldier looked with envy at his police counterpart who was a civilian with an 8-to-5 job, so it turned out to be an even greater task to teach them to appreciate the fact that the best time to attack might be at night or near dawn and that they had to get out into the rain sometimes.

Marksmanship, map reading, and learning how to create and execute an operations order proved to be easier than changing their philosophy about what a soldier does—duty versus free time. Hayes had marveled at the Filipino soldier's acceptance of duty. Duty meant hardship— traveling on foot because vehicles and even roads were limited; food was cold rations because cooking fires were easily seen; the farther the scene of encounter, the greater distance back to camp with the dead and wounded. But the Filipino soldier was a social animal—even in the boondocks, an Army encampment was always noisy and happy at night.

The result of months of training by Special Forces teams had yielded measurable improvement in mission accomplishment and overcoming basic bad habits. The U.S. gave the AFP rangers and elite paratroop units new rifles and combat gear, and marksmanship improved. Many of their old rifles were left over from the Vietnam era, and their constant use since then had worn smooth the rifling inside the barrels, so bullets would not pick up the spin they needed to follow a true trajectory to their target. The Americans also turned over to the Philippine Army older radios after the U.S. forces upgraded their own equipment, and issued the Filipinos night vision equipment. Now there could be no excuses, no more playing games and singing songs until bedtime. Hayes knew that the Filipinos had personal integrity, but they had to learn the art of war.

Like his commander, Captain Agustin was unable to sleep and was up early preparing for the mission. His company had the shortest distance to move and therefore would not push off from their present position until just before dawn, very soon now. It was almost time to wake his men. He passed Hayes and Liu on his way to the long row of tents where his troops were still sleeping. Major Hayes saluted him. "Kick ass today, Agustin!"

"Will do, Hayes." It might have seemed an insignificant moment, but Agustin would always include it when in his old age he retold the story of what happened that day, for they would never meet again.

Captain Agustin told his sergeants to roust the soldiers from their tents and whistled awake those who had covered themselves with camouflage cloths or mosquito nets. The posturing of Task Force Davao at its encampment was observed by new NPA recruits headed into the triangle, civilian-clad inductees on their way to report to Kumander Ali. They walked or biked directly past the Philippine Army soldiers bivouacked along the road between the Alah and the Banga. Farther north in the triangle, when they met Kumander Ali, they reported what they had seen, continuously updating his intelligence on the enemy.

Liu had no concerns about giving his position away. It was part of his plan to let the NPA leaders think that he was remaining in a fixed position, and he encouraged his troops to make noise while they prepared for the day. He was about to execute what he hoped would be a clever feint.

Ali's men had not observed TFD's B Company pull out just after dark the night before, and the remaining troops made enough commotion to hide their absence. Captain Bautista had moved his company of infantry out of camp two miles west. Using stealth, it had taken them all night circling north to move into position, but by the beginning of early morning half-light they had rotated to approach Ali's camp from its right flank. Before dawn the NPA camp lay directly in front of them. B Company formed into a firing line extending 100 yards from north to south and held their position far enough away from the NPA camp to avoid contact with Ali's outposts, not alert in any case at this hour.

The sleeping mujahadeen thought that the noisy army troops scattered along the road to their south were the only enemy they had to worry about, and were not overly concerned; it was too early in the day for their adversaries to get to work, they thought.

Under Captain Agustin, A Company's primary mission was to make noise, and not to get anybody killed. Any deaths would be certain to make the Manila news at noon and the CNN late report in the U.S. Eastern Time Zone, which would be bad politics. Just as soon as they could see morning mist replace the coal black night air, about thirty minutes before sunrise, they began firing their weapons sporadically, and everything else they had, from the side of the road in the general direction of Ali's camp. They were too far away to hit anyone except by accident, but they achieved the desired effect. The firing woke up Ali and his groups of followers, and after the NPA soldiers grabbed their rifles, machetes, sticks or ammo boxes they moved toward the source of the firing, their heads ducked. Agustin's men fired all the ammo they had loaded; then fell back in an orderly fashion, withdrawing to the line of their departure and off the field of battle. Just as the sun rose they returned across the road and into a defensive perimeter around Colonel Liu's position, his radio operator and immediate headquarters staff.

Within the triangle, Ali was up quickly when the firing started and bolted out of his tent, having slept in his clothing; as all of his men did, and he moved toward the sounds of the action. He found many of his undisciplined collection of fighters moving around in disarray instead of proceeding deliberately to their positions—just what Colonel Liu had counted on. Kumander Ali tried to rally them by shouting "Allah Akbar!" and firing a rifle burst into the air, but that only added to their confusion.

With A Company withdrawn, Captain Bautista's company moved forward and fired at will from their positions directly into the general area of Ali's flank as his fighters headed west, bunched together and illuminated by the morning sun, now risen and outlining them from behind. Again, as Liu had expected, many of the rebels turned to face the direction from which the new firing was coming, some throwing themselves down into the wet grass in fear, others courageously moving toward the fire, and some disenchanted recruits simply escaping all the commotion by disappearing into the jungle and starting a long walk home. Overall, the initial fighting succeeded in getting the NPA to move around, aimless and dispersed.

Three minutes after they began firing, Bautista's men paused, reloaded, and moved forward in line, now taking aimed shots. The disorganized NPA soldiers were obvious targets, picked off easily. Ali did not know which way to retreat and had difficulty communicating with the scattered groups. By default, not knowing what else to do, they held their positions, and the fighting continued, but were not effective in their own defense.

Rather than have many of his men wounded or killed, Liu radioed Captain Bautista to withdraw to the west and then to turn south as planned, regroup, and move back into defensive positions along the east-west road, next to Agustin's company, which had already returned. Bautista acknowledged and marched back to camp in good order, his troops showing new discipline and the great satisfaction of victory as they headed back to where they had pulled out the night before. There they rejoined Captain Agustin's company, poised in its position in case the rebels pursued. They need not have worried; the entire enemy camp was in disarray.

In the battle for the triangle, Liu's force had taken only five casualties, two dead and three with minor wounds from lucky hits made by the

NPA in their confusion, while sixty-two NPA had been killed and perhaps over a hundred more wounded. Liu was sure of the exact number
killed; one of his patrols found their bodies the next day stacked in an
abandoned pile and counted them before the final report of enemy KIA
was filed. Liu could have exploited his victory and killed even more of
the insurgents, but, politically, it was better to have only a few of his own
to report dead, and after all, he would really be killing his own countrymen. But he wanted to get revenge for his defeat at Koronadal, not
simply kill a bunch of half naked men, and women, fighting with knives
and stolen guns. He wanted to engage the main NPA force, wherever
they were assembling.

During the last minutes of firing before Captain Bautista's troops
broke off contact, Ugly Maria got caught in the fire from the AFP
infantry and was hit in the upper right arm with a small caliber bullet. It
was painful, and after tying it up with a rag, she looked for someone to
help her. But the loose collection of NPA groups had no medical contingent, so she had to do the best she could on her own. Some of the women
around the camp looked at the wound, which was still bleeding, pumping
regularly spaced spurts. But Maria did not belong with the other women;
she was a fighter. And she did not belong with the fighters; she was a
woman. With the fighting still going on, she was not missed when she
staggered off and sat down to rest near one of the rivers.

The next morning when she was found, her body had bloated to the
point that it was hard to tell whether it was that of a man or a woman.
In death, Ugly Maria was regarded with much the same ambiguity as
she had been in life. The new recruit who found the body didn't know
what to do with his discovery and rather than make work for himself or
someone else, he covered it with a stack of loose, green vegetation, to let
nature and the scavengers of the rain forest consume the remains.

27

Jungle Patrol

In the windless night, rain was falling straight down in buckets. It had started a few hours before, a heavy rain indicating that a front was moving in. It was not going to be a quick shower. Elaiza was crouched low, under a small canvas sheet that was too small to keep her dry, but let her observe. Thornton was pushed in tight beside her as they saw an NPA patrol moving from left to right only twenty meters in front of them.

"What direction are they headed?" Elaiza asked.

"They're pushing northeast through the brush," Thornton told her. "Let's do a map check," and he took out his compass and crumpled, moist map. "They're making a path that will bring them directly into Itig village after they cross the Banga and the main highway. If this is the Abu Sayaf patrol with the Turk and the bags, it could be our chance."

Thornton and Elaiza turned around and crawled on their stomachs toward Starke. Thornton signaled the STAGCOM team with hand movements to get down and not to move, and they stretched out in a line behind Starke, frozen in position. When Thornton reached Starke he let him know, "There's movement along the trail, many of them, not the small patrol we followed before."

"Shouldn't we let Colonel Liu know? He might have the chance to . . ."

"The hell with him. We have to let JUSMAG know. That's who we work for," Thornton said. He would have liked to surprise the Abu Sayaf patrol, but he had the duty to keep Hargens informed. "Elaiza, make some techno noise."

Elaiza stood up and walked in a perpendicular line away from the direction the enemy patrol was headed, making one step to the right at the end. "Should I draw the circle?" she asked, the request for a fire mission from JUSMAG.

"No," Thornton answered her. "We only have to tell Hargens where they are: we can get them ourselves."

Elaiza cocked her ear toward the trail the NPA were making. "I hear movement," she told him. "There's another group passing now, bigger than the first and talking loudly, speaking a dialect I don't understand."

"They're all escaping from the triangle. Liu must have attacked them. Damn him, he attacked too soon," Thornton concluded.

"Look at the map, Elaiza." Elaiza shared her scrap of canvas with Thornton again to protect the map as she studied it.

"It's a clever escape route; Task Force Davao won't know about their move."

"This messes up our chance to surprise them. Liu's already alerted them." Starke said a bit too loudly.

"I know." Thornton tried to get Starke to speak quietly, and to show by example he whispered from under the canvas cover. "We have to work with what we have. Our embassy needs to have up-to-date intelligence. They can pass it on to Liu, or not, as they please. Hargens expects me to report any and all current information. It's part of my deal."

"How many men have you counted so far?" Thornton asked Elaiza.

"Over a hundred."

"Then you were right before. This is not the Abu Sayaf hit squad that took the radio station; it's part of the main force. The entire NPA army is on the move."

"Let's pull back a few more meters; we don't want to be seen," Starke recommended. "We're way outnumbered."

"Yeah, but not for that reason. We don't know where the Turk is. This would all be useless if we didn't get him and the two bags."

Pedro, dripping, moved up to them and looked to Elaiza for some sign of what to do. He had also seen and heard the movement of the patrol. She put her finger to her lips, and he propped himself against a fallen palm tree trunk.

"The NPA are retreating after their defeat," Thornton concluded, "they're not looking for a fight right now, they're making a lot of noise, and their heads are hanging down in this pouring rain."

"Looks like they're moving their main force to the radio station in Itig, right?" Starke asked.

"Logical. They'll regroup there around it. Itig is easy for the NPA units from the north and east to get to, as they build strength," Thornton said.

"From the map, it looks like a good choice." Elaiza studied the wet map with Thornton, took out her iPod and verified the data. "Rather than stay trapped in the triangle, they can defend Itig village. If they have to retreat out of there, they could withdraw in any direction if they have to; there's jungle all around Itig."

The STAGCOM members settled down, waiting for Thornton to decide what to do next. Killing time, he said to Starke, "Know what I like about this rain?"

"You have to be kidding, like what?" Starke said, water dripping off his Oakland A's baseball cap.

"No, I'm not kidding. When it rains like this, mosquitoes can't fly."

"Not at this moment, thank God, but watch them as soon as it stops."

"Then let's get moving now." Thornton got himself together. "Liu's preemptive attack changes things. Our embassy will pass on location info to him from Elaiza's data, but he won't know it's the NPA main force pulling out of the Isulan triangle; he's probably still planning on wiping them out there."

"And I bet he doesn't know how many more of them there are now," Elaiza said.

"Quiet. Look, another group is moving forward. At this rate, they'll get a thousand men into Itig in a day," Thornton said.

"Let's get out of here. We won't be able to get to the money carrier this way. We don't know which group has it, but one of them must. We have to get to Itig before Liu messes up again. After we have the cash he can have his way with them." Thornton put away his equipment and STAGCOM changed direction. Soaked through to the skin and feeling heavy from their wet clothing and gear, they moved south and then circled around to advance parallel with the NPA route, both columns heading directly for Itig village.

STAGCOM took all night to get into position near Itig, and they were tired when they saw the village before them at dawn. Thornton had kept them moving by pointing to Elaiza and asking Pedro, "Are all Manobo women like her?" He knew her example would inspire the Otazas.

"No, she is unusual even for one of us." Pedro answered with pride.

"You'll all have your chance soon enough to do something unusual." Thornton said, wanting to take action before they all passed out from exhaustion. He gave Pedro an encouraging slap on the back and turned to Starke.

"I'm going to try to get in close and see what I can spot with my binoculars. I'll take Elaiza and Pedro with me to recon; you stay here with the other Otazas, I don't want too many of us moving at once. We've got to find out where those bags are, then maybe we can get them before Kumander Ali spends all that cash."

With that, Thornton, Elaiza and Pedro moved forward toward Itig.

28

Itig Village

The New Peoples Army camp at Itig had continued to grow with more warriors and their entourages arriving. They heard on their radios the "Call to Prayer" being announced by Radio Free Mindanao. The faithful of the village and the ever more numerous transients loitering along the main street put their abaca cloths on the ground or on the wooden floors inside the huts and bowed toward Mecca. From the single mosque in the community the mullahs chanted their rhythmical prayers in their best imitation of Arabic, and for this moment, differing views were compromised and all were united as they prayed together for a free Muslim nation. All else was momentarily quiet in the armed camp of the mujahadeen in Mindanao.

After his prayers, walking through the village to stretch his limbs, Mahir saw two women standing in front of the shacks, wearing chadors of inconspicuous neutral colors. Something in their bearing was foreign to the place. The two women seemed taller and more graceful than the

others, and were not mingling. As he approached, they moved into the
street to pass near him, and the first whispered in English, "Sheik Kemal
says your family is safe. They have received the transfer." Continuing,
she added after an almost imperceptible pause and with a slight lilt to
her voice, "And perhaps you will be with us again, if you wish." The
second shrouded female form pressed a small cloth bag into his hand as
she floated by. Mahir knew not to look more closely at them, but after
the two figures were out of sight, he opened the bag and examined its
contents. Inside was a very small chip of jade and one white jasmine
blossom. Sheik Kemal had reached out to him and confirmed what
Lateef had reported about the electronic transfer of his reward. Mahir
knew that whatever happened from now on, his family would be provided for. The feminine contact and brief touching of a hand also
excited him with anticipation for a possible return visit to the second
floor chamber in Digos.

Women who were permanent residents of the village remained inside
if they had a place with an inside. The women who had followed their
men from other regions to join the movement stayed hidden within their
personal tents, their chadors, the shapeless cloth sacks that covered
female bodies from head to ankle. Some of the wives did not cover themselves effectively, the mullahs reported, because they did not own
enough cloth; or at least they used that excuse when the temperatures
rose near 100 degrees. Naked arms were exposed and sometimes more
than just their eyes could be seen through the slits in the headscarves.

Aldrin Bumbog, chief of the original NPA faction, left the shade of
the command post when he saw Mahir walking along the street and
moved near him to engage in conversation. The two had spoken only a
few words in their brief prior meetings. To break the ice, he asked the
Turk, "Do you have wives back in your homeland?"

"Yes, I have a wife, and my first son. You must understand, my
country is Muslim, but a modern, progressive Muslim nation. In Turkey,
men are allowed only one wife under our laws."

"That doesn't sound like progress to me. In our new nation, we will
have as many as we can afford." Bumbog sounded irascible for no
apparent reason.

Mahir wanted to keep the tone pleasant and, to show his interest in the culture of his cohort's land, asked, "I thought you were permitted four?"

"Yes, true. But that is all we can afford." Bumbog regained his usual jocular demeanor and attempted a modest humor, "It is better to keep wives some years apart. A man needs an older woman when he is young to teach him, maybe two new ones during middle age for having children, and a young one when he is old, to keep him young. This also is the most convenient solution for the women. If they are with a man who can afford them, they are not forced to marry some tricycle driver."

Bumbog waited for Mahir's response, but receiving none, continued, "I noticed that you observed closely the two young ones walking by. Beware, they are the cousins of Lateef, they are not from here." The warning seemed sincere to Mahir. Obviously, Bumbog could not have known of the intimate contact between Mahir and the girls back in Digos, but the direction of the conversation made him uncomfortable, and he moved to change it.

"Your customs here are different than ours in many ways, although we all follow the law of the true prophet." Mahir was putting the conversation on safer ground.

"Yes, now we read the same words, but it was not always so. Many of our tribes have old ways still. Especially pertaining to the ways of war." Bumbog entered unexplored territory with his new comrade.

"That is usual, there must be a code of honor between men." Falling rain drained mud into the basketball court in front of them as Mahir continued, chanting a hadith almost under his breath. Mahir was a priest, in the sense that all Muslim males are priests, even if not learned in the law. Bumbog did not understand Mahir's intonations but the rhythmic quality of his voice encouraged him to confide further.

"Some of our customs in war you may find strange," Bumbog confided.

"Like what?" Mahir was curious. "In the thousand years of the Turkish Ottoman Empire having ruled most of the Western world, our soldiers encountered many strange cultures. There is nothing they have not experienced and recorded for our scholars. What do you think would surprise me?"

Bumbog paused before he answered. "Tribesmen who eat their dead enemy."

"You mean cannibals?" Mahir was frankly surprised.

"No, no, not exactly, not like I heard about across the water, in Borneo, not as a customary food, and not the entire body. But I know that warriors of the Bilaan, some are with us now in this camp, follow a tribal ritual that includes eating the flesh of their fallen foes."

Mahir did not quite comprehend, "They kill and eat other humans?"

Bumbog was not an expert on this subject, but gave his understanding. "It's like this; they have difficulty taking and keeping prisoners. What would they do with them? In war, they just want to eliminate threats to their own livelihood, or to defend their lands." Bumbog fidgeted, now a bit nervous about revealing these details to a foreigner. He lit another cigarette and tried to explain. "They spear them."

"Spear them? Don't they have guns?" Mahir's curiosity grew.

"Some have rifles, but I have not heard about what happens if they are shot, perhaps it spoils the meat," Bumbog conjectured. He had only heard the stories; his tribe did not engage in the ritual.

"So they spear enemies only in combat?" Mahir had to draw the details out of his comrade.

"No. Not only in war. In the wilderness there is a different law. A man could be speared for stealing another's horse or wife, if the chieftain of his own tribe approves the punishment."

"What, exactly, is spearing?"

"It is a way to keep peace among the rival families. If the thief is speared, a tribal war of vengeance and great loss of life can be avoided. The victim is avenged."

"So spearing is a way to keep peace."

"Yes, in a manner of speaking, peace is the outcome. The evildoer is speared, and his head is immediately cut off. The head is put on a stake in the spot where he was killed for all to see for several days. The victim's abdomen is slashed open, and the heart and liver are removed and wrapped in banana leaves. Only these parts are taken back to the camp of the avenged. The corpse of the dead is not kept for food, but the warriors viciously dismember it and spread it around the stake holding the head. After a few days, there will be no traces remaining in a hot jungle alive with hungry creatures.

"Back in the village, the heart and liver are broiled over charcoal and the warriors paint their bodies and dance around a huge bonfire. When the meat is cooked, it is cut into small slivers that are shared among the tribesmen. The ritual is performed to avenge the offense."

"Can we expect our new recruits to follow these customs now, in combat?"

"Only if it is not convenient to take prisoners. I expect that in combat there will not be time for the proper ceremonies. But if we have a great victory and take captives, there may be an opportunity. It is not a question of lack of food; the Bilaan with us could hunt monkey or take a domestic carabao more easily. But do not be surprised to see a few heads on stakes after the next victorious battle."

The two leaders of the NPA walked to the end of the village and returned along the other side of the one street to the command post. Mehmet Al Zein squatted outside the hut, cleaning dirt off his rifle ammunition and replacing the lightly oiled rounds into one of the three magazines he habitually carried. His rifle was propped against the wall of the hut. It was an unplanned opportunity for the three subordinates of Kumander Ali to talk informally together about their leader.

"Mehmet," Bumbog greeted his contemporary, "do you think you will have a chance to use that weapon soon?"

"If it be the will of God." Al Zein had been focused on his work and had not noticed the two approaching until they were leaning over him. "I hope to use it soon, the sooner the better, tomorrow would be my prayer. Are you as ready as I?"

It was a good question. Both Mahir and Bumbog knew that combat, possibly mortal combat for themselves, could be near, but they had not thought about any definite start date. Kumander Ali had briefed them about his plan for the elections, but military action could happen at any instant, and not always at a time of their choosing. Their enemies might have their own idea about when the next shot would be fired.

The newest warrior among them, Mahir addressed the two seasoned soldiers together. "Kumander Ali now sees us as being united. As the New Peoples Army, we have a chance to defeat the combined Philippine Army and National Police. Their army is better organized than I thought. I saw how they communicated while maneuvering between the rivers. The national police cut off our escape with armed checkpoints on the roads while the army maneuvered effectively in rather difficult terrain. If they can do the same with large forces, it could become challenging for us."

"That was exactly our report to Kumander Ali. He is the leader we have all accepted, and it will be his responsibility to create new tactics. We agreed to subordinate our sovereignty to him for a common cause, but our followers will not wait forever for results. He needs our help now. We must change how we fight if we want to win our freedom." Al Zein gave the opinion he had formed during his long service. He locked a full magazine of ammo into his rifle, fired two shots into the brush to check it, then leaned the weapon back against the wall and stood up to motion the other two to sit with him on the porch. Mahir and Bumbog were willing to consider new strategies with the older warrior.

Al Zein continued. "The AFP might start to launch large preemptive attacks against us, because they must show significant victories to keep the money coming to them from the foreign Jews. If we don't give them a big target, they can't achieve a large victory. Our strategy must be simple: small units of our New Peoples Army should hit many visible targets at the same time—any AFP soldier standing in a post office, a PNP officer directing traffic, a coffee shop with foreigners. Each of these small targets will result in a recognized victory for us. Our patrols will then conceal their weapons and disappear back to their homes, wait, then reach out and strike another target a few days later. We will be impossible to stop."

Mahir asked, "How do we command them? How do we resupply them?"

Bumbog explained for the Turk. "You are new here, we have been practicing for years how to achieve this. We live off the land and the taxes we collect. And the easiest solution is: we do not communicate with each other. After we leave this camp, each of us will return to our origins, but we will resurface again and again as the New Peoples Army. We will prepare for the elections that we know we will win. In the meantime, we will continue attacks against the infidels and the foreigners. Our work does not need to be coordinated."

Al Zein summarized the new strategy of the NPA. "That is the beauty of Ali's plan. That is why I supported him and agreed to accept the NPA label. We do not need to have communication; we do not need to be directed. We will act on our own. There will be no more defeats for us, only victories."

"I am trying to help you make the best of your victories, so you don't need to fight again. I need to change some of the large U.S. dollar bills I have for pesos for our immediate needs and must find a bank that can do that. "Where is the nearest one?" Mahir asked.

Bumbog gave him the directions, "On my way here I passed one. It is near; you can walk there in half an hour, a village named Bual."

Only an hour later, Mahir was leaving the Bual office of the Bank of the Philippines. He saw a fancy truck covered with banana leaves—out of place in this village. He walked down the alley. There were not many vehicles like this one in Mindanao.

Looking in the open window, Mahir saw two new M-16s on the front seat, and a map with circles and lines drawn on it. He knew he had found an enemy vehicle, so he watched it for a while. When Juanito came back from the village and went to sleep in the Pajero, Mahir returned to acquire two more guns for the NPA.

Sleeping in the cab of the Pajero, Juanito never felt the shot that ended his life.

29

Holy Warriors

After their initial military victory in the field, when they surprised Colonel Liu at Koronadal, the Muslim revolution had gained momentum. And Radio Free Mindanao did not report the NPA defeat the following day in the triangle. That unfortunate incident was considered the will of Allah, and best ignored and forgotten. Enshallah. It did not matter. The radio D.J.s and the ulamas continued to report only the earlier victory in detail every hour over the Itig station. Allah Akbar. The NPA owned the radio station now, and every family at home, every customer in open-air *ihaw ihaw* restaurants in the hamlets and the soldiers moving along the roads listened and heard the message. The commentator announced, "No longer is there an MNLF, the Abu Sayaf, or the MILF. From today there is only jihad; we are all mujahadeen. We have one mission, to be independent; we have one leader, Allah Akbar! One name now: New Peoples Army. All strugglers for independence must accept Allah and join the NPA! Libertad!"

The success of the radio station takeover and its aftermath had been spectacular. New NPA recruits were joining up every day and coming to the encampment around Itig. Especially welcomed were the old guard from the NPA who had been fighting for years and had experience and cohesiveness within their small units. Simple farmers turned insurgents had no problem accepting Allah. The tribesmen could still worship their own gods at home, and they viewed Islam as just another religion of the foreigners, as was Christianity in its various and confusing forms with strange rituals. When we die, do we wait for God or Jehovah, or for Allah to judge us? One prophet or the other from the deserts of the West sounded like the same guy to them, but at least this Allah lets us keep our guns and feeds us now, not just after we die, and he provides virgins for us in paradise if we die on jihad.

In addition to the NPA now under arms in the north, the coalition had another 7,000 men added from the MNLF in the western provinces. Kumander Ali hardly knew what to do with them all. The new enlistees would need basic equipment, and they would demand sustenance. Walking up the road in front of him at the moment were more than a hundred new men from what was once a unit of the liberation front, his own former cohorts, now accepting the combined designation of NPA. The men joining them had uniforms of a sort, and almost every one had a rifle.

Moros from the western provinces were dedicated separatists who had resisted the control of Manila for generations. It had taken some of the warriors three days to travel all the way south from the swamplands bounding Lake Lanao, mostly on foot, but part of the distance in inter-city motorized bicycles, spurred on by their increasing sense of urgency and the importance of the mission they shared, and fueled by poverty and desperation.

Ali's face was stern and showed little emotion, but his heart swelled with pride and concomitant responsibility. He was the instigator of all of this. The new troops might not know who he was, but he knew that through the informal layers of leadership, he was their commander. Even Bumbog, the leader of the original NPA, had accepted Ali and was now a loyal lieutenant.

Kumander Ali knew these new soldiers were not well organized and had no discipline and only a shaky chain of command. But if he could assemble them all in one place at one time with guns, and if he could choose that place, he would gain a big advantage over the Tagalogs in Manila. As long as Task Force Davao did not know where he would attack, he would have the initiative again. If he could defeat the Philippine army chasing him, the elections could be held without meaningful interference.

Ali was sure the Manila central government would cave in, and the NPA would win the war. But he would have to fight and win soon; time was not on his side, and without a decisive victory the alliance he had molded would be forced to disband and revert to small unit actions by local cells. They might never again have the chance to mass their combined forces and achieve ultimate victory and freedom. Ali decided to call the tribal leaders and the key men of the New Peoples Army together. This took some rounding up, as not all agreed among themselves who the key men were. But Ali achieved a quorum.

He rejoined Bumbog and the others sitting inside one of the few wooden houses available to them, an old building raised off the ground on stilts with the walls covered with colorful hangings of Maguindinaoan tapestries.

Mahir could hardly comprehend all the enthusiasm for the cause. So many signed up for the cause who were barefoot and skinny little men carrying nothing more than a *malong* sack with some fruit and a few personal belongings, bolos sheathed but sharpened, many of them bringing their wives and sometimes three or four kids under the age of five with them. He asked Lateef, sitting on the porch next to him, "Why, especially after our defeat, are so many new recruits joining up?"

"Brother"—it was only the second time Lateef had addressed Mahir in this familiar way—"these men fight for rice. They have little to lose, and hope we will feed their families and provide candy and cigarettes for them. Most have not heard about what happened to us during the encounter between the rivers, and even if they knew of that defeat, we would still be their best chance for future rice, maybe even rice with viand sometimes."

Mehmet walked up and sat with the other two. He was chewing betel nut, and stains of the red narcotic dribbled down his chin, dropping into bright puddles of tarnish on the dusty floor. He chewed leisurely while he listened to the other two discuss what to do next. He told Mahir, "The genius of Kumander Ali is his ability to see our weaknesses clearly and to turn them into our strengths." It was an eloquent statement of strategy formulation.

"Yes," agreed Mahir. "We have a saying in our country—an army of sheep led by a lion will defeat an army of lions led by a sheep."

"And we have our lion in Kumander Ali. I opposed him before; perhaps as a leader I was a sheep. That is why I agreed to adopt the name of NPA and to put my trust with him." Mehmet's concession was the single most important one that had made the wider revolution possible.

The NPA mujahadeen knew they would eventually have to fight the Philippine forces now approaching them from the south. Feeling the pressure of time, Kumander Ali announced that after the upcoming battle his followers would disperse throughout Mindanao. Operationally mobile groups would return to their home regions and make individual attacks on any government or army facility they could identify as a target. Each local cell would choose its own target. But they would wait for implementation until the decisive date: the 29th of the next month, and the time would be one minute after midnight, the first minute of the historic date, the anniversary of the original founding of the NPA. Ali explained to the newest arrivals that they could either choose to become Muslim or not be included in the new society. It made their choice to accept his plan easy; no single tribal chief could refuse as he would just be replaced by another. So it was no surprise that acceptance by the tribal leaders was unanimous.

After the other leaders had left, Mahir heard Kumander Ali explain to Lateef, "We have money now, but when we spend it, we will have it no more. Then the situation will go back to exactly what it was last year. These people will be back in their fields and villages, and nothing will have changed.

"Those who do not join us now will find their brothers will have taken over their lands and their homes, maybe even their wives, when they get home with no money or power. So they join." Kumander Ali presented his very logical plan.

Lateef understood the rationale, "We will have a local chieftain on our side in every village. All together that constitutes a new nation. We will have won."

"Our radio is reporting all good news." By saying the word "independence" and not being contradicted, Kumander Ali had solidified his position as leader of the combined and renamed NPA. "And we have named a specific date for elections."

Mahir was still dubious and asked, "Elections? How can you organize elections?"

Ali spoke tangentially, not directly answering Mahir, gazing around the room. "It is time I delegate leadership. Lateef, you have agreed to drop the Abu Sayaf name. For this, I want you to lead the military effort. Mahir, you will be one of his lieutenants."

"I cannot. I do not know this land, the languages, or this people." Mahir stood up to object. "I was not NPA, not MNLF, I am a Turk. These *peoples* with so many tribes, languages and cultures, are difficult to lead. Any military leader would have the same problem. I cannot lead them. I have little real combat experience, less here."

Ali was surprised by Mahir's reluctance, and did not respond immediately. Then he picked up the conversation again in a way that gave Mahir confidence. "I will command. But I need leaders of men in combat. You are better than most, and you speak English, which gives you an aura most others do not have. It overcomes tribal rivalries because it demonstrates that you are not from a rival tribe. My decision is easy for me. You must lead an important part of our army.

"I will be occupied with more important matters. I *will* organize the elections, and be elected." Kumander Ali continued. "Mahir, you will safeguard the money to be certain I win. I will name the polling places and appoint our representatives at each place to collect the ballots and to pay those who vote. Each man on our list will receive an American ten-dollar bill as he leaves the voting place. That is more than a week's wages for most of them, if any had work before. Women will not vote, of course; and the men not on our list will be talked to and discouraged, or rather explained the realities of living in their villages after the election with our men mixed together with them. And we *must* get the men back to their villages, away from our camps, as soon as we achieve one decisive military action in the field. We cannot support them very long, but our troops must think we can. That is why we will give each voter real money, dollars that circulate freely in their world, so the men will vote."

"I thought my duty was done when I delivered the money to you. Now you are trusting me to give it all away for you." Mahir said. "I expected to be leaving tomorrow." Mahir was still debating his options, looking for Ali to say something that would make his decision to stay easier.

"You will get a great reward; now, here, back in your home, and in paradise. I have already confirmed to Sheik Kemal that you have done your job. I had a man go to the Internet café in the village and send an e-mail to him. He has acknowledged receipt. Now this you do for Allah. Not for personal vanity, but to stop starvation, not just for this one time but for the future. When we win the election, this huge fruit farm called Mindanao will belong to us. We will feed the people, and we will be rich ourselves, not the Chinese of Davao or the Tagalog of Manila, not the Jew or the American. The wealth of the land will belong to us. As the Emir of Mindanao, I will assign to you personally the rights to all of Europe for the export of the fruits of this land, the fruit of our victory. We will construct a new port in Cotobato City, and I will own that port personally." Kumander Ali had not really thought out a national development plan to be implemented after their anticipated victory. He was creating it as he spoke; the ideas seemed to come to him directly from Allah.

As the leaders debated, more wet and exhausted troops straggled into Itig village to join the NPA. They needed rest and food after the long distances they had moved on foot during the last week. The NPA would have to establish a more permanent headquarters than they had in the triangle. Many more recruits would be moving in from Agusan and the Moro territories around Lake Lanao, and Kumander Ali would need to find a place for them.

From the position he had staked out for himself, Mahir watched at least seventy new men, with their wives, kids and pigs, who had set up shelters in the area around the radio station. About half had guns, the others carried a bolo of some sort. In his new role as exchequer for the NPA, he had the authority to pass out some of the pesos he had obtained at the bank in Bual. He gave each man a hundred pesos and a few pesos to some of the soldiers' wives to buy rice. They would surely remember when it came time to vote.

Two men came in from the jungle, carrying between them and lashed upside down on a pole a medium-sized male monkey, the whites of his eyes twinkling brilliant in the dusk. They made a fire while the monkey watched, terrified, head turning quickly back and forth, still tied to the stick, now stuck upright in the ground. When the fire died down to a bed of coals, they disemboweled the monkey, but retained the head on the carcass because the brains would be a delicacy of good eating after all the hair burned off and the body was roasted, the meat tasting sweet, the skin crispy. Some Muslims were invited to join the group but all refused tactfully, citing their religious taboos. Since more than enough goats were available to feed everybody well, nobody went hungry.

The armed camp grew quiet. Mist began to rise off the ground and the rich aroma of cooked meat hung amid the sounds of sleep. The New Peoples Army was ready.

30

Buluwan

Lake Buluwan is a shallow inland lake, a depression on a plateau filled by muddy streams running out of the surrounding mountains and rimmed by swampland on the three lower sides sloping away from mountains lesser than Mount Apo. Apo, literally "Honored One" in the Visayan dialect, dominates the topography of southwestern Mindanao as Fujiyama does central Japan. Apo rules his land.

Colonel Reginald Liu's Task Force Davao would again engage the NPA, now settling in a few miles to the north, but this time a reinforced and reorganized force would exploit the expected victory. Liu had been inspecting his troops at dawn when he was called to the telephone line he had hard-wired into the command post. It was Martin Galan, calling from Manila. Liu was able to report his limited success in the field. Galan listened to the entire report, then said, "Reggie, you have to do more, opposition to our president is growing in the senate, and the United States is pulling back from giving unconditional support. They say they are our allies, but their president has his own problems with global terrorism, and the American voters are tired of the casualty reports coming in from Iraq. Their ambassador has informed me the U.S. can only guarantee new military aid if we demonstrate that we can win the conflict that is now going on in the field, and win big, soon. They won't trickle in more aid if we get into a stalemate."

"Yes, sir, I hear you. But the insurgency of the Bangsomoro communists has gone on for a long time, and the Americans know all about it." Liu questioned his boss, "How can they expect us to change history overnight? What's new?"

"What's new, Reggie, is that we have all run out of time. The electorates of both countries don't understand what you're up against out there in the field. Now listen to me, you get this revolution ended immediately, and then report back to me so I can take positive news to the president and congress. And don't take this the wrong way. I'm not angry with you, but don't call me back with bad news. The rebels are in your area. Get to them and take them out!"

"As I told you before, I will need more troops and artillery, you know. I am already chasing a huge force that far outnumbers my one battalion of troops. You want miracles tomorrow, try sending reinforcements today!"

"I did." Galan replied. "They're on the way now. More than a colonel normally commands, but you will still be the overall commander of the task force." It was a significant commitment from the National Security Advisor to put Liu in command of a much larger force.

"I fully understand, Martin. And thanks." Liu did not often use Galan's first name in formal communication.

"Good luck, Reggie." Galan recognized in his comrade's tone their sharing of mutual trust, and closed quietly with, "Until we meet again." Colonel Liu had his marching orders.

Leaving his command post a few hours later, he saw white thunderheads billowing high above the horizon, a sign of the rainstorm certain to drench them in the afternoon when the bright day dulled. A jeep approached the command post, driving up the highway. Behind it, canvas-covered trucks towing artillery pieces came into view. The lead jeep stopped.

The officer riding shotgun addressed Liu, "Lieutenant Colonel De la Rosa reporting, sir." Salutes were exchanged. "Where should we deploy?" The reinforcements promised by Galan were moving in.

"North of Lake Buluwan and east of this highway—where you can cover the area from Mount Apo to Itig," Liu instructed the commander of the 3rd Battalion, 21st Field Artillery of the AFP. He stood tall by the highway with his hands on his hips as three batteries of 105mm Howitzers, eighteen pieces of light artillery, were pulled north.

While Liu was admiring the last of the artillery units, another jeep bounced forward over the ruts, and Liu was soon instructing a full colonel of infantry to follow De la Rosa's into positions adjacent to the artillery. Although they were both full colonels, the infantry commander had saluted Liu first and called him sir. They both knew who was in charge of whatever was going to happen next; Galan obviously had sent the message through channels that this was Liu's show. Sweat began to soak through the underarms of his uniform, and it was more than the heat of the day that caused his perspiration.

Liu felt his spirits rise. With bigger authority came bigger responsibilities—and bigger opportunities for success. He started to cross the road, then fell back to watch the rest of the infantry brigade move forward, some in trucks, most on foot. Altogether, over a thousand armed soldiers would be in the infantry brigade that Liu would have available to him. During the next twenty-four hours, two more infantry brigades checked in, their commanders reporting to Liu, and were assigned positions farther north, near the highway, with logistical tails running back to the port of General Santos City. Liu was in command of a force exceeding a full division of infantry, reinforced, and he ended the day walking among his new troops, his insignia of rank unnoticed in the dark.

* * *

The sun rises quickly near the equator. The early rays of the new day's sun reflected off the polished steel breech locks of the artillery pieces when the crews opened them for Colonel Liu's morning inspection. He trooped the line of six of the howitzers with their crews lined up and at silent attention in their positions. He went on to visit two more batteries and then the adjacent headquarters of the infantry brigades.

He was pleased at the quiet efficiency of the newly arrived units. Boxes of ammunition were stacked within a few steps of the howitzers, and beside each stack two rounds were already out of the ammo boxes, the brass-tipped detonators shimmering in the sun, ready to ignite their explosive centers on target. During his inspection tours, the only sounds were the peaceful bells of a Catholic church calling its congregation to early morning Mass and the slow wail of an imam's chant in Arabic, broadcast from speakers wired into the turret of a mosque in the same village, a village where Christians and Muslims had lived in peace for centuries until both factions began to get help from foreigners.

The commander had asked the leaders of his subordinate units to meet him in the mess tent for breakfast. Major Hayes was already there—it seemed to Colonel Liu that the American officer was always around his headquarters—and his own officers filled the tent. When he sat down in front of the large map and a blackboard, he told his officers to relax and to smoke with their coffees, if they wished.

Having arrived early, Major Hayes had a good seat, away from the smokers and beside Colonel Liu's chair. Before the Colonel started the meeting, Hayes took him aside, "Colonel, I have news. Our intelligence has discovered that the main NPA force has relocated out of the triangle and moved into Itig village."

Liu was silent for a moment while it sunk in. "Hum. Logical. They want to use the radio station, so they'll need to defend it, to put their headquarters there. It will be a nice target, easy for my artillery to determine the exact coordinates."

Liu stood up to address the officers, but when Radio Free Mindanao began the news on the half hour he turned up the volume and tuned in the rogue station so they could all hear.

The commentator reported, "The combined power of the Abu Sayaf with our friends the MNLF have joined forces with our brothers of the NPA, and all those who accept the true God and will declare their faith in public on election day. They will be the ones who will share the riches of our new nation. Together we will drive the foreign soldiers out of Mindanao. Thirty days from today elections will be held in your village.

Vote for your voice in the new Islamic Republic of Mindanao. Our leg-islature will convene in Zamboanga City on the tenth day after that, our new nation, Enshallah, will no longer pay taxes to others. And what we can change in the Philippines; others can change in the world." The announcer went on to explain the rationale; if the U.S. could invade Iraq and call elections, then the Abu Sayaf and their local supporters, now growing in number, could call elections in Mindanao.

The Itig radio station held by the NPA had announced, in effect, inde-pendence from the Republic of the Philippines, and amplified their proclamation with this shocking call to elections. A copy of the broad-cast would be on its way electronically to Manila within the minute, and copies would also be sent directly to General Hargens and Charlie Downs in Washington. Twelve time zones from Mindanao in either direction, the Chairman of the U.S. Joint Chiefs of Staff would hear it on his way to the Pentagon from his home in Fairfax Station, Virginia. It would get to the Oval Office, and the president would not be happy. In America, the turmoil would cause critics to question the direction the president was taking his nation. "Why is he getting us involved in another Iraq?" they would question. The Mindanao war could con-tribute to regime change in more than one country.

For the next hour, Liu listened to the recommendations of the other officers as they discussed various alternatives and courses of action. "We don't know exactly what we're up against at Itig, but it's big and getting bigger," Liu continued his briefing. "Before we finalize our plan and commit our main force to combat, Captain Bautista, get together a patrol of experienced men and probe the area around the radio station. Move toward the center of the NPA encampment without starting a real engagement. Approach as close as you can, determine the strength of their forces, fire some rounds at likely targets, and report what you get fired back at you."

Hayes turned to Liu. "I see by the number of new troops and artillery that you have chosen the second option."

Colonel Liu let him guess. "Which is?"

"You've massed your firepower; you're going for the big kill."

Liu answered him briefly, as he would be laying out his strategy in a few minutes to his staff in any case. "You got it. No more playing around. After almost forty years, their time is past," referring to his NPA enemy. "This will be the last time they celebrate the anniversary of their founding."

Then Hayes made his request tactfully. "I'd like to see your men in action on this one."

"OK with me, Major, but stay out of the way. You're already a nice, big target, so don't become a nice big problem, if you know what I mean." Liu had other things to worry about.

Against Liu's advice, Hayes decided to go along on Captain Bautista's patrol. As it turned out, he should have listened to the colonel.

31

Death and Virtue

Mahir and Kumander Ali entered a house beside a crudely constructed communal basketball court in the center of Itig town. They stood on the open-sided, raised platform porch comfortably shaded by a thatched roof of woven *anahaw* leaves. From their elevation they could see the intersection below them where a heavily traveled footpath crossed the road leading up a slight incline into Itig. With binoculars, Ali observed two of Liu's scouts standing near their jeep at the intersection, looking in the town's direction.

After a few minutes, a jeep appeared to pick up the scouts and return to their headquarters in time for their meal and to report that there was a straight, open avenue of approach leading directly to the radio station.

Squatting on the porch, the two NPA leaders spoke in English, the common denominator for communication. They both knew that the Philippine army would soon be coming after them and the radio station. "Brother Mahir, I trust you to protect the station while I am meeting with the tribal leaders. I have to get them started back to their villages with the money to pay the voters before election day," Ali told Mahir.

Mahir had achieved the mission he was paid to do—deliver the money to the leaders—but he had been offered a chance to accomplish much more and to embarrass the Philippine government and their foreign allies as a side benefit. The idea appealed to him, and he had his opportunity to commit to jihad, to gain favor with Allah. He had come a long way to leave too soon, so he had accepted Ali's order to lead a unit made up of recently recruited members of the NPA.

Mahir had begun to believe in a greater moral mission. Kumander Ali was vocal in his condemnation of the Philippine president for his personal support of the PSI, the Proliferation Security Initiative. The current president and recent ones before him had unintentionally justified the cause of the insurrection by involving foreign nations in their earlier negotiations with the MNLF and NPA. What happened in Mindanao was none of the business of the foreign capitalists. Mahir wondered how America would react if Russian paratroopers jumped into Arizona to enforce the rights of native American Indians? Now the ironic result of Manila's request for foreigners to help them fight their own countrymen would be the launching of a movement whose inevitable climax would be the achievement of an independent Mindanao.

After Ali retired inside the hut, Mahir found Lateef, who was trying to charge his cell phone, but there was no electricity in the village this week. Lateef was privy to Kumander Ali's ideas and intentions, and Mahir wanted to sound him out. With Lateef were three of his long-time followers, telling obscene jokes about Ugly Maria, how she looked and how she died. Lateef wanted them to change the subject and asked them for ideas about how to collect more revenue after they had control of the province. One of the men suggested burning buses that were engaged in intercity transportation; after a few buses were burned—they would let the passengers out first, of course—the bus companies would agree to pay revolutionary taxes that the new NPA government would levy on each trip, to be collected in cash from the driver at checkpoints. It was a solid plan, the man thought. For certain, Lateef needed cash to support his three wives and their extended families down through second cousins; he was the patriarch, and none of them had ever worked for pay. He and the cause could use extra revenue in the future, after the Syrian investment capital had been spent on the election. Lateef supported the suggestion, and added, "To collect revolutionary taxes, I recommend we blow up some of the heavy equipment of the international mining companies working in the Compostela Valley. That will get them to pay quickly." The strategists turned to quiet contemplation.

Mahir took the opportunity to ask Lateef, "Why does Kumander Ali trust me, why does he assign me, a foreigner, to a position of command?"

Lateef was pleased to fill in the blanks. "Kumander Ali is turning over tactical leadership for an important mission to you, Brother Mahir, because you are an ideal leader," Lateef told him. "You are more educated than most of us. And you speak Arabic and English, which will be very useful as our new nation grows in the future. But most of all because you chose to stay with us and share our struggle. Now that you are one of us, you should choose a new code name, perhaps an English alias, so we will know what to call our Turkish brother."

Mahir decided instead that he would insist that his men all address him simply as Brother. Many chieftains, even those leading only a few of their tribesmen, liked to make up tough, Hollywood-sounding nicknames, like Kumander or Commander, but as a leader he would not choose such a new name; he liked the sound of Brother in this foreign land. He had an important assignment. He commanded a unit of the newly forged NPA alliance. It was a big job.

The number of warriors was increasing by the hour as new recruits, usually groups of five to ten at a time, continued to show up. Bright smiles glowed as the campfire coals reflected enthusiasm and commitment. At home they were big fish in little ponds. Kumander Ali let them all believe that they were in charge and herded them into a loose order of battle by assigning campfire sites. Enough of them were spread around at least to protect Ali's personal headquarters from surprise.

When the minor leaders appeared at Kumander Ali's headquarters, each of them expecting to assume command, he entertained them with betel nut chews and warm Coca Cola, and then made his speech. "Be aware of the tricks of the devil. The Americans want to talk to us because they are losers. We have started a war we will win, and then we must build our nation. Get rid of the foreigners, make your swords drip with their blood, move forward with God's blessing." He gave them each a banded stack of a few hundred-dollar bills, suggesting that they share it with their followers, after exchanging the large foreign notes into pesos at a good rate. The impressed tribal leaders hastily departed with their stash as the twilight would soon turn into night. Thoughts of combat leadership were quickly forgotten, as the faction chiefs were anxious to get away before their followers heard about the windfall.

While passing into the street after counting his money, one of the important chiefs slipped his roll of cash into the crotch of his briefs, to make it more secure in case he was accosted. Realizing that he might have been observed, he made a pretense of scratching himself in various places. To complete a façade of poor personal hygiene, he made exaggerated and noisy gestures of blowing his nose into the nearby gutter where slimy water flowed slowly. He then proceeded along his way, satisfied that no one would suspect that he carried so much wealth. He felt proud about his role and his high position in the NPA hierarchy.

Distracted by the negotiations of the afternoon, Ali was not aware that Task Force Davao was on the move until Lateef informed him that forward sentries had seen movement below. Ali ordered Lateef to organize a defense immediately.

Lateef's men got lucky. They blended into the tree line below Itig town and parallel to the sugar cane field that Captain Agustin had been ordered to cross with one of the platoons from his infantry company to probe the NPA perimeter. The NPA outposts had been well instructed this time; they were ordered not to fire until Lateef fired his pistol, or they would lose a week's incentive pay of candy bars for firing too early. This was a serious threat; they held their fire.

Hayes was close to Captain Agustin as they moved forward, expecting eventually to find a guard leaning against a tree and smoking somewhere, if he was awake. But Hayes was surprised when he heard a single .45 pistol shot, followed by a hail of hostile bullets. The task force probe had been successful. Ironically, Agustin's men found the enemy, but not surreptitiously; they had been found first. Agustin's men had advanced too far forward without cover and too quickly. They were forced to back away, unaware that Mahir's NPA fire team was positioned behind a wooden pole fence outlining the field.

Major Hayes jumped away from his position and sprinted for cover away from his unseen adversaries. But an Abu Sayaf sniper fired at him and a rifle bullet hit his leg, breaking the thighbone. Hayes had been told to remain out of the line of possible fire, but because he was too far on the flank, the patrol could not rescue him while they themselves were doing the low crawl under a fusillade fired over their heads by Lateef's irregulars.

Lateef's fire team leader on the left flank saw Hayes go down, and went to end his pain and noise, but seeing that he was an American officer, thought Kumander Ali might have a better use for him, alive. He ordered two of his riflemen to wrap the American in a cloth sack and drag him back to headquarters. They tied up his wound, but did not set the broken bone sticking out through his torn trouser leg, thus they only succeeded in stopping him from bleeding to death for the time being.

Captain Agustin, after learning that Major Hayes' body had been recovered by the hostile forces, decided to advise Colonel Liu immediately on this sudden development. As soon as there was radio contact, Agustin reported, "Cardinal 6, this is Cardinal 3, observer probable KIA, body carried back by withdrawing NPA, over."

Colonel Liu understood. "Damn," he said out loud to no one in particular, "they've killed or captured Hayes. What an awful mess. I gotta get him back." And he then went back on his radio, this time to De la Rosa's artillery. "Redfire 6, this is Cardinal 6, Fire Mission, over."

They exchanged call signs and protocol, and Liu ordered, "Give me one volley of high explosive, 100 meters due south of Itig, Charlie one six four, over."

"Roger, Cardinal 6, on the way," reported the fire direction center. A minute later six artillery rounds exploded on target, but also right on the STAGCOM position.

"What the hell!" Starke yelled as the first round exploded.

Thornton knew what it was. "Damn him, Liu's started too soon again. Our surprise is ruined. We'll have to move forward. Let's get the hell outta here!"

Behind the first explosion, Thornton saw the NPA withdrawing and fired at them with his carbine. Like it or not, the battle had begun and they were suddenly in the middle of it as more rounds exploded all around them. Elaiza motioned the other Otazas forward to follow her. An NPA soldier rushed them while Thornton was kneeling near her firing his rifle, but Elaiza shot their attacker with her pistol full in the chest just as Thornton fired at a charging enemy behind her. Their eyes met in a microsecond—thank you—and then the second round of Liu's artillery hit, and with a whoop and a flash both of them were thrown up into the air, Elaiza disappearing behind a ball of fire and smoke. Pedro tackled Thornton, whose clothing was on fire, and wrestled him to the ground, rolling him to put out the flames.

"Pedro, let me up," Thornton was still dazed, but keenly aware of what had happened. "I've got to find Elaiza!"

"She's gone," was all Pedro could say. Thornton charged into the area of the blast's impact, but there was nothing to see, and he collapsed in shock and sorrow.

32

Martyrs

They gave Major Hayes an aspirin and drinking water, hoping to keep him alive; perhaps he could be traded for something. But if he died, at least his corpse would be an embarrassment to the Americans and his death in a battle with the AFP would prove to voters in the coming election that the capitalist Americans were supporting the Tagalogs in oppressing the poor farmers of Mindanao. Hayes regained consciousness at times during the night, smelling the aroma of rotting jungle undergrowth and camp refuse. But the smell of his own clotted blood and the decomposition of his festering wound forewarned him of the distinct possibility of gangrene and a short future, which could end in the Philippine jungle. He spent the night in and out of consciousness, in and out of pain.

The leaders were moderately surprised when Mahir walked into camp leading Elaiza on a rope tied around her neck, her hands bound in front of her. She did not seem special to them, just another woman,

probably one of the girls who did the cooking for the American tres-
passers. He untied her hands and put her with their other captive. They
would find a use for her.

In a moment of awareness, Hayes thought, "Does it matter? Does
anyone care? Does it make a difference if my name will be carved on a
stone memorial somewhere in Manila, or maybe just a photograph with
a heroic caption hung perpetually on the embassy wall after my body is
shipped back to Harlingen for my wife and kids to bury?"

He thought he was dreaming. Suddenly a woman was sitting beside
him; he recognized her. He mumbled a name Elaiza did not understand,
" . . . is it you?" he heard himself asking.

"Major Hayes, what have they done to you?" Elaiza tried to comfort him.

Recognition finally dawned. "Oh. Elaiza. Most of this I did to myself.
I should not be here." Hayes looked down at the plastic tape that tied his
hands. "What happened to you?"

"I'm OK. You're a mess. Don't blame yourself for what these hoodlums have done to you." Elaiza's hands were free, but one of her legs
was tied firmly to a tree on a long leash, and the armed guard who
watched them both prevented any escape. She sat by Hayes and put her
hand on his forehead.

Hayes flinched. He tried to control his pain and told Elaiza, "There
was a time before, during the first Gulf War, when I almost died in
combat. I wish I had. Am I going to die now? How would my life have
unfolded if I hadn't gone on that patrol for my idle curiosity? I don't
want my family to know how I died."

"I'll tell them,"–Elaiza looked into his eyes and touched his chin to
make him look at her–"I'll tell them the way you'd want me to." From
the way she said it, Hayes now knew he would never see them again.

Walking between the shacks carrying a cup of Nescafé, Kumander Ali
looked down at Hayes. Ali was preoccupied with planning what to do
now that he knew the Filipinos had located his headquarters. Would
they get the Americans to call in an air strike? He had heard about so-
called smart bombs which could be quietly guided downward from
unseen aircraft thousands of feet above the clouds, accurately impacting
in the common area of the camp, even before his men could leave the
area. While random ideas like these bounced around in his head, he

decided to relocate most of his military force after reeducating them with his philosophy. Then they could scatter back to their villages with money in their hands and a list of approved voters in their pockets.

Ali did not want the eternal responsibility for feeding his followers and the entourages they had brought with them on the trek. It was one thing to join up with the movement; it was another thing to live off of it. He heard but could not see a jet fly over; it was too low to be a commercial liner on a flight path into the airport at Koronadal, and too high to have seen them, unless there were some new optical technologies the Philippine Air Force had that he did not know about. Now he heard fixed-wing military aircraft whirring in the distance parallel to the coast, while two helicopters chop-chopped in the opposite direction low over the palms. He was beginning to suspect all sounds.

Mahir went over to Hayes and looked at his wound but did not touch him or his bandaged leg, tied with what was really more of a tourniquet than a bandage. The flesh had turned a speckled black below where the wound was tied off to keep blood from pumping out, probably early symptoms of gangrene.

"What does it all mean?" Mahir thought, but only asked Hayes in English, "Are you happy to die here?"

"You, Brother, have the power to let him live." Elaiza was still beside Hayes.

"Shut up, woman!" Mahir was not interested in some female's ideas about brotherhood.

"I am not happy to die anywhere just yet," Hayes answered his captor with a surly and proud, slightly crooked smile, "but I may not get my wish."

Mahir observed more than spoke, "I think you will get your chance to meet your God soon, whether it is your wish or not." He could not help throwing out his question, almost rhetorically, "Was it worth it to you?"

Hayes did not give Mahir the satisfaction of hearing his doubt, but thought, "It doesn't seem so now, but it did before. Most men dying in combat die suddenly, without having a chance to think about it; their decisions were made in their minds long before they found themselves faced with the choice." The single aspirin was not doing much good; thank God the bandage was tight. It throbbed, but it would hurt worse if blood were allowed to pump into the dying flesh. The blood vessels in his leg were lying open, and Elaiza chased away the fat, black flies attracted to the wound.

Seeing life begin to slip from his captive's grasp, Mahir thought about his own wife and son, their own future. Why take chances? He had enough now to live his dream, their dreams together. Why can man not quit when he is ahead and just live his life? Why waste it on these hopeless souls and their desperate dreams?

Neither Mahir nor Hayes would ever know the answers to the questions they were asking themselves and each other.

Mahir did not stop Elaiza from ministering to Hayes. He just left them alone.

Two women were preparing lunch for their men in a grassy patch between the huts. They had carrots today, and they peeled the skins of the vegetables and fed them to the goats. Waiting for the food to cook, a naked child defecated while several piglets waited in anticipation for him to finish. Mahir wondered why, in a society that is underfed to the point of malnutrition, the part of the vegetable that contains the most nutrients and vitamins would be discarded. They were lucky today also to have rice with the vegetables—rice steamed in covered cooking pots, rice that was imported from Vietnam, the new breadbasket of Southeast Asia. The Philippines, with all its rainfall and tropical heat and once an exporter of the grain, could no longer grow enough rice to feed its own population; land usage was being converted to more valuable crops, like banana and mango, for export to Japan and Europe. Mindanao was a fruit basket, but for the NPA in bivouac such delicacies were hard to locate, and they ate what they found. Mahir saw the impossibility of the NPA cause in this vignette; these were the lucky ones, those who had rice today. Go ahead, let them vote, nothing will change, nothing matters.

Mahir told the women to give a bowl of their rice to Elaiza. She fed it all to Hayes, except for a few spoonfuls she fed to a wounded enemy soldier propped on the other side of the tree. The latter was a human being too, and he was her countryman.

Mahir leaned against the pole holding up the corner of the tent in front of Ali's headquarters. After watching the two for a while in thought, he said to Hayes, "You have come here for an evil purpose, and you will die knowing you have died stupidly for an evil cause."

"Evil is blowing up a synagogue. Stupidity is blowing it up on a Friday, when no Jews are present, killing only your own Muslim brothers. Stupidity is blowing up a workers' barracks in Saudi Arabia, not knowing that the Americans had moved out of it two years before. Even if you think I'm evil, you must know that you are fighting for a stupid cause, and you must live knowing that." Hayes' answer to Mahir just came out spontaneously. He had not even thought about the flawed logic of his enemy before in the exact words that conveyed his thoughts, since "stupid" was a word that hit hard in this culture, especially when the hearer knew it was true.

The day became hotter, and more flies gathered. Hayes' presence was beginning to irritate his captors. Lateef approached where Mahir was standing and discreetly took charge of the situation. He ordered the guard watching Elaiza to tie her hands again and push a ball of cloth into her mouth and tape it in place. They had heard enough from the woman.

Lateef was more experienced in these matters than Mahir. Under Ali's orders, he cut the tourniquet and Hayes twitched as blood seeped rather than pulsed out of his limp body. The suddenness of the pain caused by the blood flowing into crushed muscles brought him back to life enough to say through dry lips, "I thought Allah did not allow the killing of innocent people."

Lateef was the one to answer, irritated at the insolence, "Allah does not allow the killing of innocent people, but you are a killer, and the Koran teaches that killers should be killed."

"Then you are not a true Muslim, you who pretend to be a judge, you who permit violence to guide your life." Hayes could act as judge as well as Lateef and Ali.

But Ali had already determined that since Hayes had little time to live, no matter what happened, he wanted to get the most leverage possible from his death, an event sure to stir up the Americans. Better to be proactive, execute him rather than let him die, get some good press out of it. Lateef moved Hayes inside the radio station and tied him to a stool.

Hayes' execution was broadcast in a dramatic special presentation on Radio Free Mindanao—not like the executions of infidels shown on pre-recorded videotape by Middle East TV networks. Native music set the tone and commentary continued on the air. Hayes could not be heard saying anything that seemed intelligible, but it did mean something when the embassy labs studied the recording later. The description of the proceedings was narrated in detail by the announcer, saying, "This is how we deal with nonbelievers who oppose us." Listeners heard the surreal rustlings of preparation, a stool moving on a concrete floor, steel chinking on steel, muscles moving against muscles, a muted chop, than another, a chair falling and muffled noises, people talking calmly in stage whispers, then silence. The images were more powerful imagined than when actually seen.

33

Radio Free Mindanao

For his breakfast the day after Hayes had been executed, Mahir cracked an egg and dropped it into a frying pan sizzling with cooking oil; the yolk broke and spread out crackling into a shapeless mass. He watched the sibilantly cooking egg and thought it a premonition. It seemed to resemble Mindanao on the map—a raised irregular formation in the center and bubbling arms reaching out into the turbulent sea around it, one arm reaching south toward Sabah, North Borneo, the other arm arching north toward Leyte in the Philippine Sea, with scattered island globules swimming alone in a boiling sea of fat. Mahir saw the NPA and himself snapping and sputtering against the inevitable, a foreboding of the approaching battle.

From the way Kumander Ali analyzed the situation of the New Peoples Army, they could not maintain a large army in the field for very long, but paradoxically they needed a large army to defeat Task Force Davao, which, unknown to him, was being augmented every hour with more infantry and light artillery.

Mahir found it easier to converse with Kumander Ali when Lateef was present, as a catalyst. So later that day he asked Lateef to go with him for a meeting with Ali. Mahir wanted to know what Ali intended to do now that their positions had been probed by the AFP task force. He thought the major attack was likely to happen soon, given the events of the last few days. The Americans had not yet responded to the humiliating execution of one of their officers, but the international news networks had been reporting his execution every hour after editing out the horrific sounds of his death. If Kumander Ali had wanted to make news with the manner of Hayes' death, he had certainly succeeded. In Mahir's view, if Kumander Ali took advantage of the NPA's superior strength in numbers that he enjoyed at the present moment, including the large army of new recruits, and threw the whole mass at the task force before more troops or even the Americans were brought in, he would have the advantage and a good chance to win. But he would have to act soon.

Kumander Ali, drinking his coffee from a worn-out Styrofoam cup smudged with muddy fingerprints, flipped his cigarette butt into the street. As Lateef and Mahir walked up the steps of the hut to join him on the porch, he lit another and casually offered smokes to them also— a welcome luxury, American brand cigarettes for a change, Marlboros made in the Philippines and recently seized from a merchant at a roadblock as a tax payment to the revolution. Lateef squatted down and turned his baseball cap around backwards, looking like a malnourished Latino player on the farm club of a major league team. Mahir squatted on the porch floor as there were no chairs outside; in fact there were no chairs inside, just three benches around the square table where Ali had spread out the map. They were all silent; the presence of his two subordinates seemed to indicate their curiosity about what Ali planned next, and they impatiently waited for him to get to the point where he was ready to talk.

Ali knew about the supposedly secret but openly obvious presence of American army combat troops in Mindanao. He began by telling Mahir, "If we can get the wavering Yankees to waver more, we can get them off this island and end outside influence on our culture."

"But I am also an outside influence." Mahir wondered what Ali really thought about him. "I brought in money, just like they do, the only difference is I carried it in cash. Obviously, if they know about me, I am a target for an American hit squad or an air attack for bringing in the money."

"Be sure you are, and I'm also a logical target because I'm the chief initiator bringing the Abu Sayaf and the NPA together," Ali said.

Ali sensed their unspoken questions. "Our war for Mindanao must be seen as universal, not just a local disagreement between neighbors." He knew generally that independent Islamic cells would also be waging jihad in other countries soon. "If Allah permits me, I will destroy the pride of the Yankees and Zionists who are responsible for this war." He flipped another cigarette butt into the street.

Mahir, the foreigner, added his perspective. "The world is momentarily mesmerized by images of American dead sons on television. They will have no stomach to continue a war that has no purpose for them. You don't even have oil here for them to take, only tuna fish and pineapples."

"We must define the cause not only for ourselves, but in the eyes of our enemy," said Ali, becoming as animated as Lateef had ever seen. "We must apply *ijtihad,* the critical thinking process taught by the Prophet, and determine our actions within the teachings of the Prophet. Study the book!"

For Lateef, the argument seemed simple. He saw no reason for academic debate. "There is no way to interpret the Koran except literally. It tells us whoever offends the Koran will die by the sword; he who defends it will live in paradise."

Mahir reminded them, "The Koran prohibits killing children, herdsmen or unarmed men, so we must be careful how we employ our power. I don't like the way the American captive was executed. I can't accept such actions."

"You don't understand the politics of Islam," Ali lectured him. "The West has combined their president and their pope to unite against us. The Yankees have brought in military police trained in Iraq to lead the PNP and the AFP. Their actions justify our reaction."

For another half-hour and two more rounds of cigarettes the dialogue continued. Ali's new comrades Aldrin Bumbog and Mehmet Al Zein showed up at the shack unexpectedly and joined the others on the porch. Ali took the newcomers inside where they sat down on the slatted, rough rattan benches to study the map for a while. After talking with each other quietly and continuously about their problems with camp life, Lateef invited them back to the porch and passed around a liter bottle of Fundador.

Alcohol was permitted only to Islamic warriors fighting in holy war, according to Lateef, who liked brandy and sometimes made on-the-spot interpretations of the rules based upon how he perceived the immediate situation. Alcohol was not the only personal problem Lateef had. Most of his other difficulties were in the relationships between himself and his three wives—such problems as how to manage the money he would bring home after this current undertaking. He was not looking forward to those discussions.

Kumander Ali, unable to read the Koran in Arabic, improvised his own interpretations, stretching the limits of his intellect and knowledge to fill in where he was short on dogma. "We will have justice. In one month, we will be able to follow strictly the laws of the Koran and no longer work for foreigners. Their laws will no longer be needed; we need only the law of the Koran and the codes written there. All will embrace the faith." Some of this came from his memory of the teachings of the ulamas in his village when he was young.

His speech interested Bumbog as well as Mehmet. Bumbog stated a long-standing problem in his area: "Large tracts of our land are already occupied by Christians, and ownership of tribal lands has been transferred to corporations that mass-cultivate it with cash crops. We have no place to hunt or plant, and every year they extend their fence lines."

Ali seized the moment. "The Manila government of the north asks us to renounce terrorism as a condition for their cease-fire. How do we respond?" he asked in a raised voice.

"With blood, Ali, with their blood, O Ali!" was the enthusiastic response from the four listeners. Passersby in the street joined in the clamor and fired a few shots into the air, a practice Kumander Ali immediately stopped. They were short on ammo, and some of the troops might have used their last bullets in praising him. If so, they would have to go through the rest of the campaign with empty rifles.

Mahir wondered how his purist philosophy permitted Kumander Ali under the laws of the Koran to offer him the exclusive and lucrative fruit export rights of Mindanao for commercial development. He was just as much a foreigner as the Tagalogs, even more so. But Ali's commercial proposal to Mahir was at least half the reason he was still in camp and not already on some *banka* halfway to Indonesia and back to Turkey. Mahir considered how Muslim entrepreneurs in the new independent state could make a profit legal under the laws of the Koran. How did Ali rationalize his planned bribery to get votes with the high morals of the Koran, for example? Who would do the work in the fields? How could they buy tools or fertilizer without capital investment by one of the locals, maybe even the Chinese? Although Turkey was a Muslim country, at least they used currency and traded with their Christian neighbors in Europe. How would Ali manage the great wealth he would control? Mahir listened with curiosity. Lateef merely listened, but was pleased that Mahir was with him. He had grown to like and to respect the Turk, the foreigner who could ask the innocent questions the others heard in their minds but never quite formulated and certainly dared not speak.

Mahir wanted to move into more tactical and less theoretical areas, so he put the question to Kumander Ali: "We have thirty days until the election, thirty days during which we must survive, let alone defend ourselves from the enemy pursuing us. And they are increasing in strength every day. Can we feed our own growing army and all their followers while we sit here in Sultan Kudarat doing nothing?"

Kumander Ali cut him off, showing impatience for the first time since they had met. "Allah will provide. It is not necessary for us to think about this." Then there was quiet, as the four looked at Ali, surprised by his atypical outburst.

Ali felt he had to paint the big picture and teach his followers what he believed. "The Luzon government has tried to deal with the MNLF and for over ten years we have watched sporadic peace talks, facilitated by outsiders, Malaysia, Syria, Libya, but all this time we kept the pressure on with our regular business throughout Mindanao."

By "business" the rebel commander referred to kidnapping for ransom and progressive taxation quotas that were little more than extortion, like forcing delivery trucks to pay taxes to gangs when they crossed province or even village borders, effectively stopping deliveries of foodstuffs into the most needy areas. For thirty-six years the NPA had been

kept alive by keeping the people poor, its terrorism discouraging investment. The vicious cycle was self-perpetuating: no investment, no profit,
again no investment in their provinces in northern Mindanao, and then
unemployment, discontent, hopelessness, and revolution followed in
that order.

The captured radio station in Itig, RFM, was still broadcasting news
in Visayan, the language understood by most of the people in Mindanao, and foreign to the average Filipino on the other large islands,
who spoke Tagalog or other dialects. The news came between the
reading of the Koran and prayers in Arabic, and the NPA leaders listened before they made their prayers.

RFM reported, "From North Cotobato to Zamboanga we are now
united. Neighbors from Agusan and Surigao, we wait for you to join us!
The news: In the south, the former government has admitted they
cannot supply food to the residents of T'boli, Banga, and Polomolok,
while in the north, our allies, the New Peoples Army, have freed themselves from the oppressors and now join with us here where we can take
care of ourselves, Enshallah!"

After a pause the announcer continued, "The corrupt generals and
politicians who take bribes in Manila tell us we do not have the right to
hold the elections we have already scheduled for next month. But we
learned from the Americans that we could. The Yankees taught us how
to run elections while war continues during their aggression in Iraq.
Elections will be held on schedule. This station supports the MNLF
party, the Moro Islamic Liberation Front, and the New Peoples Army."

Then, sure to arouse all who identified themselves with their roots,
the inspiring anthem began. First the low notes of the brass *agong*, then
the strings, and gradually the legendary voice of Freddie Aguilar:

Filipino against Filipino are fighting in Mindanao
Is all their blood wasted in the land of
Mindanao. Mindanao.
Is there no way to stop it?
Is there no way to end this?
Is the solution only found in war?
In this land of promise

Mindanao. Mindanao

Is there no chance to save
our brothers and our sisters in
Mindanao. Mindanao.

Mahir did not understand the Visayan words, but he felt the emotion and witnessed its effect. His instructions from Sheik Kemal in Lefkosia and the Syrian in Damascus were to support Kumander Ali in his efforts to achieve an Islamic state. And now he was witnessing the creation of that state. Others like him were organizing teams with separate missions in other countries at the same moment, intending to call local elections wherever they were. The United States could not fight them all at once, and Manila could not win alone in combat, having neither the stomach for it nor the resources. The five million U.S. dollars that Mahir had brought into Mindanao would go a long way in this part of the world. They could give 10 dollars to more than 300,000 voters, and that gesture would get them the swing vote and win the election. The rest of the money they needed for personal use, like automobiles, travel expenses, and houses made out of hollow concrete blocks not just raw wood. They might obtain a majority vote without the ten-dollar reward, but the gesture would insure a good turnout. And a minimum of sixty percent of the half million voters in the five voting provinces would be a good enough result to confuse international opinions. Perhaps they would even invite observers to witness procedures and report to the world regarding the validity of the elections.

The announcer came back on. "We, formerly known as the Moro National Liberation Front, confirm our agreement with the New Peoples Army to provide security in the South as they will in the North. Voters do not need to fear going to the election sites to vote out the imperialists."

The announcement by Radio Free Mindanao intimidated many who would otherwise have considered voting for candidates supporting the federalist movement and opposed to the NPA. Terrorist groups were integrated into their *barangays,* the small local districts, and everyone knew everyone else and their politics. If the mullahs monitoring the election did not know you or were unsure how you would vote, it would be best to stay home. The RFM newscast ended with a call to prayer, after which the station reverted to recitation of the Koran in Arabic on a looped tape that continually replayed, "*Bismilahi rahumani rahimi.*"

Mahir, Lateef, and the NPA leaders left the hut after the newscast and their personal prayer session ended, rolling up their multi-purpose prayer rugs and tucking them into their combat gear. Lateef walked with Mahir and asked him, "What is the real reason that you are with us?"

Mahir thought for a moment and replied, "For the honor of it. That is why I made the long trip, that is why I started, anyway, but I have to say that Ali's promise of other rewards is what keeps me here now, for these next few weeks. Why do you stay?"

Lateef knew his reasons and explained to Mahir, "There must be justice. We will continue the kidnapping of foreigners and Christians, like that girl we have tied and gagged over there—maybe we can trade her for something—until we have justice." He jerked his head in Elaiza's direction.

"But," Mahir was not sure if Lateef had it right, "Islam means peace. When can we end this war and begin the peace?"

"When we have restored central Islamic authority over the world, as in the time of the Prophet Muhammad." The answer was obvious to Lateef.

"How do we involve the people in an Islamic democracy? Is that possible? We are fighting for their freedom to choose their leaders and governments." Mahir was still confused by Lateef's logic.

"Democracy and Islam are like oil and water. They do not mix without adding flour. We achieve the faith of oneness because we will provide the flour, we warriors of Jihad." Lateef understood his role.

"For me, I want to get this over with and then leave here for a while. I have some things to attend to back home, and down south in Digos as well. Ali has made me an offer to work with him in the new country. I will see." Mahir looked around him at the collection of men and women who composed their army, the Islamic cell of organized terror in Mindanao. He asked Lateef, "What will you do after our victory?" They had reached their tents.

It was easier for Lateef to decide; he had no conflicts of interest. "I have no place else to go." He reflected, logically, he thought, "I will work overseas someday, unless I die in jihad and go to paradise, or perhaps move to Davao City and study to become a nurse, and then get a high-paying job in Europe. Or maybe work as a truck driver in Saudi. But sometimes, I think my time may have passed."

34

King of Battle

Wings spread, silently sailing upward on an invisible wind drafting out of the valley, Kabayan soared. The last Philippine eagle, son of renowned parents Pagkakaisa and Pag-asa, was looking for lunch, perhaps a slow-moving tarsiers monkey in the treetops or an even slower rat in the grass farther below. Kabayan observed an unfamiliar object, perhaps a rock from an erupting volcano, pass below him in slow motion as it reached the apex of its trajectory and slowed in its arc, changed pitch and began its acceleration downward toward the alluvial plain slanting away from the highest point in Mindanao, where it exploded upon contact. The object Kabayan watched was the first artillery shot fired in the battle of Mount Apo.

The AFP artillery did not need to call on their forward observers to give them estimated coordinates for the radio station; they knew exactly where it was, already marked on their maps with a bright red X. The fire direction center had the firing directions for the radio station not only memorized but pre-programmed, waiting for the inevitable order to fire.

"This way, follow me with those bags!" Mahir yelled to the cargo porters. Mahir untied Elaiza from the tree, released the gag in her mouth so she could breathe while running and pulled her with him. He had to get out of Itig with the cash.

Colonel Liu had decided to hit the surprised enemy force in Itig village with "punitive action" as authorized by Galan and ordered a barrage of five volleys from the entire battalion, a total of ninety high explosive rounds to be walked across the target area starting at the edge of Itig and progressing along its main street.

For this important fire mission, the artillery battalion commander called for high explosive munitions with fuses to explode on impact, targeting the sandbagged radio station and its dug-in defenders. After the rounds were in the air, Liu knew he could forget about RFM and that the insulting radio station at Itig and the bastards around it who made him so angry. Now it was time to decimate the enemy. Leaving the artillery to do its bloody work, he retuned to his jeep, where he gave orders to the infantry brigade commanders, "Chase them and keep firing until they surrender, then put any captives into confinement behind barbed wire until we have new orders from Manila." It would be troublesome for the junior officers and their sergeants to contain and take proper care of any survivors, and the fewer the better anyway.

In Itig, the incoming rounds raked across the road and through the city center, now clogged with men dropping their weapons and struggling around the wounded to get their bicycles. It was as if the gods of the mountain had suddenly lifted the entire town up and then dropped it back to earth in a muddy clump, so suddenly had their world changed.

A quarter of a mile from the target, natives were buying rice and hardware items in a small *sari-sari* store when an errant round penetrated the corrugated steel roof, exploding on contact. Irregular shards of metal shredded five people buying or selling canned and dried goods, and parts of them became mixed indistinguishably with their purchases. It was one small mistake of "friendly fire" that would not be worth reporting by either side.

The Itig radio station exploded, along with huts, and the village was pulverized. People with all they owned and their animals were torn apart and thrown into the air. A man mounted his bent bicycle and did his best to navigate around bodies strewn in the street and a sobbing woman holding a dead baby.

As the smoke gradually cleared after the last artillery rounds had exploded, the ear-splitting noise was replaced by absolute quiet—not a bird left to chirp. But shortly thereafter the silence suddenly ended and the wailing and screaming started. The shrill cries of the injured were heard above the low moans of a wounded dog, and a new storm commenced as a Philippine infantry brigade, held for the last two hours in attack positions, now moved quickly into the town and toward Ali's shredded hut, the almost-empty command post of a suddenly less proud New Peoples Army.

While the artillery attack was underway, the infantry soldiers maneuvered through the sugar cane fields, up the incline hill as fast as they could move, each soldier carrying assault packs of rifles, ammo attack gear, and their all-important water canteens. As they emerged from the field, the infantry continued the attack, and the troops formed into firing lines parallel to the road from where they could take aim at any suspected NPA. The riflemen fired well-aimed shots, hitting the demoralized NPA members almost at will.

Some women and children accompanying the NPA forces were felled during the crossfire, hit by stray or ricocheting bullets. They shared the tragic fate of the other innocents who had been caught by the artillery shelling.

The retreating NPA were too confused to stop and surrender or simply to drop their guns. Withering fire covered whatever direction they chose to escape.

The radio station in the center of Itig village, around which rebel soldiers and their supporting followers had been assembled, was a scattered stack of splinters and junk—the survivors now being eliminated one shot at a time by the pursuing AFP soldiers.

Colonel Liu had just congratulated the artillery unit commander and his headquarters staff, and Lieutenant Colonel De la Rosa was wrapping up his after-action report, when Thornton and the STAGCOM troopers emerged from the bush on the north side of the road. Dirty and dripping with old rain and new sweat, Thornton charged straight to Liu's command post as the briefing was breaking up.

"Reggie, you killed her!" Thornton said, not thinking about the bloody cuts on his head and body.

"What the hell happened to you?" Colonel Liu stood up and grabbed Thornton, trying to push him into a chair.

"Your damn artillery, you killed Elaiza." Thornton almost sobbed out the words.

"What are you talking about?" Liu was shocked.

"We were near Itig, trying to get close to get a look, when your artillery hit us." Thornton faced Liu directly, "What's the matter, Reggie, you attacked too soon again. You weren't supposed to do that."

"I think this is what happened." Liu surmised. "At first, we just probed Itig with an infantry platoon, to see what was there. Then your Major Hayes, who had accompanied our troops, against my advice by the way, got hit and disappeared. So we fired a few rounds of artillery to keep their heads down while we tried to locate him. You know the old left-over artillery ammunition that Uncle Sam gave us is not so accurate anymore after all the years of being stockpiled. And we had no time to calibrate those howitzers. In any case, there will be some stray rounds from every batch of ammo, old or new."

"Well, your second attack blew up STAGCOM, and killed a wonderful girl, Reggie. We had gotten close." Thornton sat down. "She was on the point, with me. Blown up by your artillery! I saw it. She just disappeared."

"Tom, you were not supposed to attack. It's your own fault." Liu felt sympathy for Thornton, but did not feel guilty. He had to tell him, "There's more. They executed Hayes." Liu told Thornton about the RFM broadcast of the beheading.

"Those bastards!" Thornton collapsed weakly on a chair and covered his eyes. "Reggie, I have to get them. I gotta get even."

Colonel Liu put a sympathetic hand on Thornton's shoulder. "We also found the Pajero in Bual, brought it here for you. The young Otaza is dead. Shot in the ear with a pistol, close range."

While Thornton was trying to absorb all the shocking information he had just learned, Liu's radio operator handed the colonel a message. He passed it on to Thornton. "You've got a meeting with Hargens in Manila. Right now. Take my helicopter. You can't do anything here."

Thornton didn't think for a second before answering Liu, "No. I'm going back to Itig."

"Then good luck to you. I thought you might do that. I had gas put in your vehicle for you. Compliments of the Philippine Army." Liu pointed to where Thornton's SUV was waiting. "And for God's sake, don't get too close to the NPA when the shooting starts again. Remember the first Rule of Combat: Friendly fire isn't friendly."

"Thanks, Reggie." Thornton was already up and running toward the Pajero. On the way he grabbed Starke and turned him around, "No time to rest yet," and motioned to the Otazas to jump into the Pajero. Wheels spun in the mud as they sped off.

Twenty minutes later Thornton drove into Itig. The village was destroyed, but they heard some sporadic firing at the far end and continued through the village, past burning huts. Thornton parked the Pajero behind a mound of rubble when he saw a group of armed men on the far side of the village.

"That must be an NPA squad. Hank, take the Otazas and circle around, cut them off. I'll attract their attention from the front," Thornton, angered and seeking revenge on any enemy he could find, ordered his men out of the vehicle.

Thornton fired a few shots from his carbine, mostly to make noise; he was too far away to be accurate, but it worked. The NPA squad faced him and returned his fire as he crawled forward. A burst of fire came at him, and he hit the dirt, rolled and came up behind a clump of thick grass. Now he was closer and took the time to take careful aim. This time he hit one of the enemy directly in the forehead, the man dropped the duffel bag he was carrying as the remainder of the NPA squad tried to retreat, just as Starke and the Otazas hit them on their flank and pursued them into the tree line.

Suddenly Thornton was standing alone where the NPA had been and checked the body of the man he had shot. His face looked like the photos he had seen of Kumander Ali. Thornton picked up the duffel bag, wondering. Could it be? He opened it; it was. He scooped up the bag of cash and tied it down on top of the Pajero among the other bags of equipment lashed on the roof. Just as he finished, Starke returned from behind a blown-up building, leading the Otazas past a squad of approaching soldiers of the AFP, entering the town to mop up.

The sergeant leading the patrol located another duffel bag, charred and barely recognizable as what it once was, and gave it a kick. The bag fell apart in blackened fibers and charred chunks of burnt paper that once were bound stacks of hundred dollar bills tumbled out. He ignored the bag and continued on, hurrying to rejoin his patrol.

The infantry soldiers of the Philippine Army walked through the village, itching to shoot anything that moved. As they took pot shots at barking dogs and stray chickens, a few burned and blackened bank notes swirled along the street in the wind.

Thornton finally had to admit there was nothing more that could be done in Itig. There was no Elaiza to be found. He drove the Pajero back to Liu's command post, but this time, he had new instructions for Starke. "Hank, take the Pajero. Use it to go back to Davao; there's nothing more for us here. Park it in front of the Lady Love, and leave the keys with Morris if you're not there. But take the long way back, and make a stop here." Thornton pointed out a gravesite on a map and showed Starke what was in one of the duffle bags lashed to the top of the Pajero.

Starke looked confused for a moment, then it hit him. "You think people don't trust you, but you trust everybody. I'll show you." He gave Thornton his friendly frown and did a slow about-face to coordinate with the Otazas, telling them to stay at Liu's CP but to be ready. He would be back when Thornton told him to be back.

After Starke drove away, the downtrodden Thornton walked over to Colonel Liu and told him, "OK, Reggie, I'll take that flight to Manila now."

35

Birds of a Feather

"Where the hell have you been? All I know about your *verdammte* antics since you went on the job with Thornton is official press releases. Where are you now?" Wolfgang Moser asked Starke when he called.

It was good to hear Moser's voice. "In town, on the way to O'Neil's place. Got time?"

"Sure, about twenty-five minutes?"

"Perfect. I'll come by your place. Be ready!" Starke was hungry for a cheeseburger and for some companionship—Moser first, for conversation, and the twins later.

From where Starke parked the Pajero, he and Moser walked together down unlit Claveria Street to the Lady Love. The city stationed two or three patrolmen on every major intersection within the city to direct traffic with hand signals because that was cheaper than installing expensive traffic lights. There were no streetlights and few traffic lights in

Davao City, and with ever-higher electricity costs, streetlights were a fantasy of the future.

A barefoot woman wearing a loose, torn dress appeared out of the early evening shadows from between two buildings and approached Moser to offer, "Do you want a girl?"

"No!" Moser was disgusted to contemplate being with the old hag and walked quickly away from the woman, but she followed him, trying to negotiate. He turned back to ask Starke, "Can you imagine a woman that ugly trying to sell herself on the street?"

"Wolfgang, don't you get it even after all your years here? She wasn't asking if you wanted *her;* she was asking if you wanted a *girl*. She probably has a stable of teenagers or even younger girls back in the alley. Maybe her own daughters or daughters of her friends, and maybe some boys, bought in the country or in the barrios around town from parents who have too many kids."

Moser was embarrassed he had been so naive and did not relax until he reached the familiar environment of the Lady Love, where Moser and Starke commandeered a booth for themselves. Morris O'Neil himself came over and plopped down beside Moser while a cute new waitress took their order for six beers, two for each, to save time. Moser recounted the recent street scene to Morris.

"I think you're right, Hank," Morris told him seriously, "there's been some rumor about a covey of quail living on the second floor above the ink refill station. But I haven't seen any of them. Where you lads been lately?" Morris asked as a half-dozen draft San Miguel beers in icy mugs were set down in front of them.

The twins showed up, and the direction of the conversation changed. Jade snuggled beside Starke, lightly touching thighs from hips to knees. "Do you want to see our new costumes?"

"Sure. Morris put up the money for your outfits?" Starke thought they both looked very sexy.

"No way. We had to pay for them ourselves, but it wasn't very much." Jasmine was standing beside Starke, resting her hand lightly on his shoulder.

"And we did a lot of the work ourselves, finishing, doing some sewing and gluing. We can make our own dresses, you know." Jade was justifiably proud of her handiwork.

Starke pretended to be surprised, "You're becoming industrious and yet conservative young ladies."

"No. Hardly that. We thought we might have to take care of ourselves alone someday." No one present believed Jasmine in the slightest.

"I suppose if it didn't cost much, it means there were very tiny amounts of material purchased. Right?" Moser liked to kid around with the twins; they were nice girls and harmless.

"You got that right, sir," they answered the D.J. simultaneously.

"Anyway, there's more coverage than with the two green sleeves." Jade turned back to Starke. "So many of the customers that come here have become regulars that we decided to change our theme. Now we'll wear only feathers!"

"Only feathers? That's interesting." Starke could imagine how the clientele would appreciate their new act.

"Yes, we start with the green sleeves as before, but then slowly take them off. The end of our old act is where the new one starts. We end it wearing only feathers."

"Yes. And the feathers are only on our face masks, winding upwards in swirls and down in spirals around our paper masks. We'll look just like Kabayan." Jade completed the image for the three men at the table.

"So, that leaves you completely *hubo hubo?*" Moser knew the Visayan phrase. The girls seemed to be becoming more aware and less naive than when he had first met them.

"Yes, except for the feathers." Jasmine laughed and continued to play with her audience.

Starke could imagine their finale. "Well, maybe later I can watch the last show?"

"You can count on seeing our last show, but not here." Jade whispered in his ear, and then flew backstage with Jasmine to get ready for their first performance of the evening.

Moser had observed the private cabaret at their table with mild amusement, but had enough. "I'll leave you gents to your vices, got to get ready for my own show."

"Break a leg!" Morris said to his back as the D.J. left the bar.

After the twins' first show they busied themselves flirting with customers, something they seemed to have gotten better at. Starke wondered about their newly found gregariousness. He finished one more beer, then left the Lady Love and walked home along the never deserted, now even darker streets, passing some of the same street people he had passed on the way in. Back in his loft, he pushed in a Willie Nelson CD and waited for the twins to come home and unfurl their feathers.

36

Old Generals and Empty Chairs

The urgency of quieting both Manila and Washington had been the reason General Hargens needed to get Thornton back to the embassy sooner rather than later. The Philippine Air Force flight out of Koronadal Airport that Liu had arranged was delayed by bad weather over the Sulu Sea, refueled in Iloilo and Batangas, and finally dropped Thornton at the Manila airport to hook up with Hargens' chopper. Hargens liked to start early, before much of the Defense Department in Washington, D.C., closed down, which meant 6 AM Manila time. He was accustomed to talking with his home office first and getting himself up to speed before the day began in Asia. Hargens was waiting for Thornton when the helicopter deposited him onto the embassy grounds and escorted him directly to the conference room.

Hargens had scheduled this meeting, following instructions from his boss, the Secretary of Defense. The U.S. Ambassador to the Philippines was the nominal chairman of today's meeting, but the ambassador was in trouble and he knew it. Ambassador Richardson had been quoted on Malaysian television while on a trip to Kuala Lumpur as saying that the situation in Mindanao was beginning to look like Iraq, a sensitive issue in Washington with overtones of political dissent. In Manila his quoted statement was viewed simply as condescending ignorance on the part of the Americans. The ambassador wanted to get himself out of the mess; perhaps Hargens' ideas and the recent successes of the Philippine Army in Mindanao could help his situation.

Most of the participants who had attended the previous meeting in this same venue, which now seemed so long ago, were already present. But Major Hayes' chair was empty. His temporary replacement had arrived from the states, a young infantry lieutenant outranked by everyone. He leaned against the wall not knowing where to sit. John Robert Mundy's place was also unoccupied; although he had not been pleasant to have around when he was alive, Mundy's loss was nevertheless felt in some way by each of them.

Thornton arrived late, and had had a lot to think about during his delay. When he got to the conference room, he glanced at the vacant chairs and thought about what might have been for the men who once sat in them. He had seen men in combat survive terrible wounds and recover to lead valuable lives, and he had witnessed men bleeding to death from apparently superficial cuts, drowning in a few minutes or dying of fever from what started as a common cold. There seemed to be no reason why some survived.

Thornton wrestled with his conscience. Was it true that passion and ignorance were a dangerous combination? If so, it is a continuing condition in Mindanao, and here in Manila it was worse. Even the embassy staff seemed to have succumbed to a global pandemic of ignorance, his buddy Hargens and a few others excluded. Hargens had the ability and the vision to see truth, or at least truth the same way Thornton saw it. Revolution and continuing threats of revolution in the southern Philippines would happen again and again as long as there were too many people chasing too little useful work. Thornton sat next to Hargens, and allowed himself to philosophize somewhat more than usual. What he said was, "Luke, I was wrong about thinking I was doing this all just for the money. I don't need it; I miss what I lost."

Hargens heard him, didn't completely understand, but had to start the meeting. He wrung his bony hands, nodded respectfully to Congressman Galan, and addressed the entire group. "Yesterday may have been a day of defeat for the NPA, but those outlaws don't know about events outside Mindanao. They're waiting for international support, for global revolt against the 'imperialistic and capitalistic' Americans, using their terms. You have to realize that's what they believe. Let's see what happens next; it's just never over."

"Well, this chapter is over, anyway." Thornton gazed around the room. "But don't you wonder, what have we really learned here, what difference will it make a hundred years from now if our photos are hanging on that wall and MacArthur is forgotten and is as irrelevant as U.S. Grant today? What have we really changed?"

"Maybe you and I remember why the old wars were fought; the newer generations don't know; they haven't studied history." The general did remember.

"We just waste our time proving once again that power always wins," Thornton answered Hargens and paused while the others thought about what he meant. He continued, "Foreigners just enforce their foreign superstitions on Filipino citizens over tribal superstitions, with missionary preaching mixed in." True to his rabble-rouser label, he could not stop.

"And thank you, U.S. government, corporations and taxpayers for funding *both* sides in this war," Thornton continued. "If America didn't send money here, and the Arabs also didn't, there would be none to steal or to be filtered off by the several levels of graft between Manila and Mindanao."

"That is truly superficial and arrogant, Mr. Thornton," interjected the ambassador, who had his own opinion and the official position to sell. Tapping his ballpoint pen a little too hard on the table, the furrow in his brow deepening, the ambassador looked as though he was ready to spit. This civilian "contractor" guy was done with his job. And tomorrow Hargens would be in his plush JUSMAG office, while Congressman Galan would be busy shuffling routine papers. But for him here in the embassy there would be new issues, new politics, the same indigenous tribes and established interest groups emerging with different icons and newer slogans, and a whole new crop of Filipino generals whom he would have to meet on the lunch and dinner circuit to learn their names and agendas. He would have to wrestle with reporters from the *Star* and the *Inquirer* and think about the delicate phrasing of the next press releases that he would have to concoct concerning what USAID and the JUSMAG advisors were up to in the field. He prayed he would not have to shut down the embassy again because of street demonstrations against America.

The conversation in the conference room was becoming testy. "The Filipino citizen needs to do more for himself to prevail against internal terrorist threats. We can't do it for you." Ambassador Richardson needed to impress Galan with the U.S. position. His country was busy in too many other places in the world to hold their hands forever.

"We didn't ask you to." Galan stated frankly. "In fact, if you remember, we didn't want you here in the first place."

Thornton had had enough. "Anyway, I'm out of here, before your next war against the Lumads. I've lost everything I care about. There can't be real peace in Mindanao until the MNLF cuts its ties with the Al Qaeda and the Abu Sayaf, and they never will. That's all they have, those poor, desperate bastards."

"OK, I know, we can't defeat a desperate populace." The time for Galan's political opportunities was growing nearer, and he was positioning himself to further his reputation and position with the electorate. "But there are criminal elements that must be wiped out so our good people, Christian and others, will be able to build a nation."

Ambassador Richardson wanted to remind all those present that the Republic of the Philippine Islands was *not* the only country in the world where the U.S. was involved, and it was far from the top of the list in importance, but said it as tactfully as a career diplomat could and still make a point: "Congressman, it is your country and your show, but we will always be your ally. You should assess the remaining strength of the NPA and give us your official report. We'll continue to assist your forces in the field, and to help with the immediate image problems you may have. The U.S. Embassy will sign a memorandum of support for the government as having successfully defeated this particular terrorist plot. You can decide the venue and how you want us to announce it. Go ahead, make some hay."

It seemed fortuitous that the new, unintroduced lieutenant who had been called out of the meeting returned at that moment, marching quietly but at a quick pace. It broke the tension. He came up behind Hargens and reported, "You will want to see this first, General Hargens; we just received it."

Hargens read the message and handed the sheet of paper to Thornton. "You won't like this, but you have to know. We received the following text that will appear in today's *Mindanao Times*. They sent it to us as a courtesy." Thornton read:

Called by a videoke bar owner, Morris O'Neil, city police were asked to investigate a suspicious situation. The resident of a flat in Claveria Street had not responded to a telephone call from a friend, although known to be in the flat. The owner of the flat supplied keys and accompanied police, who found the body of a large white man, American, Henry Starke, known to have been the occupant of the flat.

The police are releasing no additional information as the matter is under investigation. However, the owner of the building told reporters of the *Mindanao Times* that the cause of death was most unusual and not natural. It was reported that the man died due to the presence of a high-heeled spike from a lady's shoe having pierced the left eyeball and an identical spike through the other eye, both having penetrated into the brain and still in place when the detectives arrived. The apartment was otherwise undisturbed, although a U.S. one hundred dollar bill was found on the floor. Thus robbery is not the suspected motive.

On the dead man's chest, the informant learned from detectives, were an unset jade stone and a single jasmine flower. The police were not aware of the significance of these symbols, but are seeking two female friends of the deceased who shared the apartment with him, seen leaving the downtown area with a certain Lateef, known to be a criminal wanted by the PNP.

Thornton stood up, left the room and walked outside into the small garden in the open atrium centered within the political side of the embassy. As he re-read the entire article, the song Elaiza had sung while moving around the house in Toril came back to Thornton in a new version to haunt him even more: *Did you get everything you came for, Sergeant Starke, old buddy?*

Thornton thought that no one could ever find final resolution, the end of problems. But Starke had reached his end at the hands of those perfidious twins. He thought about the symbols left on his chest by those damn women. By now they had probably escaped to some village deep in the interior, waiting until the time was right to slip out clandestinely through Indonesia. Jade and Jasmine would comfortably find their way to wherever they wanted to start their next lives.

When Thornton returned to the room the atmosphere was different. He sank into his chair. Galan came to one side, Hargens the other, sheltering him from the sympathetic glances of the others.

Hargens made his offer to Thornton, "Tom, I heard about the loss of the girl and I know about your relationship with her. Obviously I can't replace her, but I'll get you on a military flight out of here, to anywhere."

"Thanks, Luke, but there's no place to go from here."

"Think about it, a house on the beach in Thailand may give you a place to hang your hat. I can get you there," Hargens said.

The lieutenant came over to Hargens again. "General, there's something you should see that's showing up on our maps in the operations center." The young officer brought a laptop to Hargens, with a live satellite view of western Mindanao on the screen. "We're picking up signals from the TIAM; we have it on high resolution."

Thornton pushed past Hargens and the lieutenant, and there it was, traced out on the ground by Elaiza using her iPod. He felt every muscle in his body contract and heard his heart pounding.

"Luke. She's alive!" Thornton saw what had attracted the ops center's attention. Paced out on the land in small, precise letters by the TIAM was a single word, TOMAS.

Thornton threw his head up and said to Hargens, "I'm going back to Mindanao."

37

Mount Apo

Mahir and the demoralized remnants of his retreating patrol were moving toward Mount Apo. Mahir had nothing left to save but his life. Maybe he could trade the woman he had dragged along with him for that. But for now he had to hide until the situation returned to some kind of normalcy. Mahir had no way of knowing the extent of Colonel Liu's effectiveness the day before in exploiting his artillery barrage with an infantry assault on Itig.

Breathing hard and stumbling over rocks, Mahir withdrew with the men in his immediate command toward higher ground as fast as he could. He untied Elaiza's hands so she could balance herself and move faster. The idea that maybe he could trade her for safe passage kept going through his mind.

Meanwhile, artillery forward observers of the AFP no longer concerned with Itig identified a platoon-sized unit of the NPA in the open and reported it as a target of opportunity, not knowing it was the Turk moving to a safer place.

A single spotting round from a 105mm howitzer landed about 400 meters from Mahir's position. Mahir knew he was in imminent danger when the next explosion occurred about 200 meters closer to him than the first impact. When sixty-five seconds later a third single round exploded a close 100 meters from him, it was clear that his position had been bracketed. The explosions splintered trees and threw up debris upon impact along a straight line leading directly back to the cannon that had fired the spotting rounds. Mahir expected that the next impact would not be another single round but rather a six-round volley impacting right on top of him, from which there would be little chance of survival.

To minimize the risk of getting into the direct line of fire, Mahir wisely chose to move perpendicular to the imaginary line established by the three impacts. He also thought perhaps he should simply shoot his captive here, as she was just slowing him down. The possibility of using her for bargaining purposes with the government forces became less advantageous with each passing minute.

After the Fire Direction Center of the Count-down Battalion, the 3/21 Field Artillery, recalculated the trajectory to the target based on reports of the impacts, Colonel Liu watched as fire direction control officers entered information from the forward observers into their computers. He had ordered a barrage of three volleys by one entire battery, and the artillery commander selected fragmentation rounds, which were calibrated to explode about thirty feet above ground, thereby inflicting maximum killing effect on the exposed enemy personnel. An officer transferred the corrected deflection and elevation data to the howitzer positions where a gunnery sergeant barked out slight alterations, changes in direction and elevation, to be cranked into the guns, determining which of the enemy would live or die. Soon the howitzers were poised to deliver their deadly munitions.

The battery commander ordered "Fire!" and the first six rounds were on the way. Immediately the howitzer crews clanked open the breeches of their guns and loaded another six rounds, which were in the air before the first six had impacted on the target, followed later by the final volley of the barrage to make a total of eighteen artillery rounds on their way to meet Mahir and his soldiers moving above the tree line on the boulder-strewn, open slopes of Mount Apo.

The Philippine Army artillerymen had correctly adjusted their firing data. One round of the first full volley took out Mahir's point man and several armed followers when the electronic detonators exploded the projectiles above them, slicing limbs from torsos exactly as intended. Three other rounds were near misses, causing casualties among the rebels and blinding a NPA squad leader bringing up his team to protect Mahir's left flank.

Mahir, his men and the woman with them ran from the rocky terrain into the jungle, but they could move only a few dozen yards in the few seconds before the next volley arrived on target. They were now in the wrong place at exactly the wrong moment. The second volley of six rounds exploded above them, and only the thick jungle canopy protected them from being shredded to bits. The artillery rounds detonated above the foliage, which bore the full force of the explosions. A shower of branches, leaves and coconut fragments covered Mahir's group. The last volley landed on Mahir's third squad, leaving a red layer of blood and torn flesh splattering the green foliage.

In a clear and open area unprotected when the barrage arrived on target, shards of steel cut three or four of Mahir's men into unrecognizable parts, making it uncertain how many men had been standing in that place. A rifleman ran toward Mahir holding his shoulder together with his right hand where his left arm had been severed, screaming as blood pumped for a few more seconds. Mahir saw men with legs shattered and white bones exposed, men living but wishing they were not. Bleeding from death wounds but not yet realizing they had been hit, two men leaned on opposite sides of a coconut palm. The leader of Mahir's second squad struggled off the barren patch with another almost dead soldier, blood soaking through the seat of his Levi's trousers. Those remaining alive on the mountain when the shelling stopped assembled near the dead and tried to hang on to their own lives, considering themselves blessed.

The exhausted survivors spiraled down the slopes of the great Mount Apo, desperately looking for any embankment or gully, however insignificant, that might protect them from the unseen but lethal artillery. Dragging with them comrades who might live, the haggard men worked their way lower into the scrub brush following Mahir's lead. With a sense of urgency, they made their way back into the forested areas where they hoped they would be swallowed up by the dense jungle.

With nine of his remaining irregulars, Mahir finally reached a point below a rounded outcropping of volcanic rock that fortunately offered some overhead cover. Once below the tree line and in a defensible position, he tried to regroup and decide what to do next. Saved by the concealing shadows of a fast approaching night, the patrol settled in.

Working as best he could to reorganize his men and keep them from deserting, Mahir did not pay much attention to Elaiza, except to notice that she was limping back and forth and moaning quietly as she appeared to rub her bruises. He knew she could not go far and could be easily recaptured or shot if she attempted to escape.

Elaiza was amazed that she had suffered only a few scratches and contusions during her flight from the artillery attack. The bloodstains on her clothing came from Mahir's men who were not so fortunate. It was reassuring to her to know that the device she switched on in her iPod would pinpoint her location and track her movements, footstep by limping footstep, as she faked her injuries. If the U.S. embassy knew exactly where she was, they would know to a great degree of accuracy also where Mahir and his team were, at least close enough for the STAGCOM team to be directed toward her and to move into a coordinated attack, certainly accurate enough to call in artillery or an air strike as had already been proven. As she paced her message on the ground, she hoped it would not be an aerial bomb attack.

* * *

Early the next morning Thornton arrived back at Liu's forward command post as the fire direction officer reported to Colonel Liu, "We have visual now, sir. When we got the coordinates from the Americans, we had one of our forward observers take up a position from where he could observe the site through his binoculars. As soon as we had daylight, he identified a tall, Arab-looking man."

"That would have to be the Turk." Liu knew it and had the fire direction center show Thornton precisely on his map the exact ravine into which the enemy patrol had descended.

"Reggie, you've got to let me go get them. That's the woman who gave us, all of us, the exact position of the rebels." Thornton was calling in his chips. "You owe her, and you owe me."

"I think she's a lot more than that to you." Liu's support for Thornton was immediate and unequivocal. "OK. Check your map; get the exact location marked from our fire direction center. So go and do what you must. Take my jeep; you'll need it where you're going."

"God, Reggie. Thanks. You should be more careful, I lose everyone who helps me."

"Hurry, I'm not making any promises about when we unload everything we have on them." Liu grabbed Thornton and gave him a quick handshake. "Now's your chance."

Liu ordered his staff to hold the scheduled artillery fire, intentionally giving Thornton a window of time to get to Elaiza.

Already halfway to the jeep, Thornton grabbed Pedro by the arm and pulled him along, "Get your brothers up and into Liu's jeep! It's time for us to be on our own. We're going to get Elaiza!" Thornton was glad to have a guy like Pedro—as well as his two remaining brothers—to back him up. It didn't take long for Pedro to react; the Otazas had been waiting for Thornton to return from Manila.

Thornton pulled his safari hat on tight and lightly touched his front trousers pocket to feel the weight of the small back-up pistol he always carried there, concealed, and flung his almost antique carbine, accurate for short-range shots, onto his shoulder, hooking its leather sling behind his canteen to be held out of the way.

While Pedro hurried Vicente and Reymundo into the back seat of the jeep, Thornton checked his map and determined his route to the coordinates where Elaiza was being held. Almost before they were loaded, Thornton drove away from the command post too fast for road conditions, the steering wheel and gearshift comfortable in his hands, reminding him of active duty in other times and places. He bumped past the tents of the infantry brigades now guarded by only a few soldiers, and raced along the main road to Bual, the village north of the artillery positions, then into the foothills of Mount Apo.

In the narrow ravine, Mahir was thinking his last thoughts: "If we had stayed in our camps the infidels would just have stayed in their homes. Our side could have enjoyed the simple pleasures of Mindanao without needing to divide this overgrown jungle and defend to the death the right to establish a new Islamic nation. What good is this dream now? We don't have the money, and we don't even know where to escape." Mahir was suddenly aware that he might never see his home and family in Turkey again.

Mahir did not know about the complete destruction of the main force at Itig; he was too far up the mountain to have observed it. His guides had erred, judging incorrectly that they would not be discovered while crossing an open plain offering only scant foliage. It had cost the lives of many NPA troops with good rifles, men and guns hard to replace.

Just as these thoughts occurred to him, Mahir was hit with a single bullet in the chest. He screamed in pain but with wild shots emptied his weapon at Thornton who was rushing down the ravine, rapidly closing the distance between them. Reymundo, crouched behind a tree, continued to empty his M-16 magazine, peppering the ravine with well-aimed shots at the few armed NPA soldiers still standing.

Thornton finally reached Mahir and saw that Elaiza was slumped on the ground, maybe dead, maybe unconscious, but definitely not reacting to what was going on around her, just a motionless heap against a pile of rocks. Infuriated, he grabbed the Turk, slamming him against the rocky wall. Blood was beginning to froth out of his mouth, but he was still conscious and struggled to defend himself, thrusting a dagger against Thornton who knocked it aside with his drawn Walther PPK. Thornton placed the barrel directly under Mahir's jaw and shouted into his ear, "Turk, I know you speak English, so listen good. Give my regards to the 72 virgins," and pulled the trigger, firing the final shot of his personal war.

Thornton dropped Mahir's lifeless corpse and ran to Elaiza. Pedro had propped her body up to a sitting position and gave a thumbs-up to Thornton who suddenly felt enormous elation and happiness. He held her in a close embrace until she stirred awake and saw who was holding her. Sobbing in relief, she threw her arms around his neck and held him as tight as she could.

"I can't hear," Elaiza said, and Thornton nodded.

"Artillery." He mouthed the word slowly, and she read Thornton's lips. "I'll take care of you."

Pedro replaced Thornton as the driver so Thornton could lift Elaiza into the front seat where he could hold her as Pedro drove. They were all anxious to get out of the area, as it would become an artillery impact area again soon.

The four men and one woman remaining of the STAGCOM team withdrew out of the ravine and were soon back at Liu's headquarters, where Liu proudly updated the enemy body count from the victory at the Itig radio station and told them about the even larger victory as the decimated enemy was forced away from the destroyed village and went in full retreat to parts unknown, perhaps never to regroup again. Thornton figured correctly that the scattered enemy was being pursued doggedly at the moment by Philippine Army troops. He secretly hoped that the seasoned soldiers of Task Force Davao had no interest at all in the hassle and administrative complications of taking captives.

As an army medic checked her, Thornton wiped beads of perspiration from Elaiza's forehead and made her drink water.

"I see you got her, did you get 'it'?" Liu asked Thornton when he realized that Elaiza was going to be OK.

"Yes, I got it too, I think," Thornton answered.

"Well, I haven't seen any bags. I was busy elsewhere when you returned. Got it?" Liu asked, a hint of a smile on his face. "In fact, we have reports of burned money drifting along what once was a street in Itig."

"Anyway, you're all lucky STAGCOM saved you from having to decide how to divvy up the percentages this time." Thornton didn't know whether Liu might have succumbed to some political deal Galan had offered, but now it seemed Liu was telling him he didn't take any deals. There would be no secret slush fund to corrupt a future election.

Liu told them, "Be careful where you go: the insurgents still are active north of here," as he headed back to the command post.

"I have three tough guys with me, Reggie."

"Four tough guys! Did you forget about me?" Elaiza gave Colonel Liu a farewell peck on the cheek.

"Get out of here, Thornton; you have some things to tend to." Liu was doing Thornton a favor, and they both knew it. "You can keep that damn old jeep."

With the motor running, Elaiza squeezed into the front seat next to Pedro who was ready to drive, and leaned against Thornton sitting beside her. As the wheels began to turn, he felt her warmth against his shoulder and they were finally able to catch their breath. The other two Otaza brothers sat in the rear.

The STAGCOM remnants jolted down the path in the jeep, Pedro doing his best to guide the vehicle north. They passed camps of reinforcements continuing to move up from General Santos City to help Task Force Davao exploit its victory and to expand operations into the northern provinces. Thornton counted enough vehicles full of men to constitute another full brigade of infantry. A brigadier general he did not recognize was in an open jeep near the head of a convoy. The entire force would soon be joining Liu in moving northwest around Mount Apo and west of Itig to cut off and kill as many of the retreating NPA as they could catch. Headquarters, AFP, at Fort Aguinaldo in Manila, would announce another entire army division had been "unleashed" with a single mission: to wipe out the New Peoples Army, having already killed its chief, Kumander Ali, the Communist insurgent leader.

The STAGCOM team drove away from the northern slopes of Mount Apo, crossed the Pulangi River at Kabakan and took the main road north to Malaybalay. They rode in silence from the hot mid-day humid heat into the cooler but still humid early evening. Pedro was chain-drinking coffee from a thermos while the others dozed or gazed out the window. When they reached the sea, they turned east and took the coastal road toward the port city of Butuan, where the brown waters of the Agusan slide a continuous load of uprooted inland trees and shrubs into the ice-blue salt water of the warm Mindanao Sea.

38

The Payoff

Thornton watched Elaiza while she slept. A few tears etched a wet pattern down her brown cheeks as they washed off yellow dust gathered during the encounter on Mount Apo. She was tough, and Thornton saw it only as strength when she could cry as she did now, thinking about how many of her countrymen had died. And tomorrow she would have to deliver Juanito's body to his mother.

The jeep bounced on the uneven pavement, and Elaiza woke. Thornton pointed to a wagon with Dole painted on the side pulled along by a small tractor, stacked high with greenish pineapples. He asked her quietly, "What do you think, are those going back to Davao City for export? Where do you think they'll end up?"

"In world markets, maybe Tokyo, Los Angeles, or Paris." She thought about what those places might look like.

"Like us someday?" Thornton teased a bit. "Or maybe the fruit will just be appropriated by leftover NPA squads on the way to Davao. The stragglers no longer have outside cash for support, and the Philippine army won't cooperate with them anymore, now that they've won."

"Some victory." Elaiza began to nod off. She rested her head on Thornton's shoulder and slid her hand under his shirt, falling asleep.

After Butuan, they turned right and followed the road south along the Agusan upstream to Prosperidad, turned right again and crossed over the river into the Manobo village where Pedro and his brothers lived and would now get back to their pig farms and taro plantings.

When they disembarked, a young girl wearing a torn Lakers tee shirt tied at the waist for a dress, took Elaiza to an amakan hut, whose walls were constructed of tough grass husks, woven close enough to keep out larger pests but loose enough to ventilate. Elaiza's cousins were surprised that she took the big white guy into the hut with her to rest after their baths from a bucket of sun-warmed water.

Elaiza was relaxed and happy to be back safely with her tribe of aunts, uncles, and cousins, and became animated after her nap, having recovered and now feeling rested after the long drive. The others were already gathered on the porch of one of the larger houses. As often as he could, Pedro did the talking, asked the questions, then answered the questions himself to the entertainment of his shyer clansmen, but today there was a new level to the meanings of the stories he told. Pedro, Reymundo, and Vicente played some quieter music and strummed slower songs then they had played at the start of their adventure. They praised Juanito, whose body Colonel Liu had had delivered and was being cleaned in one of the huts and prepared for burial. They told stories about him when he was a boy, not that long ago.

Pedro asked Thornton, somewhat rhetorically, "What's the difference between them and us anyway? Simply how we spell or say God? Desperate people do desperate things, and a desperate populace cannot be defended against itself."

Reymundo finally had something to say, not just to his brother, but as much a reflection to himself, "Here, in Agusan, the communists are the Muslims. They do not know the labels outsiders give them."

Thornton said, "How ironic. We thought we were fighting communist insurgents, but we wound up fighting a religious war as much as an economic ideology."

Elaiza had a new personal perspective after her recent experience, "The Abu Sayaf, and the others, whatever labels they or we make up, terrorize our people and make us poorer. We are well rid of them all."

"A few hooligans threatened Manila, provoking a real revolution in Mindanao, and the Muslims nearly won their civil war," Thornton said. "They had hoped, more or less correctly, that the U.S. would ignore a local war in the Philippines because U.S. forces are overstretched—too many things going on all over the world at the same time. It almost worked."

They became quiet and watched the wood fire burn down to coals, and turned on the radio, barely able to receive Wolfgang Moser's late night program from Davao City, playing his usual Strauss and Beethoven.

Then came the message for Thornton, relayed by Moser from some new point of contact at the Davao consulate. The D.J. announced, "Now my eager listeners, *Goetterdaemmerung*," but he actually played Mozart's Piano Concerto #21, a clear signal to Thornton, who smiled, remembering one of the key words they had included in the Schloss Code. In the Port of Davao, a small motorboat had pulled way from the dock, with Lateef and the twins sitting together on the deck. It headed south, toward Indonesia, but as soon as it hit international waters, the passengers heard a screeching sound and looked up in the direction of its source. The object streaking in from a very high altitude penetrated and destroyed the boat even before it exploded.

In the Manobo camp, they had the feeling Juanito would be rejoining them at any moment, but he would not, ever again. Starke would have enjoyed this evening too. Feelings of loss, yet resurrection, hung around. Strangely there was no hurry now to do anything.

During the night, Pedro packed up his gear. Thornton wanted to say good-bye and job well done, but Pedro had trouble with that sort of thing. He had not committed himself and his brothers on this mission for Thornton. He had done it for Elaiza, whom he had to protect. He was the patriarchal head of an extended family; his brothers also had their own duties to fulfill. And with the NPA incapacitated, no longer a constant threat to their fields and family, they could grow old and get fat, hook up on the Internet and converse with their daughters working overseas. Pedro looked forward to digging his own plot and growing some calabasas commercially. Maybe *Magbabaya,* the name he gave to God, would be generous to him this year, or he would have to make a special offering to that woman priestess if his personal prayers failed. He might even have to go to a Catholic mass also; just to be sure all the bases were covered. While the others slept, he left during the night without saying goodbye. He had a brother to bury tomorrow.

39

Paco Park

The first cock crowed at 4:47 AM, making an early invitation to the proximate hens well in advance of dawn or any rival crowing of competing neighborhood roosters similarly anchored by one foot, tied with plastic tape to poles near the adjacent shack, limiting the cocks' competitive activity to a six-foot radius and any hen that might intentionally or accidentally stray within.

"Tomas, give me a full body hug," were Elaiza's first words of the day. It turned out to be more than just a hug, but it was definitely full body contact. They took turns removing the remaining clothing preventing their moist skins from touching everywhere and let their perspiration and aromas mingle. Whatever the day would bring, it was a good start. He hoped she would not jump up to shower for a while, at least not until the last of the breeding cocks tied outside their window was satisfied that the sun was completely risen and silence would return. They stayed that way a long time, neither awake nor asleep.

"This is why men wage war and engage in commerce," Thornton teased her, enjoying the feel of Elaiza's smooth, lean form fitted next to his, "so they can have a few moments in their lifetimes that are this pure and simple."

"You mean rape and pillage?" she teased him back.

* * *

Thornton got up to make early morning coffee on the fire outside the hut. One of Elaiza's young nieces brought boiled rice in a big black pot directly to a table where fresh bananas, mangos, and pineapples were already laid out. Elaiza joined them, and Reymundo brought over an oval platter he had to use both hands to carry, stacked with pork he had fried, and put it in the middle of the table for all to share.

After the breakfast, Thornton loaded the borrowed jeep by himself. He and Elaiza, the last remaining members of the deactivated STAGCOM team, would be returning to Davao City. They carried only a small bag of personal items and left behind in the village equipment they would not need in their future plans; someone would make good use of it.

It took a while for Elaiza to say goodbyes to her family. It would be some time until they would meet again, and then life and the world would be different. Thornton was already in the vehicle with the motor running when she jumped in. In the early morning hours it was not unbearably hot yet, and the fresh breeze was welcome. They drove back to the hardtop road, then south, following the main highway past Elaiza's old schoolhouse and later the dirt road leading toward the sea to the east and the place of her birth. There were no NPA blockades now. The Philippine Army checkpoints were manned by men who were awake and looking like real soldiers, clean-pressed uniforms with all the buttons buttoned and rifles with clips inserted. Security had returned to Surigao del Sur, if not yet stability.

After a few hours of bouncing along the road, they passed the dam on the Agusan and later "Roasted Chickens." The trip was eerily similar to the time Elaiza had taken Kapitan Tomas on their first journey to the interior. It seemed so long ago, but had been only a few weeks.

By the grave, she took his hand this time, and he scratched his head again on the same branch sticking out over the path. "See, my mother is reaching out to touch you." She smiled, and then was surprised. Over her mother's grave was a large, white tombstone, elegantly engraved "Victoria Payen Otakan." Elaiza was puzzled, and paced around the headstone, glancing back at a pleased Thornton between paces.

"What is this for?" she asked, seeing a metal door on the rear of the stone.

"Hum, let's check it out." Thornton himself was not sure what they would find in the compartment, if anything. He came around to the back and worked the combination lock. The lock opened, and it was there, one almost full duffel bag. "We better get this to Davao."

"My mother can finally rest in peace." Elaiza helped Thornton carry the bag up the path to be sure he would not scratch his head again.

The rest of the way south there were no text messages of disaster this time, only a courteous greeting from Hargens by cell phone. "I see you two are in Agusan."

"You got us, Luke. Maybe we'll shut off the TIAM."

"Ha." Hargens chuckled. "Doesn't matter now. Liu and the Filipinos are mopping up. So, somebody got Kumander Ali, and you got the Turk after all. Did you get *it*?"

"We can talk about *it* sometime."

"Can the two of you come up to Manila for a debriefing Wednesday? I'll buy." It was not really an invitation, and not quite an order. Hargens could not order Thornton to do anything, but it was more an assumption. "Fly up tonight, do the town, rest up." Hargens thought it would be no imposition. "I'll arrange for your hotel bill to be handled as a government expense. I've got something to talk to you about."

"Can we do it, Elaiza?" Thornton asked. "Let's just go right now."

"Sure, why not, we're already in travel mode, and I can take a long bath just as easily in Manila. Besides, they have shops in Makati where I can get anything I need." Elaiza was ready for the next adventure.

"OK Luke, we're on our way."

"Roger. See you tomorrow."

Thornton finished with Hargens and called his travel agent in Davao City to book one-way tickets for himself and Elaiza. What the hell, he thought, and booked first class tickets all the way not just to Manila but onward to LAX, Los Angeles International Airport. First-class sounded good to him. After all, they had something to celebrate, and surely it would be personally rewarding to hear Hargens' insights and to spend a few hours with him before he flew back to DC. Thornton and Hargens might not meet again for a long time, if ever. You never know.

"Then one stop on the way to the airport." Thornton started to drive a little too fast.

"Let me guess, Union Bank on Bangoy Street?"

"You got it. We have a heavy bag to leave with Joel. Don't want to haul it along to Manila; rather put it all in a bank vault."

Thornton parked near the bank on Bangoy Street in front of an onion wholesaler; the sweet-sour smell of the merchant's inventory was not unpleasant, and waited while the guard helped Elaiza into the bank, carrying a large, olive-drab canvas bag.

She was back in a half-hour. "Did you get it all counted and deposited?" Thornton asked.

"Not enough time to count it exactly, but we guess about two and a half million.

"Good enough. Starke hardly took any for himself, maybe a few thousand. Let Joel count it."

"He will. He put the bag in the vault and locked himself in with it. He's sure to be in there for quite a while. Over the next week, he'll put it into seven different accounts for us, three here at Union Bank, and two for each of us in The Bank of the Philippines. Some accounts in my name and some in yours."

"Perfect. When we get wherever we're going, we can make transfers of less than ten grand at a time to stay under everybody's radar screen for money laundering."

"Which, by the way, Tomas, we are not doing. We are completely legal." Elaiza did not want Thornton to get involved with anything sticky, not anymore, and not to get any wrong ideas about her after all this together. "I just wanted to remind you we have done nothing bad. And now we'll be OK for a long time."

"You're right. I just want to avoid international electronic snoops. Anyway, I have a credit card with a big limit and first-class tickets waiting for us at the airport. We can go a long way. And maybe we can do some good things." He surprised himself when he said it.

They dropped the jeep off at a Task Force Davao checkpoint at the entrance to the airport; Liu would get it back eventually. They were early for their unplanned flight.

In Manila, it was a short taxi ride to the Paco Park Hotel. "Your General Hargens only reserved one room for us," Elaiza noted when they checked in.

"He has great sources of intelligence, part of his job spec," Thornton teased, and took Elaiza by her arm, his casual touch calming her while they walked up the two flights of steps to the first floor of the hotel and circled around the pool to their room. The bellman looked suspiciously at the two guests who had no luggage.

Alone in the early evening with nothing planned, they took a long shower and then sat by the open window, warm city air drafting up as the first street lights came on, sharing a cool Australian white wine served from a carafe on the table. Elaiza even took a sip. Finally they had time to talk. He told her about a time the previous April when he had spent a long weekend in Manila visiting Colonel Liu, lasting into the May Day weekend. It was obvious the way he told the story that they had had fun catching up. Thornton called Liu his best student, and Liu made Thornton sing old German army songs with him at parties, songs sung badly, but with good pronunciation.

"Tomas, your involvement with Colonel Liu and his friends makes you too visible. Better stay off everyone's radar screen," Elaiza said.

"It's OK. Develops contacts for my business." Thornton thought it was no big deal.

"Hanging out with those old generals serves no purpose, other than to satisfy your ego." How could she build a life with him? He would always put himself in danger of being kidnapped or eliminated. And where would that leave her? Lovingly, she told him specifically what she was worried about.

"But you work for the embassy. That makes *you* involved too," Thornton rejoined, not following her logic.

"I *did* work for the embassy. I *had* a job I was proud of. With Hayes gone, who's my boss now? I haven't heard from anyone lately. Anyway,

I'm not involved with the 'Generals of Manila' as you pretend to be." Elaiza was concerned that Thornton was about to get involved again in dangerous activities and drag her along with him. Their new life could be idyllic if he would just settle down. But that was not like him: he would need to do what he called the "right things."

"I agreed with Hargens to locate the Turk. We did that," Thornton said. "That was all. Now, no more need for the Schloss Code and such games. The Filipinos have the NPA in their sights. We have nothing more to report."

"So you're done."

"We'll see. Anyway, we've got the money and we're not going to give it back, no matter what Hargens tells us tomorrow."

"I wish none of this had happened, that no one had died, except maybe that Turk." Elaiza had had enough of this line of conversation.

Intoxicated neither by booze nor drugs but only by soft music, memories, and the uncertainties of lives always too brief, Elaiza slid into bed and pulled a thin sheet over her head. Thornton left her alone for a while, then sat down beside her and massaged her feet to calm her. One thing led to another until they were both asleep.

The next morning Thornton woke early and looked at Elaiza sleeping. Her bare body was clean, unmutilated by piercings or tattoos. Tennis and Tae Kwon Do had burned off any body fat she might have had, with only a bit visible as one feminine curve just below her abs under her tight brown skin, skin that was the same color and texture from head to toe, her only tan lines, not really tan but latté, visible where she wore wrist supports when she played tennis. She had showered the night before in herbal essences, and in the dampness of the warm morning breeze the scent of her hair was enhanced by her slight perspiration, mingled with a few lingering drops of *Innocent Angel*. Thornton hoped she would not wake for a while. "Give me a full body hug" were her first words when she looked up sleepily. They missed the hotel's buffet breakfast.

On their way to the embassy, they walked single file with Elaiza leading the way. It was easier and faster in the city to move in a column formation of two, just as they had in the jungle. The sidewalks were constricted by beggars and peddlers intruding into the right of way, but the encroachers were less insistent with their sales pitches when Elaiza was leading. She could tell them, "No, thank you" in a courteous way, while Thornton would not always be so polite. It was still better to walk than to take a taxi. The streets were already noisy and hot, the traffic smoky and congested. They crossed Paco Park and continued all the way to the plaza in front of Manila City Hall. As there were no benches or cafes offering a place to sit in the open and empty square, they squatted Asian style on the periphery of the plaza and ordered fried bananas, served on bamboo sticks from a sidewalk snack stand, and talked.

After they had eaten, Thornton felt an uncommon uncertainty surge through his system. He had no answers to the questions Elaiza had raised again about their future, and that bothered him. Out of the corner of his eye, he noticed a gracefully carved stone water fountain, and to give him time to contemplate, walked over to it to read the faded, weather-worn inscription: "The First Cavalry Division reached this point in March 1945." The First Cav had been Thornton's unit in Vietnam in 1967. Vietnam was long ago and forgotten, with no meaning to this generation in this country or maybe in any other country now, and the Second World War, which had rescued the Philippine Islands from the Japanese, was probably not remembered by the last two generations. At what point in history do past events cease to matter? He walked back to where Elaiza was still squatting and said to her, "You're right. Many events we can't control. God grant us the wisdom to accept them. Let's walk on to the embassy. They should be open by now. We'll figure it out. By the time we get there, they'll be ready for us."

At the American Embassy they were cleared quickly through security checks by the military police team at the gate to the political section and sat down side by side on an uncomfortable old wooden bench. It wasn't long until a marine corporal opened the big glass door leading to a broad hallway and motioned them to follow him to General Hargens' office.

The world had not changed much since the Philippine Army had put an end to the civil war in Mindanao, and that was good, but worthy lives had been lost or permanently changed. Countries like Venezuela, Russia, and France were having their own internal troubles, the war in the Philippines was seldom mentioned in these countries, and the Middle East hardly cared about a civil war in outpost Mindanao.

"Hello Thornton, Elaiza." The general stood up and crossed the room to them. "Job well done. Congratulations."

"What's new, Luke?" Thornton returned the handshake. "We've been out of contact for a while."

"They're still counting, but it was a big battle. At least a thousand NPA killed at last report. The Filipinos lost only fifty-three. There will be more on both sides. The Philippine Army is exploiting their victory by moving into the villages of the NPA, and they're not in the mood to take prisoners." Hargens always made his reports military.

Liu knocked lightly on the door and entered. "Guten Tag, Herr Professor," he said jokingly to Thornton. "Fraulein Otakan."

"Oh, Herr General." Thornton was surprised. Martin Galan had pinned a shiny new star on Liu's collar at a quickly arranged ceremony in the Officer's Club at Fort Bonifacio. "You got here quick."

The new general had overheard Hargens. "Many more of our citizens would have died in the next years. Not only people killed in combat, but think how many millions still waste away their lives, no work, no hope, living with disease or dying at the subsistence level without the most basic medical treatment. Thank God we took out so many of the NPA right at the start with our artillery. That broke their back."

"Yeah, you almost took us out too, with your lousy aim! Reggie, I mean, Brigadier General Liu," Thornton admonished his friend, the newest one-star general in the world, "your country will have to wrestle with who is God, or whatever you call whoever it is that you worship, for a long time, and you're not going to achieve enlightenment overnight. You just won a civil war. Now see if you can do your jobs and manage the peace."

"By the way, sirs, it wasn't that easy." Elaiza recalled vividly how Mahir Hakki looked as he died. How Major Hayes looked just before he died. Juanito lying in the hut. Images she would never forget.

"We know it wasn't easy, Miss Otakan. But you've done well and been noticed. I understand there is an embassy staff promotion in line for you." Hargens surprised her with the secret.

"That's news to me. What would I be doing?"

"Taking over tech ops, what Hayes did before," Hargens confirmed. You'd be assigned back here." It would be a big promotion for her.

General Hargens let Elaiza consider and looked at Thornton, "Tom, stay on with us. I'll write up a long-term consultancy agreement. After all this, there will be some tidying up to do. I know you can write great reports that will keep Charlie Downs and DOS satisfied. And both of you would be assigned right here, working in Manila."

It took only a second and brief eye contact between Elaiza and Thornton, who answered. "No, thanks, Luke. We're going to L.A. We've done our time in Mindanao."

On their way to the airport, Thornton and Elaiza stopped for an early dinner at La Tasca and were seated in a booth on the second floor. The classic old restaurant was almost empty as it was early for dinner in Manila, especially in a Spanish-style restaurant. The three-guitar band gave the two guests all their attention with *Granada* and other tourist standards until Thornton requested *Sombras, Nada Más,* which the lead sang beautifully, then moved away after a good tip to continue with romantic songs in Spanish from across the room. Shadows, only shadows, nothing more, *Sombras, Nada Más,* the words hurt and reminded him of other places. Thornton held Elaiza's hand in his against her bare leg under the table. In the Spanish ambiance, they ordered paella for two with a bottle of reasonably good Rioja and listened quietly to a few more songs before they spoke.

"So, what do you think the final head count will be, Kapitan Tomas? Happy with the results of your little war?" Elaiza did not like to witness the death of any living thing. It was OK to kill in combat when the alternative is to be killed and the cause is just, but she was saddened by the deaths of so many of her countrymen, of whatever religious or political persuasion. She did not blame Thornton, but was glad it was over.

"This little war would have happened whatever I did. But I can do the right things, and we came out financially well off." Sometimes she was hard to talk to.

"No more reports from us to the embassy?"

"It's over."

Elaiza frowned and looked around the room, "And you will stop such nonsense forever?" she asked.

"Yes. I promise." Thornton looked her right in the eyes, and she knew he could not lie.

"What's next for us? What happens here? What happens next in the Philippines, after we leave?" Elaiza was thinking about the family she would be leaving behind, the aunts and uncles, cousins, and her old father living alone.

"Nothing has changed here, nothing ever will. A new generation of guerrillas will rise up to avenge their fathers. The Philippines will retire ten more old generals and promote a dozen new ones to take their places. Another generation of peasants will mature into poverty." Thornton felt the inertia of the system, keeping everything in place.

"Why, why does it have to be that way?" Elaiza really wanted to know.

"I've been thinking, maybe it doesn't. How about we make some good use out of the money. We're already OK. Do you remember the mango tree and the old farmer, his handicapped wife?"

"Sure. It haunts me." Elaiza was surprised he would bring up that particular image. "Why did you think of it now?"

"I have an idea," he answered. "Let's get the check."

On the way to the airport, the idea in Thornton's head kept him ruminating and the words that a West Point general, former President of the Philippines Fidel V. Ramos once told him, reverberated—"Caring, sharing, daring. Many have to work together to make a difference." That vision would change everything for him and Elaiza—and for some others who would never expect it.

"Elaiza, let's scratch the flight to Los Angeles. What do you say we fly to Cebu?"

"I'm always ready for the next place, whatever you have in mind. We can fly to L.A. anytime, and I've never been to Cebu. I hear it's a beautiful island. Let's go!"

"We won't be there long," he told her.

He was right. Once in Cebu, Elaiza bought two ferry tickets to the city of Butuan. Now back in Mindanao, she negotiated with a taxi driver to take them into the Agusan Valley and to the place they had left only two days before.

Tomorrow she would tell him.

40

Dreams

During the long taxi ride to Prosperidad, Thornton closed his eyes and dozed in and out of daydreams. He had visions of the old farmer back in Toril cutting down the tree. The taxi hit a bump, and Thornton woke to look out the window and saw only green jungle and the bumpy brown road; the mango tree was gone. That's when it all came together. "Elaiza," he looked for the right words, "let's plant some trees."

He thought she might still be sleeping, but she asked, "What are you talking about? Are you dreaming?"

"Maybe. I saw that old man cutting down his mango tree. It made me think, and yes, maybe dream. What if we used the cash we have to buy as much land as we can, and taught farmers how to use it best?"

"But what will we do?"

"We can live OK. What would you think about living right here?"

"I'd live with you anywhere, you know that, but now I think you're nuts." She continued. "How about getting an apartment in Singapore, or going back to Toril where we have a house already and all our stuff, maybe Southern California; I don't care, heck, even Kestely, Hungary, would be fine. Anyplace, but why choose here? Here is easy for me, difficult for you."

"Well, let's just stay right here, in Agusan, and let's buy that land along the Simulao River and plant mango trees. I might like a new challenge."

"Aren't you getting risky with our child's future?"

Thornton was dumbfounded, and his jaw dropped.

Elaiza liked her surprise and smiled, but with an embryo starting to twitch inside her, she had to think about security, for her and for her child into a long future.

Thornton finally caught his breath. "We can do it, for him or for her. We care about others. We can dare and we can share. Remember what we've seen. Think about the people we've seen in these villages. The shoe shine man with his box, a simple woman dressed in jeans, white tee shirt and floppies, the girl walking to nursing school in her white dress, and countless other images, even your own uncles and aunts. What future will any of them have?

"We can still do anything we want," he continued, "but so could a lot of others. The government tries to do projects, but bureaucracy or even corruption messes it up. What if we gave the land to the farmers?"

"You sound like a communist NPA. I thought we just beat them?"

"And we can beat them again, at their own game."

"So how do you do all these wonderful things?"

"One seed at a time."

"Then let's find that farmer and start a mango plantation with him." Elaiza's eyes sparkled. "I can help. I like the feel of the earth in my hands, and you will be teaching our child. You've already planted that seed."

Epilogue

The sun rose quickly and an already warm mist shrouded the workers in the field. It was best to get the heavy work done early. Pushing nicely rooted mango seedlings into loamy soil, Elaiza Thornton was getting dirt under her nails, and it felt good, and pure. She was warm inside, feeling the child growing strong in her womb, and smiled to herself. She looked up at her Kapitan Tomas, a few meters ahead of her, hoeing the warm earth to prepare it for the seedlings. He stood up from his work and shaded his eyes with one hand, squinted into the sun and looked upwards into the distance. She followed his gaze to where a large bird struggled to rise against the wind. Reaching altitude, Kabayan floated gracefully in mid-air for a moment, but this time, he did not fly alone. No longer the last Philippine eagle, Kabayan had found his mate. The two swooped downward together to gain speed, then rose and disappeared behind the far tree line.